Neco's Rescue

Louise Furley

Jace's Elusive Woman

Isle of Orainn

Neco's Rescue

Anastasia

The Kissing Number

Capturing Dove

Auction Block

The Poser

Wrath of Wolf

Shawn's Prisoner

Rogan's Desire

Liquid Velvet

Vijay

Neco's Rescue

Chapter One

Neco Bardiche let the answering machine pick up the call. He had no desire to talk to anyone. Ever again.

As he passed the landline phone, he heard his brother's voice speaking. "Come on, Nek- pick the fuck up, I know you're there, pick up-"

Neco grabbed up the landline and growled into it, "Why are you bugging me, Josh, you know I want to be left in peace." He cradled the phone between his shoulder and ear while he headed to the kitchen for a beer.

"Nek, give it a rest," his older brother scolded, "you know damned well none of it was your fault, none. You can't let-"

Neco sighed not bothering to hide his irritation. "I don't care anymore, Josh. I'm finally getting back on my feet, you know I don't want to see or talk to anyone." *Least of all my family who keep trying to nurture and comfort me.*

His brother's sigh came through loud and clear. "Yeah, we know. But you can't just blow us off because your heart is aching. Mom is so freaked you won't return her calls. You can't just shut off family because of the tragedy."

Neco dragged a hand heavy with annoyance through his hair then sucked down half the beer before saying, "Josh, enough said. You all know I want to be by myself for a while. Just leave me alone."

"Nek, bro, I can hear that tough edge in your voice, you've turned cold. Ice cold. You sound like, I don't know, like a man who has been released after doing ten years of hard time in prison, stone-hard and empty. It's damned scary."

1

"Yeah, so? I don't fucking care."

Silence. Josh's breathing was so loud it sounded like he was right in the same room as Neco.

Josh kept his voice level, carefully submerging any sounds of reproach, "It's been like forever, bro. First you disappeared for months. We find out you buried yourself out in the damned wilderness somewhere living like a wild bear or something, climbing mountains, hunting your food. What are you Grizzly-fucking-Adams?

"Then you leave the city to go build a house in that rural town, Lark in northern Washington, and hit the bottle. You can't go through the rest of your life regretting, and blaming yourself, and drinking yourself to death. You need to come home."

Pinching between his eyes with his thumb and a finger, Neco's aggravated sigh was harsh, loud, he didn't care. "No. I'm not coming home. I moved way the hell out here in no-where's-ville to get away from people. All people."

"Even your damned family, Nek? You have to punish us along with yourself?"

Dead silence.

Josh waited. Still silence. "Okay, fine. Stay out there in the sticks and nurse your broken heart and your pride. We'll give you some more space, and then we're coming." His voice intense, imposing his will over his younger brother's, he demanded, "You hear me?"

Neco shut the phone off and set it in the cradle. He stared at it for a long time. The longer he stared the colder and harder, and emptier, his heart felt. In fact, he no longer had a heart. A stone had taken its place. He felt nothing.

Maybe down the road he'd care about his family again, but right now, after all the fucking shit that went down, he felt nothing and wanted to see no one. Just leave him alone so he can work and try to get back all he'd lost.

Well, that was never going to happen, you can't bring deceased people back. His stomach stitched with a sudden pang.

He shook off the feeling and went to get his only friend now, another beer.

Hysterical with terror, she ran for her life, down one dark street after another. The rain blinding her, the wind shoving her in so many different directions it was a job to keep upright, avoid crashing into something.

Screeching tires squealed behind her even on the slick streets as the car took the corners ruthlessly chasing after her.

She couldn't draw another pained breath. Panting like a building on fire, shallow breaths with tightening wheezes, her lungs felt like cement she'd been running so long.

Her legs heavy with fatigue were slowing down, she couldn't keep this up. But she had to keep going, if they catch her they will kill her like he had-

The car careened in front of her just as she burst out of an alley to the street.

She screamed, tried to stop and back-pedal, but it was too late- Two men jumped out of the car, grabbed her and hustled her into the back seat.

One of the men climbed in after her, the other man hopped in the front passenger seat and the car took off.

The man next to her clutched her neck, the look in his tiny mean eyes brutal. Digging his fingers into her throat he commanded with ferocious fury, "Tell me, where is it? Tell me and I'll let you go."

Trying to catch her breath, she could feel the sweat pouring down her shaking spine. Her eyes wide in horror, he held her so tightly she couldn't move her head.

His dark eyes sparking fiercely, squeezing, jerking her neck hard, he spat with threatening menace, "Goddammit, tell me now or I swear to God you're fucking dead!"

She stayed mute, trying to swallow under his tight clench, her big eyes staring unblinking with terror and hopelessness over his big hand.

He released her then hauled his fist back and socked her.

Then he hit her again and again and again until her world went black.

Chapter Two

Driving back from the store with the raging storm thundering all around him, Neco was still thinking of the earlier phone call with his brother. It got his craw up that they wouldn't just leave him alone.

Josh told Neco that he was wallowing in self-pity and to buck up and get it together, move on. How could a person move on from such devastation?

Neco shook his head, that was never going to happen. Life had changed irreparably, he would never be happy, carefree, or damned trusting ever again.

Cursing a blue streak, it was a job to keep the truck on the road. The storm was fearsome, sleeting wind slammed at the vehicle like a hurricane. The driving rain had been unrelenting torrential for hours and now the drops had turned to golf-ball sized hail.

The hail hit the windows so hard he wondered how long it would be before the glass cracked.

Cursing a blue streak, "Dammit-" he mumbled, jerking the wheel to avoid a flying branch. The rain rushed in thick opaque grey sheets making visibility almost nil.

The truck suddenly went into a wild skid, he scuffled with the wheel trying to pull the truck back into his control.

The side wheels caught the mud on the side of the road making the truck slide even worse, skating sideways until it crashed into a mess of shrubbery in a gulley.

When it came to a sudden hard stop, Neco's head snapped forward. "Great," he grumbled rubbing his neck. "Now I'll have fucking whiplash." He slammed the truck in park to take a moment and regain his bearings.

Peering out the windshield he saw the visibility had only gotten worse. He had turned the radio off when the news alert advised that the river had swollen and pretty much cut off the rural town of Lark from the main city of Sanlura.

The officials advised everyone to stay off the roads until told otherwise, besides accidents, sudden flash floods could be deadly.

"Goddammit," he swore again, slapping his palm on the steering wheel.

Muttering out loud, "All I want is to get home," he jerked the truck into drive. Cranking the wheel to steer back up on the road, he groused on, "Get a beer, plop in front of the fire, and catch the game is all I ask."

He swerved the truck back to the road, half the vehicle was still in the gulley and half on the blacktop. The tires slid, making a nasty grinding noise, but they managed to grab some traction.

Through the obscuring rain something off the road just inside the bushes caught his eye.

"What the hell-" Damn, he wanted to go home but he was drawn to see what the hell had been tossed into the gulley. An uneasy feeling crept into his gut.

As he got closer and struggled to see out the shrouded windows, the hail beat like billiard balls all around the truck, clanging and clacking as they struck hard.

Brows scrunched, Neco muttered, "It looks," he leaned closer squinting out the passenger window as he pulled up, "like a bunch of clothes."

He sat back with a scowl. "Great, some asshole thinks it's okay to toss their trash anywhere, fucking litterbugs." In a huff, he yanked the wheel to pass by it when he thought he saw- a human leg?

"*Shit-*" he wrenched the wheel to get back off the road and shifted the truck in park. Last thing he wanted was to get out in that damned storm, but, a leg? Meant there was a body…

Shoving his ball cap on, he zipped up his jacket. He tugged the collar up around his neck, took a deep breath and got out of the truck. He had to fight the wind to get the door shut behind him.

Jogging to the bundle of clothing with his head down, the hail and rain and wind slapped and beat at him. He was huffing in seconds from his laboring struggle against the hellish storm.

When he reached the clothes, he crouched down and his heart did a summersault.

It was a woman.

She was scrunched up like she'd been thrown out of a moving car and landed hard and rolled.

Neco leaned closer, his stomach clenched. She looked…dead. He'd been in the service; dead bodies didn't freak him out, but a small, slight, torn up woman dying alone on the side of the road?

He shook his head and tried to keep his dinner down. He knelt and felt for her pulse anyway.

Setting two fingers on her cold neck, he barked, "Hell!" and jerked his hand back.

She had a pulse, it was so light he almost missed it, but she was alive. "Holy shit," he ground out. Taking a few seconds to ponder the situation, he made a decision.

Yeah, he should wait for EMT, but they couldn't get through this storm, and sure, he could cause her further damage moving her, but she would surely die if he left her there much longer.

He slid his hands under her and lifted her in his arms as he stood up. The hail pounded them both. She was totally sodden, the wind tossed her hair and clothes, he couldn't see her face, but she didn't weigh much.

He bent over to shield her as best he could with his body and carried her to his truck. He had to maneuver her to lay her over his shoulder to free a hand to get the door open.

The wind fought him at every step, the rain blew under his cap blinding him. He finally wrestled the door open and gingerly laid her across the bench seat with her legs curled on the seat. Slamming the door shut, he hustled around to the driver's side.

Neco didn't spare her a glance as he floored the truck to get it out of the gulley and fishtailed onto the asphalt.

Once he got the vehicle righted and heading down the road, he glanced at her.

Her skin was as pale as a ghost, her lips blue, *damn*, what was he to do with her?

The news alerts said the river was already running over and flooding half the town cutting them off. There was no way he could get to the city to take her to the hospital. He had no choice, he had to take her home.

Like driving in a whirlwind tornado, the truck went airborne several times. It skidded and the wind pushed it sideways, but Neco finally pulled into his driveway and stopped in front of his house.

He shut off the truck, ran to the front door, got it open and then hurried back. He opened the passenger door, she hadn't moved. Her hair covered most of her face.

Taking a deep breath, he reached in and scooped her up. Closing the door with his hip, he strode quickly through the storm and finally into the dry, warm, safety of his home.

It was murky inside. He hadn't left any lights on and the storm made it darker.

Shuffling to the couch, he bent and carefully set her down. First thing he needed to do was get her dry and warm and then see how seriously she was injured.

Leaving her for a second, he hit the lights then ran and got blankets, a flannel shirt and sweatpants, and grabbed up a pair of his wool socks and hurried back to her.

She was still out.

8

He leaned over and put his ear to her chest. It barely rose, her breaths were so shallow.

"Ah, damn," he muttered in concern. He lifted the top of her, shoved a blanket under her then did her bottom half.

He needed to get her wet clothes off. But he couldn't make himself move.

She was an unconscious, helpless, injured woman and last thing he wanted to do was violate her in any way, and that meant touching her, undressing her.

Taking a deep breath, Neco picked up another blanket and laid it over her. He slipped off her shoes then slid his arm under her back to lift her up.

She was wearing a blouse and skirt. His big fingers fumbled at the tiny buttons on her blouse. It was a struggle to try to get the soaked blouse off and keep the blanket over her to protect her privacy. She could be someone's daughter or wife.

He knew how he'd feel if some strange guy stripped his sister if he had one, and leered at her helpless naked body.

As he undressed her, his stomach lurched with sickness.

Her arms and ribs, even her neck was covered with cuts and huge nasty bruises.

He dropped the blouse on the chair next to him and feeling like a pervert, slipped his hand under her back to unclasp her bra. He'd caught a glimpse of it, dusty pink, silk maybe. He'd seen more but tried to block her breasts mounding over the bra out of his mind.

They were plush and soft and- he shook his head to dispel the picture, chastising himself, "Come on, asshole, you're not some damned perv ogling an unconscious defenseless woman."

Dropping the bra, he covered her top with the blanket then went to work on her skirt. Sure, he was used to undressing women, but this was creepy.

Undoing the skirt, he tugged the wet material down her legs and tossed it on the chair. Bile gagged him as he saw a giant bruise rose over most of her hip and down her thigh, her legs were scraped up, probably from hitting the road. He prayed she didn't have any broken bones or internal damage.

He paused, he couldn't help it, she was small but her legs looked long, maybe because they were so slender with a pretty nice shape- dammit- he shook his head. "Knock it off, creep," he rebuked himself again. The girl was badly hurt and he was perving on her.

Lifting the blanket higher, he noticed that her panties matched the pink silk bra.

It was difficult, but he lowered the blanket and reached under it, grasped the sides of the swathe of sheer material and as quickly as he could, yanked them down and off and threw them at the chair, leaving her totally naked.

Neco tried in his mind to remain analytical, like a doctor examining a patient. It didn't work. Being a normal red-blooded male with his hands all over a finely built naked woman, he was burgeoning wood.

He pushed at his wet jeans cursing himself for getting a hard-on over a woman who was helpless to protect herself against his voyeurism. But, as slim as she was, she had a curvy little body. And worse was yet to come. He had to dress her.

He did the best he could without looking directly at her nudity. Finally he got her into one of his flannel shirts, sweat pants, and wool socks. Everything was huge on her.

He didn't have a bra and panties lying around so she'd have to go commando- *oh great*, his wood turned to iron.

Letting out a hard breath, at least she was no longer naked on his couch. He covered her with another blanket. Now to see to her wounds.

Shaking his head, he stared down at her and asked, "Why the hell did this have to happen to me?"

Looking up to the ceiling, he cried, "Why, God, haven't I been punished enough? I ask to be left alone and you drop an unconscious injured woman on me and make it impossible for me to get her to the hospital."

He held his palms up in supplication. "What next, huh? What else are you going to throw at me?"

The young woman laid there not moving, barely breathing, covered from head to toe in bruises.

Struck with a hint of guilt, he realized it wasn't about him, it was about her. Ashamed of his whiny tirade, Neco knelt beside the couch.

It was hard to see what color her hair was, it was soaked. But it looked maybe like golden-brown, amber? Tawny? Now where did that come from? What man uses the word tawny?

He gently pushed the wet locks off her face and groaned. It was hard to tell what she looked like, her face was swollen, cut up, and a mass of bruises.

His stomach churned, he kept smoothing her hair back, he couldn't make himself stop, like it was a compulsion. His brain was trying to protect him from comprehending the grisly job someone had done on her face.

The damage was no way from a tumble out of a car, no matter how fast it was going and how hard she landed and rolled. Some fucker had beaten her to a pulp. There were fucking fingerprints around her throat. Neco thought he was going to puke.

He forced himself to stop clawing at her hair, and got up and went to get a towel.

Carefully, he tried to dry the long wet mess with the towel. The locks had to go at least halfway down her back. Part of her was muddy and some cuts were bleeding, he needed to get her cleaned up.

Hurrying to his bathroom, he came back with washcloths, another towel, and a first aid kit.

He bathed her face, neck, back, her arms and legs, feet. Then he set about cleaning her cuts and putting antibiotic and bandages on the best he could. He wouldn't know about broken bones or a concussion until she woke up. If she ever did.

No, he wouldn't let himself think like that. No one was dying on his watch. "Huh, like it wouldn't be the first time. Crap," he snorted sarcastically, mentally beating himself up.

Anguish sucked at the pit of his stomach, memories could be a vicious enemy. He pulled his thoughts back to the present, again reminding himself that it wasn't about him right now.

When he'd done all he could, he sat back on his heels and stared at her.

She looked from what he could tell, young, maybe late teens early twenties. She had a heart-shaped face, small nose and pointy chin. Her lips, he bit back a sigh, were what they called 'pouty' in the magazines.

Her mouth was small but puffy, even battered it made a man want to stop what he was doing and suck on it. His dick had settled down somewhat and now the stupid thing was back at attention.

Studying her face, he couldn't tell what she looked like, she had too many bruises. Her eyes were purple and swollen shut, the pouty mouth had a split on the side.

Rage fired in his belly and burned up his chest. How the fuck could anyone strike this- girl, much less beat the shit out of her and throw her out of a moving car?

Maybe she threw herself out trying to get away from the bastard who was beating her. Yeah, he smiled bleakly, that little chin looked defiant. She probably gave her boyfriends, or whatever, husband maybe, a run for their money.

He tucked a pillow under her head and stood up. There wasn't much else he could do for her. He was soaking wet and cold, he needed a shower himself and dry clothes.

Leaving her tucked in, he kicked off his boots and padded down the hall to the bathroom.

Chapter Three

"What do you mean she got away?" the man snarled, glowering at the three men standing in front of him struggling not to cower.

"Explain, and fast, Harry." He was so furious he almost shattered the glass of cognac he held. If he got liquor all over his Dolce suit someone would pay with their neck.

His ebony hair was shellacked back, each strand straight and gleaming. A scowl crimped his strong face with a domineering nose and equally forceful chin. Neat winged black brows with only the faint touch of grey at his temples pointed to his age at low-forties.

"Sir, Mr. Pryce, I was, uh, trying to get the information out of her. She wouldn't talk so I uh, beat her." Thickset Harry glanced at his boss to see if that was okay, the boss nodded without changing expression.

Harry was big and hulking as hired thugs go, heavy shoulders and barrel-chested, short buzzed hair, dark round eyes and thick lips.

Harry went on awkwardly, "So, uh, somehow, I mean, she just wouldn't tell me where it was, so I beat her until she passed out. We were in a freakin' shit assed storm, couldn't see a hand in front of us, right Don?" He glanced nervously at the man who had driven the car, a tall, narrow yet muscular man who nodded nervously without looking at him.

Mr. Pryce fastidiously smoothed his silk tie in an effort to maintain his composure, but his rage was already boiling over.

His tone deliberately menacing, a snarl curling his full lip, Pryce sneered, "Yeah, so what. You let a little fucking rain stop you from getting what I want from that young woman? She's practically a child for God's sake you assholes. You better not have killed her. Besides the pictures, you know I want that bitch in my bed. How the hell did she get away if she was knocked out?"

Harry stammered, "Well, um, well," he looked at the other man with his brows lifted asking for help. "You tell him Don, tell him how bad the storm was!"

His austerely cut, doyen face scrunching into a gnarl of wrath, Pryce bellowed, "I don't give a shit how bad the fucking storm was you pussies!" His words thrust out with spittle at the three men. "It was rain goddammit, not bullets. I said tell me how a slip of a female got away from you three burly fuckers. Now!"

Don and the third man stared at Harry with their mouths clamped shut. They hoped Pryce's wrath would stay on Harry.

Harry's heavy bumpy face paled, his big Adam's apple bobbed in his thick neck with rapid hard swallows. "Well- uh, we were driving down some freakin' rural back road and I kind of nodded off. She uh, must have woken up, I guess, and before we knew it, she had opened the door and flung herself out!"

"Yeah," Don finally jumped in. If Pryce didn't believe Harry, then he and Landers, the third guy were just as dead as Harry.

Don resisted the urge to rake his long knobby fingers through his short blond hair and stuck them in his pockets instead. Shiftily glancing from Harry to Pryce, he sniffed and worked his shoulders to get his gumption up.

"Speak, you idiot!" Pryce thundered. He normally had zero patience and now he was about to pull out his gun and shoot the lot of them. These types of thugs were a dime a dozen. He could replace them with a click of his fingers.

"Yeah, yeah, okay." Don swiped at the sweat beading over his eyeballs making his lashes damp and heavy.

He explained, "I stopped the car as soon as I could, but it was dark and you couldn't see shit in the storm. We drove around, back and forth. Hell, there were hills and gullies and ravines and shit, and woods, she could have tumbled down a hill to another road or into the woods."

"We," he glanced at his compatriots who were staring at the floor, "we just couldn't find her. It was dark," he repeated.

The three men stood nervously waiting for the boss to speak.

Wandering over to stare out the window, Pryce took genteel sips at his drink.

Watching the rain still pelting the glass, he looked blankly out the window, not seeing the gloom, the thunderclouds, the streaks of lightning flashing in the black clouds.

Without turning around, his voice calm and cold as a snake's, he ordered, "Find her."

Chapter Four

Neco set his hand on her forehead for at least the tenth time. There was no denying it, she was burning up.

He glanced out the window, the sun had long set and the storm hadn't let up. There was just no way he could get her to a hospital.

Retrieving a glass of water, a bottle of aspirin, and icy wet cloths, he set them on the coffee table. Tapping out two aspirins, he crushed them then mixed them in the glass of water.

Then he rolled his arm under her back, lifting her, her head lolled back. He shifted her so her head was supported on part of his arm. Gently tilting her head back so her lips parted, he very, very slowly and carefully poured the doctored water down her throat, praying she wasn't allergic to aspirin.

When she got it all down, he laid the cold compresses over her forehead and settled a light blanket over her. Then he pulled a big cushiony easy chair over, propped his feet on a footstool and stared at her wondering what color her eyes were until he fell asleep.

Neco woke the next morning slightly disoriented. He was sprawled in the living room chair. He must have really tied one on. Nothing new, he'd been drinking nonstop since- he sat up remembering- her.

Leaning over with his forearms on his knees, he gazed at the young woman.

She hadn't moved a muscle.

Groaning, his back sore from sleeping crooked, he got up and went to her and felt her head. Still warm. "Shit," he blurted. Actually it was burning hot. And the storm hammered even harder at the windows.

All that day and all the next, he poured aspirin and water down her throat and iced her.

Neco was growing hopeless, the rain still pummeled. It lightened up occasionally but he knew it wasn't enough for the river to recede.

But, she was so sick. Her breathing grew shallower and wheezy as her skin burned like she was on fire from the inside. No way could he let her die there on his couch. No fucking way.

He had given up and was putting his boots on to take on the roads anyway and try to get her to a hospital, then- did her eyelashes flutter?

He lowered to his knees and leaned over her.

Yeah, long amber lashes spread over the bruised cheeks were fluttering.

A minute passed before she took the deepest breath she had since he found her, and her eyes cracked open.

Hell, Neco admitted to himself, he was dying to see her eyes. He'd sat worried and brooding for two days guessing what color they were.

When she peered blurrily at him under half-mast lids, he never would have imagined their stunning color.

Green. Not just green, but, there were flecks of blue and streaks of gold. They were, amazing, like crystals.

He didn't want to say they were the most beautiful eyes he's ever seen, but damn, they were. And they had now popped wide open radiating sheer terror.

She tried to sit up and punch at him, her screams were so weak and raspy it made his ears cringe. "No!" she cried. "Don't kill me! I won't tell you!" She flailed frantically at Neco until he caught her wrists and held them while gently pushing her back down on the couch.

Holding her hands next to her head so she couldn't hurt herself, at least her arms weren't broken, he said softly, "Shh, shh, honey, calm down, I'm not going to hurt you. You've been…sick."

He watched her eyes roll back in her head and she went under again.

"Damn." He sat back on his heels. Putting his hand on her head, he relaxed a little. The fever had broken, she was cooling down.

Throughout the day he fed her water and aspirin, sometimes he got a little tea with lemon and honey down her. He hovered over her, hoping for a glimpse of those amazing eyes. No, he was waiting for her to awaken so he could get her the hell out of his house and take her home. Wherever that was.

Later in the afternoon, Neco was sitting next to her reading a book and nursing a beer. He hadn't gotten trashed in days, she might need him and he couldn't be passed out. He saw her stir.

Laying the book on the end table, he leaned towards her but not in her space, he didn't want to freak her out again.

He couldn't imagine being a young defenseless woman and waking up in a strange man's house with him gawking at her. Wait until she saw what she was wearing.

Her head rolled back and forth slightly as she struggled to open her heavy lids.

Neco decided on a different tack. Without moving closer to her, he said quietly, softly, "It's okay, you are safe, I won't hurt you."

Her body stiffened, she pushed her lids up. When she saw him, the fear instantly struck her again, she opened her mouth to scream.

Knowing it would only hurt her raw throat, Neco held his hands up, palms out, nonthreatening. "Honey, calm down, I'm not going to hurt you. You've been ill."

She tried to sit up, groaned, and fell right back flat. Her eyes relaying agonizing pain flew to him waiting for his attack she couldn't stop.

Keeping his hands up, he repeated, "I swear, I am not going to hurt you. You've been sick. I'm going to come to you and help you sit up a little. Don't be frightened, again, I am not going to hurt you."

There wasn't much she could do. She was obviously in too much pain, and too weak to fight him off, she just lay there and watched him.

He knew she was scared, her chest was rising and falling like an out of control water pump. Hell, fear streamed from her big eyes.

Moving slowly, Neco knelt beside her. He said quietly, "Here, I'm going to put my arm around your back and help you sit up, okay?" He didn't expect a response and he didn't get one. She just stared in wide-eyed fright at him.

He slid his hand behind and around her back. Using his arm to support her, she fit easily into the crook of his arm, he carefully lifted her while pushing pillows behind her to prop her up.

Leaning back, he observed that she wasn't sitting straight up, but she didn't look as vulnerable as she had lying flat on her back.

Her eyes darted around the room. Her confusion increasing, along with frantically rising panic, she looked at him and croaked, "Who...where am I?"

He stood up slowly to not frighten her. "I'm going into the kitchen and making you a cup of tea and then I will be right back and explain everything to you. All right?"

She just stared mutely blinking at him, watching him walk to the kitchen.

When he returned, he could tell she'd tried to get up.

The blankets were in a pool at the foot of the couch, the pillows were on the floor, and she was flat on her back again, tears streaming down her battered face.

He hurried in with the mug of tea and set it and a plate of crackers on a table and went to her.

"Okay, it's okay," he spoke quietly. "I'm going to help you sit back up."

Trying to ignore the pain in her bruised face, and her body rigid with fear, Neco picked the pillows up and stacked them against the arm of the couch. He carefully lifted her and set her to recline against them.

Even though he moved slowly and gingerly, streaks of pain creased her face, and tears slipped out the corners of her eyes. Her agonized gaze fell to the clothes she was wearing that were obviously male and way too big for her.

The bewildered green eyes flashed to him, so awash with tears they looked like circles of turbulent seas.

When he got her settled and covered with the blanket, he handed her the tea. She just stared at it.

It took a minute for him to realize she was so battered she could barely move. Stating the obvious, "Oh, you probably can't lift your arms," he put his arm around her back again.

Ignoring the way her body went rigid again with fear, gently lifting her, he put the mug of tea to her lips and held it while she drank a few sips then he set her back down braced by the pillows.

He'd used his smallest mug and only filled it halfway, nevertheless, she still couldn't manage drinking it on her own.

He couldn't imagine how she felt lying so small and broken, confused and helpless while a big, muscle-bound stranger moved her around.

"You haven't eaten for days, or longer, you're probably starving." He reached for her hand, stuck a cracker in it and brought her hand to her mouth.

Watching her take a small bite and chew, then struggle to swallow, clearly, not only was she afraid but she was in terrible pain.

He sat patiently just watching her. She ate the cracker awkwardly then blinked at him and croaked, "How," she couldn't get anything else out.

He helped her drink some more tea and handed her another cracker before he started talking. Leaning back in his chair to give her space, he said calmly, "There's not a lot to tell. It was storming like a son-of-a-" he broke off, cleared his throat.

"Ah, I was driving down Cold Creek Road," her blank look told him she wasn't familiar with it. So she must not be from around the area.

"My truck skidded off the road. I was righting it when I saw," how to say this gently. "Well, you were kind of...unconscious, and...in a gully..."

The amber lashes flew up, her mouth dropped open, the cracker fell from her fingers.

"Here." He moved slowly, picked up the cracker and put it back in her hand. The more she moved, the more flexible her arms were becoming.

"I- I-" she gasped for breath, "don't understand." Her voice hoarse, the words cracked. "Why was I...there?"

Dragging a hand through his thick hair, his bottom lip pulled in, he shrugged his broad shoulders. "I thought you could tell me."

She blinked rapidly trying to digest this information. "Who," scraping a breath out of her sore wheezing throat, her hoarse voice barely audible, she rasped, "are you?"

At least he could answer this question. His blue eyes scanning her cuts and bruises, he replied, "I'm Neco. Neco Bardiche."

She tried to repeat it, her voice as shaky as her body, "Nayko? Nayko Bardeechay?"

His mouth quirked at her pronunciation. "Yeah, sort of. So," he sat back and crossed an ankle over a knee, "you are?"

Her face was a blank. She blinked. A lot. Her mouth opened a few times like she was going to say something and then it closed...

"Um," he cleared his throat, "it's customary when a person tells you his name that you, you know, tell him yours?" *Especially when he saved your life and you're sitting in his living room wearing his clothes.*

A wave of extreme distress crawled over her bruised face. She put a hand to her mouth, tears gathered in her huge eyes, she looked about to shatter into tiny pieces.

Worried at her despair, "What is it?" Neco asked. He put his foot down and leaned closer to her.

He could see her lips trembling behind her hand; she bit down on them to still them. She stared at him so hard, he thought she was going to faint.

Snapping roughly, he demanded, "Tell me, what's the matter?" And instantly regretted the harshness of his voice because her entire body started to shake.

Regardless of her fear of him, Neco moved to sit on the edge of the couch beside her. Facing her, he set a palm on the back of the couch but kept a bit of distance. He said more gently, "Please tell me why you're suddenly even more distressed? I only asked you what your name is."

"I- I don't know," her voice floated in disturbed wonder, the green eyes flit to the window. Curtains of rain smeared across the glass.

Looking fearfully back at him, she whispered, "Please don't hurt me. I... don't remember my name."

He leaned back. Brows drawn down in disbelief over his blue eyes, he barked, "What? What the hell are you saying?"

Afraid of his harsh, disbelieving tone, she turned her head and pushed back against the pillows to move away from him but she had nowhere to go.

Huffing in irritation, he said, "Okay, calm down, I said I wasn't going to hurt you. Explain to me, what exactly do you mean?"

Neco watched her face drain of what was left of any color under the bruising. The green orbs turned bleak and scared as they turned up to him.

"I- I don't know who I am. I don't know my name. I- I don't remember anything," a tiny wail trailed from her trembling voice. Her breaking, rasping voice rising in edging panic, she clutched the blanket to her chest. Tears rolled out and down her round bruised cheeks. "I can't remember anything."

Neco stared at her. He couldn't tell if she was lying or not, but her fear and distress seemed genuine. His lip curled, but then he'd been taken in before by a woman. That thought caused his compassion for this woman to stall, his heart stiffened.

"All right," he said quietly. "Tell me anything you can recall. Start with something simple, like your home, your house? What does it look like? Your parents? Siblings?"

The more he asked, the more distraught she became. Her eyes darted back and forth so fast he thought she'd make herself dizzying sick. He reached out and took one of her hands, held in on her lap.

The pretty lips trembled. Her lids slid down as if by closing her eyes she could remember, something, anything. Tears squeaked out the corners of her eyes. She opened them slowly, looked at him so bleakly, his felt a pang in his chest.

"I can't remember anything. It's…like, I was born just now. There's nothing," she drifted off looking to the window again as if it held the answers.

"How about work?" She was young, maybe she was still in school. "School? Friends?" His mouth pursed at her shaking head. He said swiftly, "What is your favorite food?"

She stared at him then pulled her hand from his and dropped her face into both palms.

He couldn't hear her, but he could see her shoulders shaking with silent sobs. Neco was at a loss. She'd been beaten and banged up pretty good, she might actually have amnesia from a concussion. Or from the trauma that landed her in that gully. He patted her knee over the blanket.

"Okay, okay, take a breath, we'll figure this out. Here," he got up and grabbed some tissues out of a box then sat back down and pushed them into her hands.

It took some time before she got a grip.

Neco sat silently and patiently waited.

Finally, she sniffed, wiped her eyes and blew her nose. Eyeing him guardedly, sounding lost and alone, she whispered, "I don't know what to do."

"Well," Neco kept his voice soft, "we will just go to the police. As soon as this storm abates and the river goes down, I'll take you to the hospital and then to the poli-"

"No!" her cry rasped loud, she shot a hand out and grabbed his arm. Wincing with pain at her outburst, she swallowed deeply.

A ragged breath crawled up her shuddering chest, she said more quietly, "No police. Um, thank you for your hospitality, and- and- rescuing me. I can't tell you how much I appreciate what you've done…"

She pulled her legs up out from under the blanket to slide them around him then put her palms on the couch cushion behind her and tried to push to her feet. She got halfway up, her knees buckled, she cried out in pain-

Neco stuffed a hand under her butt and the other under her back and lifted her then set her back down on the couch propped against the pillows like she was before.

She tried to lean forward, to get back up, he put his hand on her shoulder and pushed her back. Even if she wasn't weak and injured, he was twice her size and weight, and his muscles had muscles, she wasn't going to budge him.

She struggled futilely against his hand, trying to push it off her. Sobs caught in her throat, tears rushed down her face.

"No, please," she choked, "let me go, I need to go! You can't keep me here."

Legally she was right. But right now it didn't matter. "Honey, first of all you can't even stand up. You haven't eaten at the very least for several days. You're just recovering from a bad fever, you've been brutally beaten, and, judging by the road rash on your skin I'm pretty sure you either fell, were pushed, or jumped from a moving car. You are terribly injured."

Obviously in deep pain and despair, she still tried to fight him to get up to leave. Pushing at him, gasping for breath, cries of pain eked out of her sore throat.

24

Keeping his hand over the top of her chest holding her immobile, he said sternly, "You are hurting yourself further by fighting me, it won't do you any good. Stop it."

Her breathing grew shallow and rapid as she gasped for breath. Gritting her teeth against the pain, she still tried to push him away. But, he was a brick wall with arms of steel and a powerful chest to match, and wasn't budging.

Under his hand she felt so soft and delicate, and shaking with fear. Still, he couldn't keep the exasperation out of his voice.

"Listen to me. The way your eyes are still slightly unfocused, and you press your hand to your head, I think you have a concussion. And for heaven's sake, girl, look," he motioned to the window where the storm raged on.

"There's no way in hell, even if you could walk, that I would let you go out in that. Besides, we're way out in the middle of nowhere, there's nowhere for you to go."

With a heavy sigh, she ceased her struggles, her gaze fell to his hand on her chest. He moved it off her.

She looked at him then the window. "Maybe, could you please, drive me somewhere where I can, uh, catch a bus, maybe?" Her rasping voice was tiny and scared, swollen eyes desperate, confused.

"No."

"Please, I just want to – to-" she looked disoriented.

Neco crossed his arms over his big chest.

Her eyes followed his movements and widened at the way his biceps bulged under his T-shirt. Fear surged back into her beat up face.

Watching the play of emotions shoot across her poor face, he said, "You can't even say where you want to go. Tell me, if you got on a bus where you would go, how you will pay for it, and I'll take you there."

He had no intentions on taking her out in that damned storm, but he wanted her to see her situation and settle down.

She just looked more panicked. Stuttering, "I- I-" she went to get up again.

And, again, he set his hand gently but firmly on her shoulder, his large palm on her breastbone, and held her still.

Her head lowered, she stared at his hand, he didn't move it this time.

Every time she struggled to get up, Neco could see her face wreathed in pain, she was just causing more damage to her injured body.

Her gaze went from his hand to stare quizzically at her clothes. Looking back up at him, she asked, "Are these my clothes?"

He smiled wryly, they were ten times too big for her. The shirt went almost to her knees, and her feet were buried in the legs of his sweats. "Ah, I'm pretty sure you have better fashion sense." He shook his head and told her, "No, they're mine."

Puzzled, she looked down at the flannel shirt and asked, "But how did I get into-" she broke off as a flush of color brightened her hurt cheeks. She slid her appalled gaze sideways up at him. "You...didn't..."

He didn't think she really wanted to hear the answer to that question, so he moved his hand off her chest and crossed his arms again. She looked so terribly lost, confused, and now supremely embarrassed.

"Hey," he patted her knee, "how about I heat you up some soup and more tea, I'll toss another log on the fire. You sit here, relax. You're just shaken up right now. Everything will come back to you in time."

Neco patted her knee again then got up and crossed the room to the stone fireplace. He moved the iron gate, strew in some kindling, lifted a few hunks of wood off a stack in a bucket then crouched and built a fire.

He pushed the wood around with a poker for a minute then put the grate back and headed to the kitchen. Maybe if he gave her some time alone she would calm down and everything would come back to her.

He heated up some soup, made a fresh cup of tea and carried them back to the living room. "Oh shit-"

She was lying on the floor between the couch and the front door.

"Dammit, woman," he quickly set the soup and tea on a table and went and squatted down beside her. She was slightly curled on her side and crying. Her belly hitched in and out with gaping sobs.

Muttering, "Damned headstrong..." Neco picked her up in his arms.

She was so weak she couldn't even verbally protest his actions, her head fell against his shoulder.

An odd sensation roamed around inside his chest. Neco had never held a woman like this before, all nestled in his arms, her hair tickling his chin. Instead of being angry at her for trying to leave, he felt...protective.

Carrying her gently, he brought her back to the couch and set her down. Her teeth were chattering, he pulled the blankets up to her chin. Bunching the pillows behind her back again, he retrieved the soup then sat down on the couch facing her.

"Listen," he said and waited for her to look at him.

She dashed her hands at her eyes. Her face was red, the small lips puffed in and out with her misery. As injured and sick as she was, she still had the most pouty lips he'd ever seen. The kind that made a guy want to just spend hours licking and nibbling on them.

He inhaled deeply to move his thoughts on. "I told you. You can't go out in that storm. For Pete's sake, if I have to tie you down, then goddammit, girl, I will. You can't even get to the door, how far do you think you would get out there? I don't need some strange woman dying on my damned doorstep."

He dipped the spoon in the soup and said tersely, "Just calm the hell down and sit still. You do not have to be afraid of me." He held the spoon near her lips, and ordered, "Open."

Long lashes lowered over her eyes as she got control of herself again, and then opened her quivering mouth.

He slipped the spoon in like he was feeding a child, and then dipped for more.

Her tiny tongue slurped around her lips, her eyes opened and she smiled weakly. "That's good." Her expression shy, she took another spoonful. "You're right, I am hungry." Wheezing, she croaked, "I can do it." She reached for the spoon then winced.

"I got it. You want some tea?" At her nod, he handed her the mug and helped her lift it. "I don't know what you like so I put in cream this time instead of lemon, and honey for your throat."

The smile fled, her lips drooped down. Her voice a bare whisper, she admitted, "I don't know what I like either."

He took the mug from her, set it down and spooned up some more soup. "It's okay, it'll come back to you. Just rest, give your body time to heal."

He slipped the spoon in her mouth, watched her tongue sweep around her lips, it made his pants tighten. God he was a sick fuck. Lusting after a helpless injured woman. He forced his attention on the soup bowl.

Scooping up some chicken and noodles, he asked, "Why don't you want to go to the police or the hospital?" and gently shoved the spoon in as her lips parted in confusion.

She swallowed the soup, but a wall came down over her eyes. She didn't reply, and didn't look at him.

"Honey, you are really injured." He didn't want to repeat that she was covered in bruises. Every time he mentioned the bruises, she shut up again when she realized he had dressed her. And undressed her.

"You could have internal damage, the way your face is battered and bruised a concussion is definitely-" Oh shit, he'd said it anyway.

Her eyes flew open and darted around the room. Her hands went to her face. "My face? What happened? Am I- deformed? They would do that- mutilate me- I need a mirror!" She moved to get up.

"No." He put his hand on her shoulder and pushed her back and kept his hand there as her panic rose again.

"What? Why can't I see myself? Am I that ruined? I had little to begin with- now-" she lowered her head to her hands and cried.

Setting the soup bowl down, Neco gently massaged her shoulders while she wept.

She peered at him through cascading pools of green. "Why can't I see a mirror? Please tell me how bad I look, how...disfigured?"

Rubbing her shoulders, his thumbs brushing her collarbone, he thought it was weird seeing this strange woman in his clothes. He normally didn't care for it.

Women often pulled his shirt on after sex and asked him 'Aren't I cute?' A coy fish for a compliment, and a permanent latch onto him. It pissed him off and besides that, then he had no shirt to put on.

Neco had never brought a woman to this house. After...*her*...he decided he'd get what he needed from females and take off before they could ask for more. He never wanted to get trapped, get screwed over again like he had. He learned his lesson.

Women had only one job as far as he was concerned. Except of course his mother.

His gaze traveled over the girl on his couch, and here he not only had a woman in his house, in his clothes, it was one he hadn't even had sex with, and she was a total stranger.

His shirt was big on her, but he could easily see her tits rising and falling with her breaths.

Suddenly she tensed under his touch and pushed at his hands. He realized she caught him staring at her chest. Shit.

Trying to keep her in his mind as just an injured person, asexual, nothing but a patient that needed his help, he stood up to put distance between them.

"I was ah, just noticing how big my shirt was on you, and wondering, if...I had a smaller one...that would be more..." rambling foolishly, he could feel his ears burning.

He stood awkwardly with his hands on his trim hips. Now her gaze dropped to his pants, she turned red and looked away. He discreetly looked down.

He should have put on a belt after his shower. His jeans were hanging from his hipbones. Plus, the fact that his dick was growing hard again probably wasn't going to make her feel any safer. He grabbed up the empty soup bowl and strode to the kitchen.

Remembering the last time he left the room and returned to find her on the floor trying to crawl to the door, as soon as he calmed himself, he pulled his t-shirt out of the waistband and yanked it down over his pants and hurried back.

She was still on the couch, not moving.

He crept over and looked down.

She was asleep. *Thank God.* He didn't even know really what she looked like and already her proximity was causing a strain on his manhood. But, nothing was going to entice him to let her out that door.

Studying her, he tried to figure out how he could keep her from leaving while he slept. He meant it that he would restrain her, bind her, if he had to.

Yeah, hold her hostage, that will win points with the law. Doesn't matter, her word against his. He'd use soft ties.

Chapter Five

She was petrified. She couldn't remember anything past waking up on the man's couch.

Her heart jumped in her throat, so scared she was nauseous with it.

All she remembered was opening her eyes and seeing this man staring down at her. Since she was lying flat on her back and she didn't know him, her first thought was that he was going to rape her.

She tried to fight him but he was as strong as an ox, and she was so...sore...so tired, nauseous and weak. Her head spun with dizziness and it just cranked with ache after ache in between stabbing pain. What was wrong with her?

Nako, he said his name was Nako or something. What kind of name is that? But as soon as he told her his name and asked for hers, she drew a blank. About everything. She could remember nothing past waking up.

She tried to tamp down the terror. He was right, she would get it back, her life would come back to her. But, did she want it to? She shook her head in disgust, why would she think that, of course she wanted to know who she was.

She couldn't believe he found her by the side of the road in a storm. *Humph*, she grunted. That's some story. Why on earth would she even be out there?

No, she shook her head again, darn that hurt, he was up to something. Was it he that had beaten her and he was lying about it so she wouldn't go to the law on him?

Something treacherous niggled in the back of her mind, but she couldn't pull it out. It was like a whisper telling her she was in dire danger, of what, she couldn't bring up anything visual.

Then, a vague, hazy picture of an older man with his hands on her shoulders pulling her, trying to hold her against his suit coat while murmuring…something…threats? She couldn't bring the picture into focus, straining to hear his words made her head hurt worse.

One thing that pressed into her mind was that she needed to stay away from the police. She didn't know why that thought pursued, but it did. Oh God, she thought in horrid dismay, was she some sort of criminal that was hiding from the law?

She needed to get out of here. He finally left her alone and went into the kitchen. She tried to roll on her side. "*Ohh,*" she groaned with the pain of just moving.

It took forever for her to get on her side and then slide to the floor. The agony fired up her limbs, her hips, her back, even her brain hurt as she hit the floor.

She lay stunned. She could hear him in the kitchen. If he was going to assault her, why hadn't he done it already?

A feeling of dread overwhelmed her. She was sore, covered in bruises, dressed in his clothes, her stomach dropped, maybe he already had. How else did she get out of hers and into his clothes?

Surely she would have remembered undressing and redressing herself?

Mortification riddled her body, embarrassment coursed through her. He'd stripped her naked and dressed her. Yes, he must have beaten her and raped her and was going to keep her there, hold her prisoner.

But, why would he bother dressing her only to assault her again? Maybe he was expecting someone to come by. Maybe he planned to share her with other men. Her eyes rolled to the window, the storm still crashed all around the house.

That riled her to get moving. She dragged her body across the floor, but the agony, swirling stomach-turning dizziness wiped her, pressing her to the rug.

It wasn't long before she heard him curse and come to her. She tried to get away from him, but her body refused to cooperate. As she wavered in and out of consciousness, she felt him pick her up like she weighed nothing and brought her back to the couch.

He'd made her soup. It was undoubtedly poisoned. She tried to decline, but he forced the spoon in her mouth and made her swallow. Turns out it was tasty and it didn't kill her. But still, she had to go. Something banged at the back of her injured brain telling her she needed to hide.

The fact that he physically restrained her from leaving, told her he had no plans on letting her go, maybe he was recuperating from beating her and assaulting her.

He must be ready to attack her again. She had caught him staring at her breasts. He tried to play it off, but his eyes were glued to them, his pupils enlarged and burned with white heat. His erection was clearly outlined in his faded, snug jeans, oh yeah, it was obvious. But he got up instead and left the room.

Lying there, she tried to think, who was she? How did she get here? What the heck was she going to do? Her body ached, but her lids were heavy and closing.

Her last thought was remembering his words about her face. She was disfigured. Already plain, her uncle always told her, she was, and now...yawn....disfigured...

Chapter Six

Damn this floor is hard. So much for plush carpeting, Neco groaned, opening his eyes.

He turned his head slightly, ah, she was still here. He'd bedded down on the floor in front of the sofa. There was no way she could get out without touching him.

She was too weak and injured to climb over the back or an arm of the couch.

Sitting up, he stretched his long arms over his head, then combed his fingers through his dark hair. Just in case though, he'd tied one of his silk ties around her thin wrist with a knot she wouldn't be able to undo and tied it to a leg of the sofa. He quickly untied it before she woke.

He got up, folded the blankets and pillows he'd used and set them on a chair then went to look at her.

She was sleeping soundly.

He had crushed a few aspirins and put them in her tea last night, hoping they would make her so drowsy she would fall asleep before trying again to leave.

Her lashes stirred on her round cheeks. She was thin, but she had serious curves, and her cheeks were round and soft like she had just left childhood.

The bruises on her face were starting to lighten, but they still marred her face too much to see what she looked like. He was damned curious to finally see her entire unmarred features.

Aggh, he turned to head for the kitchen and make some coffee. He told himself he didn't care what she looked like.

As soon as the rain cleared and the river went back down, he was taking her ass to the first police station he came to. And that was that.

He prepared the coffee and pushed the button. It didn't take long before the smell of the rich coffee brewing drifted around the room.

Padding back to the living room, before he even got to her, he could see she was awake.

She was struggling to sit up, tears of frustration and pain glistened in her crystal green eyes.

Not wanting to alarm her, he moved towards her slowly. "Here, let me help you." He cringed at the look of fear that scrunched her face at his approach. Ignoring it, he slid his arm around her back and under her shoulders and carefully helped her to sit.

"So," he said cheerfully, "I'm fixing some bacon and eggs. How many eggs and pieces of toast do you want?"

He watched her wary gaze flow from him to the kitchen and back. She couldn't hide her hunger, it blared from her starving eyes and rumbling belly. Yet, she didn't answer him.

Mutinous little bitch, he thought. "Okay, other than the soup and a couple of crackers, I think you haven't eaten for a bit so I won't overload you. How about I just fix you one of each for now?"

Still she said nothing, her lip quivered, she bit it to still it.

Without another word, Neco swung around and went back to the kitchen. He'd seen her eyes flare with hunger at his words, the smell of bacon cooking will bring her around. Unless she was a vegetarian. Then again, she wouldn't know now, would she? He paused at the kitchen door and turned back.

She was staring at him. She blinked in consternation.

He asked, "How 'bout some coffee?"

Again she didn't respond, but he saw her lips pull in and her eyes flicked to the kitchen and back.

"I'll take that as a yes," he left the room.

The smell of bacon broiling permeated the house. Neco carried in a mug of coffee and a glass of water and set them down on the coffee table. Then pulled the table over so it was within her reach.

"I put cream and sugar in your coffee. You should take these," sitting on the edge of the couch he held his palm out, two white aspirins lay on it. She backed away from his hand like it was venomous.

He could understand her being frightened of him, she was so small and delicate, female and fine-boned, and he was big and brawny, and a total stranger.

Then there was that cold flint in his eyes, he knew it was there, he couldn't help it. Sitting next to her had to increase her anxiety quotient.

Sighing heavily, he said, "Listen, if I wanted to poison you or kill you I would have done it. The days that you were out of it, yeah," he said at her surprised look, "days. You were sick. You ran a fever. I fed you aspirin like they were candy. It brought the fever down. You are still obviously in pain and I think we need to keep a handle on that fever."

He moved his hand so it was right in front of her.

She looked at the aspirin, then picked them up off his palm. He noticed how small her hand was against his big rugged paw. Obviously she saw it too, and it made her uneasy, her fingers shook as she put the aspirin in her mouth.

He reached for the water and handed it to her, waited for her to drink, then handed her the coffee mug and left the room.

When Neco returned, she was sitting up with her back against the back of couch and her legs dangling over the front. Her mug was empty.

He said with a small smile, "Hey, you feeling better?"

Her eyes swept down shyly, she nodded. Her voice soft and still raspy from her illness, she murmured, "Yes. Thank you."

Finally. She spoke without fear screaming in her voice and eyes. "So, do you want to try to come to the kitchen or shall I bring your plate out here?"

He watched her consider his question, then she shuffled painfully to the edge of the couch.

She said firmly albeit hoarsely, "I'll go to the kitchen. I can't be some lame duck and lie here like a lazy log while you wait on me. Just," she put her hand on the arm of the couch trying to push to stand up, "give me," she puffed and winced, "a minute." She needed to get her strength up to fight him off and get away from him.

"Yeah, sure. I think you're ready for a marathon. Let me help you, okay?" He reached for her arm.

She looked warily at his hand. He could see it took an effort for her to not visibly shrink back from it. He leaned over, wrapped his hands around her upper arms and carefully lifted her to her feet.

Her body swayed, she moaned, he threw his arm around her to hold her from falling. "Okay, I think you need to just stay here. Let me get you back down-"

"No," she shook her head and moved a foot. "I can do this, I need to do this. You go about your business, I'll, uh," a gasp of pain slipped out. "I'll get there."

Boy she was a stubborn little thing. He'd been right about that soft but pointed, defiant chin. He kept his arm around her and they moved painstakingly slowly to the kitchen.

When they reached the doorway, she said, "Oh, your food is going to burn, leave me and go to it." The smell of bacon was strong, fat sizzling and spitting could be heard from the door.

"Oh shit, okay, here, stay here." He set her against the wall in the threshold, lifted her hands to brace against the wall and hurried to save his bacon.

Tying an apron around his hips, he cursed at the bacon. While trying to peel it off the pan, it kept sliding off the fork.

There was soft chuckling coming from the doorway.

He glanced over his shoulder, yeah, she was laughing at him.

"Oh yeah?" he said, putting the strips on a paper towel. "You think it's funny? A guy cooking?"

"No, that's not funny. A guy burning down his kitchen is funny."

Four pieces of toast popped. He quickly set them on a plate on the table then went to her. "I got a job for you, Miss Giggles."

He rolled his arm around her and brought her to the table and helped her to sit.

Her giggles left and the wariness returned.

He handed her a knife and a tub of butter. "You can butter the toast. Okay?"

She took the knife and stuck it in the butter. "Yes, sir, Mr. Betty Crocker, wait, make that Benny Crocker," she quipped, her grin was back. Even with a split lip she had a gorgeous smile. A drop dead gorgeous smile.

"Ha, smartie," he snorted, going back to crack some eggs. "We'll see who has to do the dishes." A grin tugged at his mouth, that shut her up. He slipped four eggs into the pan of hot bacon grease.

The thing was, now that she was talking, he didn't want her to stop. She had, well, not a cute voice, but soft and pleasant, still a little hoarse made it sexy. *Ga-* he must be tired, he couldn't remember the last time he'd wanted to talk with a woman. "How do you want yours?"

"Hmmm?" The tip of her tongue was sticking out a corner of her mouth as she carefully buttered the toast.

Damn, he wanted to suck on that little tongue, bad. "Your eggs. You want soft, hard boiled, scrambled." He looked dourly at the setting eggs. "Might be too late for scrambled."

"Oh, whatever is easiest, I don't think I'm fussy." She set a buttered piece of toast on the plate. Sitting comfortably in the pale yellow kitchen, her face seemed to relax a bit.

Like the rest of his house, the room was fairly large, scantly decorated but contained everything one would need for comfort.

The oak table sat six with matching oak chairs and yellow cushions to make them softer. The silver appliances complimented the pale yellow.

More bread popped up. He pulled them out then cursed as he tossed them from his burning fingers to a plate.

"You need to be careful, even heat can hurt a big guy like you," she chided with a chuckle at his balancing act.

He brought the plate of toast over and set it down in front of her.

She frowned. "Who's going to eat all that? You have a dozen hungry dogs hidden somewhere?" Her head twisted back and forth like she was looking for a dog to materialize.

His forehead creased. "What? What do you mean? I'm going to eat them. A guy needs a lot of fuel you know." Neco didn't move a muscle as her eyes scrolled from the top of his messy brown hair, down his chest with slabs of muscles pressing against the t-shirt, then down further to his jeans.

He'd put on a belt. He willed his dick not to rise at her attention. He didn't remember ever before feeling awkward at a woman's perusal of his body. But then, no woman had ever studied his physique so intensely. He realized he was holding his breath.

She shrugged and went to butter the toast. "I guess. You are a really big guy, you must burn a bunch of fuel and need to eat a lot."

He let out the breath and turned quickly before she could see his Johnson swelling in his jeans. Flipping an egg, he said, "My brothers are all big too, we get it from our dad."

She glanced over with interest. "How many siblings do you have?"

The eggs on one plate, he picked up the bacon and brought both plates to the table, then pivoted to retrieve the coffee pot. He poured a fresh mug for her, then filled his. He put the pot down and came and sat opposite her at the round oak table.

"Dig in, honey," he said, reaching for a piece of buttered toast. Taking a huge bite, he chewed vigorously, then he noticed she wasn't moving. "What's wrong? You don't like eggs?" He saw tears of embarrassment gathering in her eyes.

"Oh," he felt stupid. "The toast was in reach but you can't lift your arms to get the other stuff. I'm sorry, just say something, here," he got up and picked up the plate sliding an egg off onto her plate then forked a strip of bacon and set it on the plate.

He picked up a piece of toast she'd buttered and added it, then moved the plate as close to her as he could.

Her face flaming with embarrassment, she stared down at the plate. A tear of frustration escaped and plopped on the table.

"Hey," he scolded gently, his voice soft, "cut it out. You've had a rough time of it. You'll feel better in a couple of days. Already you're looking more human. You need something, don't sit there and suffer, just ask me. Okay?" He waited for her to look up at him.

When she did, his heart plunged. Her beautiful eyes glowed, the plush lips, bruised and split but still goddamned gorgeous, curved up in a grateful weak smile.

She picked up her fork and nodded slightly. "Okay," she said and cut a piece of egg. "Ooh," she crowed, chewing it, "this is truly perfect, you are really a good cook."

Feeling his ears turning red at the compliment, he shoved an entire strip of bacon into his mouth.

Chewing then swallowing quickly, he reached for his mug, gulped half of it then said, "I was in the service, we had to learn the basics anyway or starve. I really can only whip up a few things." He caught her frown. "What's wrong?"

"Nothing," she sighed. "I mean, but you said I was looking better. Please tell me what I look like. Am I scarred? I'm already plain I don't need-" she broke of mid-word, her eyes flew to his, her brows dropped over them.

"You remember something?" He set down his fork.

She closed her eyes, then shook her head. "No, I just, I mean every time you mention my face I hear like a voice in the back of my head telling me what a plain Jane I am."

She didn't mention laced with those words she had the feeling that the person...because she felt a creepy fissure run up her spine, was touching her...inappropriately? She couldn't get a clear picture and wasn't about to share such weird information with him.

Seeing her face blanch, Neco asked, "Are you all right? Did you remember something?" The look on her face made him feel sick. She obviously recalled something very unpleasant, and the way her arms stole around to cross over her body, it was sexual.

She stared at her plate, then looked self-consciously up at him. "I, uh, I'm fine. I just keep thinking if I'm already homely, how horrible will I look with scars, or worse?" Tiny lines of gloom crinkled around her sad eyes, the pretty lips drooped.

Neco studied her so hard and so long, she flinched. He shook his head, mumbled, "Sorry." He pushed back from the table and left the kitchen.

Her heart started racing, was he kicking her out? Now that she wasn't so delirious, she was scared to leave. She felt vulnerable and...fearful of...something, she couldn't put her finger on it, but it was out there.

Her eyes flashed to the kitchen window surrounded by plain white curtains. The rain had finally stopped. Would he drive her somewhere or would he make her walk?

When he came back, he was carrying a handheld mirror.

She looked at it, her brow furrowed.

With a stern tone but his voice kind, he said, "Now, listen to me first, all right?"

"Um, okay." She looked from the mirror to him. His blue eyes were bright and vibrant, glowing with health and vitality.

"All right. Now," his mouth pursed. "Ah, I hate not knowing your name. Anyway, when I found you, you had been beaten, very badly." He tried to stifle the fury in his voice he'd felt when he had found her like that. He wanted to take apart the person who did that to her, one inch of flesh at a time.

His eyes moved over her face. "So, your face has been bruised and swollen, you had some cuts, but thank goodness nothing was broken. Most of the swelling has gone down a lot, and a lot of the purple color is leaving. Don't be frightened of what you see, the rest will go away. You will not be permanently disfigured. I promise."

She held out her hand for the mirror.

"One more thing," he waited for her attention. A tawny brow arched at him.

"Every day, as the bruises have faded, you have become more and more beautiful." Her brows went up in disbelief.

"Yeah, you are a looker, honey. I don't know who filled your head with that crap about being plain. No, you are far from homely, girl." He handed her the mirror.

Her hand shaking, she moved the mirror in front of her and looked with trepidation at her reflection. She could see him watching her over the mirror.

She stared at her face and blanched. She could feel her egg coming up, she dropped the mirror and put her hands to her face.

"Hey," he got up and came and sat on the chair next to her. He set a hand on her shoulder, he could feel her crying.

"You're not looking at this right, honey. You aren't used to the bruises, I am. I've seen you worse so I can tell. You aren't looking past the bruising and the cuts. Now," he picked the mirror up and handed it to her.

"Look beyond the bruises, babe, look hard. Ignore the purple, ignore the swelling around those huge, gorgeous green eyes. Just like those marks on your arms and legs, you've seen them lessen daily, the ones on your face will too.

"Now. Really look at yourself. See those high rounded cheekbones, your pointed but soft chin making your face look like a… a fig leaf, heart-shaped I guess is a better term. You have the most kiss…um, your mouth is very pretty." He pushed the mirror into her hands.

Reluctantly she took the mirror. Holding it up, slowly she peered at one tiny spot on her face at a time. All she could see was a face that looked like a mask of purple and blue, abrasions and swelling.

Around the jumble of lumps and color and split skin, her hair was such a tangled filthy mess she couldn't even tell what color it was. She laid the mirror face down on the table and pushed it away then picked up her fork and continued eating.

Sighing, Neco got up and went back to his seat. "You'll see, I don't lie, a few more days and you will look normal. And I promise you," his elbow on the table he waved his fork at her, "you will only see beauty."

Changing the subject, she asked suddenly, "When will you make me leave?" Her voice timorous, she chewed uneasily, swallowing with difficulty around the knot in her throat. In her terror of him and the delirium, she had been frantic to run outside, get away from…well, she didn't know. She'd been frightened of him and just wanted to flee.

Common sense was sifting into her bruised brain now, and she fully comprehended she did not know who she was and where she could possibly go. She still feared Neco, but it was warm inside his home, and he has taken such tender care of her.

Glancing at the harsh outdoors, a shiver of pure panic roiled over her at the thought of him pushing her out the door and saying, 'sayonara sweetheart, you're on your own.'

He looked in shocked ire at her. "What the hell are you talking about? I'm the one who fought you, forced you to stay here. Why the hell would I throw you out?"

Instead of his napkin, he wiped his hands on his jeans. His boots were by the front door, he'd been padding around in his socks.

Shrinking slightly from his angry voice, she straightened her spine, raised her head and looked toward the window.

Neco followed her gaze, and saw the sun had broken through the angry black clouds and was streaming in the window.

For some reason, his brain fell flat. An odd hollowness spread through his stomach and up into his chest. Soon it would be time for her to go. Didn't he want her to?

Didn't he want his isolation, his privacy, to be alone, no one bugging him while he wallowed in self-pity and licked his wounds?

His attention turned to her.

She was struggling to eat while obviously stuffing her nerves. She wasn't looking at him, he figured on purpose, so she wouldn't see the normal pitiless steel in his expression that he hasn't bothered to hide the past year.

"Honey," he waited but she stared at her plate. "Look at me."

It was a few heartbeats before those green gems rolled up at him.

He reached out and patted her hand. "We, you and I, are doing nothing until you are well enough to move easily on your own, and your mind is clear enough to make a decision as to what you want to do.

"And, if we can't find out who you are, until you have a concrete workable plan as to what you're going to do, and live, you will stay here. You have any problems with that? Because I don't." Patiently he watched his words mull around in her mind.

When she nodded, doubt still etched her face. He stood up.

Starting to clear the dishes, Neco piled the plates in one hand. She struggled to her feet. He asked, "What are you doing?"

"I'm," she swallowed a groan of pain, "going to do the dishes. I need to give back, Neco." Her face was already white with the strain of standing.

"Uh huh. The only thing you are doing is lying down." He took the dishes to the sink.

Hearing her pained sob, Neco turned and saw her face streaked with pain, her eyes rolled back in her head and she was crumpling to the floor.

"Hey!" He rushed over and caught her just before her head hit the floor. "Damn, girl, what the hell is the matter with you?"

Sitting on the floor, he cradled her head and shoulders, and barked at her, "I told you to take it easy, you moved too goddamned fast."

Her wobbling eyes were mere slits from the pain and dizziness, he could hardly see the green of the irises. Feeling guilty for yelling at her, he said quietly, "You're just dizzy, it will pass, just close your eyes, I've got you."

Her skin paper white, the plush lips partially open erratically gulped shallow frantic breaths. Her eyes kept rolling. With an effort, she focused on his face for a second before her sight wobbled away again.

"Neco," her voice tight, tiny, "please don't leave me, I'm...scared..." She tried to focus on his face again. Her chest pumped with anxiety under the loose shirt.

He smoothed the tangled hair from the side of her face, her pale skin damp with tears. He said with surprise, "Geez, honey, I'm not going to-"

Like she didn't hear him, she cried, "Please, Neco," her voice grew weaker as she passed out in his arms, "don't leave me..."

God, his heart panged. She was so pale and frail. He stood up with her and carried her back to the living room and laid her on the couch.

Fluffing the pillow under her head, he pulled the blanket up to her chin, then stood over her with his hands on his hips.

Even though she was out cold, he mumbled, "You stay here and rest. Don't argue with me." Laying his hand on her head, he was relieved to feel it was cool, no fever. The concussion would cause the dizziness.

He scowled down at her, she needed to quit fighting him and just rest.

She appeared to be now breathing normally, her face no longer crushed so terribly in pain. He smoothed her hair back again, it was more of a comforting act for him than a grooming one for her.

Secure that she'd be asleep for a while, Neco went back to the kitchen. When he finished cleaning up, he took a quick peek at her.

He sucked in an inhalation of relief. Her eyes were closed, her chest rose and lowered in calm breaths. She was sleeping soundly.

Satisfied that she was peacefully resting, Neco trod down the hall to his office to get some work done.

Chapter Seven

Neco had let his work slide for most of the time she had been in his home recovering. He puttered at it here and there when he knew she was asleep.

But then, like now, those green eyes kept pushing their way into his thoughts, he couldn't keep his mind on his work.

"*Ahh,*" with a big sigh, he set his pencil down and trod quietly to the living room. Expecting to find her asleep on the couch after fainting at breakfast, he was surprised, the sofa was empty.

Grousing, "What the hell," he glanced to the front door, it was still closed and locked. He heard a noise and followed it.

She was in the bathroom, vomiting.

"Aw, fuck," the dizziness must have caused her stomach to get upset.

He turned the knob but the door was locked. He knocked softly, called out, "Hey, uh, hon, let me in so I can help you."

She didn't respond.

He said louder, "Come on, you're sick, let me in."

Her weak, "Go away," barely made it through the door, the pain and strain sucked most of the strength from her voice.

"Listen, don't be embarrassed. I told you, I was in the service, this isn't anything I haven't seen a hundred times before. Now, let me in," he waited. Nothing.

"I don't want to kick in my own door, but I will, you can't be alone like that, babe." She passes out she could choke to death on her own vomit.

"Please," her voice barely audible. "I just want to take a shower. Can I...please?"

Biting back his urgency to get to her, Neco said calmly, "Of course you can. There are clean towels right there on the rack. In the drawer are new toothbrushes, maybe a comb. Let me in so I can help you."

He tried to keep his voice sterile, like a doctor would sound, but his pants tightened nonetheless at the thought of washing her in the shower.

Or the tub. Admonishing himself for like the tenth time for thinking carnally of her when she needed his help, not his lust, he shoved angrily at his penis that was rapidly hardening at the thought of her naked. Keeping his voice cool, he said, "Hello?"

Her exasperated, "Neco," came blurred through the door. Very quietly, she said, "Please, just let me shower, alone. I will be fine. Go away."

The corner of his mouth tightened in a small grin, stubborn damned wench. Leaning his forearm on the doorframe, he said with a sigh, "All right. But I will be right here. You need me you call out. You have ten minutes and then I'm coming in. You got that?"

He could hear the slight humor in her weak tone as she responded, "Okay, Mr. Benny Crocker."

Little vixen, his grin broadened. He turned and leaned his back against the door, crossed his arms over his chest, and one foot over an ankle and waited.

The shower came on a few minutes later.

When thoughts of her scrubbing her nude body threatened to take him over, he ran work ideas through his head like math puzzles to cool his libido.

Fifteen minutes passed, he was about to call out to her again when he heard the water turn off.

He waited a second then called out, "You all right in there?" Her mumble sounded affirmative so he waited.

When he heard the knob turn, he straightened up.

The door opened slowly. She took a step to the threshold.

"Hey," he said quietly.

She looked so wan, and damp, weak, and sexy as hell. Shit, she wore only a towel tucked just above her breasts that didn't go too far past her thighs.

Her soft ivory pillows mounded over the terry cloth, long wet hair curled down her shoulders and rolled around those lush mounds. Her legs were slender...and bare. His mouth went dry...

Neco clamped his open mouth shut to keep the drool in and forced down the hot lick of desire he knew was searing through his eyes.

She looked about to topple over. Shaking himself, he moved to her, and putting his mind in the frame of if he were her brother, he slid his arm around her shoulders, helped her cross the living room back to the sofa and helped her sit down.

He set two fingertips under her chin and raised her head so he could look at her. Just a simple shower had exhausted her.

Even as her head tilted back in weakness, she tried to keep ahold of the towel bunched up in her fist in front of her.

With his hand at her back, Neco gently helped her lean back against the sofa cushions.

Watching her clutch the towel to keep it from slipping, "Let me get you some clean clothes, I didn't think, I'm sorry," he blathered as he hurried to the bathroom to pick up the discarded clothes.

He took them to his laundry room and dropped them in the hamper than moved quickly back to his room. Gathering up a fresh shirt and sweats and socks, he hurried back to her.

She was as he had left her, sitting back like a wet noodle.

"Here, these are clean." Neco tried to hand them to her but she just looked wearily at him. "Okay, I'll set them here." He set them near her on a cushion.

Then he plucked his comb out of his back pocket and set it down with the clothes. "You want me to ah, I mean, help you get dressed?"

Both of them flushed red at his words.

She shook her head, he was glad. He didn't think he could do it anyway. Well, he could, but hell, it would be tough.

"How about I let you alone for a bit to change? I'll go start some laundry, I can get your dress clean-" he could have slapped himself. He should have done that before. Not only not having any underwear on, he gulped, turned redder, she has to feel foolish wearing his clothes.

Yet, his gaze quickly rolled down her and back up, he recalled she had looked so... young...and...kind of vulnerable, and yeah...hot, in his clothes.

He'd never wear them again without thinking about her naked little body- he shook his head. What had gotten into him? He never acted the horny-brained idiot before. It must be the strange circumstances of him being a caregiver for the first time in his life. It's not like he hasn't seen more than his share of naked women. He needed to be cool, sterile minded, about this.

Lifting her head up with a little more strength, she smiled gratefully up at him. Her tired voice soft and appreciative, she said, "Thank you, Neco, for everything."

His stomach did flip-flops. Her frightened voice begging him not to leave her as she lay passing out on the kitchen floor still gripped the back of his mind.

Joking to lighten the mood, he said, "Next time, if you don't like my cooking just say so, you don't have to toss it!"

She looked about to deny what he said, then she grinned at his teasing. "Okay. But seriously, Neco, you are a great cook. Really."

He shifted from one foot to the other. "Yeah. I'm gonna get to the laundry, you holler if you need me, all right?"

"Sure. I'll be fine. I'm feeling a little better already." She was picking up his shirt as he left the room.

Neco took his time getting the laundry in the washer, as sore and weak as she still was, and with the dizziness, it might take her a while to get dressed. Last thing either of them needed was him barging in on her half-dressed.

While the washing machine was filling, he folded some clean clothes he had removed from the drier.

When he'd done all he could, he made his way down the hall to her calling out, "I'm coming, are you decent?" Both words, coming and decent, sent tingles to his groin. Damn, when had he turned into such a relentless horndog?

"It's all right, I'm dressed," she called back, but didn't sound happy.

He rounded the corner.

She was on the couch dressed in another flannel shirt of his. She had rolled the sleeves up so they didn't cover her hands, and she'd rolled the pant legs up too. Her face was set in a frown. She was staring at the comb in her hands.

"What's wrong?" Neco asked entering the room. He stopped a few feet from her.

She raised miserable eyes up to him. "I'm such a jerk, I can't even comb my stupid hair." Glaring at the comb she dropped it on the couch. "I can't lift my arms up long enough to," she broke off feeling foolish, what did he care about her hair?

A corner of his mouth tugged up. Neco moved to her, bent and picked up the comb. "What do you say I give it a try? I mean, I've never combed a girl's hair before, I might hurt you more than help you, but I'd like to give it a shot."

Her brows arched in speculation, she looked from the comb to his own mussed locks. "I don't know, you don't seem to have done too well with your own hair."

His lips curved in an abashed grin. "Ah, well, I can't say I remember brushing my hair after my shower. I'll try to do better with yours. Here," he sat down with his back against her pillows bunched up at the arm of the sofa, and lifted a leg setting it along the back of the couch cushions and left the other foot on the floor.

Gently he turned her and pulled her to sit between his open thighs.

Her shoulders were rigid, but she sat still, setting a hand on the back of the sofa to brace herself.

"Okay, tell me if I hurt you."

Her hair reached into a point just before the top of her waist. Starting at the bottom, he combed as carefully as he could making his way up one lock at a time.

She had used his soap and shampoo, but somehow it smelled different on her. His nose kept inching closer to her, inhaling her sweet scent. He made himself lean back, they were already in a fairly intimate position.

He felt like circling his arms around her and pulling her to his chest, then cupping those plump tits in both hands-

Shaking his head with a pull of his lips, he was making it worse for himself, he needed to keep his thoughts back to completely sterile. If she knew his thoughts, she'd forget her weak moment in the kitchen asking for him to stay with her, and hightail it out of there.

"How's that? How am I doing?" He drew the comb straight down a thick tress, and watched it as it waved when leaving the comb's teeth, the ends curled.

Her shoulders had finally lost their stiffness. "Hmm," her murmur was like a contented kitten's purr. "It's nice, Neco, really nice. I don't remember, but I have a feeling a man has never done this for me before."

His groin tightened at her purr. For some reason the picture of another man sitting with her like this, between his legs and brushing her hair bothered him. How ridiculous, he didn't even know her name.

"Hey," he said, "listen, I hate to keep saying 'hey' to you. How about if we give you a name, you know, temporarily so I don't have to keep saying 'hey you?'"

Her shoulders stiffened. He regretted saying anything. She must feel like shit not knowing her own name and here he was throwing it in her face.

But, surprisingly she said, "I think that's a great idea." She turned to half-face him, her wavering smile interested but unsure.

"Oh." Taken aback, Neco dropped the hand holding the comb onto his lap. Her face was only a few inches from his.

The gold and blue flecks sparkled amidst the rich green, he could tell she was getting better. The clouds were dissipating from her eyes making the colors glow sharper, clearer, greener, they were steadier.

His gaze fell to her lips. So...puffy, yet small, the cut had almost disappeared. "Yeah, let's come up with something."

Her tawny brows drew down in a frown. "But what? How do we come up with something? Maybe we could use a relative's of yours, do you have female cousins?"

He made a face. "Yeah, but no." His body didn't react to his cousins like it did to her. He wasn't going there. His gaze left her and wandered around the room. "Um, let's see, chair, flower, mirror, what do you think about Miss Painting?" He smiled at her giggle.

She playfully slapped his arm. "You're being silly."

Nodding with a grin, he kept looking. "I know, but I'm looking for inspiration." He rubbed her drying silken tresses between his fingers, tugging on them to watch them spring back into wavy curls.

Not only was her fresh scent coiling delicately around him, but the warmth of her body drew at him too, enticing him to pull that fragrant warm curvy body into his arms.

He looked her over, taking in the soft, curly tresses. "How about Amber, or Tawny, like your hair?"

She made a face. "No, sounds like a stripper or a model or something. Somehow I think I'm, um, simpler than that. Keep thinking."

Under his breath, he muttered, "You are anything but simple, honey." He kept looking around thinking about each thing he saw, then he noticed his duffle bag he took the gym was by the door. Duffle? No, that's stupid, suitcase, case,

"Hey, I've got it, what about like Casey?"

Her brow threaded considering it. Deciding she liked it, she smiled up at him. "I think that's good, what do you think? How would I spell it?"

His gaze flickered over her face, down to her lips curved up in a happy, relaxed smile.

Finally. He said with a mirrored smile, "I think it's a cute name. We can spell it Casey, or Casee, or Casie, or Casi, what do you like?"

The puffy lips pulled in. "I don't know. I'm afraid since I have no recall I'll say something dopey."

"You would never sound dopey. Let's go with Casie, it will be less common. And you," he plucked up a tendril of hair and laid it back behind her shoulder, "are anything but common."

Their eyes locked, Neco could feel his neck growing warm, he licked his lips. He set his hands on her shoulders while he swung his leg around.

"You ah, I mean, I think your hair is pretty well combed. Parts are drying." Around her he was in a constant state of arousal and it was affecting his language.

Normally calm yet cold, he was finding himself uh-ing and um-ing, stammering stupidly, not his usual confident self. No, he was still confident in his own strength, it's just that she tied up his tongue. Yeah. Now there's a thought to run with. Their tongues and what they could do with them. He shook his head with his eyes closed. Not helping. Move on.

His tone admiring, he said, "Your hair is waving into fat curls." He stood up quickly.

Picking up a lock, she studied it. "I was kind of curious what it looked like. It's been so grubby I couldn't really tell before."

Nodding, Neco said, "Me too."

They both watched her move the lock around catching the light.

He murmured appreciatively, "It's like an amber gold-ish brown, like a lion's mane, golden brown, um, sort of." His neck grew hotter. What a goofy description. He needed to lose whatever this sappiness was that was coming over him and man up like his brother had said.

Physically, he straightened his back and shoulders, mentally, he fortified his thoughts to stay off her other than as a person he was obliged to help. That was all.

His mouth compressed in a hard line, brows down, last thing he needed was to get moony over some broad. Then he saw her playing with her hair, so interested in such a simple thing, her lids started drooping with weariness, his mouth softened.

"All right, *Casie*," he tried out her new name and was rewarded with a sweet sleepy smile.

Just the trivial thing of having a name urged some confidence into her. It showed in the vibrancy of her sweet voice. "I've felt so lost, Neco, now at least feel like I have something of my own, even if it's not...real."

Then, hell, her lips were pulling in sad again.

"Hey, *Casie*," he said cheerfully, "how about you take a nap and I'll get some work done, then we can have lunch and see how you feel. Maybe you'll feel well enough to take a little walk around the yard? The rain has finally stopped and the ground is drying. I can take you on a tour."

Covering a yawn with the back of her hand, she nodded. "Okay. But I haven't even seen your house yet." As her lids drifted closed, she murmured, "But that's all right. I understand you not trusting me...I'm a stranger you picked up on the side of the road...like roadkill..."

"Casie," he liked her new name. Neco bent and lifted her to arrange her to lie down more comfortably, and pulled the blanket over her.

"I haven't taken you through my house because you haven't been well enough or had the strength to move much. Now, go to sleep and dream of my famous melted ham and cheese sandwiches."

Her smile made him smile.

Tucking the blanket around her, he sniffed her hair, so sweet, *arggh*, he stood up. All right, enough sissying around, he had work to do.

Chapter Eight

When Neco came to get her for lunch, he smiled right away.

She was sitting up looking much more animated than before.

"Hey," he said, "you look like you feel a lot better."

With a flick of her head, she tossed her long curls back behind her and grinned. "Yes. The shower and nap really did me wonders."

"Good, come on then, it's lunchtime." He moved near her and held his arm out for her to take.

She wrapped delicate fingers around his brawny forearm, her skin so pale against his tanned arm covered with dark hair. He helped her up and was surprised how much more easily she moved across the room to the kitchen.

"You look like you've done this before," he quipped pulling out a chair for her.

"I guess walking is like riding a bike." She grinned at his teasing.

He already had grilled the sandwiches and had them warming in the oven. He took them out, added tomatoes then set them on the table along with potato chips and pickles that were already there.

"You want a soda? Or I have juice, milk, beer?"

"Oh, thanks, sure, I'll have a beer. Make it a frosty one with lots of foam." A laugh burst right out of her at the look on his face. "Gee, I'm kidding, get a sense of humor already. I would like a soda if you have one, thank you."

Taking a bite of a potato chip, she scooped her hand under her mouth to catch the crumbs as she laughed at the look on his face.

"Oh yeah? We'll see who has a sense of humor, Missy." He took ice and a bottle of soda out of the fridge, filled two glasses and set them on the table, then sat down on the chair beside her.

Watching her nibble her ham and cheese, he asked, "How is it?"

She dabbed at her mouth with a napkin and went to take another bite, "You must have been a chef, Neco, you are the best cook I've ever-" Realizing she didn't know if she knew any chefs, she chewed the sandwich and reached for her drink.

"Unfortunately, I only have a small repertoire of things I can cook." Taking a handful of chips, Neco tossed a couple in his mouth and dropped the rest on his plate.

"Casie," he smiled at the name. "I really like our choice. Anyway," he turned serious, "you're going to drive yourself bonkers if every time you remember that you don't remember and get upset.

"It will come to you. You need to relax and let that itty bitty noggin," he reached over and tapped his knuckles lightly on her head, "get some rest and heal." He grinned at her expression.

"Like I said, sweetheart, paybacks," he said, "are a bitch. Remember laughing at my burning bacon and calling me Bennie Crocker?"

"Huh." She bit off the end of a pickle spear and said sweetly, "At least I don't have a big giant egghead like some people I know."

Both hands holding his sandwich, he paused with his mouth open in midair ready to take a bite. "It is not egg-shaped. I happen to have a large but well-formed head," he took a huge bite.

That sent her into gales of laughter, so much so she started choking.

"Casie!" Neco reached over and patted her on the back. "You okay?"

She coughed, her eyes watered. She nodded, grabbed her soda and washed it down her throat. Wiping at an eye with a grin, she croaked, "You sure have a way with paybacks big guy, making a girl choke like that."

Damn, he'd like to make her choke on something all right. "Yeah, and make sure you remember that. Don't fight with the big boys if you don't want to get hurt."

His hand was still on her shoulder. Shoving the rest of his sandwich in his mouth, he wiped his face with his napkin and found himself absently stroking her neck.

Her body stiffened slightly, he gave her back another pat then nonchalantly drew his hand back. Clearing his throat, his ears heated red, not looking at her, he said, "You're all right now?"

Still wiping at her eyes, she nodded. "Yes. Even if you have a big misshapen head you're still a good cook." She finished her sandwich and licked her fingers.

Popping in the last of his chips, Neco leaned back and perused her. Finally there was some natural healthy color in her cheeks and she didn't look so ill, or so bone-tired. The bruises kept dissipating by the day. And she was being jokey.

He already found her amazingly desirable, but now, the helpless injured waif was turning into a stunning, bright woman with a very enjoyable personality. Hell, he was so screwed.

"I will take both of those as a compliment. Come on, you done?" He stood up and picked up his plate and reached for hers.

Casie pushed from the table. "Wait, Neco, let me do the dishes. I have to contribute something to my-"

"No." He headed for the sink. "I'll do them later. Right now, we're going for a tour of the house and then a walk outside if you survive the tour. Are those the shoes you're wearing?" He raised a brow indicating her socks. Well, technically his socks.

Grinning, she replied, "No, I," then she frowned. "I don't know, uh, do I have shoes?" She looked embarrassed to not know something so mundane.

"You do. They're by the front door next to mine. They're all dry now."

Her eyes lowered to the table, again she was mortified she didn't even know if she had shoes.

Neco pulled her chair to the side and crouched in front of her. He took one of her hands, waited until she leveled her eyes on his then said, "Let it go, baby, just get through each moment and move on. It'll all come together one day and you'll regret the torment you wasted on punishing yourself for not remembering things."

He looked into her sad eyes wishing he could make her laugh again. Seeing an errant tear roll out, he dabbed at it with a fingertip then cupped her face.

Their faces close, he said softly, "I wish I could fix it for you, honey, but I can't. You have to let nature take its course and stop bucking it."

Another tear slid out, she swiped at it and sniffed. "I know. It's just," she sighed and tilted her head towards his. "I feel like I'm in a- a hole I can't get out, and there's something dangerous waiting outside it. It's a nightmare."

Neco nodded. He knew. She wasn't aware that while she was ill he had held her as she slept fitfully, crying out in her sleep about someone with dark gruesome eyes mauling her, and she seemed to be running half the night in her sleep.

He didn't tell her because there was no way it would not upset her further. She needed tranquility and a feeling of security right now.

"But you're not alone. You have me on your side." He pretended to frown. "Hey, are you saying my house is like a big black hole? The nerve of you, little girl!"

That did make her laugh. Her lips curved up and her eyes sparkled. He still cupped her chin, before he knew it, he leaned in and kissed her.

As soon as he felt those tender lips, he knew he'd made a mistake. He only wanted more. Quickly breaking from her, he patted her on the head and stood up like he was just being kind to a child, or a little sister.

Right. He should apologize, but he didn't want to put any emphasis on it. What if she freaked, got scared of him again and fled?

"Hey," he said, "you were going to get your shoes?"

Cheeks pinking, she blinked at him like she wasn't sure of what just happened. Making light of it too, she slid off the chair to her feet, mumbled, "Yes," and trod out of the kitchen to the living room.

Neco let out a whoosh of a breath and leaned his hips back against the table for support. What the heck was wrong with him taking advantage of this vulnerable woman? What an asshole, first a light kiss next he'll be climbing all over her.

He took a minute to slow his breath, and let his pants loosen around his hard-on. If a tiny kiss brought on so much wood, he needed to keep his hands off her.

When he was back in control, he combed his fingers through his hair thinking about when she had looked askance at him, at his own tousled hair when he'd offered to comb hers. With a smile, he sauntered into the living room to begin her tour.

Neco showed her his office, and a den, then they stood in the doorway of his room, neither seemed to think it was wise to go inside.

"It's nice, big," she commented on the masculine room.

His bed was large enough for a man of his size to be comfortable. The dresser and tables were heavy dark wood, plain blue curtains at the window matched the carpet and the bed linens.

There were no pictures on the walls or on any of the tables. "How come you don't have any photos around?" She asked him, "Don't you love your family?"

Neco felt his blood lurch through his veins recalling when he had thought he was going to be starting his own family.

As wretched as that time had been, he had thought he'd never get over it, yet now, all he could think about was picking her up and carrying her to his bed.

Before he had her naked again in his mind, he shrugged. Standing next to her in the doorway, he set his hand on the door frame over her head, and said, "Yeah, sure. I just, I'm just not a picture kind of guy. Let me show you the other rooms."

He dropped a hand on her shoulder to steer her from his room where too many ideas of him and her on his bed were crowding into his head, and moved her down the hall.

"This is another bathroom," he indicated a large gold and white bathroom. "There's one in my bedroom as well."

Neco let her peek in then lowered his hand to her waist to usher her down the hall. So much for keeping his hands to himself. His hands were like iron and her body a magnet; he had to make a concerted effort to not touch her. And he was failing miserably.

He showed her two more bedrooms, one in browns and tans, the other in pale blue, then he brought her to a fourth room.

"Oh, Neco, it's very pretty," Casie said, poking her head in.

"It's mostly for my mother when she visits." He didn't mention she hadn't been to his house yet because he didn't want anyone there. Not even family.

"I have a couple of aunts and cousins that can use it too. But for right now," his hand still on the curve of her tiny waist, he brought her into the room. "I want you to make yourself at home in here."

She froze.

Neco dropped his hand and crossed his arms, waiting for her reaction.

Her gaze flickered around the pink and darker rose room. The curtains were soft flowery with the bedspread matching. The wall was pale pink and the carpet a deep rose. The furniture was white, and feminine.

Neco had hired a decorator to do most of the house. All he said was keep everything low key and masculine, but make one room feminine for his female relatives that might visit.

He never thought in his wildest dreams he would be telling a woman, not a female relative, that she was welcome to stay there.

"Casie?"

She wrapped her arms around her body. "I don't, um, what are you saying? Aren't I to leave soon?"

Neco stuffed his hands in his pockets and shrugged. "Like I said earlier, I would like you to stay here until you're truly on the mend, and maybe until we find out who you are."

Her eyes flit to him and quickly away. "That may take…a long time."

He nodded with another casual shrug. "I know."

She took a step further into the room and looked around. "I…Neco, I can't put you out like that. I would be fine on the couch for another day or so then I should…go…you know." She tried to turn and hide it, but he saw the distressing tears of being a stranger to herself gather in her eyes.

Personally, he had surprised himself with his offer. What happened to his plan of being a recluse for the rest of his life?

Following her in, he drew his arm in a sweeping motion as he said, "I obviously have a lot of room." He lightly gripped her upper arms pulling her around to face him.

"Casie, I would feel like shit knowing you were wandering around out there, with no money, no job, no ID, no identity. I mean, you really have nowhere to go, aw come on, honey don't cry."

His stomach twisted at the miserable look on her face. He never could take a woman's tears and hers were worse than anyone's. He pulled her against his chest, set her head to rest on his chest and wrapped his arms around her.

Her body shook against him wracking with sobs. She turned her face against his chest and cried helplessly.

Damn, Neco could feel his entire body tightening up like it was getting screwed into a bolt. He felt horrible for her pain, and he was going to be feeling some pain himself in a minute. His cock was swelling in his jeans.

He turned slightly so she wouldn't feel it, he didn't want her running out of the house thinking he was going to jump her.

He patted her head while saying soothingly, "It's okay, Casie. You'll stay with me until we get this figured out. No matter how long it takes. Got all the time in the world. All right?"

He clipped her chin with his finger and thumb and raised her head.

The green eyes were like storm tossed seas, she looked scared, and the uncertainty of her life stressed her face. He wiped at her tears with his thumbs.

She looked so forlorn his heart broke for her. "Come on, it's decided. You will stay in here from now on. I kept you on the couch because I was worried for your health and wanted to be near you. But you're well enough now to sleep on your own."

His groin twitched at that, it wanted her to sleep with him. Shaking his head at his relentless lustful thoughts, his voice gruff, he said, "Ah, so, you're staying in here and we're not going to talk about it anymore. You want to take a walk outside or not?"

Her smile was small and tremulous, but it was there. She nodded.

"Fine. Let's go." He said it but he didn't move.

She just kept looking up at him with her big sad eyes, he couldn't resist. He brought his lips down on hers and kissed her as gently as he could make himself, then stopped and stepped back holding her arms.

"I, ah, I'm sorry, Casie, I just feel so bad for you. I get carried away trying to comfort you. Don't be afraid of me, or be offended, okay? I shouldn't have done that."

Damn he had zero resistance when it came to her. He needed to get a grip before he chased her right on out of his home, which he admitted to himself, was the last thing he wanted.

She stared blankly at him, then smiled. "You are so good to me, Neco, and you don't even know me. Do you treat your girlfriends, uh, girlfriend, oh uh, I didn't think. You must have a girlfriend, what is she going to think about me being here! Oh

Neco, I need to go!" Panic infusing her voice, she pushed at his chest for him to let her go, but he held her.

She saw the pained look that crossed his face. The gentleness was gone, replaced by impregnable steel, the blue eyes turned cold and empty.

He released her and started for the door. "Let's go before it starts to rain again." His shoulders spanned the doorway they were so broad as he left the room.

Casie followed him down the hall.

On the way, he grabbed a baseball hat off a hook and dropped it on her head. "You're too pale, even though it's still chilly, you need to take the sun slowly."

Next to the door, he plucked a sweatshirt and a suede jacket off hooks. He helped her put the jacket on and then drew the sweatshirt over his head.

Opening the door, he nodded for her to pass through. His hand itched to set on her waist like before and usher her, but he needed to gird up his self-control and keep his hands to himself.

Especially if she was going to stay around for a while. His cock jumped in anticipation at the thought of keeping her. Keeping her? Where had that come from?

Neco grit his teeth, he needed to bury his carnal, and now possessive thoughts of Casie and get better at treating her like a friend. A sister. With a rocking body and green eyes that seared him to his soul. He followed her out and closed the door.

She stood outside the door on the walk and took a deep breath, dropped her head back and held her arms out to her sides. "Oh, Neco, it feels so good, it smells so good."

He chuckled. "Are you saying my man cave stinks?"

She admonished with a choked laugh. "No, you silly, of course not. It's just, you know, I've been inside for, I don't really know how long I've been here."

"Whatever." He wasn't going to get started again on talk about her leaving. She starts thinking about how long she's been here, she already thinks she's an imposition, it might push her to leave now.

So much for his self-control, he took her hand and started walking.

The stone path wound around the back of the house. In the front, he had a great expanse of lawn, acres surrounded by forest on one side. His closest neighbor was a farmer a mile down the road. They followed the path to the back.

"Neco," she said softly.

"Hmm?"

"How come you live out here, so far out, alone?"

He absently squeezed her fingers until she made a tiny sound. "Sorry." He loosened his grip but held onto her hand. It was so small, and smooth, and delicate. "How about we save that stuff for another time, okay? Let's enjoy this moment."

She looked up at the tall, physically fit handsome man beside her and smiled with a nod.

He showed her his patio. It was up on a brick terrace, three steps led down to the grass.

"I'm working on getting this fixed up. I like grilling and this is perfect for it."

Strolling down the steps to the grass, he asked, "Do you like grilled food?" He could have bitten his tongue. Quickly he said, "Honey, ignore it every time I shove my big foot in my mouth. I hate myself for keeping bringing it up, making you think about your memory loss."

Holding his hand, she reached up and stroked the side of his rough face. "It's all right, you have big feet so you can make big goofy mistakes."

He grinned down at her, feeling the heat of her palm on his skin. "Ah, I'm thinking another payback is due…"

Giggling in his face, she dropped her hand. "Be kind, remember, I'm sick."

"Sure, I'll remember," he bent and scooped her up in his arms.

Shrieking, "Neco!" her legs flailed. She threw her arms around his neck exclaiming, "What are you doing?"

LOUISE FURLEY

"You said remember you're sick. When you were really ill, I carried you everywhere, I'm just reminding you. Plus, I'm letting you know who is in charge around here, brawn beats beauty." He swung around in a circle laughing at her shrieks.

Her giggles filled the air, making him smile, and his heart warm. He set her on her feet.

As soon as she landed on her feet her pants slid down,

"Whoa!" She just barely caught them as they almost went past her hips. She scolded him with a stifled smile, "Look what you've done, you made me laugh my pants off!"

A flush ran up his neck, he knew she had nothing on under the sweat pants. "Uh, actually, I made you laugh *my* pants off." That didn't help.

"I should have given you a belt but I didn't think of it. I don't think my belts would fit you anyway. I guess you need to hang onto them."

She tugged them up and twisted the waist in a knot to keep them up. Bringing the conversation back to an impersonal level, she asked, "How much property do you have, Neco?"

His eyes were on her pants. He remembered the wet swatch of lace panties he'd pulled off her while she was incapacitated-Damn, he needed to get laid. Not with her.

He needed to go pick up some strange and get rid of the constant hard-on she made him have. Whacking off in the shower was not cutting it because he was picturing her when he was doing it. His luck and he'd be thinking of Casie while he was doing some woman he picked up in a bar. Damn, he was sliding into a no win zone.

He jerked his eyes off her and faced the woods, his neck burned red. "I have, oh, around sixty acres."

"Wow, that's a lot of property."

"Yeah, come on, there's a lake, let me show you." He took her hand and they strolled down the small incline towards the trees.

As they walked, he said lightly, "Casie, when you were," should he get her upset all over again? He had to, they had to work

67

with the things she said, her excited utterances. Like the police use when coming on a scene. Usually the first thing the person blurts out is the truth. Maybe.

When he didn't keep talking, she asked, "When I was what?"

"Now, don't get upset, I think we need to discuss things that you say without realizing it."

Her eyes skewed sideways up at him, she said nothing.

"So, the day I gave you the mirror, you said, your words were something like, 'they would mutilate me' do you remember saying that?"

She tried to pull her hand from his as a wall came down over her face.

He held onto her. "I'm not trying to hurt you, Casie, you must know that by now." He tipped his head sideways to see her expression.

But she had shut everything down.

"It's all right if you don't want to talk about it, no pressure. Let's just go to the lake."

Her feet dragged, looking up at him, her brow wrinkled, she was biting her lip. "It's not that, I mean, I want to talk about whatever will help, but," her gaze fell to the ground in front of them.

"But what?" He gave her hand a gentle squeeze.

Her slight shoulders rose then lowered in a half shrug, "It's hard to explain, I don't want to sound…peculiar."

He stopped and cupped her chin. Smiling at her, he brushed aside tendrils wisping in her face from the breeze. "You are in an untenable situation, honey, nothing you could say would be peculiar. How about trusting me?"

Her lips parted, she shut them and frowned.

It was dangerous for him to touch her, he was realizing that day by day. But it was like his hands, his mouth, itched to feel her soft skin, lick those plump lips…he let go of her chin.

His palm slid down her neck, over her shoulder and down her arm to take her hand again. He didn't miss the slight shiver that stirred her body. "Talk to me, Casie."

Taking a deep breath, she let it out with her words, "I don't actually remember saying that. But when you just said the words, I could sort of hear the idea echo in my head, like it was true. I feel as if I truly believe someone would not hesitate to…hurt me, seriously hurt me…"

Her breath cut in sharply, her step faltered. Someone had seriously hurt her. She kept the feeling to herself that someone had maybe tried to assault her, or…

He caught her up, held her steady. "All right, let's let it go for now." Shit, he was trying to get her to think about some freak mutilating her. They had no idea what had happened to her before he found her in the storm.

She'll have nightmares for sure tonight. Where has his head been this last week? He should have let it go.

Locking their fingers, he led her along the trail through the woods. They walked under the canopy of trees smelling of crisp freshness.

A week ago there'd been a warm spell and the buds started popping. The sweet smell blended with the earthy scent of the wet ground. The couple was quiet in their own thoughts as they meandered.

When they came to the end of the trail, they could see the shimmering water of the blue lake.

"Neco look!" She tugged her hand free and ran forward. "There are ducks!"

She slowed right away so not to scare them off.

They moved anyway. She followed them, chattering away at them.

Smiling, Neco stuck his hands in his pockets and strolled behind her enjoying the laughter in her voice, the gaiety in her skip. Her pretty hair rippling in the breeze, streaks of gold highlighted from the sun within the amber locks.

She looked funny, but endearing in his big clothes, like a child playing dress-up in her daddy's clothes. His dick twitched. But even the loose clothing couldn't hide her sensuous curvy body. She wasn't a child, and he sure as hell wasn't her father. Probably less than ten years separated them.

He sat on a picnic table, his feet on the bench, his forearms resting on his knees, watching her chase the ducks wishing he'd thought to bring bread for her to feed them.

It didn't take really very long before he noticed her shoulders slump, her step slow, she pushed her hair back with both hands. She was tiring.

He'd let her play for too long. He chided himself, he sounded like a parent. Neco shoved off the table and strode over to her.

"Casie, it's time to go."

She frowned at him. "No, not yet. Can't we stay a little longer?"

Again she reminded him of a child asking to stay out later. He smiled with indulgence, but he could see although she wanted to stay, the weariness was dimming the light in her eyes, her step was unsteady.

"The lake will be here tomorrow, and so will the ducks. We need to go, you have gotten overtired." He held a hand out to her.

She stubbornly ignored his hand and looked longingly at the lake and the ducks. When she swayed he knew she had gone too far.

He put his hands on her shoulders and turned her back towards the way they came through the woods. "Time to go, honey." When she started walking he took her hand.

Walking back through the woods seemed to take longer than getting there, her steps grew shorter and slower.

When they exited the woods and started up the lawn, Neco bent and lifted her, holding her tightly against his chest.

When she started to protest he said, "Shh, we're almost home, put your arms around my neck."

His words were like warm tea relaxing her. She softened in his arms and wrapped an arm behind his neck. Her other arm crossed over his chest locking her hands. It drew her body closer against his.

Striding over the grass still partially brown from the winter, he tucked his nose in her fresh smelling hair and easily carried her up to the house.

At the door, he set her on her feet so he could open it.

They went inside and Neco kicked off his boots at the door. He helped her off with the jacket, then she shuffled across the foyer to the living room to the couch and wearily sat down.

In another second, her head was on the arm of the sofa.

After peeling off his sweatshirt and hanging that and the jacket up, Neco trod over to the sofa and looked down at her.

She was already asleep. He thought, *I guess we'll wait until tomorrow to move her into the rose room,* and knelt beside the couch to remove her shoes.

Neco lifted her and laid her back down so she was stretched out with her head on the pillow, and tucked the blanket around her.

He went into the kitchen, rustled up a beer and a sandwich and sat in an easy chair with the remote. He put the game on mute and watched it, periodically glancing over at her to make sure Casie was all right.

Chapter Nine

He woke up stretching his back, hell it was tight from sleeping in the chair all night.

A smell wafted through the room. He sniffed. What was that?

The remote was still in his hand, he shut the TV off and set the remote on the table beside the chair and looked over at the couch.

It was empty. The blankets were neatly folded and placed under the neatly stacked pillows. His stomach suddenly felt like a fist was clenching it, *she was gone*?

His eyes flew to the door, his stomach relaxed, her shoes were by the door. He could hear noise coming from his kitchen.

Raking his fingers through his hair, really, he reminded himself that he needed to work on his grooming. But in the meantime, a tantalizing smell grew stronger the closer he got to kitchen. He could hear humming.

Stepping into the doorway, he saw a sight he thought he'd never see, a woman at his stove cooking. Even Kandi hadn't cooked for him.

Seeing a woman there, in this case Casie, didn't make him feel sick or resentful like he thought it would. Maybe it was just this particular woman.

Casie had his apron on over the sweats and flannel shirt, and she was pouring some kind of batter into the big saucepan. He looked at the counter, it was lined with eggs, flour, sugar, milk, vanilla, a bowl, he could smell the sausages sizzling.

"May the real Betty Crocker please stand up," he said watching her jump and almost drop her measuring cup.

"Neco! You startled me!" She ran her finger under the spout of the cup to catch the dripping batter and set the cup with a clatter in the sink.

He moved in further, his socks silent on the white tile floor. Stretching the kinks out of his neck, he asked, "What are you doing?"

The redundant look she gave him made him grin. "Okay, duh, you're cooking. What are you cooking?" He trod closer to see. "Those look like pancakes," he licked his lips and inhaled deeply.

The side of her mouth turned up. "You're smart, you must be a college boy."

"Yeah? You think you're funny?" He slid right up behind her and slipped his hands around her waist to clasp his long fingers together over her belly.

"Neco! Stop it, you're going to make me make the pancakes lopsided!"

"Hmmm," he shuffled his nose through her hair to put his lips on her neck and pulled her against him. "They'll still taste like pancakes."

"But they'll look funny," she pouted trying to flip one.

Lifting the side of her hair he kissed her neck, mumbled against her ear, "I'll eat the funny ones."

Switching to tongs, she reached for the sizzling sausages. "I'll hold you to that." She didn't make any effort to push away from him. A tiny snicker slipped out. "I can picture the funny pancakes telling jokes inside your stomach and laughing."

"Hmm," he smiled against her neck. Nipping little kisses down her throat, he tucked more hair out of the way so he could reach more of her neck, and lightly sucked her smooth skin.

Hugging her against his body, he was vaguely aware his brain was shutting down and his hands and mouth were in control.

Her head tilting to the side with a tiny breathy moan, Casie set down the tongs and put her hands on his thick forearms wrapped around her.

Her moan went straight to his groin. Neco kissed and sucked her neck, then he slid a hand under her jaw turning her sideways in his arms, and lowered his lips on hers.

She responded with a shade of innocence, like she hadn't had a lot of practice kissing. That was fine by him. His thumb brushing the hollow under her cheek, he licked her lips trying to push them open further.

When they parted, he slipped his tongue in, tasting her, *damn she tastes good.* His arms tightened, and his mouth moved more fervently over hers, then she stiffened.

Reluctantly, he ended the kiss. Letting go of her face, Neco slid his hands down the side of her waist over the sweet part where it curved in, and moved back from her.

She didn't look at him, just picked up the tongs; he could see her hand tremble. From fear or passion? He was already feeling a flush of guilt. What had he been thinking?

That was just it, he hadn't thought at all. His hands, body, mouth, had taken over. But, she had responded, he didn't mistake that. One thing he did know, was when a woman was responding to his touch.

"I need to wash up, then I'll set the table, okay?" he asked, speaking to the back of her head.

She nodded wordlessly.

Fuck, he hoped he hadn't finally done something stupid enough to run her off. "Okay, I'll be right back." She still didn't turn around. He quietly left the kitchen.

In his bathroom, he threw cold water in his face while berating his actions. What was he, a horny teenager who couldn't control himself?

Neco looked in the mirror. The same guy he'd always seen looked back at him, but with harder eyes and a tense jaw, compressed lips. Kandi had done that to him. Ruined him with her betrayal.

The sting of guilt stabbed him in the chest when he remembered the tragedy of what happened after he found his wife and one of his best friends, and partner, together in their bed.

Neco shook his head hard, scrubbed his hands down his face and threw more water at it. He had put all that in the past. At least he tried, but there it was raising its ugly head.

Right now he'd felt so fresh, so pure with Casie, but his past was tarnishing his feelings. Dammit, he had no right to think of Casie in any way except as him helping out another person in need.

He let out a deep sigh, but the person in need was so hot, and sweet, he felt so protective of her. He'd never felt that way ever in his life before, except with his family.

Every time he thought of Casie leaving, his stomach clenched. When he pictured her with another man he wanted to slam his fist through the wall. He was losing it over a woman he had known only a short time, and, actually, didn't really know.

But, he did know that he thought of her every minute, and the dread of the day when she would say she was leaving scraped at the inside of his chest, where his heart was encased.

He fixed his clothes, he could shower after breakfast. He didn't want to leave her alone long enough for her to decide to flee.

Making his way back to the kitchen, he noticed the air still smelled like pancakes, but the humming had stopped.

"All righty," he said jauntily entering the kitchen. He saw her back go slightly rigid. "I'll get the plates and silverware, do you want juice?"

She turned holding a plate of pancakes, not looking at him. "Sure." She set it on the table and went back for the sausages and toast.

Neco got the plates, silverware, coffee mugs, the maple syrup, blueberry jam and butter were already on the table. He grabbed the coffee pot and filled the mugs then retrieved the cream from the fridge. By then, she was setting the sausages down.

"Gee, Casie," he said cheerfully as if he hadn't just tried to suck her lips off her face a few minutes ago, "this smells great, I can't wait to dig in."

He put the coffee pot back on the counter and pulled a chair out for her. "Here, sit." Sticking a fork in the pancakes, he asked her, "How many you want? Six? Eight?"

Finally, she smiled. "I'll start with one. I made all those for you, you eat so much, like enough for an entire football team." She added a spoonful of sugar to her coffee and a splotch of cream, just like Neco always made it for her, and stirred it.

Chuckling, he put a cake on her plate and put five on his and sat down. Layering on the butter, he poured a ton of syrup all over them. It pooled around the pancakes like an amber moat.

Cutting off a big hunk, he shoved it in his mouth and looked at her. Seeing a tiny smirk on her face, through the mouthful he asked, "What?"

She was staring at him like he was an animal in the zoo. Smiling, she daintily cut her own cake, put on a bit of butter, a little syrup and gracefully ate a bite.

"Honey," shoveling in more he said while chewing, "you act like you've never seen a man eat before." Cutting a big chunk, he swirled it in the moat of syrup and watched her blink a few times, but then she smiled.

"Maybe I've just never seen a man like *you*, eat before."

His fork paused halfway to his mouth, the syrup dripped on the table, he quirked a brow at her. "I'm not sure if that's an insult, or, what." His eyes narrowing at her in a tease, he gobbled the rest of his cakes before she got through one.

They ate in silence for a while ignoring the elephant in the room.

Then Casie said, "I have been completely self-absorbed since I've been here."

His eyes flicked to her, he started to shake his head, she kept talking, "I have. I don't know anything about you. Tell me what you do. You know, work and stuff."

Holding a piece of buttered toast in his fingers, he said, "You mean now or like when I was younger." With less animalism, he bit off the end of a sausage.

"Oh," she sipped some coffee, set the mug down. "I'd like to know everything. Why don't we start with now and work backwards." She smiled her interest at him.

Damn, she had the prettiest smile he'd ever seen. There was barely a trace left of her bruises, the swelling had gone down, she was every bit as beautiful as he'd thought under all that abuse.

High, young, round cheekbones that now had a soft pink tint in them that matched the pink in her lips. His attention caught on those damned puffy lips, he pulled his gaze away from them with effort, they made his thoughts lead to other things better kept locked away.

She had sort of a pointy chin but it was softly rounded and made her large eyes look even bigger. Her complexion was so pure the Ivory baby would die for, and those green eyes, hell, like the tide, they sucked him in.

"Um, Neco? Casie to Neco, come in Neco."

He grinned at her. It was the first time she'd used the name Casie to refer to herself.

"I was wool gathering. Okay, me. Well, right now I'm in the Marine reserves and I work with computers. That's why I can do most of my work at home. You gonna eat any more pancakes?"

"No. Go ahead disposal, eat the rest." She asked, "You were in the military"

Making fast work of the last two pancakes, he picked up the last sausage and chewed on the end of it. "I was in the Marines, Special Operations 1st Battalion, earned an Honorable Discharge. While there I got my degree in Computer Forensics."

Her head cocked with curiosity, brows high in ambiguity. "I get the Marines, but what is computer forensics? You study dead computers?"

After devouring his blueberry buttered toast, licking the tips of each of his fingers, he wiped them and his mouth on a paper napkin then balled the napkin up and dropped it next to his plate.

He pushed his plate forward to lay his forearms on the table. "Computer Forensic Science is also known as Digital Forensics. It's the preservation, recovery and analysis of information stored on computers or electronic media.

"It can involve reconstruction of a computer to determine potential evidence, for example for computer crime or misuse, fraud, or theft of business secrets, destruction of intellectual property, and a bunch of other stuff."

Her eyes flew back and forth as she comprehended what he was saying. "What do you, uh, specifically do?"

A thick shoulder shrugged with his answer. "Sometimes I recover deleted, encrypted, or damaged information that can help in investigations for litigations."

"Huh." She looked away briefly while she digested the information. "So, what do you do it for, I mean for whom?"

He shrugged again. "Sometimes for lawyers or private detectives, but mostly for the..." He thought about how much he should tell her about who really employed him. "Let's just say I do a lot of work for the government."

"Oh." She checked out his arms in the t-shirt. "On TV, guys in the military have tattoos, but you don't have any?"

The lopsided grin gentled his hard face. "Yeah, I do. On my biceps." He lifted one short sleeve.

The sleeves were exceptionally long, usually the bottoms of the tats showed when he wore short sleeves.

"This one on my right arm was my Force Reconnaissance Unit." He pushed up the other sleeve and said, "This is my battalion. Every time we went on a bender we ended up in a tattoo parlor. I stopped with these two. I wasn't crazy about permanent drawings all over my body that I might eventually get bored with. And neither was my mother."

He smiled at the memory of how mad she was when she'd seen them. She'd cried, "My baby, your beautiful skin, how could you!"

Casie pushed her sleeves up then twisted her arms to see all of her own skin.

"What are you doing?"

"I'm looking to see if I have any tattoos." She reached for the hem of the shirt like she was going to lift it up.

"You don't."

She instantly dropped the shirt, her cheeks stained a dark pink. She started to get up from the table, he caught her hand holding her in her seat.

It was kind of weird, he knew her body better than she did. But not every inch of it. She knew he'd changed her clothes, but they hadn't talked about it. She looked so unnerved every time it came up he'd change the subject.

But he didn't want her modesty, or self-consciousness, or dormant thoughts that he'd taken liberties with her body while she was out cold to get between them, keeping things awkward and her on edge.

She looked at his hand holding her down, he ignored it.

"Casie, I had to get your wet clothes off you, you were half frozen and at death's door. I explained to you that I couldn't take you to the hospital and you were getting hypothermia, I had to do it. I did the best I could to secure your modesty, I swear. I didn't see every, ah, you know, part of you, the, important parts, private...stuff. So, chill out, okay?"

A dark look passed over her face.

Trying to read her expression, Neco was about to ask when he frowned, hard. His lids lowered in a squint, the anger in his voice made his words very low and glacial.

"Casie, shit. You must know me by now that I did not do anything to you. You think I might have...raped you?"

Furious with the silent accusation, it was so offensive to think that he would- *hell*, no wonder she was so afraid of him half the time.

Neco watched her trying to fight her dark thoughts, reconciling the man she thought she was getting to know with a psychopathic reprobate.

Her face grew deeper red, she kept her eyes on the table. Her tight swallow was the only sign she wanted to say something, but didn't.

He let out a harsh breath, dragged a hand through his hair then kept his palm braced on the back of his head as he regarded her. He was so angry his shoulders raised rigid, eyes tapered to slits and his mouth was a tough line.

His words stilted, harsh, he ground them out, "Casie, look at me."

She appeared on the edge of flight. Shifting anxiously, she tried to pull her hand out from under his and get up. But he refused to release his grip on her.

"We're not leaving this table until we work this out. Now," he couldn't help the harsh anger that clung to his voice, "look at me."

He waited, then started to calm when he saw she was growing more distressed. Hell, he was talking about raping her and here he was holding her captive and barking at her.

Gentling his voice, he said softly, "Please, Casie, look at me."

It took a minute before she rolled her eyes slowly up to meet his discordant gaze. The fear, and disconcerted feeling of not having anything to attach her soul to, to ground herself, exuded from the large green orbs.

It was difficult, but Neco softened his rigid body, loosened the planes of his face. Scaring her more with his fierce, angry countenance, bowing his intimidating big body towards her wasn't going to help.

"Casie," he looked her in the eye. "I swear, I did not touch you inappropriately, and I sure as hell did not assault or molest you in any way." He studied her, watching the conflicting thoughts flutter around her face that still burned red with discomfiture and mortification.

When she said nothing, he sighed. "Casie, there clearly is no way I can prove anything at this point. You have to trust that you would maybe feel in your body, ah, if anything had happened."

He moved his chair a hair closer to her disregarding the flash of nerves in her eyes. The way he held her hand down she couldn't move away from him.

"I can only tell you that I did not do anything wrong to you while you were unconscious. You have to trust that, trust me, my word, believe what I say, for us to be at peace with each other." His body slumped somewhat.

"If you can't, it would be impossible for you to stay here. I can't bear for you to be terrified of me, and you shouldn't have to live like that. I would have to take you to the police as I sure as heck wouldn't let you walk out that door with nowhere to go."

Taking a deep breath he said, "Now, do you believe me?"

Her pupils flared and flickered with her frightened thoughts at his words, but her eyes stayed on his. Still, she said nothing.

"You need to talk to me, Casie. Tell me what you are thinking." Neco rounded his back into his chair but kept his hand over hers.

Some of the redness dissipated, the tight lines that had dug in around her mouth with the anxiety of the conversation softened until they disappeared.

Her eyes dropped, he squeezed her hand gently, she raised them and looked at him. He sat in earnest, warmth in the deep depth of his blue eyes asking her to trust him.

Clearing her throat, she said a bit wobbly, "I, uh, Neco, I do trust you. I don't think a man could have been so caring, and taken such good care of a woman he had...uh, attacked.

"You have been nothing but kind and patient and caring with me. I think, um, that there is something in my...past, that is mingling with the present. Making me distrustful...of all men. I couldn't separate it from you."

His thumb stroked her hand. "Honey, we'll find out what happened. If someone hurt you," his belly twisted at the thought of her being raped, everything about her screamed virgin, "it won't happen again." That's for sure, because he would go and personally take care of the problem.

Neco's brain burned with fury at someone harming her, physically, mentally, especially sexually. It was a struggle, but he needed to put the fire out in his mind for now, and get them through this. "Casie-"

"No, Neco." The flaxen highlights in the tawny hair glinted like sparkly sand with the shake of her head. Her smile was true and sure, "I do trust you. I do believe you. I need to separate you in my mind from whatever happened. Can you be patient with me?"

He stared at her unblinking, trying to keep back the tears that stung the backs of his eyes. Seeing her struggle to trust him, to *want* to trust him, and the hell of her past that was lurking in the back recesses of her brain that made it so hard.

His throat constricted, he blinked rapidly to stifle the stinging. His Adam's apple bobbed with a swallow, his lips pulled in then pursed. Stroking her hand, he murmured, "Of course. Anything that will help you be at ease."

"I'm..." the corners of her mouth tugged in, "sorry I hurt you."

Coughing into his hand to break from the emotion of the moment for both of them, Neco said, "It's all right. I understand. Your mind has gone through suffering, it knows it, it just can't bring it into focus. But you have to understand, I had to do what I did to you to help you. I did no more, no less than necessary. Are you all right with that?"

He knew he couldn't bear for her to be in his house and look at him and think the possibility that he had raped her and might again. It made him feel God-awful. Especially when he was realizing more and more that he wanted a relationship with her, and not just as friends.

He wanted to kiss her again, and he couldn't do that if there were any lingering doubts about him on her behalf.

Casie lowered her head, then raised it in a slow, steady nod. "I know. Neco." Her lashes swept over her cheeks before she looked at him again.

"I know you did what you had to. I am grateful, I truly am. I'm grateful for you saving my life and every caring thing you've done for me since. I didn't mean to hurt you. I...do believe you, and uh, I trust you."

Neco's heart did a flip, he bit back his smile. He squeezed her hand then pulled from her. "Casie, I know it's wrong to hold you against your will like I just did. I don't mean to bully you, but I want us to be good. And if you had fled we wouldn't have resolved anything. So, are we good?"

A soft smile turned up the edges of her mouth making his heart flop after the flip. She said, "Yes. I think I'm the one that needs to offer you an apology."

He stood up and said firmly, "No. You don't. You thought what a woman in your situation would have. What I ask is, I'd like not to have to discuss this again. It stirs you up and distresses the hell out of me. All right?"

Her smile broadened with the shake of her head. Tossing the hair back that fell over her breast she said, "I'm good with that. Let's move on."

Letting his own face shift into a gentle, relieved smile, he said, "Great. So now, I'm going to do these dishes then I have to head into my office to work. I need to put in a few hours. What do you say," her eyes had lowered to the tablecloth, he touched her arm to get her attention back on him.

"The news said the roads are clear and I need to go into town for a couple of errands. How about we go to this little diner for lunch?"

She blinked at him without saying anything. Her hand went to her face.

Understanding, he said kindly, "Casie, you look fine. I promise you. Your bruises are almost gone. No one will stare at you." Maybe not at the bruises, but the men will assuredly gawk and the ladies will frown.

He still couldn't believe anyone had ever told her she was plain. It was a vast understatement to even say she was beautiful.

"I- I don't have any money." The woebegone look took over her face.

He rolled his eyes. "I know that, honey. Besides, when I take a woman on a date, I'm old fashioned, I pay."

Seeing her lips pull in, he said quickly, "I mean, when I invite a woman out, any female, even just a friend, you know, I take care of the check…"

Damn he was stuttering like a kid. "Listen, just put your skirt and blouse on and everything will be fine."

Chapter Ten

$\mathcal{A}$round 12:30, Casie was perched in an easy chair in her skirt and blouse with her legs curled up on the seat.

While waiting for Neco, she flipped through a sports magazine. It was mostly about football, she wrinkled her nose, as bored as she was with the magazine she assumed that she wasn't interested in sports.

But, he only had sports or science magazines. She glanced at the other end-table, there were a few financial and some computer magazines. Even the newspaper was folded to the sports section.

Of course, if he'd had magazines on makeup or shoes she'd be thinking differently about him, she put her hand over her mouth to cover her giggle.

"What's so funny, missy?" Strolling in wearing jeans and a button-down shirt, he smiled at her. "For some reason, I have a funny feeling you were thinking about me. What were you laughing about?"

Casie set the magazine down and moved her legs to hang over the edge of the chair and smiled at him.

She'd been so sick and out of it, she was starting to realize not only was he a nice guy, humorous, attentive to her needs and gentle with her, but he was a really good looking guy.

Dark wavy hair and sky blue eyes that sometimes were warm, but mostly they were like blue ice with, it seemed, suppressed rage, and she'd seen the hurt in them many times.

She'd heard him speaking tersely on the phone sometimes before slamming it down, and one time he yanked the cord right out the wall.

His rough anger made her nervous, but she knew he wouldn't hurt her so she relaxed and didn't let it bother her. Too much.

She kept studying him. Hard angled face, strong nose that looked like it might have been broken at least once as well as strong high cheekbones and squarish jaw, and…full, but…masculine lips that could kiss a girl into the ground.

Many inches over six feet of pure hunky lean muscle, Neco Bardiche would turn any girl's head. The giggles switched to a blush that ran up her face.

"Ah, okay, now I'm really interested. What makes you giggle and blush at the same time, while you're looking at me?" He stood in front of her, buttoning a cuff of one sleeve.

She put her palms on her hot cheeks and shook her head. "Nothing. Never mind. Are you done working?" She slid her butt to the end of the chair and her feet hit the floor.

He cocked his head at her while buttoning the other cuff like he was trying to read her mind. It only made her blush harder. "You're not going to tell me?"

She pushed to her feet. "No, it was nothing."

"Uh huh. All right, keep your secrets. You ready to go?" He took in the skirt and blouse she wore. Seeing them gave him a sick feeling in the pit of his stomach.

They were the clothes she was wearing when he found her dying by the side of the road. Hell, there were holes and bloodstains he hadn't been able to bleach out. Dragging a hand through his hair, he frowned, she had to wear them, she couldn't very well wear his clothes in town.

"What's the matter, Neco?" Moving to him, Casie touched his arm, concern pulling her eyebrows in.

86

He looked at the delicate fingers setting lightly on his sleeve then up to her face. He patted her hand with a smile. "Nothing, let's go, I'm hungry."

"You're always hungry. You are like a bottomless pit," she teased as they went to put their shoes on.

"I work it off, sweetheart, we can't all be pin thin like you." He held out his brown suede jacket for her to put on.

Fortunately with her amnesia she wasn't annoyed at his teasing, she didn't know if what he said was insulting her or just making an observation.

He stood behind her holding the jacket as she slid in one arm then the other. When it was on, Neco didn't let go of it. He slid his hands across the front of her to hug her against him.

It felt good to be wrapped up safe and secure in his strong arms, but Casie wasn't sure where he was going when he would cuddle her like he does, and kiss her. Her lids lowered as she remembered his mouth scorching on hers, his lips on her neck, sucking...

"Casie?"

She blinked, and shook her head.

He held her shoulders and turned her around to face him. Worry wrinkles furrowed in his forehead. "You all right, sweetheart? Do you need to lie down?"

Smiling, she pulled from his hands and turned around to the door. "I'm perfectly fine, just a little tired and a lot hungry."

Neco opened the door and waited for her to go out before locking it behind them. They walked to his truck. He held the passenger door open then looked at her and then the high step up to get inside. "Here, tiny," he teased, "let me help you up." He put his hands around her waist and lifted her onto the seat.

Sliding inside, Casie noticed he stared at her legs when she swung them inside the truck. Was he looking for lingering bruises that might make people stare at her?

Closing her door, he went around, hopped in behind the wheel and turned the ignition and the heat on. "You warm enough? It'll take a minute for the heat to crank up."

She burrowed into his jacket. "I'm fine. I'm a lot better now, you don't need to worry about me anymore." She felt his eyes boring into the side of her head.

Clicking her seatbelt on, she turned to look at him with her brows raised. "Is something wrong?"

"No, everything is fine. Just because you're feeling better doesn't mean you're well. I still need to watch you for signs of that concussion worsening. You think I don't see when you try to hide your bouts of dizziness and small winces from places that still pain you. You still tire fairly quickly."

He caught the ends of the jacket's fluffy collar and drew it up more snuggly around her heart face. "But I do notice. So you need to keep taking it easy and letting me take care of you."

"Oh, Neco," she sighed. "I've already been so much of a burden and bothersome to you."

He drove down the gravel drive to the street.

Passing pastures of winter grass that were turning green, Neco said, "Casie, you are not a burden. It is not bothersome for me to care for you. I don't mind at all." His expression indicated he was surprised at his own words.

They were driving through the countryside, her nose almost stuck to the side window. Changing the subject, Casie asked, "Are you from here? Were you born in this town?"

When he didn't answer right away she turned to him.

His jaw was hard and set, mouth clamped, crinkles around his eyes looked pinched as he stared hard out the window. He had one hand on the wheel and it visibly tightened.

"Neco? Are you all right?" She reached out and touched his arm.

He glanced at her, saw her concern and smiled bleakly. "Sure, yeah, I'm fine. To answer your question, no, I wasn't born in Lark. I was born in the city, on the other side of Sanlura."

That neither place was familiar to her was obvious by her blank look at the names. She asked, "Is your family here, in, uh, Lark?"

He shook his head. "No. They're in Sanlura."

"Hmm." She looked back out the window. "So why are you living here. Don't you like being close to them?" Glancing at him she saw his jaw go rigid again. But then it reluctantly softened slightly.

"I do like being close to my family. Just not right now."

She started to speak but he cut her off, "I really don't want to talk about it right now." He looked quickly at her then back at the road.

Her lips were pulled in like she'd been chastised.

"Honey," he said kindly and patted her leg. "It's just a…not a long story, but a complicated one and I don't want to go into it right now. I don't want to drag the mood down. But, if later, down the road, you still want to know, I'll tell you. All right?" He kept his hand on her leg.

It felt like his big palm on her leg was burning through to her core. Trying to ignore it, Casie said cheerfully, "Okay. I want this to be a nice day. I agree, let's not do anything to bring it down." She shot him a cheery smile.

He returned her smile and squeezed her leg, and again left his hand there. They both were highly conscious of it.

He didn't move it until he parked in front of the diner.

It was a little late for rush hour lunchtime so there was plenty of parking. He hurried around to get her door but she'd already opened it.

"Wait, Casie, it's a high step, I don't want you to break your neck, let me help you." His eyes were trained on her legs as she pulled her skirt down that got pushed up when she slid to the edge of the seat to get out.

"Put your hands on my shoulders," he told her while he held her arm.

On the sidewalk, while he locked the truck, Casie looked around.

Lark was a small town, on the rustic side, the street was lined with grocers and pharmacies, bars and shops. People were bustling up and down the walks. A few nodded or waved at Neco, he nodded back without smiling.

The diner had a silver steel front with cherry red trim, red door and red sign. Neco held the door for her and she stepped shyly inside.

He didn't expect it because he was pretty sure she wasn't from around the area, but Neco still kept a discreet eye out for someone looking at Casie like they recognized her. He said nothing to her about it, she was already acutely uncomfortable just being out and not having any idea of her identity.

A dozen heads turned as they entered. They didn't look away. People blatantly stared with curiosity at her.

Casie pulled her long hair around to cover the side of her face. "Neco," she whispered. He bent his head down to hear her.

An urgency tightening her voice, she said quietly, "My bruises, cuts, they're staring, I must look awful." She started to turn back to the door. "Please, can we go home?"

Neco swung his arm around her waist. "No, you look beautiful, I swear to you. Your bruises can't even be seen except really up close. They're staring because this is a small town and most everyone knows everyone, and because, like I said," he hugged her to him as they followed the hostess to their booth, "you are an extraordinarily beautiful woman. Believe me."

He helped her off with her jacket, then shrugged out of his and set them on the booth seat.

She still looked doubtful, keeping her eyes lowered as she slid over the red vinyl seat.

Neco sat on the other side. He had hesitated, he really wanted to sit next to her, but decided it was better for him to keep his distance. He was in a state of arousal every time he was near her, laying eyes on her, make that even thinking about her brought on a damned boner.

He thanked the attractive hostess as she handed him a menu. She smiled broadly at him but he didn't even glance at her.

The server came right to the table. "Hi there, handsome," she greeted Neco with a blatant invitation in her dark eyes.

Neco said to Casie, "What do you want to drink, honey?"

She opened her menu. "Um…" She asked the waitress who was staring boldly at Neco like she wanted to eat him, "Do you have unsweetened ice tea?"

The hostess didn't answer, she kept staring at Neco. He was looking at his menu. He looked up at the twenty-something with blonde hair, a lot of makeup and brazen smile.

Frowning, he said coldly to the server, "The lady asked you a question."

At first the waitress looked offended at his tone, then she turned up the wattage on her smile. Leering at Neco in undeniable solicitation, she said to him, "Sorry, hon." Without turning to Casie, she muttered with unconcealed disinterest and annoyance, "Yeah, we have it, is that what you want?"

"Yes, please." Her voice came out small, Casie felt in the way. The woman was clearly attracted to Neco.

"I'll have the same. Thanks." Neco dismissed her without another glance and set his hand over one of Casie's. "You look sad, baby, is everything okay?"

Her lips turned in a semblance of a wan smile, green eyes flipped up to his then immediately lowered to the table. "I'm fine, Neco. But, I," she took a breath, her gaze darted to the side, flitting over at the customers that were still staring.

"What, Casie? Don't look at them, they'll stop in a minute. But what?" He squeezed her hand gently. Her face was such an open book, she was completely unaware her every emotion blared across it.

Her shoulders moved in a small shrug. "That woman. The, uh, waitress," she trailed off again.

"The waitress, what about her?" His dark brows arched puzzled as to what was upsetting her.

Casie pulled her hand out from under his and folded both in her lap. "She, uh, is obviously interested in you, and I feel…you know…in the way. She likes you and you might get a date with her if I wasn't here."

Neco blinked rapidly at her in puzzlement. He had barely noticed the woman except she annoyed him by deliberately and rudely ignoring Casie.

He folded his arms on the table and leaned towards Casie. The position made his biceps bulge huge even in the loose shirt. "Casie, she's hit on me like half a dozen times. Every time I come in here she flirts and gives me her number. If I had any interest in her I would have already done something about it."

"Oh, so you've dated her?" She didn't know why this bothered her so much. "I know she was looking at me wondering why such a dud was with you."

He laughed like she was being ridiculous. "No, we have not dated and we are not going to date because I have zero interest in her." He didn't mention also that he didn't really date. He had sex, but he didn't date, at least not any more.

Frowning, he said, "Now stop being so," he tried to think of a word that wouldn't hurt her feelings.

Her head tilted down, lids lowered over her eyes. Peering up slightly through the long lashes that curled up at the very ends, she asked quietly, "So…what?"

"Damn girl, sometimes you have the sultriest looks."

Her head straightened, lids popped up. "What?"

Neco shook his head with a laugh. "Never mind. You keep disparaging yourself, and you don't even know you. I like you, and if you were as wretched looking as you say you are, it makes me look like I have horrendous taste in the women I date, and that is far from the truth."

His gaze swept her soft face and he realized his taste was changing. She was nothing like the brash, flagrantly sexual women he normally saw. Then again, he chose them more for their easiness, than their actual looks. A means to a quick end. A release, nothing more.

He'd dated when he was younger, had a few serious relationships, but then between the boxing circuits and the military it left little room to give any one woman the attention she required, and deserved.

Then Kandi came along and changed everything. He didn't realize he was staring so hard at Casie until her lids levered down over her eyes, shielding her from his intense perusal.

Lowering her head again, Casie looked up at him with a patronizing smile. She reminded him, "Neco, we are not dating." Pink blossomed up her neck and over her cheeks, but she kept her eyes on his.

With a slight smile of gratefulness, she said, "You rescued me like I was a stray cat. You are kindhearted and keep helping me. Even a caring person would take care of an ugly cat."

Wailing, "Oh Lord," he rolled his eyes. The server returned and set their drinks down. "Baby, you are not-"

"You ready to order?" Her full attention on Neco, the waitress cut him off trying to draw his attention to her.

He ignored her. Looking at Casie with a tender smile, he asked, "What would you like, honey?"

She started at his use of the endearment honey. Sure he'd called her that at the house, but he was being kind to her like you would speak kindly to an invalid, but out in public it made them sound like they were-

"Casie?"

She peered up from the menu. His eyes were not their normal chilled blue. Right now the blues were settled on her warmly like a baby boy's blue flannel blanket.

Casie turned her attention to the server even though the woman never looked at her. "I would like a burger with some fries, please, Miss, um, Tempest." She read the nametag, Tempest M.

"Sure. How you want that cooked?" Tempest's eyes were on her pad as she wrote so she didn't see the suddenly panicked look on Casie's face.

Neco said, "Honey, last time it wasn't cooked enough for you, why don't you try medium this time?"

Casie's weak smile of relief she gave him warmed his heart. Their eyes stayed connected.

Purposely breaking their connection, the waitress bent towards Neco trying to give him a look down the front of her uniform. She'd unbuttoned several buttons when she had first seen him come in. Every time he came into the diner she was more determined to get him to ask her out.

She tried asking him out for a drink, or whatever he would like, but he always politely shot her down. Said he was really busy but that it was kind of her to ask.

Kind? Hell, she wanted to jump his damned bones, kindness had nothing to do with the heat that burned between her legs the moment her eyes caught the handsome bruiser coming in the door.

Tempest had wondered if he was gay, she couldn't believe the man didn't run with her obvious offer of sex. She knew she was built and pretty, she had her pick of the hottest males in Lark. But, she knew men, and this guy was straight as an iron rod. There he was sitting next to Miss Goody Two Shoes, maybe he liked the young and dumb types?

Neco stared at his menu.

Tempest set a palm on the booth and leaned over further. "See anything you'd like, sugarpie?" Most men fell drooling into her abundant cleavage, she had to fight half of them off with a whack of her check pad.

He closed the menu and handed it to her. "I'd like you to knock off the flirting shit, Tempest, and I'll have the same as the lady, a hamburger, medium, with fries. Thanks." His gaze never even went in her direction, he smiled at Casie.

Tempest flounced off in a huff.

Neco grabbed up packs of sugar, tore them open and dumped the sugar in his tea, half of the sugar missed the glass and spilled on the table.

"Cut it out," he said jokingly at Casie's giggles. "I have big fingers and that's not a large glass. We can't all be all ladylike and dainty like you, you know."

With a burst of laughter, she threw her head back. When she stopped laughing and looked at him, her eyes were glistening with laughing tears.

He regarded her with a pretend offended look, his bottom lip pushed out in a pout.

It made her grin harder. "I'm sorry," she giggled. "I was just picturing you with those big 'ol thick fingers, pinky in the air and eating all dainty and proper, elegantly chewing a fancy cucumber sandwich, dabbing primly at your lips with a napkin."

She burst out laughing again. Slapping her hand over her mouth, her merry eyes twinkling at him over her hand.

A crooked grin softened his tough countenance. He said softly, "I like it when you laugh, Casie, it makes me smile, it feels good." The color in his face darkened and his eyes glazed over as he remembered when he'd brought her home thinking she was going to die.

He had wondered then what she would sound like, look like, happy. And now he knew. He liked it. A lot.

Then he slid over on the booth and stood up. "I need to wash my hands, and there's a guy at the other end of the diner I need a quick word with. I'll be right back, don't get into any trouble."

She was still laughing at him when he left the table, grinning.

Casie stuck her fork in her lemon then squeezed it over her tea. When all the juice was out of it, she dropped it in the glass. Peeling the paper off her straw, she plunked it in, swished the ice around then bent her head to suck on it. It was good, even without sugar.

"Hey there, gorgeous."

A man stopped by the table. Casie kept her head down assuming he was speaking to the person behind her.

But, he leaned a hip against her booth, facing her. He bent a little towards her and said, "Hi honey, you are definitely new in town. I would have remembered you if I'd seen you before."

Keeping her head down, her lips on her straw, Casie peered up at him. Why was he talking to her? Maybe he was a friend of Neco's. She raised her head and gave him a cool but polite smile. "Can I help you?"

He was quite handsome in a more stylish sense, while Neco's looks were tougher.

Neco was as good looking as this man, but in a strong masculine way. Casie preferred Neco's more rugged type of male.

95

The stranger probably did all right with the women. His black hair was combed straight off his tanned face. He had light scrub on his jaw, a classical nose, solid jaw and dark eyes that were at the moment scrolling up and down her body. She shifted uncomfortably under his scrutiny.

"What's your name, sweetness?" He had a deep, sensuous voice, and dimple slices on both sides of his face.

Casie glanced around looking for Neco, hoping he'd hurry back. She didn't know what to say. Casie wasn't her real name, and they hadn't made up a last name for her. She was at a loss and it showed.

The man set his palm on the table like the server had done and leaned closer, boxing her in. If she wanted to get out she would have to make a scene.

His chuckle was sensuous and velvety. "Damn, gorgeous and shy, what a package." He held his hand out to her and introduced himself. "I'm Rex King." He waited patiently with a friendly smile while she very slowly, hesitantly, put her hand in his, then he shook it gently.

He had a huge hand, like Neco's but not as calloused as Neco's, he apparently didn't do as much labor.

The little of his life he'd talked about, Neco said he had lived for a while deep in the wilderness, living off the land, hunting and mountain climbing and such. And he sparred with his brothers, and liked to chop wood year round for the fireplace.

King was wearing sharply pressed black slacks and a severely starched, long-sleeved navy blue shirt. Several buttons were undone, gold chains twinkled in the black hair that was visible under the open lapel.

His shoes were black and as highly polished as his hair. He looked a few years older than Neco, maybe around 32 or 33.

He kept hold of her hand, she mumbled, "Um, pleased to meet you," and tried to peer around him, but he moved slightly to block her view.

He laughed. "My, aren't we the polite one?" His teeth were big and bright white, so white they gleamed.

Made her think of the big bad wolf in the nursery rhymes. *Oh, that was odd*, she remembered nursery rhymes. Maybe she was getting some memory back.

Feeling bittersweet about that, it would mean leaving Neco, she had to tug to get her hand back. She gave him another tight polite smile.

"A quiet woman," he said with teasing wonder. "Never thought I'd see the day. Just tell me your first name, little green eyes."

He said it so firmly, almost commanding, but wrapped in a cajoling soft voice.

Avoiding looking directly at him she responded with a breathy whisper, "Um, uh, it's Casie." How embarrassing, did she always stammer so awkwardly?

His smile broadened. "Now, that's a cute name. Listen sugar, I own the exotic dance club down the road, the King's Palace." The smile showed more teeth. "Ah, I see by the blush you are appalled at my type of business."

Not wanting to insult him, she shook her head and said swiftly, "No, not at- at all. I'm just…uh," she didn't know what to say. Her face got redder and his smile got bigger.

Rex moved slightly closer to her. "You are so pretty, honey, and that's a damned understatement. I'm thinking you would be a big draw in my club. You have the sexiest green eyes I've ever seen, a face like a damned water-lily, and a raging, fresh, young bod."

Peering at her through slightly squinted eyes, he said with appreciation, "That skin is amazing, no makeup and it's as pure as top shelf cream."

She had no idea what to say to his absurd words. It was like he was trying out his amateur poetry on her.

*****

"Yeah," Rex shook his head in wonder at the jewel sitting so anxiously in front of him. He actually had a crazy urge to touch her, what a new experience for him!

Seeing her confusion, he chuckled. Somehow the little broad had no idea how sexy she was. It only made her hotter. Sexy and youthful innocence, and blushingly awkward, all together was a cock burning combination.

Rex could picture her on his center stage in only a G-string and stilettoes. Right now those high plump breasts strained with graceful sensuality at the blouse, the tiny waist curved in at the waistband of her skirt.

He'd gotten a glimpse of her shapely yet still girlish legs before she tucked them self-consciously under the booth.

He'd bet she had an ass on her to kill for, he'd have to wait to see that. The anticipation of that was curiously hot, seething hot. He felt his cock stir in a way it hadn't in a long time.

Rex lived 24/7 practically, with naked women. It took a lot these days to get him really excited. And this little, soft feminine package was doing it with one look at her.

His voice as deep and roughly soft and sensuous as molten velvet, he coaxed, "A dancer, sweetness. I think you would make a great dancer at my club, what do you think?" He tried to reach for her hand but she clasped them together in her lap.

"I...don't think I dance. I don't really know...I, what are you saying?"

Behind the smile, he was thinking, *hell, hot and blushes like a young girl, she could make him a lot of money, that is after he got between her legs first.*

"Let me make this more...um clear. I'm offering you a job to dance in my club. That would be as an exotic dancer."

Rex watched the confusion swirl around her face. Could a young woman these days be that naïve she didn't get what he was offering her? "Sugar, I'm offering you a job as a stripper. You can make enormous amounts of cake."

Her brows wrinkled adorably. "Cake? I don't under-"

"Dough baby, bread, dinero, bucks. You can make primo cash dancing naked in my club."

He had to bite his tongue to keep from laughing as he saw the comprehension dawn on her face. The blush deepened and she was repelled. Damn she was cute.

"Sir, I...no, no thank you. Um," she craned her neck searching for someone to rescue her. How demure, sweet helplessness. And hot.

Seeing she was getting upset, Rex moved closer, half sitting on the table. Facing her so she was in the curve of his body, he set a hand on her shoulder.

"Okay, sugar, calm down. You could start out as a barmaid. You can keep your clothes on." *Not that there's much more to the barmaid's outfit, at least her tits would almost be covered, her nipples anyway, that should give her some confidence...*

He resisted letting his gaze dip down to her breasts. Some women would love the fascinated interest and would preen in his obvious attraction, Rex could tell it would only shut this one down.

She was too modest and too shy. He couldn't believe he had to suppress the erotic shiver bolting the length of his body. What a first.

Casie shifted in her seat trying to politely get his hand off her shoulder, but he was edging even closer to her. Demurring, "No, thank you," she wiggled, but he only clutched her more tightly.

"Sugar, I don't know what you're doing for work now, but I promise you, you can earn ten times, more than ten times what you're earning now. How 'bout you come with me right now and we can-" he broke off at her look of dismay and shaking head.

"All right, just give me your phone number and I'll take you out to dinner and we can get to know each other bet-"

"What the hell are you doing, King? Back the fuck off."

Casie had never heard Neco sound so angry. He didn't yell, but it was worse, there was a deeply quiet, coarse menace in his low voice.

He moved between Rex and Casie. Neco didn't touch Rex, he didn't have to, his body and expression were so formidable and threatening, his physical presence was like a tangible, moving concrete wall.

Rex slid his hip off the table and took a step back.

Neatly concealing his own ire, Rex turned to greet Neco. "Hey, Bardiche, what's going on?" His bland polite expression hid that he was not pleased that the person sitting with his new little found treasure was Neco Bardiche.

He had hoped it was another woman, or at the least, not such a powerful man. Bardiche was damned intimidating even when you weren't hitting on his woman.

Dispensing with any pleasantries, Neco said plainly, "What's going on is, you're going to get your ass away from her, way away, and stay away. If that's confusing you let me know and I'll spell it out more clearly for you."

Neco was barely holding the proprietary anger from his voice, but it was all over his dark face. Even the blue eyes had darkened with aggressive warning. His big shoulders pumped, a vein beat violently at his temple.

"Hey now, Bardiche, take a pill. I'm just offering the young lady a job. It's between her and me, and really none of your business." Now Rex's own voice was deepening in irritation.

Neco moved within inches of Rex and got in his face. Scarcely keeping his anger leashed, he growled, "She doesn't need a job. And she is my business. I said it nicely, now fuck off."

Rex scowled at him but didn't move. They were almost eyeball-to-eyeball, however Neco had an inch or two on him.

Growling his own anger, Rex, sneered, "Why don't you let her answer for herself instead of acting like her pit-bull bodyguard? You think because you were a champion boxer and some kind of fucking special ops you can throw your weight around? I'm not afraid of you, Bardiche, why don't *you* fuck off?"

The fact that this piece of trash strip joint owner was all over Casie and trying to get her to leave with him, made his brain burn with such blazing black fury, Neco had to fight to keep aware of where he was.

He couldn't brawl inside the diner. And he would no way put Casie in harm's way. Brow a heavy low line, his hands rolled in huge tight fists, he looked about to explode. "Let's take this outside, King-"

"No," Casie said so suddenly and calmly both men gaped at her. "Both of you stop."

She nodded to Rex with a stiff yet courteous smile. "Thank you, Mr. King, for your kind offer, but I decline. Neco, the waitress is standing there with our food. Please sit down so we can eat."

Impressed with her gracious assertiveness, Rex said with a respectful smile, "All right. You've made yourself clear, little green eyes. Just remember though, if you need a job, I can fit you in...anywhere. Or, just anytime you'd like to get to know me better, just call the club. I know where all the best dining and hotspots are. You'd look great on my arm, babe, just think about that."

He snatched up her hand and kissed the back of it. "I'll remember you, Casie," then he walked off just as Neco was reaching for him.

"Neco," Casie said quietly, "you're drawing attention, please sit down."

Chapter Eleven

Neco forced his infuriated gaze to move from King's receding back to Casie sitting so tensely, demure and pretty, struggling to squelch her skyrocketing agitation that the two men had come close to throwing blows. Over her.

Neco had to work to rein in his rage and slow his harsh breathing. He was reacting like a fierce dragon, all puffed up and breathing fire.

For some reason, Casie brought out the protectiveness in him, and unfamiliar possessiveness, neither was a feeling he was accustomed to. He couldn't stop the fury that had taken him over when he saw the son of a bitch hanging all over her, stripping her with his ravaging gangster's eyes.

Letting out his wrath with a long exhale, he muttered, "Yeah, okay." He slid into the seat across from her and scrubbed his face with his hands as the server set their food down.

Tempest winked at him and brushed her arm across his when she put her plate in front of him.

He ignored her like she was nothing but a pesky fly. First King, now the wanton waitress. He needed to get a grip on his possessive anger or they would never be able to leave the house again.

When Tempest left, he laid his forearms on the table on either side of his plate and watched Casie pour ketchup on her fries acting like nothing had happened. "Casie…"

"Hmmm?" She picked up a long fry with her fingers and bit off half of it.

"You okay? That guy is a fuck- uh, damned creep, don't even talk to him if you see him again. It'll only encourage him."

One brow arched over a glistening emerald eye in slight indignation. "Are you telling me who I can and can't talk to?" The rest of the fry slipped into her mouth, she licked her fingers.

Neco stared at her fingers in her mouth, the little pink tongue licking them, the soft lips sucking at them. He blinked then cleared his throat.

"No, of course not. It's just, in the, you know, situation you're in right now your judgment might be impaired. I don't want to see you fall into something you aren't aware of."

He shifted uncomfortably when she gazed steadily back at him, the rebuke clear in the green orbs.

"I am not a child, Neco, I'm sure even with amnesia I still have common sense."

"I'm not saying you don't, and, we don't know how old you are, you look young as shit, so," he picked up his burger with both hands and took a huge bite.

"So?" She took her knife and cut her hamburger in half, stuffing the tomato back in that slipped out the side.

Speaking through his mouthful, Neco shrugged, "I'm just saying, I mean don't get all bent out of shape, but you might not even be legal. Not of age to serve alcohol."

That gave her pause. Thinking about it, she sipped her iced tea. Eyes wide in question, she asked, "How old do you have to be to work in a bar?"

His mouth dropped open, then he chewed and swallowed the lump of meat and bun. Wiping the back of his hand across his mouth, he frowned at her. "Casie, you don't want to work in a bar, and you sure as hell don't want to work for that scum. It's not just a bar, it's a strip joint."

103

He snatched up his tea and gulped down almost all of it. Scowling at the glass, he shook it with a sharp annoyance to loosen the stuck ice cubes.

Silently, Casie contemplated her food before picking up a ketchup laden fry.

"Casie? Tell me you're not thinking about working for that fucker?" He set his burger down and glared at her.

She shrugged gracefully. "I don't know, I need a job. And I'm thinking he wouldn't be too hung up on the fact that I don't have any ID. He said I could work as a barmaid." Stirring her tea with the straw, the melting cubes chinked around the glass.

Neco leaned across the table, his blue eyes sparking ire. "Listen to me Casie-"

"How is everything, handsome?" The waitress butted in standing with her back to Casie.

Neco raked both hands through his hair mussing the wavy locks. He shot an irritated look at the interrupting woman while trying to look around her to see Casie, but the server kept moving to block her from his view.

He glared up at her. "Do you mind? We're having a conversation here," his carved lips pulled in to keep from saying more.

"All right, handsome, don't get your nuts in a nettle. God how I love a domineering man," Tempest sighed and fluffed her blonde hair with long turquoise nails.

Lowering her voice with a coy smile and eyelash flutter, she cooed, "In all things..." Then she set a small folded paper next to his plate and sashayed her ass as hard as she could away with a coquettish look back at him over her shoulder.

"Casie-"

"You see, Neco? I'm in your way. I need to get on my feet, give you your space." Her sad gaze floated to the paper, then up to stare blankly out the window.

Compressing his hand into a tight fist, Neco spouted angrily, "I told you I have no interest in that bitch." Taking a deep breath, he worked to quiet his voice. "Sorry."

Reaching across the table, he took her hand and squeezed it for her to look at him. When she did, he said, "Honey, we talked about this. Slow down, there is no hurry for you to do anything. Right now, you just stay with me until you're fully healed and we can start working on finding out your identity. Take one step at a time."

Shaking her head, she protested, "But I can't impose on you any-"

He squeezed her hand firmly. "Again, we've talked about this, Casie. You are not an imposition. It would be more of an imposition if I had to worry about you running around town all alone and confused. Geez, just thinking about you working at that asshole's club I-"

He shook his head with a creeped-out shiver. "Please, just give it some time. Just stay with me, let me give you security and care."

She looked at him, her plate, the window, back to him. "But for how long, Neco? How long before I've outstayed my welcome?"

The corner of his mouth edged up. "Honey, you can't possibly outstay your welcome." Feelings for her were already starting to make themselves at home in his heart.

Neco cleared his throat again, then said, "Let's just take this a little at a time. Can we not talk about you leaving again, or getting a job for at least a few weeks?"

Casie pulled her hand from his and tucked both hands under her thighs. She studied him carefully to judge how serious he was.

He was gazing at her steadily, his mouth firm but with a warm smile, a corner pulled in expressing his hope that she'd say yes and let it go.

She acquiesced with a soft exhale and unsure nod. "Um, okay."

When he looked relieved, she said quickly, "But you have to tell me the second I'm on your nerves. Or if you want to bring a lady friend home, your girlfriend, oh," she put a hand in front of her mouth. "Neco, what should I do when you want to bring a date home?"

His face twisted, brows slashed down, irritated again. His voice rumbling, he growled, "Would you stop worrying about my love life? I've told you, I am not seeing anyone. Seriously honey, it has nothing to do with you." *Or it hadn't until you came onto the scene.*

Looking her sincerely in the eye, he said, "I am not interested in being involved with anyone right now." Any *other* woman that is.

"But a man has needs," she said.

Rolling his eyes, he held a hand up. "Don't go there, Casie. I have no desire to have sex with anyone right now. Trust me, I won't be picking up any women and bringing them home." His eyes slid away briefly when he said he didn't want to have sex with anyone, that wasn't exactly true, he meant anyone *else.*

"So, can you just settle down for a while, honey? I don't want to have this conversation every other day. You can hardly heal properly if you're constantly worried that you're a problem and need to go."

Not answering his question, Casie said, "You keep calling me honey. Aren't you worried people will get the wrong idea?"

His gaze wandered from her thick wavy amber hair to the prismatic green eyes. He didn't look down further, he didn't need a boner when they were getting ready to leave. It was the reason why he wasn't sitting next to her.

Truth be told, he was hardly aware he was calling her that, it just came out naturally.

He smiled warmly at her. "It's just, Casie, that you are so sweet and all silky amber, like honey." He pushed his plate away and clasped his hands on the table. "You'll learn that I don't care what people think."

Her lids lowered to hide her expression. Trying to sound casual, she said, "Um, so, just so I know and don't make a fool of myself, if you are going to, you know," there goes that blush again, she resisted covering her cheeks with her hands.

106

"If you plan to stay over at a woman's house, would you, I mean, I know I would worry if you didn't come home all night. I mean," the color rushed into her face hot and pink.

She rushed on, "Of course it's none of my business what you do, but, like I said, I would worry. So, would you be, you know, letting me know if you weren't…coming…home…just send like a text…" Her ramblings trailed off with awkwardness and the sight of his face turning dark again.

The planes in Neco's face hardened further at her every word. Why did she keep assuming he was going to drag women home all the time and bang them practically in front of her?

Then, seeing how distressed she was, he loosened the deep furrows in his forehead. He raised his slashing brows and tried to smile, but it was difficult. By God she was so stubborn and selfless, and totally oblivious of his flaming desire for her.

"Casie, this is the last time we're going to discuss this. Listen to me," he spoke slowly, his words deliberately methodical. "I do not want to date or pick up any women." Hell, talk about her oblivion, he was blindly oblivious to other women since Casie had come into his life.

"Therefore, I will not be bringing anyone home, and I will not be staying at someone's house. If for some strange reason, due to a family emergency or something like that and I'm going to be really late or not come home at all, I will call you. I promise.

"I would not want to sit all night worried to death if you were out without a word, I sure wouldn't want to inflict the same thing on you." *Not that you're gonna be out without me anyway.* "So, my little worry wart, can we close this subject now and move on?"

Her face unreadable, she looked at him. He stared back calmly. She couldn't see he was holding his breath.

"Um, all right. For now. But you promise to tell me if you-"

"Great!" He twisted and waved at their server. "You want any dessert, hon- Casie?"

She shook her head. He had finished off the other half of her burger and the rest of her fries.

She drained her tea. "I'm stuffed."

Tempest hurried right over.

Neco said, "Just bring the check, Tempest."

"Don't you want-"

"No. The check. Please." He shot her a hard look, then picked up the paper she'd left by his plate, dropped it on the plate and handed the plate to her.

He turned from her scowl, dismissing her. Even if he wasn't sitting with the most beautiful girl in the world, Neco would not be interested in her harsh, ridden hard and put away wet looks, especially one that flirts with him and gives him notes while he's with another woman. That's just low class and pure slutty.

Tempest wrote up the bill and laid it on the table. When Neco went to pick it up, she set her hand over his. Still not giving up, "Listen," she whispered, "when you drop the child here at her home, why don't you come back and-"

He yanked his hand out from under hers. Without a word, he took out his wallet set some bills on the check and said to Casie, "You ready, *honey?*"

Neco couldn't help but smile at her sweet blush. He scooped up their jackets and stood up forcing the waitress to stand back. He moved to Casie with his hand out.

Casie wriggled out of the seat and took his hand.

After helping her on with her jacket and slipping into his own, Neco led her down the aisle and out the door.

Exclaiming, "Ah, fresh air," he breathed deeply. His mouth twisted, next time he came into town he needed to have a talk with that bitch. Tell Tempest to keep her hands to herself, don't give him any more notes.

And, if he brings Casie in again, *when* he brings her in again, he slid a glance at her and smiled, she was relaxed right now, damn he loved that. He'll give the owner of the diner a call, Jonathan Bravo, and tell him he doesn't want Tempest near them.

If she comes on as strong again as she did today and he is with Casie, chances are he'll blow his cool. Alone, he can just brush her off, but he could see how it embarrassed Casie and pushed her to back away from him thinking he wanted to date Tempest.

Casie turned her face up to feel the sun on it. Her head still tipped back soaking in the warmth, she asked, "What was on that paper she gave you?"

Before he could answer, a grimace pulled her lips. "I'm sorry," she kept her face tilted up. "I keep speaking out of turn, it's none of my business."

He took her hand. "I don't know, I didn't look at it. I assume it was her phone number, again. Come on, I have somewhere I want to take you."

She smiled up at him. "Where?"

He lifted her hand and kissed her knuckles. "You're looking healthier, you have roses in your cheeks." He brushed her face with his fingertips, making her cheeks brighten further. They started down the street.

"Where are we going?" Casie asked, her head swiveling to look inside every window they passed.

"You need some clothes, babe."

She stopped. "What?"

Neco knew she would react this way. He shored up his patience, turned and faced her. "I really don't want to argue about this, Casie."

Her brow knit. "About what?"

"You need clothes that fit you. You can't wear my clothes out in public, and I can't stand to see that skirt and blouse on you."

Her lip pursed, she looked down at herself. Hurt in her voice, she said, "What's wrong with my clothes? You should have told me how bad I looked, I wouldn't have come."

His eyes rolled heavenward, then centered on her. Shaking his head, he said, "Your clothes," his lips thinned, "it's just that those are what you were wearing when I...found you. They continually remind me of how close to death you were." He said matter of fact, "I would like to burn them."

Her amber brows hopped. "I-"

"You, need clothes. Let's go," he tugged her to start walking.

"Wait," she put a hand on his wrist to stop him. Her face flamed in her usual embarrassment. "Neco, you know I don't have any money, I can't-"

He kept pulling her with him. "Yeah, yeah, I know. I said I don't want to argue with you. I'm buying them. Come on, this way," he headed to a clothes shop.

"Neco, no-"

He paused with his hand on the door handle of the shop. Facing her, he said calmly, "Casie, you need clothes. You have no money. I do. I'm paying for them. Do not make us fight about it in the store. Just give in gracefully."

Still talking, he swung the door open and set his hand on her lower back and literally pushed her inside. "I think sweaters because it's still cold. A couple of pairs of Jeans? You want dresses?"

"Neco," she whispered as a clerk came hurrying towards them, "I don't even know my size."

"Don't worry about it, baby." He grinned at the clerk.

A woman in her forties, curly brown hair, on the angular side in a pants suit, smiling helpful and friendly asked, "Can I help you?"

Neco slipped his hand around Casie's waist and said, "Yes, thank you. She needs some clothes. She, ah, lost some weight and isn't quite sure of her size now." His lips pulled in hiding his grin at the gasp from Casie.

She may not have her memory, but every woman hated thinking they were fat, and he had just implied she had been overweight.

"Miss, uh," he smiled politely at the clerk.

"Ford, Lynette Ford." She smiled at him and then at Casie.

"Miss Ford," Neco said, "I have some errands to run. Casie here needs some clothes. Can you help her?"

Her hands clasped in front of her, Miss Ford nodded. "Yes, of course." She said to Casie, "I don't know how much weight you lost, dear, but you are very slender. I hope you aren't planning on

110

losing any more weight, you're already dangerously on the thin side."

As Casie's indignant mouth opened to say something, the clerk asked, "What are you looking for, dear?"

Before Casie could respond, Neco said, "She needs some sweaters, blouses, t-shirts, several pairs of jeans, and some slacks. Let's see," his brow furrowed as he glanced around at the merchandise.

"Yes, also boots, shoes, sneakers, a couple of dresses, heels, maybe at least two pairs of shorts, and," he put his fingers to his chin eyeing Casie up and down.

"Neco," she balked.

But he looked at Miss Ford. "She needs at least a couple of week's worth or more of under...things." Now he was a shade embarrassed. "And a sweatshirt and a warm jacket, hat, gloves, what else?"

"Oh my gosh, Neco, *please*," Casie cried, but he ignored her.

"I'm not interested in the price of items. Just get what looks good and is comfortable, and what she needs. She needs girl stuff too, like toiletries, brushes and things. She's on vacation for a few months, and her suitcases were lost and she needs everything replaced. Don't forget nightgowns, slippers and the like."

He pulled out his wallet, slipped a credit card out then handed it to the clerk, "Here. Put everything on this and get her what she needs. Don't let her talk you out of anything," he said with a grin at Casie's red face.

Miss Ford was studying Casie's figure.

Neco had a twinge of concern that the woman was probably thinking Casie was being kept by him, that she was his mistress. He didn't care what she thought, but he didn't want Casie to feel humiliated.

But the woman seemed kind, like she wanted to take Casie under her wing. Besides, Casie was way too naïve to even think of them in terms of mistress and lover, sugar daddy, whatever. Slipping his wallet back in his pocket, he bent to speak privately in Casie's ear.

"Um," Miss Ford turned from them. "I'll just go start collecting things I think will be right for you, dear." She immediately took off to begin her project.

Other than them, the boutique was empty. Another clerk poked her head out of the back room when they'd first entered, but never came out.

Neco put a hand on Casie's small waist pulling her slightly closer to him. He could feel her warmth, scent her pleasant natural fragrance. "Honey," he smiled at her frown, "don't think. Just do as I ask. If it makes you feel better you can think about paying me back way down the road."

He had no intentions of ever taking any money from her, but if she thought he would, and it made her feel better and be more agreeable to accepting his help then he'd let her think it.

Shit, she needs clothes, and since he got his work rolling and recouped his losses, his investments with his brothers are off the charts, he now has more money than he could ever spend.

His fingers clenched her waist, damn she was soft and firm at the same time. It was all he could do to keep from pulling her into his arms.

"Neco, I don't know what to say," Casie murmured, clearly discomfited and confused and grateful.

"Just have fun, honey. I'll be back in," he glanced at his watch, "about 1- 1 and half hours. You think that will be enough time?"

Her bewildered expression brought a smile to his face. He was smiling a lot more lately. Strange, a few weeks ago he thought he'd never smile again.

Before he thought about it, he bent and kissed the top of her head. "Thank you for saving me," he whispered.

Her forehead creased in confusion. "But I didn't-"

Miss Ford approached them with several blouses on hangers. "I've put some things in a fitting room number two, my dear, for whenever you're ready."

"All right. Casie go on, I need to speak with Miss Ford a minute."

Casie gave him a lost look. Neco brushed his knuckles gently down her cheek. "Go on. Remember, don't think. Just do this for me."

Uncertainty straining her face, Casie nodded and left for the fitting room, leaving Neco with the clerk.

Watching Casie's hot little tush sway in the skirt he was hoping to burn, as she walked away, Neco said, "Miss Ford, I meant what I said. Get her enough outfits for like a month or two's worth. Don't let her see the prices of things, just get them."

"Well, I'm not sure of the style you, or she is looking for. I mean, do you want…" Her narrow cheeks turned pink. "I mean, she's a beautiful girl with a very slender but stunning figure. Do you want her to show it off, or-"

His face darkened. "No," he said quickly. He cleared his throat with a low sound before saying, "I mean, dress her like the beautiful young lady that she is. Not prim and prudish, be fashionable, but no deep cleavage or see-through, skintight or micro-short skirts, or-"

"Yes sir, I get it." She smiled with indulgence. She was trying to figure out their relationship. He treated the young woman like he was her father, but he was too young for that. Maybe like a brother, but he sure didn't look at her that way.

And, she seemed too sweet and uncomfortable with his generosity to be a kept woman. Oh well, it was none of her business.

Neco's eyes wandered to a section near them that contained sleepwear. A nightgown caught his eye. He moved to the hangers and looked at a few more things that interested him. She might like pajamas, but hell, he liked the nightgowns.

He pulled off several and handed them to the clerk. If Casie wanted pajamas she could wear his. The thought made his dick twitch. Shoving down the urge to picture her in just his pajama top…or better, just the bottoms- the clerk was waiting.

She was watching him with a knowing smile. "I'll see that she has everything she needs."

"All right, thanks. Here's my number, call me immediately if anything, well, is not right. She's been ill and I don't want her to get over tired. Or, ah, leave without me. Her illness has caused her to have bouts of dizziness and confusion."

As he handed her a business card, he said, "Oh, and no perfume." He didn't want anything masking that sweet natural scent of her.

"I'll be back in an hour or so. Get whatever you think she needs, not necessarily what she wants. She will try to resist accepting things, just be firm but, you know, don't let her feel uncomfortable try to be-"

"Of course," Miss Ford smiled assuredly with a firm nod. "I am not overbearing and I will be discrete. I understand what you're looking for."

Neco saw Casie peeking out of the fitting room at him. He grinned and wiggled his fingers at her then left the shop.

Chapter Twelve

*O*t was closer to two hours before Neco got back to the shop.

He got done what he needed to but when he got in his truck his brother Logan called.

Of the four brothers, Josh was oldest at 28, then Neco at almost 27, his brother Logan was only a year younger than him but he thought he could tell Neco what to do. Even Chaz, the youngest about to hit 25 thought he could boss them all around.

He was eager to get back to Casie, he wasn't comfortable leaving her alone for so long. She still had symptoms from the concussion, dizziness and disorientation. All he needed was for her to wander out of the shop disoriented.

With her confused condition and the amnesia, he worried people could sway her to agree to things that might not be in her best interest. Like that fucker Rex King. He periodically texted Miss Ford to stay in touch.

"Yeah, Lo, what do you want?" he said impatiently into his cell.

"Hey, bro, what the hell kind of greeting is that?" A slight hint of mirth negated the roughness of his brother Logan's words.

"What happened to leaving me alone, giving me the space I asked for? Josh has been hounding me, you call five times a week, what-"

Logan broke in, the mirth gone, "You're our brother, asshole. First off all, we don't have to do anything you say. Second, we're your fucking brothers, we have the right to bug you, muscle into your life, care about you. Hassle you about this idiotic self-imposed isolation, guilt, and depression you're drowning in."

"Lo-"

"None of it was your fault, you shithead. The bitch tricked you into marriage with that pregnancy crap. And Holten was not a good friend, or partner. I think he ended things the way he did because he was jealous of you, he wanted your life. He wanted to be Neco Bardiche. He wanted your job, your money, your wife-"

"I'm busy, Logan, can we do this some other time?" Neco was tired of people trying to tell him how he should feel.

His heavy sigh rumbling through the wires, Logan said, "Fine. Keep being an ass. But Ma and Dad and we all deserve to be treated better."

Silence. Letting go of his perturbed brusqueness, Neco exhaled his anger. "Yeah, I know. I'm sorry. You're right."

The grin back in his voice, Logan said, "Chaz's birthday is soon. We're doing a big barbeque-pool party thing at the house. You are expected to be there."

"How many people will be there? Is the number set?"

"Huh? What kind of question is that? Of course not, it's a party, everyone we know and don't know will be there."

Then Logan's brother radar came through with hopeful suspicion. "You aren't thinking of bringing someone are you? Like a chick? Tell me, Neco-"

"Conversation is over. Tell Ma I'll call her this weekend. Now, I gotta go, tell everyone I said hey, and bug off." He clicked off as his brother snickered with rapid questions asking if he was seeing a woman.

Shoving the phone in his pocket, Neco took a deep breath and blew it out. He loved his family, but they all thought they had the right to poke their noses into his business.

Not that he would do any less if the situation was reversed. He drove back to the shop and hurried inside, excited to see how things had gone.

When he opened the door, he saw Casie sitting in a chair with her hands folded, head lowered, she looked unhappy.

Miss Ford was standing over her yakking. Ford heard the door open and smiled over at him. She left Casie who never looked up and strode over to him.

There were a few other patrons in there now and the other clerk was out and about.

His eyes on Casie, Neco asked quietly, "How did it go?"

"Come to the register, dear." She nudged him to the counter. "Here's your card," she handed him his credit card. "You need to sign here," she pointed at the receipt.

Barely glancing at the bill, Neco's attention was still on Casie. "What happened? Is she all right?"

Miss Ford handed him his copy with a cheerful smile. "She's fine, Mr. Bardiche. She appears to be quite tired, like you said, it's apparent that she's been ill and is still recovering. Also, as you said she would, she resisted me all the way. I just kept giving her things to try on as distractions while I put the items to purchase in the basket."

The clerk smiled with fond indulgence glancing at Casie. "She really is a dear. But from what I can discern, she's not much of a chatterbug anyway."

He nodded with a small smile. "Yeah, I know."

"Plus, forgive me if I'm speaking out of turn, but I think she's feeling, embarrassed. I think she's embarrassed to accept all this from someone. From you. That she feels uncomfortable that she can't pay for the things herself."

She glanced over at Casie again with affection. "You have found yourself a woman that hasn't got a greedy bone in her body."

Nodding, his eyes still on Casie, her head was still lowered, Neco smiled. "I know."

"If I may say," Ford confided, "she seems so…lost, and scared." She turned to Neco. "But she thinks highly of you."

He brightened, his brows rose. "Really? How can you tell?"

She set a hand on his arm. "Dear, she smiles and seems calmer when she mentions your name. Instead of looking at the clothes she was trying on she kept looking out the window mumbling, 'Is he going to come back? When is he coming back?'

"I don't think she thought I could hear her. She seemed, I don't know, like she was afraid you weren't going to come back for her. I told her you were checking in here and there by phone, but she still seemed…worried."

Mumbling, "Thanks," Neco's brows drew down between his eyes and he moved from the clerk towards Casie. "Casie," he said softly as he neared her.

Her head came up. When Casie saw him, her face broke into a happy smile. "Neco, you came back!" She jumped to her feet and ran to him and threw herself into his arms.

She surprised him, she never touched him, Neco was always the one pawing her. His heart warmed as he enclosed her in his arms. He set the side of his face on the top of her head. "Casie, don't be ridiculous, why would I not return for you?"

He chuckled, stroking her hair. "I'm not insane, I left my credit card with thousands of dollars limit on it."

Reminded of why they were there, self-conscious of her actions Casie pulled back. She lifted the long tawny hair and pushed it behind her shoulders.

Chucking two fingers under her chin to lift it, Neco couldn't help laying a soft kiss on her lips, then he said, "Come on, honey, show me how you spent my money." It sounded to him like he was talking to her like a husband. He expected the old painful pang in his heart at the thought, and was surprised when he didn't feel anything but happy.

She took his hand and drew him to the register, her face blazing with mortification at the pile of bags hanging on the rack. "Neco, she, Miss Ford, insisted. I tried to stop her. We can put the stuff back right now. Give her your card, she can credit you-"

"Hush, Casie, we're not doing this. Just say, 'Thank you, Neco.'" His smile was teasing and warm.

"Um, thank- you, Neco. But you-"

"That's enough, let's go home. Put on your jacket, the temperature has dropped like a rock through an iced pond." He gathered up the bags.

Casie hurried to carry some too. He motioned with his head, "I got this, honey, just go to the truck."

Casie said to the clerk, "Thank you Miss Ford, for all your help. I appreciate your kindness and patience."

"My pleasure, dear, any time. Enjoy your purchases." The clerk gently touched Casie on her shoulder with fondness.

"Sure," Neco grumbled as Casie hurried to hold the door open for him, "you can thank everyone so easily...except me."

Her skin paled. "Oh, Neco, I'm sorry, I didn't mean to be-"

"I'm teasing, baby, hush, help me put this stuff in the truck." He bent and kissed her on the tip of the nose before she could blink. His keys in his hand, he pushed the remote and Casie went to open the doors for him.

Once he put all the bags in the backseat of his truck, he went to the passenger side and opened the door for her.

Casie came around the side to get in the truck.

His pupils flared as his gaze stroked over her. "You look nice, Casie, really nice."

Her new jeans were only slightly snug on her perfect ass and her thin but shapely legs. Under her new jacket, the burgundy sweater she wore was loose enough for modesty but the way her breasts moved under it was mesmerizing.

Her unassuming but luminous sexiness made Neco's head spin. She was soft and supple and feminine and graceful. He wanted her in his bed so badly his brain rippled with a crashing wave of desire that washed like lightning through him.

Where he found the waitress, Tempest's blatant attempt to look sexy with her big tits exposed in the deeply cut cleavage, and crammed into her skin-tight uniform distasteful and a turnoff,

Casie's sensuality was completely understated, yet it struck furtively hard and swift like an arrow, bang straight to his crotch.

Her femininity painted a man from the inside out but the sensation was so enigmatic, he couldn't put his finger on it, why he felt it so intensely, or what the precise feeling was.

It felt like fizzy air, like an ethereal sensuous cloak over his entire body. Pinpricks raised his flesh, reacting to her without even touching that soft skin.

It was in the siren's song of the green crystalline orbs that tugged at his groin. The way his hands curled to touch her, the way his body of its own accord just inched nearer and nearer to her, craving the feel of her pressed against him.

Yeah, her sensuality was soft dynamite, and she was so unaware of it. But the men weren't.

Rex King clearly wanted to haul her out of the booth at the diner and take her with him right then and there.

Casie's sexiness struck men hot and quick, like a flicked match firing before he was even consciously aware of it. So blazing, King would have likely tried to fuck her in his car not able to wait until he got her to his place.

Then knowing what a huge money making draw she would be with her unusual contradiction of shy explosive sex appeal, he would have put her naked on his stage in the evenings, and in his bed at night.

Swallowing down the rage coiling up his body, Neco had to fight to loosen every muscle that turned rigid at the thought of that bastard getting his hands on her. He had to literally stop and get his control straightened out.

Slamming a lid down on his anger, he stood behind Casie to help her climb into his truck. A double-edged sword, he got a great view of that perfect ass, but now his pants tightened more. He had to force himself not to palm his erection at the sight of her butt in his face before she slid in.

On the drive home, Neco was quiet, trying to sort out his funky feelings.

Casie watched the city pass until they were on the two-lane country road. Houses came fewer and further apart, barns and crops dotted in between farming spreads.

Dark clouds were rolling in, a few snowflakes rushed by. She turned sideways in her seat to face him.

Peripherally he could see her looking at him, but he kept his eyes on the road.

"Neco?"

"Yeah, honey?"

She smiled at his continuing to use the term of endearment. "I…" She lifted her arm and laid it across the back of the seat.

Catching that sweet smile, Neco had the urge to shift closer to her, but resisted it. The seatbelts would inhibit closeness anyway.

He glanced at her to encourage her to continue her thought. His mouth softened, she didn't smile often.

The sun poked through the burgeoning clouds, a fingertip of light streaming in the side window picked out the highlights of her hair and lit the side of her face.

His gaze dropped down the front of her then he swiftly focused his vision back on the road, but his neck grew warm anyway. She looked so damned sexy in that sweater, it made him want to stop the truck, lean her back against the seat, cover her mouth with his and run his palms up under the burgundy-

"I want you to know how truly I appreciate your generosity. I'm…overwhelmed." She knuckled under an eye.

Glancing at her again, he saw her emotion. "Casie, I wanted to do it, you need clothes. Just accept them, and know that you look incredible in those jeans and that sweater." His gaze sauntered up the front of her. "I can't wait to see the other stuff on you."

"Neco," her cheeks heated. "I…don't know what to say, except, uh, thank you and I will pay you back as soon as-"

He turned his scowl to the road. "Just leave it at thank you, Casie. Please."

She was quiet, he looked back at her.

121

Her lashes lowered over her eyes concealing them, the smile was gone. She was sitting slightly turned sideways towards him with her one leg half-curled on the seat.

"Hey," he set his hand on her leg, "what's wrong?"

Her line of vision was at his shirt collar, not in his eyes. Her unsettled gaze rolled up slow and guarded, "Are you mad at me? I didn't mean to say something to upset you."

With a smile, he patted her leg. "No, of course not. I just want you to be comfortable, get well, feel safe and happy. The clothes are a done deal. You thanked me, now we don't have to talk about them again, except for me to tell you how great you look in them."

Without turning his head, his grin canted at her, and she returned it with a small lift of her lips.

She shifted a bit in her seat but didn't move from him. He left his hand on her leg. Her gaze rose to the top of his head, her question unexpected and tentative, "Can I touch your hair?"

He blinked. His eyes flit sideways to her and back to the window. The question, 'why' was on his lips but he muzzled it. Who cared why? She was asking to touch him. "Sure," sounding casual, he repressed the instant excitement that rippled inside him.

Smiling like a kid waiting for an ice cream cone, she scooted as close to him as she could get with the seatbelt on.

It was a bench-seat with a middle seatbelt. He wanted to tell her to move over to the middle seat but didn't want to change the mood. Whatever it was.

Reserved, but with ingenuous interest, Casie lightly touched the side of his hair. "Is that okay?"

Was she kidding? "Sure. Do what you feel like," he tried to sound nonchalant, "*mi* body *es su* body."

"Okay. Thanks."

She was thanking *him*?

Casie spread her fingers and sifted them along the side of his head through his wavy locks. "Your hair is thick and soft, Neco."

"Uh huh." He moved both hands to grip the wheel.

"I've been curious to see if it's as soft as it looks, it is." She moved her fingers deeper and drew them back through the dark waves. "It feels really nice, can I feel more?"

A woman had never asked him if she could touch him before. It was Casie being her shy, polite self. Whatever her reasons, he wasn't moving. "Touch anything you want, honey, anything."

"You're funny," she giggled so engagingly his heart twitched.

He had to fight the intense urge to pull over to the side of the road and climb all over her, and she was only touching his damned hair. *Shit- he was as bad as that asshole King.* "Yeah, that's me, a regular clown," he shot her a quick smile. "Anything else you're curious to feel?"

The blush crept up her cheeks. "Kind of."

"Geez, go ahead. Feel free. I'm yours to explore." He couldn't look at her, his dick was already hard enough to drill a hole through solid rock. His last glimpse, he saw her tits jostling under the sweater with the rocking of the truck. His palms itched to see if they were as supple as they looked.

"Okay. Can I touch your arms? You have the biggest muscles I've ever seen. I think. I'm not sure, but they're really big. Are they hard?"

He almost choked, the tips of his ears burned red. "I guess, why don't you find out?" He casually added, "Why don't you move over then you won't have to stretch."

"Is that all right? Are you sure?"

"Come." He patted the seat between them.

She unbuckled her belt and slid over then buckled the belt in the middle.

Neco's stomach clenched, his fingers tightened so hard it was surprising the wheel didn't bend under his fingers.

She set her small hand on his huge arm then gingerly ran her palm over his bicep. He shivered. She said quickly, "Oh, should I stop-"

"*No,*" came out with a harsh breath. "I mean, please," he cleared his throat, "explore all you want."

At his nod of assurance, she said, "Okay," and her other hand came up and she used both to try to encircle his bicep and giggled when she couldn't.

"Neco, your arms are bigger than my legs!" Laughing at her efforts as she tried to squeeze his muscles.

He smiled at her childlike glee. So refreshing to be with a transparent, non-gold-digging, sweet woman who excavated joy from the simplest of things.

Stroking his arm, feeling the steel sinew and cut hollows, she asked, "Do you lift weights?"

The gulp caught in his throat, he could feel goose-bumps rise along his forearms. "Yeah." Freakin' strangest foreplay he'd ever engaged in. Hair and bicep touching, who knew it could be such an aphrodisiac?

Her hand roamed up to his shoulder, she felt the muscles flex under her fingers. "I heard Mr. King say you were a boxer. Do you still box? Doesn't it hurt?"

"Huh," his snort mildly sarcastic. "Sure it hurts when I get hit. The object is to duck the blows while you pound yours home. I still box. My brother Josh and I did some championship stuff before we went into the service. We keep up with it with my other brothers too, it helps lighten the tension."

Murmuring, "Hmmm," she continued caressing his arm, his shoulder, probing, squeezing.

Neco willed her to explore down the rest of his body but kept his mouth shut and his hands on the wheel.

Sure she had amnesia, but Casie was acting like a pure, totally inexperienced virgin. If she was experienced in sex, wouldn't that be like muscle memory? He didn't care one way or the other, he wanted her regardless of her past. Although, being her first and only would be…

"Your body is interesting, Neco."

"Yeah? How so?"

"Part of you is so soft, like your hair, but your arms are hard as rocks, your shoulders are huge," she absently ran her hand down his arm.

He mentioned, "My chest is kinda pumped too," hoping she'd get the hint.

Her head tilted, she looked at him, the long hair poured over her shoulder.

"Don't you want to find out?" he asked, prompting.

"Is it all right? It seems like, maybe I'm like being forward or something. I mean, is it proper if we're not...involved?" She hesitated.

He shrugged with casual indifference. "It's fine. Maybe it'll help you remember something." Hell, that was totally lame, besides, last thing he wanted was to make her think of some other guy when she had her hands on him.

She wriggled in her seat to face him more and curled both legs on the seat. "Okay." She reached out gingerly and set her palm on his chest, touching him very lightly like she was afraid he'd break.

"I'm a tough guy, honey, you can press harder."

Giggling, she set her hand more firmly on his chest and spread her fingers across one pectoral.

Neco suppressed the shudder that ran from her touch down his chest and straight to his crotch.

"Gosh, Neco, you really are a strong man." She stroked and skimmed over the hills of his chest, and squeezed each rocky slab of muscle with almost childlike curiosity.

With a touch of wonder, as if she'd never seen a man's naked chest before, she said, "I can feel the hair on your chest that's under your shirt."

Neco was in seventh Heaven.

They were heading up his driveway, he hated for her to stop caressing him. It was tough on his dick, but it felt so good he didn't want it to end.

It wasn't in the forefront of her mind that they were being quite intimate with her hands on him and almost cuddled up against him stroking his body, but they were.

He was dying to take his shirt off, feel her hands on his bare skin, but he knew that would freak her out. He had considered a half-a-dozen times to keep driving around the block. Unfortunately they were home and she'd likely notice if he passed his house a hundred times.

Parking, he turned off the truck.

Suddenly shy, Casie undid her seatbelt and shifted away from him. She reached for the door handle.

"Casie, wait." Neco reached for her arm.

She turned back to him waiting.

Eyes half lazy with desire and half vivid with lust, he said, "C'mere," he wrapped his hands around her arms and pulled her to him.

"Neco-"

"Shh, just a second." He drew her over his lap and put one hand cradling her head and the other around her back.

Her eyes were wide, lips parted in uncertain surprise, he took advantage of it and locked his mouth over hers.

She stiffened but didn't struggle or pull away.

Sealing their mouths, he was gentle at first, but then he felt her lips move against his. A steady ache beat in his throbbing groin, his kiss turned harder, more demanding.

He pushed his tongue in her mouth to see what she tasted like, he'd had a hint before, he wanted more now.

Her response was tentative, inexperienced, so goddamned sweet. His body taut and vibrating like a tuning fork, Neco could have come in his pants. Another minute of kissing her and he'd be pulling her clothes off.

Neco fought through the thick haze of passion that was rapidly clouding his head. They were in the truck, if anyone saw them she would die of embarrassment. He softly broke the kiss and looked down at her.

Her heavy lids revealed only a hint of green that looked as passionately hazy as he felt. Her lips were still parted from being pulled from the kiss, the pink petals damp from his mouth. His dick jumped. But she also looked deeply tired.

"Neco," her voice shaky, "if I can do anything to thank you for...for..."

The thought that maybe she would think he expected her to pay for the clothes with sex was like cold water thrown in his face.

Carefully, he gripped her upper arms and moved her back to sit against the seat. She looked befuddled, suddenly uneasy.

His fingertips slid softly down the side of her face. "Casie, I kissed you because I wanted to, had to. You don't owe me anything."

"But, I don't have anything to offer-"

"Dammit, Casie!" he barked. "You don't owe me. I don't want fucking- sex- or anything for my help. You make me feel like," he dragged a hand down his face. "How far were you willing to go to pay me back?"

She flinched, moved back, her spine rigid. "Are you calling me a- a- whore?" Her voice broke, she turned and fumbled with the door.

Before he could reach her she wrenched it open, tumbled out almost falling, she steadied herself and ran.

"Casie!" Dammit, he was such an ass.

By the time Neco got his seatbelt unbuckled, his door open and got around the side of the truck she was gone.

"Casie!" he shouted, combing his fingers through his hair. A long hunk of bangs flopped over his eye, he impatiently shoved it back.

The sun was sinking low in the sky, a late-season fluke of snowflakes plummeted from low heavy clouds. The air had an icy chill.

He grabbed his jacket and pulled it on as he jogged around the side of the house and to the back.

There was no sign of her.

Chapter Thirteen

"Casie!" His eyes shot around the vast backyard and to the woods.

No, she wouldn't be stupid enough-

Neco ran towards the forest.

She thought he had called her a whore. She was a fragile, spooked, disoriented woman still not well, yeah, she would be stupid enough to run into the woods. For a sick woman she was fast, there was no sign of her.

The snowflakes were quickly covering even his footprints as he ran. The thought of how terribly tired she looked before she fled made its way into his mind, spurring him to move faster.

He tromped through the woods calling her name, looking for her footprints. The snow was growing thicker, the flakes fatter, the sun was weak, it was rapidly getting colder. She had no hat, no gloves, she only had on a light jacket and sneakers.

"Casie!" Damn, she stays out here even for a short time she'll fucking freeze to death. Damned fool woman.

He didn't know how long he searched for her.

The longer he looked, the more fear climbed up his craw. Brushing flakes off his hair, he dashed a hand across his cold nose. He trod back around a different path and finally saw some winter grass mushed down and a broken branch on a bush.

He didn't call for her in case she ran from him. He had hurt her feelings, threw their close time they'd shared in the truck in her face.

There, he saw color and hurried to it. He could hear her crying, his heart retched.

"Casie," he said quietly.

She was rolled up in a ball next to a tree. Her body shook with such fierce shivers, he could hear her teeth chattering before he even got near her.

When he reached her, he crouched down. "Baby," he murmured, smoothing her hair off her face.

She stifled her cries when she heard him, but her chest hitched with them.

"Dammit, girl." Neco shrugged out of his jacket and draped it over her, then shoved his hands under her, lifting her up in his arms as he stood.

"Please," her jaw shuddered so intensely the words shook out, "l-leave me."

He didn't bother saying anything; it was ridiculous for her to think he'd leave her there to die in the woods. Neco carried her high and tight to his chest cringing at the sobs that choked in her throat.

He tromped back to the house.

When he got there, he set her down keeping an arm around her to hold her up and close to him. Opening the door, he picked her back up and strode inside, kicking the door closed behind him.

Her body was shivering so hard Neco had to tighten his arms to keep hold of her. He set her on the couch, bent over her and removed his jacket and unbuttoned her sodden light jacket. She tried to fight him when he pulled it off her.

Struggling to keep his temper from exploding, his voice tersely gruff with the effort, he said, "Don't fight me, Casie, you won't win and you'll hurt yourself. Just stop."

Tossing the jacket, he gripped the hem of her sweater soaking wet from the snow to lift it over her head, but she cried out and wrapped her arms around her body.

Did she *want* to be sick? Dead? The woman needed a damned keeper.

Beside himself with pissed off agitation that she had put herself in such peril, Neco reluctantly let go of her sweater because she was so distraught. He had half a mind to just do it. Ignore her resistance, just bully over her, strip those clothes off and redress her quickly in dry clothing.

Maybe adding a few hard smacks on her butt to knock some sense into her, and, he sighed, to release some of his panic and fury at her for scaring him so badly.

Growling crossly, he stood up and said, "All right." Snatching the blanket off the end of the couch he wrapped it around her.

"I'm getting towels and dry clothes, you take these soaked things off by the time I get back or I'm doing it."

About to leave, he swung around. Eyes tapered with anger, pointing a furious finger at her, he snarled fiercely, "And don't even think of leaving. If you go near that door I swear to God I will drag you back, paddle your ass and tie you down. I fucking mean it."

Her head down staring at the floor she stuttered through clattering teeth, "D- d- don't yell at me- I t- told you I was nothing but- but trouble." She looked so miserable, freezing, with streams of soaked hair hanging over half her face in wavy strips, the ends dripped on her knees.

She wouldn't look at him through the wet tresses twisting over her green eyes, just tucked her frozen hands between her legs, stared at the floor and shivered violently.

Furious, he stomped back over to her, bent down with his hands on his knees and got in her face. "Trust me, Casie, I will do a lot more than yell at you if you even think of moving your ass off that fucking couch."

Standing up, he glared down at her.

Her face was white, teeth chattering a mile a minute, her hair dripping over her face. He knew he was scaring her, towering over her and threatening her, but by God, he dragged a hand through his hair, she could have died out there.

He glared his threat hard at her for another few seconds to make sure she got that he wasn't messing around.

Not used to Neco, the big muscular man with a chest made of rocks and arms to match, yelling at her and cursing her, a furious Neco was a fearsome sight, Casie shrank from him.

"You- you're cursing at me, and being mean. I know I'm trouble, just let me go back out. I'll disappear and you won't have to keep taking care of- of me, any…more…" The rest of her words broke off through her chattering teeth. She woefully struggled to cease the tears that sprung and rolled over her cheeks and down, adding to her wet knees.

His breath whooshed out in aggrieved disbelief that she kept thinking so little of herself that she would roll over and die.

He could see she still suffered from the concussion, the disorientation still made her eyes wobble slightly. She looked dizzy again from putting herself through what she just did, but he refused to weaken. If he was too soft, she'd be out the door and putting herself in danger again.

Kneeling beside the couch, he whipped his hand out and clutched her jaw raising her head. Her mouth vibrated in his hand from her shivering.

"Enough of this shit, Casie. You are not leaving. Just take off those wet clothes and do not leave that couch."

Her eyes wavered away from his, he shook her lightly forcing her to look at him.

The ends of her lashes were still fringed with either tears or melted snow, she lowered them until he could no longer see the hopelessness in the green irises.

Gently, he kissed the top of her head to take some of the bite out of his words, then stood up and left the room leaving her huddled under the blanket, shivering and staring at the floor.

Between her exhaustion and lingering concussion, he knew she wasn't thinking straight and was being hit with both depression and despair, and hurt feelings.

Plus, who knows if she'd been abused, beaten, possibly raped, he cringed, her ego could be completely crushed. It would explain why she kept thinking so little of herself.

In his room, Neco took out one of his flannel shirts and sweatpants, smiled wryly. He had just bought her a closet full of clothes and she was still going to wear his. It didn't bother him, he liked seeing her all snuggled up in his clothes, it was like she was wrapped in his arms.

Ahh, Neco hesitated before going back into the living room, he stood in the hall and listened. He didn't want to barge in on her half-dressed. Last thing he wanted was to spook her, add to her humiliation. He heard her rustling around, when it stopped, he coughed and went in.

She was sitting huddled under the blanket, her wet clothes were on the floor.

He went to her and set the dry clothes on the sofa. Keeping his voice level and without inflection, which was extremely difficult considering how pissed he was, and knowing she was buck naked under that blanket making him hard.

He asked even though he knew what her answer would be, "Do you want help?"

She picked up the clothes and held them to her chest outside the blanket and shook her head.

"I'll be in the kitchen if you need me." He disappeared into the kitchen.

After making a hot cup of tea, when he returned, she was dressed and pulling his socks on. He set the tea on the end table within her reach and sat on the couch next to her.

Ignoring the nervous look she sent him, he picked up a towel, put it over her head and vigorously rubbed her hair.

When he got most of the dampness out, Neco moved the towel and said, "Drink the tea." He wrapped the blanket back around her.

Casie pulled the blanket up to her chin, still shivering. Her voice shook from her rattling teeth. "N- Neco-"

Nodding at the tea, he said curtly, "Go on, drink it." He knew he was being bossy, but hell, that was the way it was, she didn't like it, too bad.

Leaning back against the cushion, he breathed in deeply. He couldn't believe the relief he felt that she was sitting a few inches from him, all warm and dry and safe, and so heartbreakingly, ethereally pretty with her sad aura.

The frightened eyes underlined in dark shadows that rolled up to him every few minutes, so big in her creamy face, seemed even larger tonight. So big they were taking up more than half her face leaving little room for the small nose and puffy lips.

He wanted to pull her petite body into his big arms, tuck her safe against his chest and smell her fresh scent, and stroke her back until she was basking in his care and affection, and was no longer looking so lost and afraid.

Picking up the tea, she cupped the warm mug in her hands and sipped the steamy brew.

He had put plenty of cream and sugar in it. Neco maneuvered to sit behind her and adjusted her to sit in front of him between his legs with her back to his chest.

Before she could ask what he was doing, he took his comb out of his back pocket and drew it through her hair like he'd done when she was first getting well.

He felt her shoulders tighten, but as he combed the knots out and the locks started drying, she slowly relaxed. Quietly, next to her ear, he asked, "Are you hungry?"

Sipping her tea, she shook her head.

By the time he got her hair combed it was almost dry. He set the comb on the table, grasped her shoulders and moved her to face him.

"Casie," he said, watching her tired eyes with the hurt roiling in them look at him then drop. He cupped her chin, raising her head to look at him.

"Casie," he said again. "I'm really sorry what happened in the truck. I wasn't insinuating, ah, I mean I wasn't calling you a," he hated the word applied to her, "whore."

133

She tried to move her jaw from his grasp but he held onto her.

"No, listen to me." He tipped her chin so their eyes locked. "What I was trying to say was, that I, I mean I was afraid you were thinking you owed me for the clothes and you didn't have any way of paying me back other than…"

He exhaled hard. "I didn't want you to ever think I expected anything, ah, physical from you, ever. Nothing you don't want to give me willingly, and never for payment or gratitude." His gaze flickered around her face, but he couldn't read her.

She pulled from his grasp. "You pretty much said I was going to…screw you to pay for what I owe you. I don't know if you were saying you expected me to, or that I thought I should, either way, that's called being a whore."

Bending slightly towards her, he stared down at her, she stared down at her hands.

"I did not say that, at least what I was saying, *again*, is that you *do not* owe me anything. Anything intimate between you and I must be what we both want and for no other reason. I didn't say you were going to have sex with me, I was trying to be clear that I would never expect it or accept it as some kind of payment."

He waited for her to speak but she didn't. He remembered her slight protest when he had pulled her over his lap in the truck, and he had ignored her and kissed her anyway.

"Casie, did you, uh, kiss me because you wanted to, or because I was forcing myself on you, or because you thought I wanted it as gratitude?"

Her eyes flew up to his, her lips parted. She laid her palm on the side of his face that was rough with his evening shadow. "You…took me by surprise."

His crestfallen look pinched around the blue eyes. He gazed at her, he wanted to kiss her now, but he knew it was not a great idea. Especially after he just gotten done yelling at and threatening her.

And, judging by what she just said, he wouldn't be kissing her again anyway, that she didn't want it. Last thing he wanted was to force a woman to kiss him or be in his arms if she didn't want to.

Still, the urge to just grab her up and make love to her was insanely intense. Maybe he needed to get away from her before he acted on his irresistible impulses.

Then she said, "But I liked it, Neco." Casie smiled shyly ducking her head. Her eyes now firmly on his, she went on, "I kissed you back because I...liked it. I...like you."

Surprised, Neco sat back and stared hard at her to read the truth.

The emerald eyes with gold and blue flecks were pure and guileless.

His gaze fell to her lips.

Even with the tea, dry clothes, and blankets she was still shivering.

He pulled his lips in to hide his grin, just nodded benignly. "Okay." The inside of his chest felt vise tight, he put his hands around her, and pulled her against his chest then pulled the blanket up around them both.

What a helluva wonderful feeling sitting on his couch with her wrapped warm and snuggly in his arms.

When her head rested comfortably on his shoulder, he wrapped his arms more tightly around her holding her close and said, "Just to get it straight, baby, you do not owe me a thing. There are never strings attached to my help. If I'm forcing myself on you, and you don't want it, you need to tell me right away. All right?"

Her head bobbed up and down against his shoulder, mumbling on a yawn, "Uh huh."

"Like right now. Are you okay with me holding you?"

"Hmmm, yes." She burrowed closer in the crook of his arm.

His sigh happy and weary, he slid his hand through her hair and caressed down her arm. He asked quietly, "Can we start over?" His rumbling voice vibrated against her side. "Can we be friends again?" Tilting his head he peered down at her and saw her tired smile.

"I'd like that." She snuggled against him.

Another deep, contented sigh and Neco cuddled her in his embrace. Relaxing back into the sofa cushions, he cradled her head that rested against his shoulder. She settled peacefully in his arms, her shivering had finally stopped.

A few minutes later he could feel her body turn boneless, melting against him, and he realized she was asleep.

Enjoying the feel of her curled up, safe, and trusting in his arms, Neco sat there for a long time until he knew she was sound asleep.

Carefully, he got up and laid her down on the sofa, slipped a pillow under her head and added another blanket tucking it over her.

Neco shrugged his jacket on and went outside to the truck. He brought the bags inside and took them to the rose room.

He hung her blouses in the closet and folded the sweaters and put them away in the drawers. It gave him a sense of permanency.

Lifting a bra, feeling a little pervy, he neatly folded her lingerie, trying not to linger over the silk and satin. Still, feeling their softness against his rough fingers as pictures of Casie in the black lace sprinkled into his mind….he quickly stuffed everything in the drawers.

He left the personal things like her brush and comb and girl stuff for her to put away. He'd already intruded too much into her private things.

He may have paid for them, but they were hers. Neco felt such a peace buying the clothes and things for Casie, he'd never even thought to, or wanted to, buy anything for Kandi or any other woman. A sour taste suddenly made his saliva seep unpleasantly and his lips curl.

Swallowing away the offensive thought of Kandi, he took a look around the room. It looked like a woman was living there, his heart smiled. The only thing better would be if her body was in his room, in his bed.

He hit the lights with a sigh.

Back in the living room, he made sure she was still sleeping peacefully, he worried she would relapse and get sick again.

She looked so damned frail, just a small lump under the blankets. Yet, the more he'd gotten to know her, he saw she was only physically frail, she had a backbone. A smile lifted the corners of his mouth.

Casie had stood up to him and that asshole King in the diner. And it took some balls, or, whatever ladies have, to run into the woods to get away from him when she was hurt and insulted. Foolhardy, but ballsy.

He got a beer and settled into the easy chair with the remote and kept one eye on the TV and one eye on her until he fell asleep too.

Chapter Fourteen

Vittorio Pryce hurled the phone at the wall gaining no satisfaction when it crashed and burst into pieces before volleying in fragments and clattering to every edge of the cherry wood floor.

His sister Dimitria's tsk-tsking only added to his rage.

Two years younger than Vittorio's 43 years, Dimitria Pryce Falcona pushed a button on her cell and murmured into it.

"I don't fucking want to hear it, Dimi," Pryce snarled at his sister, then snapped his mouth shut and glared at her as a timid maid responded to Dimitria's call hurrying into the room with a small whisk broom and dustpan.

Quickly and efficiently, she swept up the broken fragments and like a mouse scurried out again without a sound or looking at either Vittorio or Dimitria.

"This is all because you thought with your dick instead of your head, Vito, you couldn't wait to take that girl. It's bad enough you pawed and groped her even before her tiny buds starting growing into real breasts." Sniffing her disdain, Dimitria crossed her long arms under her bosom.

The black satin dress rustled with her movements, the skirt swaying at her legs below her knees. Her hair twisted up in a strict bun. Sleek black like her brother's, her polished locks under expensive salon care, rivaled the black satin of her dress. Eyes almost as dark glittered her reproachful annoyance at Vittorio.

138

His sigh heavy and labored, Vittorio trod across the richly thick carpet past the luxuriant yellow and blue print furniture to the inlaid rosewood and layered glass bar.

He swiped up a bottle, yanked the glass stopper off and poured the brandied spirits into a decanter. Carelessly dropping the stopper on the table, he snapped back an angry drink.

The stiff pendulum shaped dress rustled as Dimitria moved to him. "You married Evaline to get close to her sister, Joanna, in turn, to get close to Joanna's toddler daughter. Oh yes, Vito," she curled her lip in disgust at him, "it was clear from the start how you desired that child.

"The predatory gleam in your eyes you thought you hid under those secretive lids of yours when you watched her was like binoculars baring your sick soul. Clearly revealing you were biding your time until she was of legal age to take. That's why Joanna and Dillon moved far away, practically keeping her in seclusion to keep her out of your depraved grasp."

A hand in his trouser pocket, the suit jacket tucked behind his arm, Vittorio sipped mildly without comment. One eye slightly tapered at his sister, he was thinking, *she'd laid the rouge on a little thick today, her cheeks were frigid red. Like her cold cold heart.* That made him chuckle.

Her eyes narrowed at him. "This isn't funny, Vito. You made me extend an invitation for the girl to come see me for a visit while on her first break at the college. Her parents were right to fear letting her out of their sight for the first time in her life. Oh yes," she snorted elegantly.

"No one knew you had flown in to be at my home too. Like a vulture hiding high up in the trees waiting for the tiny mouse to get close enough for you to swoop in and grab her with your talons.

"But no, you couldn't wait to figure out how to do it right. Divorce Evaline and…oh, I don't know," her eyes rose upwards as she thought, brushing the flat of her palm up the underneath of her severe bun.

"You could have tried to buy the girl off to marry you, offer anyone enough money and they're yours. Or, find someone to blackmail her for some trumped up thing, maybe a false drug charge-"

"Dimitria. Shut. Up." Black brows like a hawk's nose slashed sharply between his arrogant eyes. His annoyance growing, he swallowed the rest of his drink and poured another.

She swept in front of him and set her hand on the edge of the glass table. "Even that one ludicrous idea you had once of abducting her and keeping her prisoner in your mansion. It's certainly large enough no one would come across her, then getting her pregnant thereby forcing her to marry you-"

Vito stalked away from her to stare out the window. Gripping the goblet, the other hand in his pocket crushed into a tight fist. He stood between the dark burgundy drapes held back by golden tasseled ropes.

Coming to stand right behind him, her voice low, cool and harsh, she sneered, "But no. You couldn't keep it in your pants until you'd fleshed out a plan. Now that she is of legal age you cornered her alone in my library, physically restrained her and forced her on her back, tore her clothes. My God, Vito you libidinous bastard."

She choked back a mirthless laugh. "Yes, you almost got her, you were just about to thrust your swine's cock into that child when Evaline burst in."

Vito swung around, his face dark and vicious. He spat, "Yes, goddammit. I should never have told you everything, Dimi. That stupid cow Evaline beat on my back screeching, punching me and screaming like a fucking fishwife. I barely got my pants zipped when she slugged me in the jaw, about knocked me off my feet."

His eyes pitch black like sharp cinders recalled his fury at his wife's interrupting his rape of the girl that he'd wanted since she was barely out of diapers.

He'd finally had the girl's parents tricked into letting her visit her Auntie Dimi and he'd mindlessly lunged at his chance at her.

Those huge crystalline green eyes just floored him, intoxicated him every time they turned in his direction. And every time, he'd felt the yearning burning in his loins like wildfire.

Not normally a pedophile, there was just something about her, his niece by marriage, even as a child that made him desire her above all else. He furtively touched her anywhere, everywhere, that he got a chance.

His desire only flamed hotter each time over the years when he'd catch a glimpse of her at family get-togethers, as she filled out all curvy and dainty. The beautiful, lustrous hair grew in thick waves, damn, he'd lain awake night after night scheming how to get to her.

And what he'd do to her when he did. He thought of the chains and cuffs, whips, collars, and other accouterments he had for the other women he expended his lust on while waiting for her.

Dimitria was angry at her brother, but she loved him. Patting his arm, she rubbed his shoulder and nodded. "It was enough for the girl to get away. Her mistake was," she watched her brother's face crease lividly with the memory.

"Yes," he sighed, drank the last drop and went to pour another. "Hearing Evaline's screams as I was beating the life out of her, the girl came back, dammit. With her phone in her hand. She was dialing 911, but-"

Dimitria slid her arm around his shoulders, she was only inches shorter than his 6'2''.

Nodding, she agreed, "I know. I think she was reflexively hitting the camera button without even knowing it, thinking she was punching the 911. She got clear pictures of you with your belt around Evaline's neck as she took her last choking, gasping...breath."

This time Vito downed the drink in one long gulp. Wiping his mouth with the back of his hand, he sighed.

"She ran before I could catch her. I know she couldn't have been thinking clearly, but she was afraid to go to the police. She knew I had Chief Constable Gerald Konrad in my pocket.

"When shit for brains Harry caught her the first time, he managed to get out of her that she'd hidden the phone. I'd preferred he hadn't beaten her, I wanted to save that pleasure for myself when I discipline her for running from me, and train her to comply with my orders." He sighed.

"I need to get my hands on that cell. The little bitch managed to give Harry the slip, fucking twice!" He bashed his fist on the glass table- it broke under the weight of his punch, slicing his hand.

"Vito!" Dimi grabbed a towel and wrapped it around his bleeding hand. "Calm down, they'll find her, don't worry." She used her free hand to dial for the maid to bring first aid.

"They will find her and bring her back to you. I will help you keep her this time. Her parents think she's on an extended vacation with me. I will send them emails pretending to be from her in a few weeks, then I can claim she returned to school. She can disappear off the map and no one will know you have her."

Her face darkened with avarice greed, she said snakily, "And then we can share her."

Vito sank to his knees cradling his injured hand in his arms. "But when, Dimi? When?" His voice high and strident and needy, he whined, "I want her here now. I must get those photos, but more than that, Dimi," his head bowed as he cried, "*I need her*."

Dimi knelt down beside him holding his head against her breast she stroked his hair. "Shh, now, brother dear. Harry told you this morning, it's only a matter of time. They've traced her to that little dippy town…what did he say the name of it was?"

Vittorio exhaled his forsaken ache, "Lark."

Chapter Fifteen

*T*he next week they made an uneasy truce.

Neco insisted Casie move into the rose room and sleep there. But it was hell for him to lie in bed at night and think about her sleeping in her nightgown down the hall.

He had chosen the nightgowns with Miss Ford while Casie had been getting undressed in the fitting room. He'd gone fairly conservative for her modesty, but he couldn't help the man in him that desired sheer, feminine, frilly, even some lace on her.

Since no one would be seeing them but him, and he was ever hopeful that he would be, he went slightly more risqué with them.

He had compromised by choosing gowns that were just above the knee, and one to the ankle for the chillier nights. All were just on the underside of sexy but not fully revealing.

But then again, he thought back, there was that almost sheer fuchsia one. Chiffon-light, her breasts would be slightly visible through the material as would the curve of that tiny waist and...yeah, well, maybe even her private parts.

The color was the only thing keeping it from being fully transparent. Holding the gown in his hands he had imagined his palms under it on her naked waist and sliding up to cup her breasts. Okay, he was being a bit of a horndog, again.

Worse though, after he chose the nightgowns, while he went about his errands that day, he had pictured himself peeling each one off her, sometimes slow, languid, smoldering while he stroked and kissed every piece of skin that was left bare as he removed the gown, and sometimes just yanking one off as he pushed her on her back and onto his bed.

He wanted her in his bed. Or, actually anywhere. On the floor, standing up against the wall, in the kitchen with her spread out on the counter, or bent over the kitchen table, he fully admitted it to himself, he wanted her.

To be honest, he'd wanted her since the second he'd held her in his arms that day he'd found her in the storm, and it only grew stronger every day. He'd felt possessive of her at that very moment. Since he found her, that made her his. Wasn't possession 9/10ths of the law?

A chuckle bubbled out, yeah, sure, and what cave did he crawl out of?

Besides feeling possessive, and protective of her, he desired her. Sure, she was beautiful and smoking hot, but she was sweet, had a cute sense of humor. She was way smarter than she gave herself credit for.

Neco really enjoyed talking to her, just holding her, and really, really wished he could kiss her again. But he was afraid if he tried, she would go running from him again. Nonetheless, there was no denying to himself, he was going to do it.

The past few days he was patient and tender with her as she was weakened again from her foray into the freezing woods. Thankfully, she was working through it, exercising and taking walks with him daily.

Neco wandered into the kitchen. "What are you doing?"

She smiled at him over her shoulder, she was up to her elbows in flour. The long amber hair was pinned up, several tendrils had escaped and curled around her face making the shape of it even more ivy-like with the tendrils like soft wavy stems.

"I think I'm making bread. I'm not sure, we'll find out later. I made something for dinner."

"Oh yeah?" He moved closer to her, remembering the last time they were there he'd held her and kissed her. "Something besides funny pancakes?"

Her laughter was contagious. "I think so. My hands are just moving, taking out ingredients, measuring, stirring, it's like they hold the memories my brain does not."

She swiped at her nose with her elbow, leaving flour on the tip. "It should be ready in a few hours. I think. You did a great job with the groceries." She sprinkled a tiny bit of flour on the counter then started kneading the dough.

"Yes, well, I can read a list you know. I'm sure not going to argue if you want to cook something other than my staples of steak and spaghetti and eggs."

Her laughter rang prettily in the room. "Your only repertoire. Don't get me wrong, you do them all great, but variety, you know what they say."

"That's not necessarily true in all things, baby." He came up behind her and slipped his arms around her, hugging her to his chest.

"Hmmm," she hummed and kept kneading the dough, but she didn't freeze when he held her or push him away.

Neco stuck his nose in her hair and inhaled deeply, he had missed smelling her. He held her more tightly and nuzzled her neck.

Her kneading slowed, when he put his lips on her neck, she stopped altogether.

He sucked and kissed her neck, licked behind her ear, kissed her jaw, then moved his lips down to her collarbone where he sucked her skin until he'd marked her.

She tilted her head and leaned into him, arching her neck slightly so he could reach her easier. The most delicious barely uttered moans came from deep in her throat, and went straight to his dick making it hard as hell.

Neco moved his hand up to cup her jaw to turn her head so he could capture her mouth for his kiss, when the phone rang.

"Shit," he groaned against her skin.

"Neco," she giggled admonishing him.

"Sorry." He tipped her face up and gave her a quick kiss then released her go to answer the phone. He had been expecting a business call, otherwise he would have turned it off and ignored it.

Grabbing up the phone, Neco trod to his office to take the call.

He stayed in his office and worked for hours until he smelled something incredibly delicious. Bread baking?

Casie had set the table and put a candle she'd found in the center of it.

When Neco came in, his neatly combed dark hair waved damply around his face from a quick wash.

Her hands clasped behind her back, peering up through long lashes, Casie shyly asked him, "Can you light the candle? I couldn't find any matches." She went back into the kitchen before he could reply.

When she returned, the candle was glowing making the dining area cozy and romantic.

She set a dish on the table next to a bowl of salad and the bread she'd baked, then stood awkwardly twisting her fingers together. "Um, thank you. It makes everything look...uh...soft and pretty."

Just like you. "Hey," Neco stood in front of her, set his hand gently on the back of her neck, tipping her head up slightly.

Smiling gently, his voice soft, quiet, he said, "You don't have to be shy with me, Casie. I think I've shown you that I'll do just about anything to make you happy." His gaze went from her eyes to her lips, then moved slowly back up to her sparkling green orbs.

Still demure, unsure, her gaze dipped from his warm blue eyes to his mouth where it lingered before moving back up.

His fingers tightening slightly on her nape, his heated blues were drawn back down to her lips. Cradling her head with his big hand he lowered his head, whispered against her lips, "Don't be shy with me, Casie, learn to trust me, I won't hurt you."

146

He lightly licked her top lip, then her bottom, then he tasted the seam between them nudging them open for his tongue to surge inside, and took her with him in a scorching seductive kiss.

Her breathing quickened, she pressed her hands against his stomach. Neco could feel her responding to his kiss but felt the uncertainty still in her hands.

Within moments his body grew so hard it hurt. His fingers twined in the thick lush amber waves. His other hand lowered, molding over her bottom, gripping it to pull her to him and he ground his hips against hers.

He was rapidly losing himself in her, but her hands were turning stiff. Slowly he loosened his fingers, he needed to let go of her. It wasn't easy.

"I, ah," his one hand still netting her head, he brushed her lips with his thumb. "We should eat..." Anymore of that hot kissing and he'd be bending her over a chair.

His dick was on board with his crude thoughts, it strained against his jeans. Moving from her before she could see his erection, he went to the table.

Ordering, "Come," he pulled out a chair for her, then took his place across the table.

Shy again, her head slanted to one shoulder. Her glowing eyes slid from his heated gaze and lowered shyly to the table. "You are so good to me, Neco, I..." her mouth closed.

"You what?" He folded his hands on the table, hating that she still had a wall up between them.

One shoulder shrugged slightly, she looked up at him. "You've done so much for me, I don't know how I'll ever repay you for-"

"Goddammit, Casie," he snapped, slapping a hand on the table. "Fucking stop it. How many times do I have to tell you that I do what I want because I want to? I am not looking for payment."

His eyes narrowed across the table at her. "Don't you ever let me kiss you if you don't want it."

Her lashes flew up then quickly dropped covering her eyes, her plush lips compressed in a line.

"Casie, look at me!" he barked, then rolled his eyes. He was trying to gain her confidence and yelling at her sure as hell wasn't the way to get it.

"Hey," his voice softened. "I'm sorry. I didn't mean to yell." He combed a hand through his hair in frustration.

She raised her lids and perused him steadily. "I hate it when you yell and curse at me."

His lips pulled in chagrined, nodding. Abashed, he shoved a damp lock of hair out of his eyes. "I know, I'm sorry. I'm not cursing at you, honey, it's...I get frustrated that you might be kissing me as payment. I just want it clear that if you don't want to kiss me, you say no and that's it. No recriminations. I won't throw you out, hell, it's all I can do to keep you here as it is."

"Okay."

"Okay what, Casie?" He wanted badly to touch her but it wasn't the right time. "I want you to stay with me."

Her brow furrowed. "I am, I mean, for now."

He was pushing her, he needed to back off. "Of course. Hey, let's eat this fabulous dinner you prepared, all right?" Neco smiled agreeably at her then reached for the serving spoon.

Looking relieved, she took a sip of water and nodded. Passing him the butter, she said, "Neco, tell me more about your work, and your family."

They ate while he rambled on about his brothers who all worked for the FBI as agents, and he explained how he conducted some of his own investigations.

Gobbling down gooey, cheesy lasagna with meatballs and sausage tucked tastily inside, Neco chomped a piece of homemade garlic bread. "Yeah, baby," he spoke with his mouth full, "you can cook."

They washed the dishes together. Neco dried and put away the last piece of silverware and saw Casie yawn.

"All right, honey, that's enough for you." He handed her the towel to dry her hands. "Why don't you go to bed? I have more work to do."

"You work a lot, Neco." She yawned as he turned her and gave her little push towards the door.

"Uh huh, and I have more to do. This week will be 12-14 hour days, I have a deadline." He walked her down the hall.

Pausing in the middle of the hall, he suggested, "How about when I get caught up we can spend some time, trying to find out who you are."

Right away her shoulders moved up near her ears. He could feel her back tense. "We can go to the police-"

She swung around to him, then stopped and started walking again. "I...would rather try to find out without involving the...police."

"Why? Do you get a bad feeling when I mention the police? You get...disturbed whenever I bring them up."

Shaking her head, she admitted, "I don't know, maybe I'm a criminal."

Her voice edgy, a shade of fear threading through it, she told him, "I...I have dreams I'm hiding, running...for my life. It uh," she stood with her back to him. "It might mean I'm hiding from the police," she nervously rubbed her hands over her arms.

Her voice and head lowered. "I, would rather know what I've done before I...turn myself in...you know?"

"Hey," he caught her arm, gently turned her to face him. "If it comes to that, I will get you a lawyer. But," he said firmly, "you are not a criminal. I can't believe amnesia changes a person's core. I mean, you know how to bake bread, honey, villains don't bake." He grinned at her weak smile.

"I know you, Casie, I think better than you know yourself." He brushed his palm down her arm. "For now, we'll see what we can find out without going to the police. All right?"

"Neco, you are so good to me." She cocked her head to peer up at him in bafflement. "I don't know why. Maybe it's because you're just the nicest man in the whole world." She reached her hand out slowly and tentatively stroked his face

His skin tingling from her touch, Neco caught her hand and held it briefly. A frown crossed his face, his gaze flit to their hands then back to her eyes.

Thinking about how he wanted to throw her on the table and fuck her mindless, he said, "I hate to say it, but I am not that nice."

She wasn't ready yet for him to tell her how he feels about her.

They walked to the door of the rose room. He tipped her head up to his. "Sweet dreams, baby," and kissed her gently, then let her go quickly while he could.

He wanted to go into the room with her, lay her down, peel off her clothes and cover her body with his... he moved away and headed back down the hall to his office.

The next afternoon, Neco rubbed the back of his head and clicked the back button, he'd missed something. Scanning each page, he stopped when he found it.

Reading the page, he scratched his fingertips over his temple while making notes. Another couple days and this part of his investigation would be finished. Thank God, he wanted to spend more time with Casie-

Screams reverberating down the hall made his hair stand straight up- shit- *Casie-*

He jumped up and raced down the hall yelling, "Baby, are you all-" he slowed when he neared her room.

"What the hell are you doing here?" he asked the man standing in the open doorway to the rose room.

Chapter Sixteen

$\mathcal{C}$he man turned and grinned at him. "That any way to greet your brother, Nek?"

"Goddammit, Josh." Neco moved up and gave him a shove out of the doorway. He looked inside and his jaw dropped.

Casie was wearing nothing but spikey high-heeled sandals and the tiny black lace panties he never thought he'd be lucky enough to see her in.

Her back was to the door, her hot little ass cheeks were mostly exposed in the high-cut panties, her bare legs looked miles long because the rest of her was bare. Her hair was pinned in a loose messy bun on top of her head.

Her slender back curved up from her tiny waist. She was partially turned towards them, covering her naked breasts with her hands, which wasn't really doing much good, was he drooling?

"*Shit-*"

"Boy, you said it!" Josh crowed next to him.

"Neco!" Casie screeched at the two men standing there gawking at her like some kind of cartoon characters.

"Fuck." Neco grabbed the doorknob and pulled the door closed. Turning to his brother, he repeated, "What the hell are you doing here?"

Josh tried peering back into the room, but Neco had closed the door and gave him another shove.

"Huh, more like what the hell is *she* doing here? Since when do you bring your bitches home?"

"Dammit Josh," Neco scowled at him. "She's not a bitch. Go in the kitchen, I'll be there in a minute." He turned to the door and started to open it.

His brother was trying to look around him inside the room. "Josh," Neco pushed him again. "Go, I'll be there in a minute."

"Shit, Nek, she's smoking."

"I know."

"You're holding a princess prisoner in your castle?" Josh joked.

"Yeah, actually, I did keep her here against her will." He rubbed the side of his face recalling how he had kept her from leaving when she was so sick.

"What the fuck? Are you kidding?" That had Josh's interest.

"No, get in the kitchen, I'll explain in a minute."

Josh looked at him with pride. "Geez, my little brother has turned into a damned outlaw. Kidnapping gorgeous women, got himself his own sex-slave, cool!"

Making shooing motions at him, "Don't be an ass, now go," Neco said. Opening the door, he slipped inside, quickly closing the door in his grinning brother's face.

Casie had grabbed a robe and was slipping into it. Obviously upset, her hands were shaking as she tried to tie the sash but kept fumbling it.

"Baby," Neco hurried over to her. "It's all right, it's only my brother. I didn't know he was coming over, he let himself in."

She couldn't get the sash tied, frustrated tears were gathering in her traumatized eyes.

Neco said, "Here, let me." Trying to keep his eyes averted from the flashes of breasts and belly and black lace exposed from her inept scrabbling, Neco grasped the edges of the robe and closed it.

He took the sash ends from her shaking hands and neatly tied them keeping the robe secured.

"I'm sorry Casie, he didn't mean anything, he didn't know you were here." Neco set his hands on her waist.

Wiping a hand across her eyes with a sniff, Casie said, "I know, I just freaked. I was going to try on one of the dresses you got me and I saw him in the mirror and screamed. Thank goodness," her smile unnerved, "I had my back to the door." She tucked escaping hair back into the bun.

"Hmmm, yeah." His big hands spanning her waist, Neco looked down the front of her as he pulled her closer. He didn't tell her the view from the back was almost as good as the view from the front.

Of course she had panties on and her hands over her tits, but then, the panties were tiny, and her hands were small and her tits were-

"How about you put that dress on anyway and come out and meet him?" He hated that his brother was undoubtedly going to have the same dreams as he was tonight of a mostly naked Casie uselessly trying to cover her plump bare breasts.

"Oh, Neco, I'm so embarrassed." She lowered her head, her cheeks flaming.

"No doubt." He offered, "But you weren't totally nude." He took a breath, feeling his manhood still swelling. Damn he was such a little schoolboy. It wasn't like he hadn't seen his fair share of naked women. Yet, Casie was in a league all of her own, and it was a major league.

"You have to meet him sometime. Come on out now, he's really a good guy when he's not lurking and perving."

Pouting, she said in a small voice, "Why did he sneak in here then?"

"Ah," Neco pushed his hand across his face, scrubbed over his jaw. "I've been avoiding my family. He threatened he'd come by, but I thought it would be in week or two, not now."

"Why are you avoiding your family?"

That had slipped out, he hadn't meant to say it. He cupped her face with one hand. "It's complicated."

"I see. You don't have to tell me, it's none of my business." Those pretty pink lips pulled in with pretended indifference.

She was expressing normal curiosity when she asked him questions, but then she constantly backtracked thinking she was intruding.

"Casie," he sighed. "I'll tell you, just not now. It's long and complicated." And mortally horrid.

"So," she looked up through her lashes. "I guess you were expecting me to be gone by the time he…came by?"

The hand on her waist tightened, the other splayed along the side of her head. His fingers constricted around her face at the wringing sadness in her voice.

He hated to keep hearing her feelings of low self-worth. It was the amnesia causing her to continuously feel like she was nothing, that she was no one, that she technically didn't exist.

He stroked his thumb over her chin, addictively enjoying the softness of her skin. "Casie," he sighed again. "How much clearer can I make this?"

Bending to her, he touched her lips with his. Unsure about her willingness until he felt her lips pulse against his, his dick jerked in reaction to it. He kissed her, sealing their mouths so tight, so hot, it felt like a branding iron was scorching his skin.

Slanting his head, Neco pushed her lips apart and thrust his tongue inside, making no mistake about his desire for her.

Through the light robe, he could feel her naked warmth pressing against him, her plush breasts wedged against the hardness of his chest. He could feel her heart beating against his, their pulses raced together.

Pressing his burgeoning erection into her belly, there was no way she couldn't mistake it through the light fabric, then he reminded himself that his brother was there. That cooled him, slightly.

When he leaned his head back from hers, he saw her eyes were closed, lips still parted. He kissed her softly. "Casie," he spoke gently and waited for those sultry eyes to open to him.

Her hands were clutching his shoulders, he had pulled her up tight in firm contact with his torso. Raising heavy lids over the glazed green orbs, raspy voice clotted with passion, she whispered, "Neco?"

He looked down at her breasts thrust up against his chest, the robe spread apart slightly, giving him a tantalizing glimpse of her rounded globes.

His hands had a mind of their own, he carefully spread the lapels of the robe and nestled his face in her cleavage. Moving his hands to spread on her back, he held her taut while he kissed the top swells of her full breasts.

Keeping a hand on her back, he moved the other to push a lapel aside more so he could kiss and lick his way down until he was about to take her pebbled pink nipple in his mouth-

"Neco," Casie moaned his name with a breathy yearning, arching her back making it easier for him to suck her rounded flesh, "your brother," she reminded him, her hands slid down to clench in his shirt.

He dropped his head on her bosom with a heavy sigh. Then he smiled up at her. "Yes, I forgot. Not the time for this." He kissed the swell of each rounded mound then closed her robe and kissed her on the mouth.

His heart soared, she responded, and talk about erotic. Following his lead, she tried to do to him what he did to her, taste his lips, slid her small tongue across his teeth, sucked on his tongue.

He drew his hands up to cup the bottoms of her breasts and felt her stiffen. Lowering his hands back to her waist, he moved back slightly.

"Casie, I...I'm not going to say I'm sorry. I've held back from touching you intimately although I've been dying to. You want me to stop you have to say so."

Her voice small, tense, the words crawled around the knot in her throat. "You, uh, didn't answer my question, Neco. Did you expect me to be gone by the time your brother came to check on you?"

"Ahh, Casie," he groaned. Setting his hands on her shoulders, he clenched them. "No, goddammit. I want you here. I want you to stay here. I don't want you to leave. Ever." He never thought he'd ever be saying those words to a woman, but there it was.

Her face wreathed with puzzlement and doubt. "You don't know me. Why are you saying that?" She pushed from his arms, stepping away from him. "I can't stay here, I shouldn't be here now. I could be a criminal, a wanted person. I should go, now- before we get too- too-"

He grabbed her arms, squeezing them in angst at her distress. "Stop it, Casie. You are not a bad person, and you aren't going anywhere. Not until we can be sure you are okay and safe. You hear me?"

He realized he was shaking her and loosened his grip. "Let me ask you this," he stroked his hands up and down her arms.

Lips trembling slightly, she whispered, "What?"

"Do you like me, Casie?" When her lips parted, he said, "I mean more than just a friend." He squeezed her arms again with emphasis, "I mean…more."

He scanned her face, all over, her mouth, her eyes, seeking her feelings for him.

Her mouth opened, no words came out.

He sighed, his face fell. "It's okay, honey, you don't have to say-"

"Yes."

His brows popped. "Yes? Yes you like me more than just a friend? I'm talking about romantically, intimately, Casie. I want a relationship with you." Still holding her arms his thumbs rubbed small circles over the robe.

"I…" Her eyes dropped then rose to his. "I do, Neco. But I'm so unsure about… everything…"

Suppressing his grin, he pulled her into his arms and pressed her head against his chest.

"It's all right, honey. One step at a time. We'll talk more later, all right?" The relief and joy that his feelings were reciprocated, likely not as strong as his were, it didn't matter. At least she was thinking of him more in terms of as a man than just a friend, a caretaker. It was enough for now.

He could barely stem his elation. If his brother wasn't here-damn, he kept forgetting Josh was waiting in the kitchen.

Twining her arms around his waist, she nodded, her weak smile pressed on his chest.

"Okay, get dressed and come out and meet my brother." He held her chin and kissed her.

As she went up on her toes responding, his hands dropped to her arms clutching them, pulling her close to him, the kiss deepened.

When it threatened to sweep them away, Neco bolstered his thinning will power and drew from her. "Ah," he sighed stroking her face, gazing into her dazed eyes. "Sorry, I just can't help myself. You are just the most kissable woman I've ever-" *don't go there*- "Let's leave it at I really like kissing you."

The one good thing about her amnesia was that she could not think of or compare him to any other man. If only when she got her memory back that one characteristic of the amnesia would stay. Shaking his head, he was being too fanciful.

"I need to get dressed. You need to go, stop touching me." Smiling softly, Casie gathered up the front of her rope together and moved a few steps from him, out of arm's reach.

"Yeah." One last long gaze stroking her body, Neco left her to her privacy.

He strode into the kitchen tucking his shirt into his jeans.

His brother was sitting on a stool at the counter rolling a beer bottle between his hands. Josh's brow arched at Neco fixing his clothes.

With a smirk and a chug of the beer, Josh said, "So, it looks like I interrupted something. It looks like that broad is like actually living in the pink room. Is she? I don't know how I noticed anything other than that smoking body, but I caught a glimpse of clothes around and stuff on the dresser."

Scowling at his brother, Neco got himself a beer and joined him at the counter. "She is not a broad, Josh, or a bitch, or a chick.

Her name is Casie. Sort of." He swigged the beer, licking his lips as he toed out a stool and sat down.

"You didn't answer my question, bro, is she living here?" Josh took a sip, set the beer down, cocked his head sideways at him. "What do you mean 'sort of?' Is that her name or not?"

Neco steepled his fingers around his bottle and half-turned to face his brother. "It's a long story."

"I've got time."

Shooting a quick glance at the hall to make sure she wasn't there, Neco quickly gave his brother the run-down on how he and Casie met.

When he finished, Josh's eyebrows were like crescents over startled eyes and his mouth dropped open. He spurted in awe, "Whew, helluva story, bro. So this is what you do when shutting off your family. Rescue beautiful damsels in distress, and keep them hidden under lock and key.

"My luck, if it'd been me, she'd be a 60-year-old fattie. You totally lucked out with that bitch- uh, damned fine woman." His lips smacked together in a smirky grin before turning serious.

"I don't understand, you saved her life, nursed her back to health, why is she still here? It's not like you to keep a woman around. Except for that slut you married, and thank God that didn't last long." At his brother's warning scowl, he said quickly, "Anyway, seriously, why is she still here?"

A corner of his lip quirked up as a brow drew down. Neco replied, "First, she doesn't know who she is. I can't toss her out on the streets. Second," he shrugged and tipped the bottle to his lips and drank, "I want her here."

Josh stared at him, his mouth twisted in disbelief. "She's not your type."

"Oh yeah?" His brow arched. "What is my type?"

"You know, lusty, strong, blowsy, fake tits and big lips, tall enough so you don't have to bend over so far. Experienced and sturdy enough to take your rough and tough big body, ones that drop to their knees and unbutton your jeans within moments of meeting you.

"Personally, I don't know what you see in them. I mean, I know what you see in them, a good rough lay, quick blowjobs. But, I can't believe I'm saying this, pinch me, there's more to a woman than just a good fuck. You do them and dump them, Nek.

"You don't get to know them; you don't take them to dinner, to the movies unless pushed into it. You despise cuddling and after sex talk, and you never bring them around to meet the family."

"I don't want to get to know them Josh, that's why I choose the ones I do." Neco smiled wryly at Josh. "How the hell did you learn so much about me and my women?"

"We're brothers, Nek. We talk, hang out together, or used to, remember?"

"Huh," Neco snorted sucking his beer.

"Ever since Kandi you got worse. You're even harder and harsher with women."

"Shut up, Josh, you know I don't want to talk about her."

"Anyway," Josh continued, "even with that quick look, I can see this girl is different. She, I don't know, she looks really feminine, ladylike, her body is hot but like…delicate. She's smaller, daintier than the women you usually bang. She's got class, and, she was genuinely freaked when I walked in on her. Your other women would have flaunted their wares at me. This one you're screwing seems…like, sweet kind of."

"I'm not screwing her Josh."

His brother swung his head at him with an incredulous expression. "What? With that body? She's fucking gorgeous with a totally bitable ass and unbelievable tits. Nek, you're shitting me. Why is she here then?"

"Lower your voice, Josh."

"Don't you want to fuck her, Neco?"

"Shh, dammit, Josh, keep it down and clean it up."

"Aha, she's got you wrapped around her little finger already, I can see it. And you're not even fuck- uh, sleeping with her? What's the matter with her, why don't you want to do her?"

"Josh, man, keep it down. I do want to…sleep with her. But I'm taking things slow. She's fragile and shy and very skittish. I don't want to freak her out by jumping her and have her rabbit. She already did once." He quickly picked up his beer and drank it down.

He wasn't about to tell him about her running off into the woods. Josh would think she's nuts. But, Josh doesn't know what she's been through, how tough it is to live not knowing who she is, and be wholly dependent on a total stranger, a man, and one who wants in her panties, bad.

Besides, Neco was sure she'd suffered some serious trauma at some point and he didn't want to do anything to re-traumatize her by pouncing on her.

"Bro, you need to watch your back, you don't know who this babe is."

"Shh!" Neco snapped, he could hear her bedroom door open. "Be nice to her."

His grin leering, Josh replied, "Not a problem, Nek. You don't want to do her, I sure do." He went to stand up.

Neco slammed his hand on his brother's chest stopping him like a Mack truck. "Stay the hell away from her, Josh," he growled at him.

Grinning wider, Josh looked down at this brother's hand planted on his chest. "Why don't you just pound your fists on your chest and bellow 'mine!'" He smirked at Neco's scowl. "Well, you claiming her or not? She on the free list or what?"

"Just cool it, brother." Letting out a whoosh of air, Neco looked up as Casie entered the room.

Josh let out a low cat-whistle.

Neco punched him in the arm, growled, "Knock it off, Josh." But his eyes popped too.

Casie was wearing a form-fitting dress with a halter-top and the sandals with the high spiked heels. The snug top cradled her breasts, clearly she wasn't wearing a bra. Thank God it was warm inside, the dress was light enough her nipples would pop right through.

Both men jumped to their feet. Neco said, "Geez, Casie, that dress. Hell woman, I told Miss Ford nothing too- too-"

160

"Sexy?" Josh helped.

Neco shot him a dirty look then turned back to sweep another glance over Casie's dress. Hot flames of desire sparked in his blue eyes. "That's, ah, you look nice, honey."

"Real nice," Josh offered.

"Shut up, Josh. Come and have a seat, Casie, meet my brother." Beads of sweat popped along his hairline. She was wearing more than she had been when they had seen her a moment ago, but hell, it was almost even sexier.

Neco knew his eyes were glued to her chest, but he couldn't tear them away. The skirt was short and swirled around her legs above the knees showcasing those spectacular limbs. Her amazing rack swayed and jostled as she sat down. He licked his dry lips, swallowed hard.

Pulling her hair to the side, she fussed with it looking down at herself. "I didn't try this on, Neco, Miss Ford added some things I didn't even see, like nightgowns and stuff. She just kept clucking saying you would like them." She frowned at the dress.

Neco's eyes flashed to his brother with a scowl.

Josh was gaping at her breasts as much as he was.

She crossed her legs, both brothers' gazes followed her movements, the skirt slid up her thighs.

Neco mumbled, "She was right about that." Sure, he loved the dress, if they were there alone, and she wasn't leaving the house in it.

The urge to untie the back of the halter from around her neck and let it slide down to her waist fought with the itch in Neco's palms to curve over those slender thighs and start sliding up.

Using his most charming voice, Josh said smoothly, "It's nice to meet you, Casie. Sorry about earlier, I didn't know you were here. I would never have intruded on you that way if I had."

He shot a glance at Neco indicating it wouldn't have happened if Neco had let his family know what was going on in his life. He took a few steps closer to her. Seeing the wary look on her face, he paused, and moved more slowly.

Taking Casie's hand, Josh lifted it and kissed the back of it while looking her in the eye. "I heard a noise in the bedroom and thought it was Nek. Can you forgive me, beautiful, for my bungling?" He kissed her hand again.

He was so charming and handsome; Casie couldn't help but smile at him. "Of course, Josh, I know you didn't do it on purpose. I'd like to forget all about it. Okay?"

Holding her hand against his lips, Josh said, "Sure, sweetheart. I'll…try…to get the picture out of my head." His gaze drifted over her curves so nicely displayed in the hot dress, he thought, *and this picture too-*

Neco reached over, caught his brother's arm and pulled it from Casie, making him let go of her hand. "Her name is Casie, not sweetheart," he growled gruffly.

Josh snickered, his smirk irritated Neco like Josh knew it would.

Casie stood up. "I think I would be more comfortable in jeans. You guys probably want to get caught up and you don't need me in your way."

"No!" Both men spoke together.

Neco glared at Josh and said to Casie, "Honey, you're not interrupting anything."

Josh stood up too. "It's all right, bro. I was only stopping by for a minute. Ma wanted me to scold you some more and remind you of the barbeque. It's far enough off she said that maybe you'll get over your snit and be friendlier, not sit in a corner drinking and scowling at everyone as usual." He ducked with a laugh as Neco swung at his head.

Neco ground at him, "Shut the hell up, bro."

"Well, it was nice to meet you, Josh." Casie slightly bowed her head. "I'll leave you two boys to beat on each other."

"Sure, Casie, a real pleasure meeting you too." Josh grinned big at her.

Both men watched her hips sway somehow saucy and demure at the same time as she turned and strode from them down the hall and back to her room.

"You bringing her to the BBQ?" Josh asked, still staring at where she disappeared, clearly hoping he would say yes.

"Not if you don't keep your fucking rapacious eyes and hands off her." Neco mirrored his brother staring at the empty hall like he was hoping she'd come right back.

"Hey now, watch that language, bro," Josh teased and ducked again at Neco's swing.

Chapter Seventeen

Twenty minutes earlier, Casie's mind had been buzzing, her thoughts tense wondering what she should do.

Standing in front of the full-length mirror, she had hesitated before reaching for the dress. How odd that her own body was as a stranger's. She eyed herself critically, but couldn't tell if she had a decent figure or not.

It was weird, she felt like a voyeur. She clapped a hand over her mouth to cover her giggle. She was a Peeping Casie. Shaking her head, how ridiculous-

The door squeaked slightly as it opened, she heard a sharp intake of breath and looked in the mirror at the same time her hands instinctually covered her bare breasts.

A man was standing there gawking at her! She screamed, his face turned red but he didn't move. His feet stayed planted as his eyes devoured her.

She screamed again and then Neco was there shoving the man out of the doorway. But then Neco stood there unmoving, his expression inscrutable, the blue eyes wide and unblinking.

He started to close the door, but then that other man poked his head in the doorway again. Neco shoved him again, and closed the door.

She could hear the male voices outside the door. Neco didn't sound angry, more like irritated. The other man's voice sounded oddly like Neco's only without the rough edge.

Come to think of it, the men looked a lot alike. Tall, heavily muscled yet lean, dark hair and blue eyes. Shaking herself out of her shock, Casie grabbed for the robe draped over the chair. She'd barely slung it on when the door opened slowly.

She could feel her face burning with mortification. Two men, veritable strangers, had been gawking at her and she was wearing only a wisp of lace panties that didn't do much to cover her butt cheeks, and a pair of outrageously high heeled sandals. More of Miss Ford's choices.

Neco had moved towards her, she tried to get the robe tied before he reached her but her hands were shaking so badly she couldn't make the sash work.

Neco calmly took the belt out of her hands and neatly tied it. She was grateful, he was a gentleman and looked away from her nude body every time the robe slipped partially open. His large strong presence made her feel safe, and cared for.

"Baby," Neco had said, "he's my brother, he didn't know you were here."

Then Neco put his large hands on her waist. She could feel the slight pressure from his thick fingers squeezing her, revealing he wasn't as calm as he acted.

He was talking, but she didn't hear his words, a flush had roiled up her body from his hands on her to cloud her head. Before she could clear her brain, he lowered his head and kissed her. He didn't just kiss her, he consumed her.

She barely felt his big hand move to her back pulling her tight against his hard body. His mouth was going so crazy on hers, pulling her in, drowning her with his raging desire. So electrifying, he heated her up with his searing hunger.

His lips overwhelmed her, sucking her tongue he besieged her mouth, beguiling her to reciprocate, enticing her to learn the taste of him.

Casie felt her core frying like the bacon in the pan. She felt...wet, and tingling between her legs. She could feel herself melting into him, he felt so unbelievably good. Her breasts mashed against his rock hard chest as he pulled her in and under his heady spell.

He ground his hips at hers, his erection, the thick hard ridge of him pressed urgently at her stomach. Oh gosh, what was she getting into? She tried to grapple back her control, but, oh, could the man kiss!

Her robe parted, she hadn't noticed until she felt his mouth leave hers and travel with wet lusty kisses down her neck and to the tops of her breasts. Casie's mind was actually going black, as if she would swoon with the raw sensuous feelings he evoked in her.

He groaned against her breast then kissed it. She felt her own shudder all the way down to her sex. Her fingers dug into his shoulders as she clung to him wanting more.

When his tongue sought her nipple she thought of his brother, *what was she doing*? What kind of sleaze was she, letting Neco ravish her while his brother was just in the other room?

Protesting, "Neco," she had pushed at him, suddenly shocked at her wanton behavior.

Kissing her swollen flesh a last time, he stopped and closed her robe. He looked disappointed, but not angry.

They were both panting, if he felt anywhere near as dizzy with desire as she did it was a wonder he could stand. As it was, she was holding onto fistfuls of his shirt. If he let go of her, with her legs so rubbery she would fall, but he didn't, his hands circled her waist again.

She knew he was unaware how hard he was squeezing her. But it was okay, it grounded her, pulled her back from that storm of desire that made her so hot she couldn't draw a coherent thought.

Neco was talking, the deep rumble of his voice kept the fire stirring in her loins. He had moved slightly from her, yet she could see he was still hard, his manhood bulged in his jeans.

166

Unsure of her experience with men, still, he seemed awfully big. She swallowed hard, dragged her eyes to his face and tried to hear what he was saying.

His deep voice heavily masculine and gruff trying to rein in his passion, Neco whispered, "I want to be more than just friends with you, Casie." No kidding.

Things were so confusing. She had no idea who she was, was she a good person? Or running from the law? Did she have family looking for her? A boyfriend?

Her face reddened at the thought that she might be involved with a man and she was here, half naked, making out with a man that she really didn't know either. But Neco was so kind and caring, amusing, and *hot*.

His mouth was like magic, she wanted to feel those big hard hands stroking her bare skin and gripping her- shaking her head, Casie pushed her loosening hair back up and worked to clear her fevered mind.

She had raised her eyes to his, he had looked so...serious. And so ruggedly beautiful he took her breath away. The dark hair was tousled, his jaw covered with scruff, he hadn't shaved today.

She brought her hand to her own face, it was stinging slightly from his beard. But not unpleasantly sore, not so sore she wouldn't relish kissing him again right now.

Neco had caught her chin to get her attention. "Casie, I am romantically interested in you. I want to have an intimate relationship with you...do you feel the same way?"

Pushing aside her hunger for his kiss, and the thought that she might belong to another man and was cheating on him, she looked at his intense blue eyes.

She replied with a skip in her voice and hesitation, "I...want to be more than friends with you, too."

He had looked so pleased, his fingers clinched her waist hard.

"But Neco," she had to make him understand. "I am terribly confused. I could be someone you don't want to know." She tried to convince him but he lowered his mouth to hers and raised those big hard hands to palm her breasts.

She could feel herself falling back, craving his touch, wanting more. If she didn't stop him he would have her naked and on her back. She could feel the powerful lust in his touch, his rapid thick breathing, ravening desire fairly crackled in the hooded blue eyes, and his steel hardened shaft pressed against her.

She gently, and halfheartedly pushed at him. "No. Please." Again he stopped right away then drew her into his strong arms and cuddled her.

"We'll talk later. Come out and meet my brother." He'd kissed her and left her alone.

The minute she had walked into the kitchen their secretive whispers halted and the two of them stared at her like she was a lamb who'd just walked into their lion's lair, they were practically licking their chops.

Josh Bardiche was sweet and charming, friendly and likable. She took his flirting with a grain of salt. She could see the more he did it the madder Neco appeared, and then he did it more with a teasing glint in his mischievous eyes.

She left them to their conversation sliding back into the privacy of her room. This time she locked the door.

Neco worked half the night.

Casie slipped in quietly and set his dinner on the desk next to his computer. He was on the phone but he reached for her, she smiled and stepped out of his reach. She didn't want to be the cause of his work taking longer because she was a distraction. She went to bed.

When she got up the next day he was already in his office, and on the phone again.

As she passed by she could hear the agitation in his voice, she paused and peeked in.

He was standing in front of the window dragging a hand through his hair like he did when agitated. He was adamantly shaking his head and now gestured angrily with his hand. It was none of her business, but she lingered beside the open door anyway and eavesdropped.

He kept his voice low but it was deep with anger, "You are not listening to me Andrew," he paused, then, "yes, yes, I know you are my lawyer, I heard what you said, but I'm telling you I don't want my wife to even see the papers for the sale of the house in Sanlura."

The rest of his words flew around Casie's head, she heard nothing but the words, *my wife*. Her blood froze, her heart pounded so hard in her chest she thought it would burst right out.

Her mind swirled, she couldn't think, 'my wife,' he was married. *How could he- oh my gosh, what a fool I've been, I have to get out of here-*

Neco must have two houses. Maybe his wife doesn't know about this one, maybe this is where he brings his mistresses. Her lungs collapsed, she couldn't draw a breath, her heart felt like it was literally breaking, splintering into pieces.

He was so kind, and smart and funny, and even with a haunted look in the depths of his blue eyes he was so handsome, and he lit a blazing fire in her. She had missed their time together these past few days while he worked so much.

Casie had thought he genuinely wanted a relationship with her. Her lips twisted, all he wanted was to get in her pants. She has been living in a fairy tale.

She moved as fast as her numb legs would take her. *Where can I go? What can I do?* Her thoughts muddled and frantic, she was in a panic- she had to get out of the house.

She ran to her bedroom, *huh,* she snorted, not hers after all. Grabbing a piece of paper and a pen, her hand shaking like a leaf, she wrote him a quick note:

Thank you, Neco for your care and hospitality.
I'll leave the clothes, maybe your *wife* can wear them.
Regards,
Casie

A tiny tear plopped on the paper. Sniffing back the rest of them, she set the note on her bed, grabbed her jacket, toothbrush and comb and hurried down the hall.

Neco was on his phone, she ran into the kitchen and grabbed up the landline. She called information for that place Mr. King owned. He said he'd give her a job.

When she got the number, she dialed. A bored voice told her Mr. King was away for the week.

"Okay," she huffed on a tight breath as panic gripped her stomach. What to do now? "Can you maybe leave him a message? Tell him Casie called about a job."

She was about to hang up when the person on the other line quickly said, "Hold on a sec, let me get him on three-way."

Not sure what was going on, Casie held the phone praying they would hurry up before Neco came out. She couldn't face him.

"Hello?" His voice deeply sexy and virile, and excited, "Is this little green eyes?"

She let out her breath. "Yes, Casie. I need a job Mr. King, you said-"

"What about Neco Bardiche? Is he-"

"I'm not with him anymore. I...need to find a place to stay, can you recommend-"

"Tell me where you are, I'll have a car come and get you. I'm out of town but you can stay for now with my Manager, Sasha. She'll get you started. I'm assuming," he said with a low chuckle, "you're more of the mind to be a barmaid, not dancing right now?"

Casie swallowed her pain. "Yes, no, I mean yes to being a server."

As soon as they were done making arrangements, she quietly hung the phone up and slipped out the side door.

She hurried down the street. It would be a while before the car would get from the city and she didn't want to be out front when it came. Neco might see her and cause a scene, and she couldn't take it.

Chapter Eighteen

Rubbing his eyes, Neco felt a kink in his neck.

Waking slowly, he realized he'd fallen asleep on his desk. The sun was streaming through the window. He peered at his watch, it was eight o'clock.

His long arms stretching over his head, he yawned and smiled. Hopefully, Casie had the coffee on. She tended to be an early riser.

His mind traveled back to a few days ago when Josh had been there and he and Casie had finally started getting physical. Smiling broadly, his dick twitched and started hardening at the thought of her. It seemed she was ready to move towards a more permanent relationship with him.

Neco would have started intimate moves on her already since she pretty much gave the go ahead, but work had burst into uber overtime. He hadn't had a moment except to gobble food Casie brought to him while he kept working.

Standing up with a yawn, he couldn't help the grin that spread across his face. Life was finally turning around for him. He had a nice house, the work was paying hand over fist, and Casie, his heart raced, he couldn't wait to put his hands on her.

Combing his fingers through his hair, he decided it would be best to shower and shave before he went in and gave her a morning kiss. Whistling a cheerful tune he went straight to his bathroom.

Showered and dressed, Neco headed straight for the kitchen. His lips pushed out, frowning, the kitchen was empty. There was no evidence of Casie being there at all.

Grumbling out loud, "Huh," he thought, *she never sleep this late, maybe she was ill again.* Leaving the kitchen, he strode quickly back down the other hall to the rose room.

Not wanting to startle her if she was asleep, he slowly pushed the door open.

The room was empty.

"What the hell," the bathroom door was open so he knew she wasn't in there. Maybe she was out walking. The frown deepened, he really didn't like her out wandering around without him.

They were far from town and surrounded by fields and woods. Plus, someone had hurt her and could possibly do it again if he came across her.

Neco was about to turn and go outside to look for her when he saw the note.

Two steps and he bent and picked it up. His stomach was twisting even before he started to read it. Her leaving him a note could only mean one thing, that she'd left him. But her things were still in the room, maybe he was being-

He scanned the few lines of the note and his twisting stomach plummeted like it was filled with lead. His wife. She must have heard him on the phone with Andrew.

Blasting, "Fuck!" moving anxiously out of the room, he hurried to his office where his cell was, and dialed Josh.

"Hey, bro what's up?" Josh's cheerful voice came over the wire.

"Dammit Josh, she's gone," Neco's fear rushed out with his words.

"What? Calm down, you talking about Casie?"

"Yeah, goddammit, who else? She overheard me talking to Andrew about Kandi and assumed we were still married. She left me a note, Josh, there's a fucking teardrop on the paper."

His voice fraught with desperation, he'd hurt her so badly she'd cried. Damn. He raked a hand through his hair and wiped over his eyes.

Josh asked him, "Where would she go?"

"Nowhere, I don't know, she doesn't know anybody, she doesn't even know who she is. She has no money, no car, fuck Josh, I don't know."

"All right, I'm on my way, I'm actually close to your side of town right now. I'll help you look for her. Hold it together until I get there." Josh hung up.

Neco stood like a rock, what to do? He turned towards the window, would she run to the woods again?

He decided to search the perimeter first.

It was still chilly outside, he charged all around the lawn. But there was no trace of her out back. When he came around front, Josh was getting out of his car.

"Thanks for coming." Neco met him in the driveway.

"Of course. Gee Nek, you look like hell."

"Thanks. I feel like it." His hair was a mess from repeatedly dragging his fingers through it, his face was pinched and pale with worry. "I checked around the outside, there had been a light coating of snow early yesterday evening, there are no footprints. I don't know where to look."

"Yeah, listen, there's-"

"You don't understand, Josh, she's been sick, she's frail and scared. I was the only one she could depend on and I-" He choked. "I made her cry, Josh! Shit I can't take it if she's lying injured somewhere and it's my fault-"

"I know, shut up for a second." Josh touched his arm. "Down the street from here, about a mile, I noticed oil on the side of the road."

Scowling like he wanted to shove his fist through a wall, Neco snarled, "Yeah? So what? Why do I give a shit about some damned-"

"I was here a couple of days ago, there's not a lot of traffic on this road. Most people take the main highway skirting this rural section. I would have noticed that oil before, Nek, like I did on the way here now. There's not much to see the few miles into this area."

"So, what the hell are you saying?"

"I'm saying I think she got in a car."

Neco stared at him, his blood chilled. "You saying you think she hitched into town?"

Josh nodded. "There's no trace of her around here, she has no vehicle, no money. Yes, I think she caught a ride."

Pondering this, Neco tried to keep his panic down. Maybe a nice woman or elderly couple picked her up, it doesn't necessarily have to be some rapist-killer like he was thinking. He turned and started for the house.

"Where are you going?" Josh strode after him.

"She must be in town. There's nowhere else for her to go. I'm gonna go look for her."

"Uh," Josh decided to keep to himself the idea that her ride could have taken her all the way out of the town of Lark and into another city. He hopped in Neco's truck and the two men took off to search for her.

They went to the shop where Neco had bought her clothes.

Miss Ford was worried when he told her Casie was missing. "No, dear, I haven't seen her since the day you were here. Is she okay? She was so darling."

"Yes, she is. If you hear from her," he handed her a business card. "Call me right away. Thanks."

They checked out grocery stores and pharmacies, shops after shops, but no one saw anyone of her description.

It had grown late. The brothers ate fast food on the somber way back home.

Neco parked the truck and sat staring out the window.

"She'll be all right, Nek, she's a smart girl."

"Josh, she doesn't even know her real name. She's young, and still gets dizzy and disoriented from the concussion. And, her judgment, well," he crushed his burger wrapper in his hand and stuffed it hard into the paper bag. "She hasn't shown the best judgment." He explained about her running into the freezing woods.

Josh shook his head. "She's got to be a lot better now, Nek. She was still recovering then, she probably was confused."

Neco swiveled in his seat to look bleakly at his brother. "Yeah, and she was running from me because I'd hurt her, just like now."

The brothers sat in silence.

"I'm going to head home, I'll be back tomorrow to help look for her. Just," Josh opened his door and patted his brother on the arm, "hang in there." He didn't know what else to say. He couldn't declare the platitude that they would find her and everything would be all right, chances were they wouldn't.

When he got in his car, Neco was still sitting in his truck staring out at nothing.

After a sleepless night and another fruitless search the next day, Josh dropped Neco off and set out for his own home.

Neco stood in the driveway with his head in his hands.

He couldn't believe it. The best thing in the world that had ever happened to him had fallen in his lap and he had not held on tight enough to it.

Well, hell, he thought bitterly, that was how life had been treating him, why should anything change now? Yet, he couldn't bear to give up on her.

The thought that maybe whoever had beaten her had found her inched in his frantic brain, he pushed the thought away, he could not let his mind go there.

Trudging up the gravel drive, he ran over the past few weeks in his mind.

Finding her half-dead, nursing her back to health, buying her clothes, the feel of her body in his hands on his lips, he shook his head. He couldn't go there, he'd start bawling. The diner they'd had lunch in, he'd asked around there too but no one had-

He slapped his palm on his forehead. Of course! Fishing his keys out of his pocket he ran for his truck and raced back to town.

Neco parked in front of the King's Palace Gentlemen's Club.

The parking lot circled the entire building, and it was packed with cars. What the hell, was every man in town here?

Pocketing his keys, his heart pounded against the inside of his chest as he made his way to the entrance.

The music was so loud the boom-boom of it could be heard all the way outside. The windows were blacked out since it was a strip club.

The door opened and closed every few seconds as mostly men traveled in and out of the club. A few women clung to a few arms but they were few and far apart.

Pulling the door open, Neco stepped inside.

It was dim, of course, so people could pretend they couldn't be seen so they could act any way they wanted.

Neco moved to the side, stepping into the shadows.

There were three stages.

A girl was in the center one, a spotlight lit her up like a starship. She had already peeled off her top, she was now doing away with the pasties, freeing her tits completely. She tossed each pasty out to the audience, men near the stage shouted and jumped up to catch them.

The stripper danced to the end of the stage and shook her big globs of flesh at the man sitting the closest to the stage. Her breasts were big but not particularly attractive. They drooped and jiggled loosely.

The man reached out a drunken hand to grab a tit but she laughed and danced out of his reach. She made her way to the pole in the middle of the stage. Now in only a G-string, she shook her ample ass as she moved to coil seductively around the pole.

Neco prayed that if she was there, that Casie was not dancing. He didn't think she would, but desperate people did desperate things. She had no legitimate way to support herself, to even get food. He couldn't bear to think about her being desperate, he just wanted her back home safe with him.

Adjusting his vision to the dark room, he scanned the bar.

There were barmaids and other women, all scantily clothed, hanging around the men perched on stools ordering one drink after another.

One man sat on a stool with a girl on either side of him. He spanked both their half-bare asses, then grabbed their cheeks squeezing as hard as he could, the girls squealed then giggled.

Casie wasn't at the bar.

Neco searched the rest of the room table by table. He was starting to feel let down, hopelessness invaded his bones like the flu, when he saw off in the corner, a fat man with a bad toupee holding onto a barmaid's arm trying to drag her onto his lap.

It was her. His Casie.

"Motherfucker," Neco muttered savagely, long-legging it across the room. His heart now banging clear out of his chest, the blood raced through his veins with screaming relief, and dire worry that she would refuse to come home with him, his pulse must be off the charts.

He had to muscle his way through small crowds, some men objected, he ignored them keeping his eyes on Casie.

Her beautiful hair was tied back in a long thick braid, it flopped and twitched on her back as she tried to disengage the man's meaty fist from around her slim arm while pushing back with her feet. The stilettoes weren't giving her much traction.

Neco came right up next to her.

"Casie," he gruffed, his expression to the fat man grabbing her was black with warning.

But the man was too busy ogling down the front of her miniscule top and pulling her on his lap.

Hearing his voice, she turned with a big smile like she was ecstatic to see him, then, she remembered, her face fell, the tears sprung quickly. She swiftly turned her head from him so he couldn't see how hurt she was, the braid slapping her back.

While choking down sudden sobs that clamored up her throat, she mumbled, "What are you doing here?" Showing her hurt, she said bitterly, "Come to watch the show? Find yourself a new mistress?"

"Hey fella," the fat guy slobbered drunkenly, "git yer own gal, thisn's mine. C'mere sweetie, give ol' Chuckie a kiss, I got a big lap for you, babygirl." He tugged on her arm so hard he almost pulled it out of its socket.

"This one's taken, man." Neco wound his fingers around the fat guy's fat wrist and squeezed.

Still trying to pull from the drunk's grasp, Casie cried, "No, Neco stop, I'll get fired!"

Snapping, "Good," Neco told the man, "let her go or I'll break it." He squeezed and painfully bent the man's wrist until it cracked.

Looking green, the man gasped and released her with a gag of nausea.

Cradling his injured wrist with his other hand, the fat guy bellyached, "Hey, that hurt, you sonuvabitch." Grimacing, he glared at Neco then snarled at Casie, "You best come and be friendly wit me little girl, or I'll see you're out of a fuckin' job." He held out his good hand to grab at her again.

Neco threw his arm around Casie and turned her from the fat man and started walking away with her. She dug in her heels.

"Stop, Neco. What do you think you're doing? Are you mad that you didn't get to- to- screw me before I found out about your wife? Well," she dashed at her tears trying to pull out of his grasp. "It's too late, get yourself another gullible woman." She jerked her body from his but he held her tighter.

"I'm taking you out of here, Casie, this is not the place for you to work." He didn't stop moving towards the exit.

She struggled to push him away. When he wouldn't let her go, she said, "You can't tell me where I can and can't work," and refused to go any further.

Smoothing the frown from his face, Neco wrapped his long fingers around her upper arms holding her gently. He said quietly, "Casie, I'm looking out for you." His irises turned to cobalt blue, the only indication he was so damned thrilled to find her and that she was fine.

"I can make my own choices, leave me alone." Her shoulders bunched up, she tried twisting from his grasp.

"Baby, right now your judgment is messed up, you aren't thinking right." He started walking again holding onto her arm.

"I am too, let me go. Anything is better than being with a cheat and a liar." The pain in her voice matched the tears blurring her eyes, but her mouth trembled with anger.

"Honey, who ran out into the damned woods in the dark of night in the freezing cold?"

She fought his hold. "It doesn't matter. I should have stayed there instead of letting myself get seduced by you. You- you're married. You're no better than a cheating rutting dog."

He stopped trying to walk with her and put both his hands on her shoulders moving her out of the main path of the crowd. "Casie, I am not married. She is my ex-wife. I swear to God."

She hesitated, narrowed her eyes at him, then closed them and shoved at him, unfortunately her strength was nothing compared to his, he didn't budge. "That's what they all say. Leave me alone."

He pulled her closer, lowered his head to get in her face. "Baby, listen to me, I can prove it. I have divorce papers, actually they are annulment papers. I should have told you about her but," he sighed painfully, "it was a brutal wretched time that I wanted to put behind me."

His voice was so filled with such anguish it gave Casie pause. "I- don't understand," she stopped struggling.

Neco still held her slim shoulders absently massaging them. Taking a deep jagged breath, he said, "I slept with her once. Picked her up in a bar and thought that was it. One time, move on. But she contacted me, and although I'd used a rubber she told me she was pregnant."

Casie had softened briefly, but hearing he was a father and hadn't told her that either burned her moral code worse than the fact he had a wife. "So you are a cheating, no-good dead-beat dad that isn't supporting his-"

He actually laughed out loud at that. Shaking his head with gratitude, he said, "No, that was the thing. Kandi told me she was pregnant so I'd marry her. Said she was from a good Catholic family and her parents would kill her, blah, blah, blah, and it was my kid. So, yeah, I did the right thing."

"But, you only had sex once?" Casie didn't know what she was feeling right now. She was so happy he was here, she'd thought of nothing else since she'd been gone.

Every minute of every day she had forced herself to push him out of her tormented mind, it wasn't meant to be, he was a dog that preyed on helpless women.

But, his hands felt so warm and solid on her shoulders, there was clear pain in his eyes darkening the blue so much they almost looked obsidian, the skin was pinched around them.

He looked bone tired, like he hadn't gotten any sleep, same as her. So handsome, her heart fluttered, she'd missed looking at him, talking to him, kissing him.

"Honey," he chuckled, "it only takes once. I used a condom, but she said there must have been a tear. She was so adamant, insisting I marry her, she cried and carried on. I thought it might not be mine, after all, I picked her up in a bar and she took me right to her place, ah," Casie didn't need to know the dirty details, last thing he wanted was for her to have a picture in her mind of him in bed with another woman.

"Anyway, I figured I could get a paternity test when the baby was born, but in the meantime," he sighed, "I married her to give the child my name, make him or her legitimate."

Her face a twist of anguish and fierce anger at being taken in by him, telling herself he was lying, Casie pulled from him again.

Neco held her taut. "Casie, she wasn't pregnant. It was totally a ruse to get me to marry her. Yeah, I was stupid to fall for it. I just didn't think it was right for the baby if I waited to do a paternity before marrying his or her mother."

180

He studied Casie's face. He was so relieved to find her he could weep. He didn't want to, but he needed to tell her the rest of the repugnant story.

"Shortly after we were married, just before I found out she wasn't really pregnant, I caught her in bed with one of my best friends, Marco. Marco was also my business partner. There were three of us guys that shared the partnership."

His face so distressed while he told his sordid story, Casie whispered, "Oh, Neco, I'm sorry," and stopped struggling.

Looking up at him, she saw his face was quilted with gouging hurt, guilt, fury and remorse. It was an effort, but she resisted her urge to caress his poor face to soothe him.

He smiled mirthlessly at her. Stroking her hair he went on, "It gets worse. Marco was embezzling from the company. When I kicked Kandi out, she told on him. She bragged that he was stealing and was going to take her away to an exotic land far-far away with the money he'd embezzled."

His lips curled sarcastically with the memory of a malignant, nasty Kandi snarling at him like a shrew when she realized he really meant they were through.

Since he was going to seek an annulment she would not even be able to go after spousal support, the scheming gold digger had decided to throw her lot in with the embezzler.

Neco gently touched Casie's face. "I was...well I was glad to get out from Kandi's clutches. What a greedy waspish viper, hell, I didn't even like her.

"I was hurt and betrayed by my friend, Marco, but I didn't want to press charges. It was enough that I got rid of her. Regrettably, our other partner wanted to nail his hide to the wall. So, Marco was arrested and was looking at ten or more years, it wasn't his first offense."

"That must have been so hard for you." Casie felt his pain. She was compassionate, sad for them all.

They were getting jostled while they talked over the music. Neco had moved them close to the wall, not the best place for the spilling of the guts. Clearly, she wasn't going to leave with him unless he gave her a good reason to trust him.

He would have just tossed her over his shoulder, taken her home and talked about everything there, most likely though, he'd get arrested for abduction before he could get her to his truck.

"It was. Still, it gets worse." He watched her brows rise in incredulity, questioning how much worse could it get?

"Marco owed money all over town. He gambled and got himself in deep. I wished he'd come to me, but he kept everything a deep dark secret.

"When he was sent to jail, he...couldn't take it. He knew the men he owed money to would hurt him even on the inside. He knew they would hurt him bad, probably, undoubtedly ah, maim him, permanently as a lesson to him as well as others.

"While he was out on bond, they sent him word they were coming for him. He was too scared, he...took his own life." Neco winced at Casie's sharp gasp. Her hands went over her mouth, eyes wide with shock and disbelief.

"No," she shook her head murmuring against her hands, her face filled with shock and sadness for him.

"The point is, Casie, I couldn't lay all that shit on you. Not so soon. You had enough of your own issues."

Other than the amnesia, she had no tangible baggage to bring into their relationship, and that made everything so pure and fresh, he had hated to throw his dirt on it.

"So that was what your brother kept hinting at that you would drink and scowl when visiting your family."

His mouth nicked in at the corner, his skin darkened slightly with brief shame. "Yes. I'm sorry to admit, I fell into the bottle to numb my pain."

He kept stroking her face, he was so damned grateful he was touching her again that his knees were weak.

"I hated everything and everyone. I was conned by a tramp. The business we'd built went into the red from the embezzling and bad publicity, we lost all our money and the business fell into bankruptcy. I had been betrayed by my friend, and then felt such guilt that he committed suicide over something…that maybe I could have prevented. I don't know. I couldn't bear the loss of him and my feelings of guilt."

Neco looked at Casie, his mouth a wry purse. "The irony is, he wouldn't have met Kandi if it hadn't been for me. Maybe things would have turned out differently if I never-"

"Neco, you aren't responsible for his actions. Only he is." She cocked her head at him. "So, what about your wife? Were you so devastated you didn't want any more relationships?"

Nodding, he said, "Sort of. I couldn't believe I was taken in by her. As I said, I didn't even like her. It was one drunken night of nameless sex that changed my life forever."

He squeezed her shoulder and reminded her, "Ex-wife. Not wife. Actually, not either. I know I misspoke while talking to my lawyer. We never had sex again after that first time. I could barely stand to look at her.

"She was grasping and nasty, bitchy to my friends and family. The conversation you overheard was about Kandi trying to get her greedy little hands on my house in the city and I was telling my lawyer to keep my paperwork away from her. I didn't even want him talking to her.

"She had a lawyer. I paid for him, but the grasping bitch took half that money for herself and now she owes him money. She is a pretty girl with the morals and kindness of a rattlesnake. She fucked Marco just to screw with him and get back at me for not loving her."

He took a breath, watching Casie gazing raptly at him. She stopped fighting his hold on her. Her face was filled with compassion for what had happened.

"Anyway," he sighed, weary having to dredge all the shit back up again. "Like I said, my business was ruined from the embezzlement, I lost everything including my home. I borrowed money to buy a tiny piece of land and built the house in the city, Sanlura, with my own sweat and help from friends in the construction business.

"I had to rebuild my life, and income, from the ground up. I was selling that city house for profit, that's why my lawyer called the other day, to tell me Kandi was trying to get her claws onto half the sale."

"Neco, please, you don't have to tell me all-"

He cut her off, "Yes I do. But trust, me, Casie, if I had a child I would have done right by it. I would have taken custody of the baby if I could. My mother, brothers, would have helped me raise it. I mean, everything I lost was just money, it could be replaced with hard work. But, Marco," he shook his head with sad guilt, "people can't be replaced."

Neco was quiet for a second as he struggled to get control of his emotions. Marco's betrayal both in stealing from their business as well as sleeping Neco's wife, and then his death had shaken him to the core.

"So, the end of the story is that fortunately I got the annulment easy enough because she lied about the pregnancy. She keeps calling me, wants us to get back togeth-" he shook his head. "Whatever. Come on, let me take you home."

She hesitated, protesting, "But, I'm working, Neco, I can't just walk out,"

"Yes you can. You don't belong in this sleaze joint."

"But I need to earn money." She looked around, the bartender was glaring at her and pointing at her. Two huge men were shoving through the crowd towards them.

"Casie, we'll figure something out. Rex King isn't going to just let you sell a few drinks and shake your ass, he wants you, honey, in his bed. He will pursue you into the ground. I know, baby, because I feel as strongly attracted to you as he does."

The corners of his mouth tugged up. "I know him though, he's more unscrupulous, and isn't going to care if you say no. Anyway, when he's used you, he'll make you so indebted to him he'll put you up on that stage and make you dance naked for the money. Rumor is, he's drugged unwilling women and forced them to dance before." He motioned to the stage with his head.

A different woman was up there, looking fairly haggard. She was squatting with her knees spread near the end of the stage so men could put money in her G-string.

Pretending clumsiness or drunkenness, the men pawed and pinched at her privates as they tucked the dollars in. A few of them were boldly groping her bare breasts, she didn't seem to notice, or care.

Casie blanched. While working, she had forced herself to not look at the stage. She was mortified to even be in the building much less working there. She'd had to fight off lascivious men left and right, her butt was sore from men swatting and pinching it when she hurried by.

She regarded Neco. He looked so strong and safe, she'd missed him so much. "What is it you want from me, Neco?" She peered up at him, his eyes had never left her face.

He caressed her shoulders gently as he answered, "Casie, I think it's clear that I want you. I want you body and soul. Yes, I want to make love to you. God knows it's been hard as hell to keep my hands off you."

He leaned over and kissed her lightly. "But, that isn't all. I want all of you. I was being 100% honest with you when I said I want a relationship with you. However," he pushed aside the long heavy braid and kissed her neck, "if you don't want me, I won't dog you down. I still want you to stay with me until we find a safe place for you to be."

She cupped his face with both hands and said softly, "Take me home, Neco."

His grin so broad it hurt, he replied, "Okay." Suddenly aware of what she was wearing, or not wearing, he shrugged out of his jacket and dropped it over her shoulders.

"These fucking men are staring at you like they want to pick the meat off your bones." He lifted her braid out from under the collar letting it tumble down her back.

She was wearing a tiny top that exposed a lot of cleavage. The strip of leather had fringe that draped from the bit of breasts that were covered and bounced like crazy every time she moved.

The leather shorts she wore were like bikini shorts, tight and showed half her butt. Neco was holding the lapels of the jacket when the bouncers arrived.

One of the men barked at her, "Casie, get your ass back to work. This ain't no break time. You been talking long enough with this guy. Unless you're taking him in the back for a lapdance or blowjob, and he pays the money up front, get your ass back to work."

Her face brightened to the shade of a beet. "I-I-" she stammered, now so mortified she wished the floor would open up and swallow her.

"She's done working, pal," Neco said, yanking the suede jacket with the big lamb's wool collar closed over her, he started to button it.

The other big guy said, "Oh yeah? Who the fuck are you? The bitch is on the schedule until 2. You can come back then and get her."

The first guy snorted with a rude laugh. "Good luck with that when Mr. King returns. He's got his eye on her for himself. But right now, she's going back to work. Let's go," he reached for her.

Neco moved her behind him. "I said she's done. She quit. We're leaving."

The bouncer's face squashed in with his anger, his hands rolled into huge fists. "Oh yeah, pretty boy? Says who?"

Neco stood calmly looking from one man to the other. It was hard to tell them apart. They were both giants heavy with muscle and weight. They had the dull look of boxers that had been punched too many times.

The one growled, reaching to grab Casie out from behind Neco. "You go away peacefully," he said to Neco, "and give us no more trouble and I won't break your fuckin' neck. Come on, bitch."

Like lightning, Neco smashed both fists down on the man's arm that reached for Casie. The man screamed as it broke. Neco bashed his fist straight into his nose, and the giant tumbled to the ground.

"What the fuck-" the other bouncer came after Neco.

Keeping Casie behind him, Neco slammed his heavy boot right into the man's knee, the crack was loud enough to be heard over the music, he howled but still threw his fist out to connect with Neco's jaw.

Except Neco was too fast. He jerked his head back as the fist went flying by then punched the man in the stomach.

When the bouncer doubled over with a wail, Neco brought his knee up like a hammer into his jaw. The bouncer didn't make another sound as he hit the floor.

Ignoring the stunned attention of the gathering crowd, "Come on, let's go," Neco took Casie's hand and pulled her through the blathering people cheering and yelling for more fighting, more blood, and hurried out the door.

Shocked over his instant and vicious brutality, Casie stammered, "But- but Neco, my jacket and things are at Sasha's, the manager's apartment."

"Forget them, I'll buy you more."

She tripped alongside him as he led her across the lot.

Grinning as he wrapped an arm around her to hold her steady Neco said, "Not used to the heels yet?"

Sighing wearily, she answered ruefully, "No. My feet are killing me, same as my butt." Pink stained her cheeks at her admission.

He glanced at her puzzled as he opened the door to his truck.

"Why does your-" Seeing her red face, he got it, the patrons had been manhandling her. His scowl dark and furious, he put his hands around her waist to lift her into the vehicle.

They didn't talk as he bundled her into the truck and sped off for home.

Chapter Nineteen

*T*he next week Neco stayed in his office to avoid Casie. He wanted to give her time to settle down without hovering over her, let her have some space to determine how she feels about him.

She was worried he'd be arrested for battery on those bouncers. Neco wasn't. Rex King had so much shady stuff going on he wouldn't want the cops nosing around.

He heard the landline ring and went out to answer it.

Casie was in the living room reading a book. Hearing Neco say her name she got up and went into the kitchen with her head knitted in puzzled curiosity.

Neco was frowning at the phone. He said into it, "How did you get this number?" Nodding, he muttered, "Caller ID." His eyes flicked over to Casie when she came in.

He spoke in the phone, "Who did you say this was?" The frown deepened as he passed the phone to Casie and said grimly, "It's for you."

He was bothered about the call; the person wouldn't say his name and no one except Josh knew she was staying with him. He stood and shamelessly listened.

As far as Neco was concerned, she was still highly vulnerable as her memory had not returned. Someone had hurt her, and that someone was still out there.

One of Neco's other brothers, Logan, did a lot of investigating with the FBI. Neco had him trying to find out what he could, discreetly, about Casie. He'd sent him her fingerprints but she wasn't in any systems, and there weren't any missing persons' wants on her.

Surprise made Casie's voice very soft as she answered the phone, "Hello?"

Neco watched her expression go from baffled to realization as she listened. She knew who was on the phone and her face turned red in embarrassment.

Her eyes flashed to Neco as she said, "Yes, hello Mr. King," and quickly looked away from Neco as his brows drew down hard between his eyes, deepening the masculine ridge of his forehead.

Neco crossed his arms and stared at her with obvious impatience and annoyance.

Casie's gaze went downcast as she listened. "I am so sorry, Mr. King. I didn't mean to leave in the middle of my shift-" her mouth closed as she was cut off.

Neco's face grew harder and darker.

She couldn't look at him. Nodding while listening, she said, "I'm sorry, something came up, I had to leave. No, no I don't think, I mean no, I won't be back." She kept nodding as King talked.

It was all Neco could do to not snatch the phone out of her hands and throw it across the room.

Her voice became strained as she grew agitated. "No, really, you're right, I should have given my notice. Yes, I know you did a lot for me, Mr. King, okay, um, Rex. I appreciate all your-" In front of her it looked like Neco was going explode.

She was quiet as she listened. Then she said, "I do appreciate it, but I have to decline your offer. I'm afraid I have to quit-" She was cut off again, her eyes flit to Neco and quickly away.

"No, thank you, Mr. King, yes, um, Rex, but I have to resign, I'm so sorry," shaking her head she still listened.

Then her face grew redder, she shuffled her feet and stared at the floor. "No, Rex, really, there's nothing you can say. No, I don't think dinner would help, I-" He cut her off again.

After he'd said a few more words, Casie replied, "No really, it's nice of you to offer. Jewelry? Certainly not-"

"Fuck it." Neco grabbed the phone out of her hand and barked into it, "She quit, King. Resigned. End of story. Don't call her again."

Angry words poured from the receiver.

Crushing the phone in his hand, Neco snarled into it, "Because I gave me the right to." He slammed the phone in its cradle and let out a fierce breath.

Casie's mouth dropped open. "Neco, you shouldn't have done that. It was my place to tell him I quit."

"Yeah." He scrubbed his hands down his face then tossed his head back, and forked his dark hair back out of his eyes. "I know. You're right. It's just that you did and he wasn't taking no for an answer. Honey," he went to touch her then dropped his hand.

"I know the man. He's a vile shark and he wants you. Since you slipped out of his clutches, he's not going to give up easily. Trust me, if he gets his hands on you, he will make you pay for leaving the club, and especially for leaving with me, and for turning down his advances."

Crossing her arms, she regarded him with a stern rebuke. "I understand. But still, you can't speak for me. It's enough that I let you drag me out of there without finishing my shift and giving proper notice."

"Casie, if I hadn't been there, that customer, that fat asshole would have had you on his lap and you can imagine where that would have gone. You were simply not strong enough to fight him off."

He shivered, feeling ill just thinking about what clearly would have happened to her if he hadn't gotten her out of there.

If the fat guy didn't get her, King was due in later that night, he sure would have. It was a strip club, whatever happened the police wouldn't have cared, she was on her own. King had the cops in his pocket.

The pink in her cheeks paled when she remembered how she had struggled for all she was worth to get away from that customer and couldn't.

She had prayed the bouncers would come and stop him, but he was a regular customer, a wealthy customer who spread a lot of money around the club, and was a close friend of Rex King's. The bouncers would have looked the other way.

Still, "I know you mean well, Neco, but I need to fight my own battles. Don't do that again." She put her hands on his shoulders and kissed his cheek to take the sting out of the rebuke.

Keeping his hands clasped behind his back so he wouldn't pull her into a hot embrace, Neco plastered an abashed look on his face. Nonetheless, secretly he knew he would do what he had to do to protect her. Casie was so naïve; she doesn't know what kind of a vicious ruthless fuck that man is.

Neco wanted to divert her from the conversation, the whole thing pissed him off so much he wanted to go fuck King up and he knew he couldn't. Well he could, but he'd be in jail and that would leave her unprotected. Not happening. At least not now.

To change the subject, he said, "Tomorrow my family is having a barbeque pool party. Would you like to go with me?"

They had done little as a couple and he wanted to take things up a notch. Having her meet his family would show her how serious he was about her.

"Um, I don't know, Neco. I feel like I'm living a lie not knowing who I am. I don't want to be dishonest with people that are important to you."

God he wanted to touch her so badly. "They will understand. It didn't slow Josh down any from hitting on you. Come with me. My family really wants me to come and I haven't seen them in…quite a while. I won't go if you don't go with me."

"Neco, that's blackmail!"

"Only if it works."

"How are they having a pool party, it's still cold out?"

"Well, they call it that because most of the gathering is around the pool and patio. But you're right. No one will be in the water, but there will be a lot of food getting eaten. It's been steadily getting warmer and it's supposed to be more temperate and sunny tomorrow. We both could do with a pleasant break. What do you say?"

He looked so hopeful that she had to smile. She said with some reticence, "Okay."

"Good, it's settled. Now, I have to get back to work so that I'll be free tomorrow. We'll have dinner together later tonight?"

"Yes. I already have something in the oven, kind of like a cheesy pot pie."

"You are too good to me." Keeping his hands locked behind him, Neco bent, kissed her quickly and left to go back to his office.

Chapter Twenty

The next day, they headed to the barbecue.

Driving on the way over, Neco held Casie's hand and couldn't stop looking over at her.

He had already spoken with Josh and told him to brief his family on her background so there would be no awkward questions that she couldn't answer. He wanted to have fun with her, not put her in the spotlight.

His parents' house was huge.

Casie's eyes stretched wide as he pulled up the drive.

It was brick with two stories and white columns striped the front. The street was lined with cars as was the wide driveway. He pulled up on the grass next to Josh's car.

Appalled, "Neco! You're ruining the grass!" she reproached.

"That's what expensive gardeners are for. Come on." He shut off the truck and ran around to get her. He knew she was going to be shy and uncomfortable.

They both wore jeans. In a long sleeved thermal, Neco decided to leave his jacket in the car.

Casie wore a frilly white blouse. She slipped out of her waist-length jacket and left it in the truck too.

He clasped her hand and brought her through a side door into the house.

Voices, some loud, some laughing trailed from the kitchen area. Neco went there first.

The rooms were big and bright and open, expensively decorated but tastefully comfortable.

They walked through a glassed porch and passed through a mudroom, then to a wide hall that led to several other halls in different directions. Casie was already lost.

The kitchen was sunny with large windows, cheerful cherry reds and yellow tiled splash-back with white and yellow ruffled curtains.

His mother was right where he knew she'd be. A bunch of people were chatting in clusters in the big kitchen.

Outside the glass doors there was a bigger crowd of people, most of which were gathered in groups around the massive pool.

Neco said quietly, "Ma."

The woman facing the oven froze. Then she turned around, her face lit up like Haley's Comet. "Neco!" she screeched his name and threw her arms open.

Neco released Casie's hand and went to her. They hugged, it was clear Melody Bardiche was crying.

Neco held her to his strong, broad shoulders and patted her back. "Come on, Ma, stop it. You act like I've been gone for years." Still she wept against his shirt.

Casie stood back, keenly aware all the eyes in the room went from the mother and son reunion, to her.

Neco pulled his mother back and said, "All right, Ma, I brought someone to meet you." He stepped back to put his arm around Casie, and drew her forward.

Keeping his arm around her shoulders, Neco said, "Casie, this is my mother, Melody Bardiche."

Melody was wiping her eyes without shame or embarrassment. She said kindly to Casie, "So nice to meet you, dear. Josh has told us a little bit about you. Please know that you are welcome in our home."

Her shoulder-length hair was still dark brown; she had hazel eyes and a kind, pretty face. She was on the slight side of plump. Without hesitation, she reached out and gave Casie a hug.

"Um," Casie hated being the center of attention. She said softly, "Thank you, Mrs. Bardiche, it's nice to meet you."

"Oh, honey, call me Melody, or Mel as my family and friends do. Any friend of Neco's is a friend of ours."

Especially other than that horrible woman he'd foolishly married, Neco hadn't brought a girl home since he was in high school.

Melody smiled at Casie but turned to her son and patted his face. The smile left briefly as she scolded him, "You have been so bad, Neco, not being in contact with us. I do not expect that behavior to continue."

Casie looked at Neco with wonder.

He looked downright embarrassed and thoroughly chastened. It was nice to see *him* blush for a change.

"I know, Ma. I'm sorry, I'll do better. I promise. I'm in a better frame of mind now." His arm still around Casie, he looked down at her and gave her a hug, making it clear what had put him in a better space.

"And the drinking?" Melody asked with an arched brow.

"Geez, Ma, that's kind of personal." He looked more uncomfortable when she didn't back down.

Her hands on her hips, she admonished, "I'm your mother, there is nothing too personal from me."

His eyes rolled, with a crooked grin he sighed. "I drink beer, and some liquor on occasion. I stopped the heavy drinking. I no longer want to shut off my feelings. I'm here aren't I? Satisfied?"

Melody grinned wide. "Yes, my babies are all here and doing well and seem happy. That's all I ask for." She said to Casie, "Always keep in mind, Neco's bark is worse than his bite."

"Sure, unless he's really pissed then you'd better hide," Josh drawled from the doorway.

Melody shook a finger at him. "Language, Joshua." Josh had the grace to look abashed at the reprimand.

195

"Sorry, Ma." He gave Casie a quick hug smirking over her shoulder at Neco. "Hi honey, glad to see you're safe and sound. Come on, Neco, Casie, come outside and get some beer and barbecue. The weather is cooperating, it's really nice out for a change." He grinned at his mother and beckoned to his brother.

"All right. I'll talk with you later, Ma, okay?" Neco gave her a kiss on the cheek.

She smiled, nodded, wiped an eye. "You'd better. I expect some mother and son time. Your father, as you know is in Kentucky visiting Aunt Jeannie, you heard she's not doing well?"

"Josh told me. I called her yesterday. She sounds like she's on the mend. Okay, we're heading outside." He kissed her cheek again then took Casie's hand and they followed Josh outside to where the party was in full swing.

"Come and meet my other brothers, Casie." Neco pulled her into the throng.

People covered the back yard. Most were scattered around the pool and the deck where the grills were. They sprawled on lawn chairs, sat at round patio tables or just wandered around with plates piled with food in their hands mingling.

The back yard was a couple of acres of neatly maintained grass, budding trees, and when the spring hits hard it will be abundantly laced with colorful flowers.

Neco went to the coolers where the drinks were. "You want a beer, Casie?" he asked, lifting the lid and digging through the ice.

"Um, I don't know." Her gaze hopped and rolled around the yard taking in the sights.

People of all ages from little babies up to white-haired elderly folks were laughing, visiting, chowing down.

He took out a bottle and flipped the lid off and handed it to her. "Here, try it."

As she accepted it, his eyes tapered slightly at her. "Are you...actually, shit we don't know if you're legal to drink, maybe you shouldn't."

She had already taken it and brought it near her mouth and wrinkled her nose. "It's kind of pungent."

Grinning, he agreed, "Yeah. Try a sip."

She took a tiny swallow and then another. Making a face, she handed it back to him. "I think I'd rather have a soda."

Chuckling, Neco reached back in the cooler and took out a can of soda, pulled the tab back and handed it to her. "At least I know you won't be stumbling around the yard drunk as a skunk."

At her baleful look, he took a big swig and exhaled loudly, "Ah, that's good. Don't worry, Casie, when I was drowning my sorrows I just sat alone brooding silently, hating the world, and myself.

"The only trouble I got in was a few barroom brawls. I'm past that now. It was childish and selfish, when I realized it I stopped. Well, I stopped the heavy drinking and fighting. But, I couldn't abide being around cheerful people when my friend…"

He took a swig. "You know, was dead. When I felt I could have done something for him, and, I had been tricked into a marriage. I felt all types a fool, and I'd lost everything I'd built, worked hard for. It was a bleak time I had to work through."

"Are you okay with drinking beer?" she asked concerned at the can of alcohol in his hand.

Shrugging, he held the bottle out and looked at it. "Yes. You've seen me drink in the time you've lived with me. I went through a dark period, I handled it badly, but I'm fine now. Let's get something to eat."

As they passed through the crowd, Neco stopped here and there introducing Casie to people, some friends, a lot of neighbors, and a few relatives.

Music played from speakers, food and drink flowed and people were boisterous and loud.

At the table lined with food, Neco handed her a plate. Rubbing his stomach, eyeballing all the food like a kid in a candy store, he exclaimed, "I am starving, I think I want some of everything!"

Beside him, Casie agreed with enthusiasm, "I have a feeling I'm going to indulge way too much today. Everything looks so delicious."

Setting a hand briefly on her nape, Neco said softly, "That's okay, Cas, you can stand to put on a few pounds. Between your illness and then," he bit his lip, "the thing with us and that, *job*, you've barely eaten enough to keep a flea alive. So, don't hold back." He bent and kissed the top of her head.

The table was filled with tangy barbecue pork and beef, both ribs and pulled, wings, potato and macaroni salads and a variety of other salads, coleslaw, casseroles, hamburgers, and a ton of desserts.

They loaded their plates and went to find a table to sit at. Neco spotted his brother Josh and a couple of their friends at a patio table, he and Casie joined them.

"Whoa, bro, you're doing all right, I see," said one of the men Neco introduced as Jimmy. He had buzzed short blond hair and blue eyes, and was big and square like a football jock. He blatantly scoured Casie from head to toe.

"I am." Neco got Casie a chair and then found one for himself. Plopping down beside Casie, he dug right into his food.

"So, Casie," Josh smiled at her while sucking on a rib, "is he treating you all right? Because if he isn't, I have a big house with plenty of room-"

"She's fine, Josh, shut up and eat," Neco growled at him.

The other men at the table slid surreptitious glances at her. It was inevitable men would desire her; Neco couldn't put her in a nun's outfit and keep her at home. "Where's Logan and Chaz?" he asked Josh where their other brothers were.

Through a mouthful and licking his fingers, Josh said, "They were both here early on. They had to work, so they ate and ran. You'll have to come here again, Casie, to meet the rest of the brood."

A girl sat down next to Josh and slid her hand on his thigh.

"Hey, Josh, I've been looking all over for you." The girl with curly blonde hair tilted her head and turned to face him blocking out the rest of the people at the table. She was wearing short-shorts and a tight shirt and she was maneuvering herself to get as close to Josh as she could.

Josh looked over her head and winked at his brother and Casie, set his rib down and leaned into the girl. "Cath, I've been right here eating my fill. But I could fill up something else..."

She slid her hand around his neck and pulled him in with a long, noisy, wet kiss.

"Get a room," half the table called out.

Catherine stroked her hand down Josh's big chest and fluttered her eyelashes at him. "I'm game, big boy, what about you?"

Josh picked up his beer, downed the whole thing, set the bottle down and wiped his mouth with the back of his hand. He stood up and grabbed the girl's hand, pulling her to her feet. "We'll see you all later."

Without another word, holding her hand, Josh strode quickly across the yard to the front where his truck was parked.

Casie whispered to Neco, "Is that his girlfriend?"

A burst of laughter spewed from the man on the other side of Neco.

Neco leaned over and told her, "No, Josh is in between girls right now. Catherine Snow has the hots for him and she doesn't hide it."

"But why are they leaving? There's food and drink and people here."

Neco slipped his hand under her chin lifting her head. "You are the sweetest thing, Casie," he kissed her not caring they had an audience. Then he whispered in her ear, "They left to have some alone time, you know what I mean?" Seeing it dawn on her, Neco kissed her again.

Feeling stupid, Casie picked up her fork and dug into her potato salad. The friends at the table chuckled good-naturedly and got down to talking and eating.

Neco was in a conversation with the man sitting next to Jimmy. Karl was a friend from middle school.

Casie touched Neco's arm to get his attention, she whispered, "I need to use the bathroom."

"Okay," he started to push his chair back. "I'll take you."

She stood up. "No, you stay and visit with your friends, I can find my way." She smiled at his frown, he was too protective. Patting his shoulder, she moved away heading for the house.

Neco watched her walk away, the frown still on his face. Too much had gone on, he hated to have her out of his sight. He knew he needed to give her, her space, still, it was tough for him to let go though.

Sighing, he turned to Karl with a quick smile. "I'm sorry, Karl, you were saying?" Keeping an eye on the house, he shifted part of his attention back to his friend.

When Casie reached the house, she asked the first person she saw where the bathroom was. She was advised there were many and was given directions to the closest ones.

After finishing her business, Casie washed her hands and finger-combed her hair. She hadn't brought a purse, there was no reason, she really had nothing to put in one.

Leaving the door open to the lavish bathroom, she ventured out and wondered if anyone would be annoyed if she peeked around a little.

She had to pass several rooms to get back to an outside door, so she poked her head inside a few on her way.

There was a morning room. Surrounded by windows, the pretty peach and white room looked plush and soft.

Next was a library of sorts. Or den. She didn't know what they called it. It was cool browns and beiges with big comfy chairs and bookcases overflowing with every kind of book.

Her shoes sunk into the thick carpet as she wandered into the room. Currently, at Neco's house, she was reading a murder mystery.

Moving to scroll over the bounty of books, Casie wondered what kinds of books she liked. She was really into the murder mystery but there were so many genres to read surely her tastes ran in several directions.

A huge variety of books lined the bookcase; history, reference, action, romance, mysteries, books about music and science, a few art and some about ballet, there were even ancient tales like Homer's Iliad.

Oddly, Casie was familiar with the tale. Interesting. She hadn't lost all of her memory. That gave her hope that the rest would return. She pondered how would her life change again?

She was living with Neco and he made it clear that he would like it to become permanent. They hadn't really discussed it though. Did he mean as just friends, or as boyfriend and girlfriend, did he want to marry her?

Or was it all really temporary, that he meant for her to stay with him until her memory returned? Her stomach twisted at the thought of leaving him.

Would she joyously and with relief return to her old life, was it a happy life? There was still doubt that she might be in a relationship with a man. It's what held her back every time Neco had his hands on her and obviously wanting to be fully intimate with her.

He'd said as much. But would she be cheating? Time was moving on, if she had a real love for another man wouldn't that be in the back of her mind? And wouldn't he be looking for her?

Neco had told her he and his brothers had researched missing persons and there was nothing out there describing her. That in itself was so odd, and kind of depressing.

Did no one notice she wasn't around? Her parents? A sibling or friend, or even employer, a co-worker? Did no one care about her? Was she such a dreadful person that people might actually be happy she'd vanished? It was all so perplexing, and distressing.

Then again, when she disappeared from Neco's home, he went searching for her. Even had his brother help him. He'd told her they'd checked shops and the hospital and hotels, everywhere they could think of, even the store where he'd bought her clothes.

If Neco, who barely knew her looked for her, surely someone out there must have cared for her as well.

The only reason she pushed Neco away was because of the moral issue of cheating, not because she felt any pull to another man. At this point, the craving of making love with Neco was so strong she was having a hard time resisting it.

She wanted to be with him. Even thinking about his intense blue eyes, soft yet masculine mouth that kissed her insanely into insensibility, those big hands that set her body on fire, suddenly a shiver ruptured over her entire body. Gosh, she waved at her face to dissipate the sudden heat; she needed to get her mind on something else.

Focusing on the row of books at eye level, Casie ran her fingers across a few of them to see if any caught her interest.

Pulling out a couple of books, she glanced at them before putting them back on the shelf. So intent on the books she didn't hear someone enter the room until they spoke.

"So, you are the little whore that Neco is shacking up with." The snide voice made Casie twirl around in surprise.

Chapter Twenty-One

"I beg your pardon?" Casie responded to the woman standing there glowering insidious resentment at her.

The woman's red hair went past her shoulders. Judging by the tiny tight curls near her temples, it looked naturally very curly but had been blown out straight and heavy gloss applied until it gleamed.

Her high arched brows were the identical, same precise shade of red as her hair, not a hint darker or lighter. The smattering of freckles she tried to hide with makeup indicated she was a true redhead, but there was something too sleek with the look of the color that implied that she'd had a lot of salon help to maintain the richness of the color.

The black liner slashing over her dark blue eyes went up in a cat's eye peak at the corners.

She was much taller and sturdier than Casie with her big bust and matching hips. The perfectly round breasts that were flaunted in the deeply low cut dress looked surgically enhanced.

Her manicured hands were planted on her hips, and glossy red lips pulled back in a sneer. Her sneering contempt of Casie clearly indicated she was finding the smaller, more delicate woman lacking.

"Oh," the woman said nastily, "I have the right person. Just as described. Petite, skinny but built, how much did you pay for your tits, honey?"

Half appalled and half amused at the question, Casie did not respond. When alone, her inspection of her own stranger's body revealed she had high firm breasts, and they were plump and soft.

A speck of pink tinged her cheeks at the thought of touching herself. She did shower and dress, it was not easy to avoid touching oneself.

The woman squinted at Casie, the sneer deepened in irritation. "Yeah, you have the long wavy tawny hair described to me, which is no doubt died by a cheap salon."

She sniffed her derision. "And you are practically a child. Certainly not experienced or womanly enough to handle a brawny lusty man like Neco Bardiche. He picked me up in a bar so clearly I'm the kind he likes, not you."

She took a few steps closer to Casie then said with smug knowledge, "He likes it rough, you know." Her study of Casie was filled with contempt. "You are way too delicate to be able to take what he dishes out. Yeah, you are definitely not his type."

Her face flaming with this information, Casie's gaze flicked from the woman to the door. "I don't know what you are talking about. Now, if you'll excuse me," she started to cross the floor to go past the woman and out the door, but the larger woman stood in her way.

"No, you slut, you stay here. I followed you here to get alone with you without anyone nosing in. You and I have some talking to do." Her elbows stuck out like batwings, her fingers curled fiercely on her generous hips.

The sapphire blue dress that almost matched her dark eyes was on the dressy side for a patio barbeque. It clung to her body like a second skin from the severely low cut top to the tops of her thighs. The wedged six-inch heels matched the dress but had a shimmer to them.

Pushing down a feeling of tense vulnerability, Casie tried to keep from frowning at her. She was not going to let this woman intimidate her. "I'm sorry, but you are wrong. We have nothing to discuss. I don't know who you are, I don't want to know who you are, and I am leaving." She marched up to walk past her but the woman moved in the path between Casie and the door.

"No. You are not leaving until I've had my say. Now," she swept the long red hair back off her shoulders and smoothed the sides ensuring it was still sleek.

The sneer seemed to be a permanent characteristic of her face and voice, as did the contempt. "I am Kandi Bardiche." She smiled smugly at Casie's aghast expression.

"I see you know who I am. Good. Then you know that you are fucking around with a married man. That makes you a home-wrecking slut, and an adulterer."

"I'm leaving, I don't have to listen to you." Casie went to sweep past her, but Kandi suddenly reached out and gave Casie a hard shove.

Casie stumbled then caught her balance. Her stunned look at the woman getting physical with her only made the woman's smug smile broader, more confident.

"You stay right where you are, bitch. I know you won't call for help because there's no way you would want the Bardiches, or anyone else for that matter to hear you causing a scene. You're the interloper here, you are the one that would get tossed out if there was a fracas. Now back to what I was saying."

The smug smile morphed to an ugly grimace as Kandi pointed at Casie and announced, "Neco is mine. He is my husband and you are whoring man-thief. He does not want that skinny little body of yours. You'll see, I'm saving you heartache down the road. He will only fuck you then toss your scrawny fragile ass to the curb when he's had his fill.

"So, do everyone a favor and get your shit and yourself out of his house so I can move back where I belong." Her command was imparted with a queenly lift of her chin. She looked down at Casie like she was an insignificant, disgusting bug.

Although her stomach felt like there were Mexican jumping beans hopping around in it, Casie replied calmly, "Neco is a big boy, he can make his own decisions. And you will not tell me what to do. Now get out of my way-" she stormed towards Kandi thinking she could rush past her but Kandi was like a bulldog with long arms. She reached out and slammed her hands into Casie's chest giving her a powerball smashing shove.

This time Casie stumbled backwards and landed so hard on her butt she almost saw stars.

Kandi declared, "Not until you hear me out. Neco is in love with me. We had a little spat but it's over and he wants me back. He's using you to make me jealous. He calls me almost every day! He sees me when you're not around."

Stunned, Casie looked up and said irately, "I don't give a damn what you say, I've had enough of being pushed around. I am leaving and you are not stopping me." Before she could stand up, a furious voice erupted from the door behind Kandi.

"Goddammit, Kandi, what the hell are you doing here?" Without waiting for her to reply, Neco pushed past her and strode to Casie who was kneeling.

He grasped her arm to help her up, and asked with angry concern, "Are you all right baby? I'm so sorry." He cupped her chin gently to see her face. "Did she hit you? If she harmed a hair on your head I swear I'll-"

Casie muttered, "I'm fine. Your *wife* wanted to warn me about you."

Neco's scowl could sink a ship it was so fierce. He said harshly, "She is not my wife. She never was my wife. Do not call her that." He took a deep breath, uttered on the exhale, "Fuck me that I fell for her lying bullshit."

His other hand swept with a deliberate display of possession down Casie's back to stay in the inward curve just above her bottom.

Neither looked at Kandi who was huffing and puffing behind them.

Casie told him, "She said you two only had a little tiff, that you love her and you call her all the time, you still see her and you're getting back togeth-"

He cut her off repeating roughly, "No. No. No. No. And no." Still holding her chin, his hand curled under the side of her face, his long fingers caressed her soft skin.

"Do not listen to her, Casie. Just remember what I told you, it was all the truth. Ask my brother, hell, ask my mother what she did. I want nothing to do with her. Think about what she said that I have been seeing her. Have I left the house at all without you?"

"Neco, darling," Kandi cooed, moving towards the couple. "I've missed you."

Casie pulled from Neco's hands and stepped away from him. Staring at the ground, she fixed her blouse that had ridden up when she had fallen.

Before Neco could respond, Kandi threw herself into his arms. She smacked her lips right on his and kissed him like she was drowning and he was air.

Mashing her voluptuous body against his chest and rubbing on him, she raked her hands up his shoulders to clutch his hair and purred, "That tiny slut could not take your big manly body like I can. She's too small and frail, you'd break her like a bull and a china doll, hon."

Resisting Neco pushing at her shoulders, Kandi exclaimed, "Sweetheart, forgive me, you know you're the only man for me! I was just, oh, young and foolish, but I know now what I really want and that's you." She wriggled her body blatantly sexually against him. "You know how good the sex was between us."

Casie started walking quickly to the door.

"Oh, hell no." Neco gripped Kandi's wrists jerking her hands out of his hair and swung her away from him. "Cut the shit, Kandi," he snapped. "We had sex precisely one time. After you tricked me into marriage I never so much as laid a finger on you. Everything about you is a huge turnoff.

"You are so damned tawdry I wouldn't have even picked you up in the bar that night, unfortunately I was plastered and horny and you were quick easy pickings. You smeared your body all over me while I finished my drink. You know I want nothing to do with you. Stay the hell away from me, and Casie."

He jogged after Casie who was already moving rapidly down the hall searching frantically for a way out of the house.

He caught up with her in front of the morning room.

"Casie-"

"I need to go, Neco." She kept walking.

Grabbing her arms, he moved Casie forcefully into the room and closed the door. He held her, waiting for her to catch her breath.

Speaking through panting gasps, Casie said angrily, "Neco, let go of me. Do not push me around. I've had it with people treating me like I'm a puppet and pushing and shoving and pulling at me." She put her palms against his chest trying to push him away.

He released her and stepped back. "I'm sorry, Casie, but I couldn't let you run out with her wicked words in your mind. She is a gluttonous amoral creature without a care as to how she hurts people." He tucked his hands in his pockets to keep from reaching for her.

"I explained all about her to you. She went after you to try to ruin things between you and me out of spite. Please don't let her sick evilness ruin what we're trying to build."

Casie stood silently letting his words churn in her mind. She remembered when he had told her all about Kandi's deceit and his friend who embezzled from him then killed himself. Neco had been aching with misery at all that had happened.

Both his mother and brother insinuated he'd gone under and had been drinking too much and avoiding people, especially them, and how hurt they were over his shutting them out.

Her crystalline gaze scanned his face, studying the strong jaw set with suppressed fury at Kandi's actions. His cheekbones hard under the blue eyes that begged her to trust him, believe him.

"Technically," he said with rough feeling tightening his voice, "we were never married. I got an annulment. I have the papers." He slowly reached out to wind his fingers around her upper arms.

"Casie, I didn't want her then, and I sure as hell don't want her now." Slowly he pulled her gently closer to him. As usual the need to touch her overwhelmed him, he slipped a hand behind her neck to cradle it, his fingers stroked under her hair.

"Neco, everything is always so…mixed up. I just don't know what to do, believe, about you, about me…" Her voice trembled with uncertainty and resistance, yet she didn't try to pull from his grasp.

"I know. I hate that things have to be so chaotic and confusing. But I'm not confused about what I feel, what I want. And that is you. I want you, Casie, do not doubt that."

"She said her name is Kandi Bardiche."

Keeping his patience although he'd like nothing better than to go strangle Kandi, Neco said, "Casie, she cannot legally use my name, and if she does my lawyer slaps her with a lawsuit in a heartbeat."

Seeing Kandi's toxic shit mulling over Casie's face, Neco said, "I can see there's some other crap she fed you. What else did she say?"

Clearing her throat, unfortunately her shyness took over and she said awkwardly, "She said you, uh, like big women because you're a big man, that I am too small…too fragile for you. That you are, uh, rough when you…uh," the blush rode up to her hairline.

Slightly embarrassed himself, no man likes to discuss his past relationships, his prior sex with other women, especially with the one woman he really cares about.

Gently but emphatically Neco told her, "I would never hurt you, Casie, if that's what you're worried about, honey. Never. As far as you being too small or fragile, what you are is dainty and feminine and it turns me on like there's no tomorrow. "Look how perfect we fit together."

Moving his hand from her arm to her back, he drew her to him, and cradled the back of her head to hold firm for his kiss.

As soon as their lips touched, like she was the blasting cap and he was dynamite, his body turned hard, fast. The heat radiated off Neco's skin as he seized her mouth and consumed her with aching need, with hunger, and with throbbing desire.

The kiss was so intense Casie's legs turned to jelly. She leaned against him as she soared mindless, her body responding and reciprocating without thought. She kissed him with all the feelings he ignited in her.

They were both giving into the desire that burned between them. The blood rushed to Neco's head pushing out any coherent thought, all he wanted was to be with her. He reached down, put his hands under her butt and lifted her so her legs straddled his waist.

Their mouths meshed, tongues tangled. She clutched his shoulders then moved to twine them around his neck, and then she stroked her palms up to hold the back of his head. Neco carried her to the divan and sat down with her still straddling him.

His hands went between them and he deftly unbuttoned her blouse. She cupped his face, keeping their mouths fused. When he pushed the blouse off her shoulders and put his hands around her ribs, her head fell back, her neck arched.

Neco moved his mouth to kiss her cheek, her jaw, he lifted her hair to kiss behind her ear, then licked and sucked his way down her neck.

His lips on her flesh, he whispered while nipping and feasting on her skin, "Like honey, Casie, you look like silken honey, you smell like golden honey and damned if you don't taste like sweet honey."

Casie's soft moan urged him to love her. His manhood was like an iron rod, he was dying to press it against her, but he couldn't get close enough in the position they were in.

"Casie," he growled against her neck. "I want you, I want you now." Her response was to wrap her arms around his neck and pull his head up to join their mouths.

His hands back on her ribs, he moved them up to cover her breasts over the silk bra and was rewarded with a soft edgy whimper. He gripped her supple flesh, molding it between his long fingers.

A growl of crazed hunger hissed through his teeth releasing a frenzy of potent fuel searing through him. In his fierce zeal, he too roughly crushed and stroked her plump breasts in his large hands. Too vehemently brushed his thumbs over her hardening nipples until hoarse cries scratched from her throat. Yet, she didn't withdraw from his touch.

"Baby," he groaned, "I need you naked." He tugged at a silk cup trying to pull it down so he could get his hands, and mouth, on her bare nipple but the bra was too tight.

While his hands greedily fondled her breasts, Casie leaned back to fumble at the buttons on his shirt.

He reached around to unclasp her bra, his eyes devouring her soft mounds plumped over the silk. His fingers feverishly working the clasp he-

There were voices right outside the door. They froze.

"Shit Casie, I don't think I locked the door." He yanked her blouse closed, picked her up and set her on the couch then buttoned his shirt as he hurried across the room.

As his hand was about to turn the lock, the door opened.

A man with his arms around a girl tumbled in.

"Logan, shit, what are you doing?"

Neco's younger brother peeled his mouth off the girl he was holding. His eyes blue like Neco's looked at him then over his shoulder at Casie sitting on the couch, a smirk took over the shock of finding the room occupied.

Snickering, "Hell, brother, looks like the same thing you are," Logan leaned over to get a better view of Casie who sat with her arms crossed over her chest.

"We weren't doing any-"

"Skip it, Nek. Your hair is a mess and she looks about to die of mortification." Logan chuckled nodding in Casie's direction. "But I am glad to see you man." He let go of the girl so suddenly she swayed, and Logan threw his arms around Neco. The brothers hugged.

"Hey," the girl giggled, "we gonna all have fun together? I'm game." She lifted the hem of her dress revealing she wasn't wearing anything under it and like she was going to pull it off over her head.

"No!" Neco and Logan said at the same time.

"Why not? I've never done brothers before. I mean of course I have, but not at the same time." She peered over at Casie who looked like she wanted to morph into a vapor and float away. Grinning, the woman offered, "I don't mind another girl."

She said to Casie, "You are hot, we can do some stuff too, right hon? Men really dig two hot chicks getting it on, especially if everyone is naked!"

"Logan," Neco growled moving to block their view of Casie, "call off your tiger."

Laughing, Logan pushed at the girl's hands to make her drop her skirt.

"Looo-gaan," she whined with a pout. Slurring her words, "Come on, let's parteee with them. She and I can start and then you guys can join in," she'd obviously had a lot to drink.

Grinning at Neco, she gushed, "You are as cute as your brother. You wanna watch your girlfriend and me play in the lady pond together? I bet her titties are as nice as mine. We'll rub our naked tits together and you guys can judge us, right Logan?"

When she reached a hand out to touch Neco, Logan dropped his arms around her to hold her arms down. Looking at his brother's annoyed face, he said with a grin, "Not today...uh, what'd you say your name was?"

The girl's arms drifted up to slink around Logan's neck. "Brittney, handsome, how many times I gotta tell you. Gimmie kiss," she slobbered over his mouth.

"Logan, Ma said you were at work." Neco turned slightly so his brother and the girl's backs were to Casie.

Logan put his hand on Brittney's face turning it from his so he could talk. "Yeah, did for an hour. Chaz is shutting things down so I came back and was minding my own business when this lovely thing plopped her sweet ass in my lap, and, the rest you know. Right...uh..."

"Brittney," she pouted trying to kiss him.

"Whatever. So, is that-"

"How about later, bro?" Neco said discreetly. At the moment the last thing Casie would want would be to have a conversation with anyone right now.

The side of his mouth curling up in a leer, Logan peered around his brother to see Casie pulling her long hair over the front of her chest. "You know, Nek, now that Brittney mentioned it, the two girls naked together would be hot-"

"Stuff it, Lo," Neco barked at his brother sweeping the picture of the two young women naked together out of his mind.

"We're out of here. We'll leave you to..." he trailed off glancing at Casie. She'd managed to get her blouse buttoned but she looked mortified.

He held his hand out. "C'mere honey, let's let them have some privacy." His voice sarcastic, he said, "It seems to be in short shrift around here."

Casie got up and keeping her eyes on Neco walked over to the others.

Neco slid his arm around her shoulders. "Lo, this is Casie. Honey, this is my brother, Logan, and uh..."

"*Brittney*," the girl slurred with vague irritation.

"Uh huh." Neco said to Logan, "We're leaving. You two can get to know each other later. Maybe dinner at my house next week?" He arched a brow in question.

Logan mirrored him with both brows raised in surprise. He'd heard about Casie but it seemed Neco was more serious about this girl than Logan had gathered. "Sure, that'd be great."

He smiled big and friendly at Casie. "It's nice to meet you. I'd shake, but," he nodded at Brittney who was hanging onto his neck looking like she was going to pass out. He had both arms around her holding her up. Her dress was caught up under his hands exposing her naked butt.

Casie quickly glanced away from the pair and murmured, "Um, I understand. It's nice to meet you too, Logan."

"Okay, we're out of here," Neco said, maneuvering Casie to the door.

Over her head, Logan shot his brother a wink and a grin. "Nice, bro, real nice. Can't wait for dinner. Call me. I'm thinking these two girls together sounds like a great-"

"No. I'll call you."

"Looo-gaaan, I wanna fool around..." Brittney wailed. Her neck arched, she gazed up at him with dazed eyes and her mouth lurching open.

"Sure, babe." Logan winked at Neco again as Neco led Casie out and closed the door.

Chapter Twenty-Two

"That was really embarrassing," Casie said quietly as they strode hand-in-hand down the hall.

"Yeah, well. For you. But if you'd walked in on my brothers as often as I have when they were…let's say occupied, you'd take it with a grain of salt." They headed for the front door.

Her voice hushed, Casie said, "I guess it works all ways, they've walked in on you, too?"

Neco stopped walking. Setting his hands on her shoulders he bent and gave her a light kiss. "Casie, I want you to understand. I'm going to say it as plain as I can. I am only interested in you. I don't care about or want to think about anyone that I was with before you."

"But, after me-"

He squeezed her shoulders. "There isn't going to be anyone after you, Casie. I want us to be permanent. When we get your life straightened out I plan on asking you to marry me."

He smiled at her shooting brows. "Yeah. I'm serious. I told you I was. I don't intend on sleeping with another woman other than you, ever."

He tucked a lock of hair behind her ear and caressed her face. "If you don't want me, you need to speak up, because I'm done waiting. I want to let the world know you are mine."

"But, Neco," she protested, her face pinched in apprehension. "We don't know who I am. For heaven's sake, I could be a wanted criminal, married, maybe even have kids. You can't take the chance that-"

"I can and will. I want us to be a couple. If down the road we find out who you are, if there are complications, we'll deal with them then. Together."

"But- but- if I'm married, I'd be cheating-"

"First off, you're not wearing a ring. Trust me, any guy has you and he's branding you immediately to cock-block other men. Now, let me ask you this, Casie. Do you feel like there's a part of you, your soul, that's attached to a man? I know you've thought about it."

Her eyes closed, lips compressed. She shook her head then looked at him. "No. I keep thinking if I loved someone I would feel something, a loss...or a lack...something. All I feel is my interest in...you."

Groaning happily, "Ah, sweetheart," Neco said and pulled her in crushing her against his chest. He held her for a minute. Her head on his chest, she slipped her hands around his waist.

He leaned back, asked, "Let me be sure, Casie. You do want a relationship with me?"

Shyly she smiled and nodded. "Yes. I've tried to deny it, suppress it, I can't."

"You've made me the happiest man, Casie." Cupping her face, Neco gazed tenderly into her pretty eyes and said, "We'll deal with whatever comes up, together. You need to trust me. People like Kandi are going to say things. Some people just enjoy hurting other people for no reason.

"Whatever is said, or you think you hear, anything, you need to come to me. Don't believe everything, and don't let shit fester. And whatever you do, do not run from me. Talk to me. Promise me."

Serious and thoughtful, Casie replied, "I know I've been quick to believe things people say, but that's because I don't really know me, it's, hard to explain. It's difficult to be firm in the face of hurtful things when I…you know, don't know."

"I understand. Just, all I ask is that we talk before you ever make a decision, or leave me again. Now, do you want to stay with me? Live at my house? Before you respond, know 100% that I want you to."

She didn't hesitate, "Yes."

Their eyes linked unwavering. Touching his face, the desolation Casie had felt still apparent, she said miserably, "When I was away from you those days at the club, I was sick at heart. The little bit I slept, I dreamed of you. Being without you was," her face scrunched, "horrible. I felt empty."

Smoothing her features out, she smiled weakly. "Working in that disgusting bar and constantly dodging lascivious hands of repulsive crude men just made me appreciate that much more what a great guy you are."

Wincing, Neco dropped his hands to her shoulders and squeezed them. "Baby, we can't talk too much about that time. Picturing those fuckers with their hands on you boils my blood. It makes me want to go and pulverize every one of them. It's…"

His fingers dug into her shoulders. "It makes me sick to my stomach thinking of them touching you, and it pains me that they hurt you, humiliated you, violated your body. It's all I can do," his hands tightened into fists, "to not go there. I have to force my truck to keep going by when I'm anywhere near the fuck- uh, damned place. "I…" he lowered his head and shook it.

"I had been so terrified that I'd lost you. I can't keep reliving it, baby." He looked up at her and stroked her face. "And neither can you."

Cocking her head to the side, Casie pushed away her abhorrence of her time at the club and replaced it with a slender smile. "You're right. It's behind us. Both of us."

She slipped her arms around his waist and briefly laid her face against his chest. The side of her face resting on his soft cotton shirt, the rocky muscles under it somehow cradled her instead of being painful.

Casie inhaled his masculine scent, she couldn't describe it, it was just…manly, strong and comforting, and sexy.

After he had brought her back from the Palace, when he was working in his office, she would slip into his room and pick up a pillow, and, she suppressed her blush, she wasn't about to tell him she sniffed his pillows.

He held her for a few moments soaking in the happiness. "I can feel you smiling, honey." Her squeeze of his waist made him grin. He set his fingers to web the side of her head, holding her gently against his chest.

Then he said, "Okay. One more thing to settle before we leave."

"Yes?"

He laughed. "Now that's a good answer to my question."

"You didn't ask a question."

"I know, but you answered it anyway."

"Stop teasing me, what did I say yes to?"

"When we get home, I would like to continue what we started here in the other room. I want to make love to you, with you. Do you? I mean, want to make love with me?"

He skimmed his hands over her shoulders then up to hold her face, lifting it to look in her eyes. His heart melted as she held his gaze, steady, sure, happy.

Yet, she did hesitate to answer him. The empty black hole of her unknown past strained to suck her down. Seeing the warmth and affection in his unwavering, warm blues, there was honesty and security, protection and yes, the possession was clear in the robust irises.

She would be his alone, he would never share her with another man.

Casie cared so much for Neco she could feel her heart bursting, and her legs almost shaking with the desire for him that he elicited by just being close to her, looking at her the way he did.

She wanted his big hands rough on her body, caressing, gripping, teasing. His mouth tearing her up like he was so good at, and the rest. She wasn't sure what she really knew about...sex... her eyes slid sideways to him, her lips turned up.

Neco was strong and a good man. He would take care of her, be gentle and guiding until they were both sure before he...let loose.

She remembered Kandi's poisonous words that Neco would break her like a china doll, that he was too big for her, like an ox.

Casie lifted her hair off her neck resetting it to wave down her back. She trusted that he would lead her, show her what to do, and he would never hurt her. He was right, they would deal with any complications as they arose.

Taking a deep, strong breath, she smiled, shy as always, nevertheless she said a solid, "Yes."

His heart leaped, but he stayed calm. Still keeping their eyes linked, Neco spoke with careful conviction, "You have to be sure, baby. I don't want to if you aren't a hundred percent. I can wait. I will wait."

Holding her face, he feathered his strong fingers, the pads stroking her soft skin. Her hesitation gave him pause. He knew she was thinking about the unknown, who she was, and Kandi's venomous words.

Casie stood on her tiptoes and cupped his rugged face and kissed him. Looping her hands around his neck, she pulled his head down for a steeping, groin burning kiss, while pressing her soft woman's curves into his hard body.

This time she took control of his mouth, nipping at his bottom lip then his top, licking between them. Kissing the corners of his mouth she boldly pushed her tongue in searching for his.

Casie felt his shock at her boldness, for only a second, then his arms went around her to hug her tight while he ground back at her mouth. His tongue accepting hers, danced with it, sucked it. They sighed in unison.

Casie pulled back and grinned up at him. "Yes, I'm ready Neco." She slipped from his befuddled grasp and started for the door.

Neco blinked out of the fire-lusted haze she'd just put him in, pushed down on his pounding erection and blindly followed her.

Just as they reached the door someone called his name.

He turned around. Combing his fingers through his hair trying to flatten it, he quickly dropped his hands clasping them in front of his pants to hide his hard-on.

His mother was rushing to him squealing, "Neco, wait!" She took a breath as she reached them. "Your cousin Trent cut his arm. It's pretty bad. Your truck is the only one not blocked in. Do you think you can-"

Neco swallowed his frustration, smiled and nodded. "Of course, Ma, we'll take him to the hospital." He reached to take Casie's hand and twined their fingers.

"Oh, thank you, dear. Aunt Jessica will meet you there. She's not in town. She needs to drive in from Platterston." Melody set a hand on his broad shoulder, and gave him a kiss on the cheek.

Stepping back, she remonstrated him, "And don't you dare wait so long again to see me. I won't stand for it, Neco Antonio Bardiche. You hear me? I will come and camp on your doorstep. I gave you space to lick your wounds and you just got further and further from us."

"Yeah, okay, Ma, please," red crept up his neck. He could feel Casie squeezing his hand. He knew she was laughing at him for being scolded like a child.

Melody Bardiche turned her warm friendly smile to Casie and beamed at her. "You dear, are welcome any time, with or without him. You are such a darling girl, and I have never seen my son so happy."

"Ma," Neco tugged at Casie who was grinning at his mother, they both looked conspiratorial, like they were planning his demise.

There was a commotion, several people hurried into the living room. One of them, a young man of around 16 had a bunch of cloths wrapped around his arm, they were oozing red.

Neco went right over to him. "Hey Trent, nice job. Come on, let's get to my truck." He opened the door and the group headed for his truck.

Tucking Casie between himself and Trent, Neco burned rubber out of the driveway and raced off for the hospital.

Chapter Twenty-Three

*H*arry Fletcher and Don Demelien had hunted around asking questions at bars, grocery stores, drug stores, hotels, apartment complexes, and now they headed into the diner in Lark for lunch.

They shimmied up on stools and ordered food. The heftier Harry asked for chili, and lanky blond Don ordered a tuna sandwich.

"Ah, I'm fucking exhausted. I can't believe we can't find one small fucking woman. Especially a knockout like that bitch. People'd remember her." Grumbling, Harry set his elbows on the counter and twined his thick fingers together in front of his face.

Stretching his long neck from driving around for weeks, Don groused, "Yeah, I thought we got lucky when we got the word she'd been spotted in this puny town, but it's like she disappeared into thin air. She has to be hiding out. No one has seen her. Maybe we should have stayed with Max and Hoss in Sanlura where they're searching."

Harry grunted as the server plunked his chili down in front of him. He pulled out a bottle of Tums and set it beside the spicy dish then opened several packs of crackers. After crumbling the crackers into his chili, he picked up his soupspoon to stir the chili and glanced up at the waitress.

His gaze blatantly trolled down her body and back up to latch onto her tits that were about hanging out of the uniform.

She chuckled and leaned over with her forearms on the counter. The top spread open further. Harry, and now Don too could see all the way to the beginning of her areoles.

"Hey, you two big hunks must be new around here. You truck drivers passing through?"

Harry stirred his dish then lifted a spoonful and slurped it through his thick lips. His brown round eyes never leaving her chest, chewing sloppily, he said, "Nah, we're here looking for someone."

She folded her arms and leaned over further.

Harry didn't move, just kept eating with his eyes on her cleavage. Don's neck stretched as he bent to get a better view.

Her forearms braced on the counter, fully aware both men were ogling her half-exposed bosom, the server asked, "What kind of someone are you looking for, handsome?" Her breasts rested on her arms so they molded further out of the top.

"Uh," so intent on the view, Harry almost forgot why they were there. Chili dribbled from a corner of his mouth, he wiped at it with the back of his hand. "Yeah, my uh, cousin, yeah, she ran away. My aunt sent us to find her."

Chomping his sandwich, Don said, "Maybe you seen her?" He pulled a dog-eared picture out and held it up so the waitress could see it. "This picture is a couple years old but she don't look much different."

Her eyes shifted lazily from Harry to Don trying to decide which one she'd meet up with later, then looked at the picture and snorted with insulted irritation. "Sure, I've seen that bitch."

"What?" Both men's eyes popped up to her face, mouths dropped open in surprise. They had just about given up.

Harry squinted one eye at her. "You seen her? You sure?"

She nodded. "Oh yeah. She's petite, like a little dainty porcelain doll, but with, like Rex said, bitchin' nice tits. She has long wavy golden-brown hair and big green eyes like cut glass, right?"

Her bitter resentment at the girl being with the guy she had found so hot, and chased after every time he came into the diner flowed right out of her sneering mouth and spiteful eyes.

Taking out a cell so he could make a note on it, Don asked, "Where? Where can we find her?"

Tempest Miller shrugged. "I'm not sure. I've heard there was new talent at the Palace. The men were all a-fucking-twitter about some young meat, the way they described her sounded like this bitch. She was only there a couple nights."

Quickly gobbling down his chili, Harry pulled his wallet out. "Where's the Palace? What is it?"

"It's a tittie bar, a sort of upper class strip club. It's called the King's Palace. Rex King owns it. It's on the outskirts of Lark and closer to Sanlura. So, one of you boys want some fun later?" Tempest moved her arms closer together to plump her breasts up more.

Salivating, Don's gaze was super-glued to her chest. "Yeah, when-"

"No. We gotta go. Come on, Don Juan." Harry dropped bills on the counter. He said to Tempest, "I'll call for ya later, babe." He grabbed Don's arm and dragged him off the stool and out the door.

Chapter Twenty-Four

*N*eco's plan was to take Trent into the emergency room and stay with him until his mother showed up, then he was grabbing Casie and high-tailing it home.

He was already undressing her in his mind. But then, the best laid plans- Aunt Jessica was several hours away. Trent was a minor, Neco and Casie had to settle down and wait for her.

Casie was curled up in a chair.

Neco crouched in front of her. "Here, baby," he held a soda he had gotten from a machine out to her.

Her lids were like heavy drapes she had a hard time opening. Peeping out from under them she smiled at Neco declining the soda. "No thanks, you go ahead."

"Baby, I'm so sorry about this. If I had known we'd have to stay so long I would have had Logan take you home."

A grin split her sleepy face. "Sure. I doubt you could have pulled him away from his girl."

His grunt was with brotherly affection. "He would do as I told him to."

"It doesn't matter, Neco. I would have wanted to be here with you anyway. You couldn't leave your cousin alone."

Trent had almost cut his arm to the bone. He had required surgery and was now resting in a room.

Neco plopped on the chair beside her. "Yeah," he covered a yawn, "but I didn't realize it would take half the night for my aunt to get here."

"It's okay, Neco, really. As long as I'm with you I'm happy."

His heart filled to the brim, Neco brushed her face with his hand then held her jaw in his palm, leaned over and kissed her.

Sitting back, he sighed grumpily. "So much for our private evening." With a disappointed smile, his eyes slid over to her, rolling heatedly from her face, down her body and back up.

Her eyes were closing, she murmured a soft, "Hmmm, disa...point...ed..." and she was out.

His smile turned tender, she always brought out the nurturing side of him, one he never knew he had.

Neco got up and went to his truck, returned with his jacket and laid it over her.

Jessica didn't get there until almost dawn.

Neco filled her in on her son's condition and the room he was staying in then he scooped Casie up in his arms and carried her still asleep to his truck and drove them home.

When they arrived, she stirred enough to go inside and to her room where she flopped on the bed and was back out like a light.

Chuckling, Neco pulled her shoes off and tucked the blanket over her and turned off the lamp. Standing in the doorway watching her, he thought wryly, he had wanted to put her into a bed, but this wasn't what he had planned.

He trudged off to his own room barely getting his clothes off before stumbling face-first into his own pillows.

The next morning Casie was setting a stack of pancakes on the table when he came into the kitchen. "Good morning, sleepyhead," she greeted him with a grin.

"Hmm," he bent and kissed her quickly then pulled out a chair, plopped down and yawned. Scratching his head with both hands, he said through another yawn, "Some of us didn't sleep away the night curled up in a chair in the hospital lounge."

226

He reached for the pancakes and without waiting for Casie to give him a serving fork, he picked up several cakes and dropped them on his plate.

"Ah, someone needs his coffee," Casie commented hurrying to the counter to return with the pot. "Here you go, cranky," she poured him a mugful.

Before she could move back, he turned sideways in his chair, strung out an arm, wrapped it around her waist and pulled her right up against him.

"Neco! Be careful!" She held the pot away from him.

Putting both hands on her butt cheeks, he squeezed them and pulled her in tight.

She was handicapped to stop him with the hot coffeepot in her hand.

He pressed his face to her chest and nuzzled her breasts. She was barefoot and braless under a snug white T-shirt and pajama bottoms that she had stolen from his drawer. His fingers slid under the waistband of the pajamas and he started tugging them down.

"No- wait- Neco, I have a cake in the oven and I need to shower, and the landline has rung several times leaving messages that sounded work related."

She tried to pull from him but he latched his teeth over a nipple that protruded from the thin shirt and grabbed her ass again with both hands gripping it, robustly kneading it hard.

Sucking and nibbling her nipple through the shirt, he moved his big hands from her butt to her ribcage.

"Neco…" She tried to squirm from him, but he held her from getting away.

He grinned up at her looking boyish with his hair flopping in his eyes. "I just wanted a taste for now, to hold me." He let her go with a smack on the butt laughing at her protesting squeal and picked up his coffee.

"Yeah," he took a healthy swig before setting it down to attack his flapjacks. "I heard the damned phone ringing. I have conference calls scheduled all day." Pouring a gallon of syrup and a huge pat of butter on his cakes, he waited until she sat down.

He started, "What I'd like to do, baby," staring at the wet spot he'd made on her shirt sucking her nipple into a tight bead, he waited until she neatly cut her pancakes into little bites.

Slipping a lightly syrupy morsel into her mouth she looked at him in question. "Yes?"

"I would really like to take you out to dinner. We haven't gone on a real date, and I'd like to. What do you say?"

"Tonight?"

"Of course. I would have liked to spend all day with you," he wiggled his eyebrows lasciviously, "but I can't. So, we can do dinner."

"That would be really nice, Neco. I would like that. What should I wear?"

He contemplated her question while studying her body.

"I quite like what you have on now. I can see your nipples," he grinned. "They're growing hard because they can hear me talking about them. It's all I can do, baby, is to not get out of this seat and come over and grope the shit out of those crazy breasts of yours. And the pajamas, my pajamas by the way, I bought you nightgowns because I was thinking easy access." He smirked at the appalled pink that stained her cheeks.

"It's okay though," he shrugged, stuffed in a big forkful of pancake and chewed heartily while cutting another chunk. "Those pajamas will come off just as easily. I'm thinking you have no panties on under them?"

"Oh my gosh, Neco! Stop it!" She almost choked on her food. Her cheeks were like tomatoes, high and round and embarrassingly red.

It was such a turn-on teasing her. "Do you like dirty sex-talk, baby? 'Cause I'm thinking you might be getting a little damp between those pretty little legs of yours." He nonchalantly chewed his food while she looked like she was going to burst of pure mortification.

He noticed she clamped her thighs together, his eyes narrowed at them, then raised up to see the heat filling her big green eyes. She quickly lowered them but he knew what he saw.

His dick hammered in his pants. "Oh shit, Casie, you *are* wet. Oh fuck, baby." He dropped his fork and stared at her. "I want so badly to clear this table and lay you on it, right now, shit."

Her eyes darted back and forth, Casie looked like she was going to run. Then she looked up at him and her limbs trembled.

White-hot fire burned in his blue eyes, he looked at her so smoldering she felt she was going to sizzle like the bacon in the pan. "Uh, Neco," she set her palms on the table as if preparing for flight.

He took a giant breath and exhaled hard. "Take it easy, honey. I want you so bad I can taste it. Hmm, now I want to taste you, and I don't mean only your mouth." His sultry gaze dropped to her lower body and his tongue rolled over his lips.

"I can get those pants off in one move, lay you on this table, spread those lily white thighs and put my mouth right on your-"

"Neco, please!" Embarrassment, nerves, and desire constricted her throat so much she could hardly squeak a word out.

Leaning back in his chair, Neco put his hand on his boner and pressed it, with a groan. He shifted it so it wasn't pinching and smiled wolfishly at Casie.

"Don't worry, honey. I know I need to take my time the first time with you, and probably more than just the first," he watched the blush deepen.

"As much as I want to take you right now on this table, or the floor, or against the wall," she was almost scarlet, "we will do it right. At the right time, with all the time we need, with no damned phones or injured cousins or obnoxious brothers barging in. We come home tonight I'm hanging a 'Do Not Disturb' sign on the front door. All right?"

Casie struggled so hard to gather her poise, he had to smother a chuckle.

She mumbled, "Um, o…kay." Her fingertips fidgeted pushing at the place mat. "Back to my question, uh, Neco, what should I wear?"

Bright ebony pupils dilated with his scorching gaze stroked her breasts pressing full and firm in the tight white shirt.

Steadying her voice, she said firmly, "Seriously, Neco."

His grin filling his face, he scratched at his jaw, he hadn't shaved yet today. He had already thought about taking her to dinner tonight, he'd shave right before they went out. "I think one of those dresses Mrs. Ford said I would like would be fine."

Her brows rose. "I thought you said they weren't right? Not what you told her to get?"

Finishing his breakfast, he chuckled. "Yes, well, that was before I thought we could for sure have a relationship, and my brother isn't here to ogle you, and you'll be on my arm. Otherwise," he shrugged one shoulder popping in the last bite, "I wouldn't let you out the door alone in one of those dresses."

"Neco," she chided, "I am a grown woman. I can wear what I want where I want."

"Sure, baby, you just keep thinking that." He wiped his hands and mouth on his napkin and stood up. "I have to get into the office. I think we should leave around...seven? I'll make reservations, okay?"

"I, uh, sure. I'll be ready-" She broke off warily as he trod around the table to stand in front of her.

"I just want to kiss you good morning, honey, don't look at me like I'm going to eat you alive." Smiling evilly he muttered, "But that does sound so delicious, my mouth is watering."

He bent and settled his lips on hers and slid his hand under the T-shirt to rest on her warm belly. He felt her abs contract at the contact and smiled against her lips.

Her blushes were so cute and such a turn-on, he wanted to roam his hands all over her body, up the T and down the inside of the pajamas, but he forced himself to let go of her and stand back.

Wrinkles of worried bewilderment etched her forehead. Something bothersome had wormed its way inside her brain.

"What, baby?"

Her finger tracing an empty pattern on the table, looking down at the table, she peered up at him, slight shame curved into the etchings. "It's just," she pushed her hair back with both hands and shrugged a sigh.

"I don't know. Right now I couldn't tell you, or myself," a wry mirthless laugh cut off her sad smile, "if I've ever had sex...uh, you know... before. I mean..." The color suffused right up her neck to her cheeks, she clapped her hands over them. "Darn I hate when I blush like a child."

A tender smile tipped up the side of his mouth. Neco brushed two fingers down her flaming cheeks. "Ah, you wouldn't feel that way if you saw how sexy and adorable it makes you look."

Her lips in a moue of indulgence pulled back in a weak grin. "Um, anyway, as I said, I can't tell if I'm, like, you know, a virgin, or if I've had a baby, or... gee Neco, I could actually be uh, you know, promiscuous." She shook her head at his snort of disbelief.

"No, it could be true. I have no feelings one way or the other. I could be a..." her voice quieted, "loose woman. You deserve so much better than that-"

The two fingers stroking her face went over her lips, his brows drew down in a strong frown. "Casie, stop trying to figure yourself out. I feel as if I know you, better than you do yourself, and I love you."

His deep voice grew louder in autocratic annoyance, "Whatever your past, if you were a damned hooker, assassin, thief, honey, I love you. Let me repeat myself." His hand drifted to her shoulder with a soft squeeze, as his voice softened with it. "We will work out everything, no matter what it is, together."

His fingers clenched along her collarbone one by one. The corners of his mouth turned down, then he lifted her chin to link their eyes. "It is I who doesn't deserve you."

"Neco, but what if-"

"No more, baby. Stop dwelling. We take every moment as it comes." He didn't want to ask her this question and make her more uncomfortable, but it would help with things later tonight. "Baby, don't be embarrassed, please, but I need to ask, as crazy as it sounds. Do you use, um, tampons when...you know?"

As predicted her cheeks blew up with color. "Neco, really, how can you ask-"

His lip pulled in, shaking his head. "The reason is, well, we don't know if you are a virgin or...not. If I know you use...tampons, then technically the deed is done and I can feel easier that I won't hurt you. Do you, ah, understand what I'm saying?"

Her fingers curled in loose fists over her lower face as her skin darkened and her eyes lowered.

He repeated, "Do you understand what I'm saying, Casie? If you use tam-"

"Yes, for heaven's sake," she blurted. "Yes, yes. Can we stop talking about it now?"

A grin broke over his face. "Okay, gotcha. Sorry, honey, but you don't need to be embarrassed with me. You will grow more at ease with me, in time. Now, I'll be in my office if you need me. Make sure you're thinking about tonight..."

Shooting her another wolfish grin, he padded out of the kitchen and down the hall leaving her wide-eyed, greatly embarrassed, and...hot.

Chapter Twenty-Five

Neco had chosen an upscale restaurant in the center of Sanlura.

It was a drive to get there but he wanted the best for Casie. She was going to drive him nuts all through dinner anyway in that damned dress.

He kept his eyes on the windshield to keep himself from being able to get too good of a look at her. Nonetheless, his eyes shifted over her every other mile. She about made him drop dead when she had come out of her room.

He had finished his work, showered, shaved, dressed in black slacks, blue shirt and tie, and a dark blue jacket over it. He had just pulled his dress boots on and was standing up to wait for her when she entered the living room.

He knew his eyes had bugged out, he couldn't stop them. "Damn, Casie." The black pupils swelled to take up almost all of the blue in his irises in his instant arousal. His eyes trolled her body like he was fitting her for a body suit.

The green and blue print dress tied around the back of her neck like the other one had, but this one dipped in the front exposing just a hint of the swells of her breasts. That devious Mrs. Ford had snuck in another halter, apparently somebody thought they were playing cupid, at his libido's expense!

The dress was snug enough to outline her beautiful breasts but not sturdy enough to stop them from jiggling when she moved. He felt his dick growing hard and knew it would be like that all evening.

The skirt was flowy and twirled around her legs just below her thighs. How was he going to keep his hands off her all night? He should have ordered take-out and stayed home. His balls were already tight and pained.

She had stood with her hands clasped behind her back causing those amazing breasts to push out further. She looked like Marilyn Monroe in her coy youth.

But Casie's face crinkled with worry. "Do I look all right? I can go change. I feel kind of," she nervously skimmed her palms down the sides of her breasts to her waist to her hips.

Neco's eyes followed her every move. It was all he could do to keep his tongue inside his hanging mouth. He snapped it closed. "Yes, I mean, you look great, Casie. Good enough to lick all over."

The edges of his mouth turned up at the pink heat that moved into her cheeks. "And that's something I do plan on doing."

The back of the dress left her skin bare, he spread his hand across her back groaning at the warm softness of her.

As he walked her to the door, he said, "I only have one question."

Going out the door with him, as he locked it behind them, she said, "What is that?"

He helped her into his truck, closed her door and went around to get into the driver's side. "Do you have panties on under that?"

Neco behaved himself at dinner, mostly. When he had made the reservations he had asked for a table, not a booth. He knew if he was sitting beside her in the intimacy of a booth in the candlelit restaurant he would be all up and down her dress.

The lighting in the restaurant was mellow golden that blended romantically with the candles on each table issuing soft light but bright enough a person could read their menu.

The interior was round, booths lined the walls and dark blue tablecloths donned the tables scattered throughout the rest of the room.

Most of the wall area was covered with a mural of what looked like narrow crooked streets of a Mediterranean country intertwined with lush colorful flowers and glimpses of the exotic azure sea.

The owner of the restaurant was a friend of Neco's so Neco was well known. The server came, Neco ordered a bottle of wine and fried calamari as an appetizer then Casie ordered the shrimp diablo and he chose the filet.

They talked about what Casie would like to do once her life was back on track.

She told him, "I would like to get a job, or go to school, but I don't know if I already went to school…or," she sighed munching on a shrimp.

Periodically Neco patted her hand. "I know it's frustrating, sweetheart. You don't have to do anything. I know you feel lazy, useless, but it is what it is right now. I think your memory is returning in bits and pieces, am I right?" Stabbing a piece of steak, he washed it down with a sip of burgundy wine.

Her eyes flew to his then quickly lowered. "I'm…not sure."

Cutting another slice of beef, he said casually, "Every so often your face goes stiff and you blank out, like you're somewhere else then your face gets all…stressed. I had to come into your room last night and wake you from that nightmare."

He set his cutlery down. "Tell me baby. Don't ever be afraid to talk to me no matter how bad you think it is." His words were true and strong, but he felt butterflies in his stomach at the thought of her memory returning and what it could mean to them. Plus, he felt she was still frail and he worried what she remembered was going to frighten her to death.

"I need to know everything, baby, to be able to help you. You have to trust me." He wanted to add that he would be her husband at some point and she needed to be fully open to him and trusting he would love her and take care of her no matter what.

Unfortunately, he knew that would make her even more nervous. She kept telling him she could do nothing until she knew for sure who she was and what she had run from.

Casie picked up the tail of a shrimp holding it between her thumb and finger and absently fidgeted with it. "Honestly, Neco, it's nothing concrete I can explain. I," her eyes flicked away from him.

"Tell me anyway." He reached across the table to hold her hand, his gaze straight and steady on her.

Taking a breath, she held it, then let it out slowly. "It's…I have been getting flashes of…oh Neco, please…"

He scooted his chair closer to hers and gripped her hand tighter. Bending his head to her, he murmured, "Tell me, baby. Look at me."

It took her a minute before she brought her eyes back to him. His blues were strong and caring, willing her to trust him.

"I see like blips of…a man… He's on top of me, shoving between my legs, ripping at my clothes. I'm screaming, I," gulping hard, she rubbed her hand over her eyes as if to clean them.

Aw shit, Neco drew the hand he held up to stop her. "Casie, baby."

Gulping down her terror, she dug her shaking fingers into her chin. Taking a deep tremulous breath, she kept going. "Then, I mean I can't focus on his face, but then today I saw, like the film blips again and he, I think it's the same man…he's leaning over a– a woman. There's a, like he has a belt I think around her neck. His back is hunched over her, I can't see his face. He…"

Sucking in another deep breath, she went on. "He was turning. He had almost completely turned around to face me but not quite." She looked down at her palm with a blank stare. "I- I think there's something in my hand."

Closing her eyes. "I can't…I don't know what it is." Shrugging, her lids rose slowly, she picked up her wine and took a sip then carefully set the glass down.

"Anything else?" he prompted.

Her eyes were doing that blanked out thing, she was there with him but not. When he saw her shoulders brace and the color seep from her bright cheeks, he shifted so that his body blocked her from the view of the rest of the patrons.

Her shoulder rose in a slight shrug. "Just, uh, I'm running, crying. I can't see who is chasing me. I think later I am in a car."

Her eyes scrunched closed. Wincing, she cried, "It hurts, Neco, it hurts!" With a tiny wail, she lifted her hands to cover her face like she was being hit.

"Baby," Neco pulled her against him, wrapping his arms around her. "Shh," he soothed, "it's all right, it's over. You are fine now, and safe, hush baby." He stroked her hair while she buried her face in his chest. He could feel the muscles in his stomach clenching.

She was remembering possibly being raped, or an attempt to, then maybe a murder, and now the pain of the beating she got in the car, that was right before he'd found her. His heart just ached like crazy at her pain, and sheer fury and frustration of not having been there to stop the assaults.

After few minutes, Casie collected herself and sat back in her chair, tears clung to the ends of her lashes like raindrops. She picked up her linen napkin and dried her eyes.

Quietly, a rasp in her voice, she said, "The thing is, Neco, what I'm really afraid of…is that I was part of the- the- murder. Maybe it was a gun in my hands, and that's why I was running, running from the police," her voice rose as she fell into panic again.

Neco put his arm around her shoulder and hugged her to him. "Shh, sweetheart, you are not part of a murder. It's more likely you witnessed one and the perpetrator was the one chasing you." He watched his words toss around her face as she tried to fit them like puzzle pieces into her flashbacks.

"Neco," her voice a weak thread he had to strain to hear her, "I'm so scared."

Hugging her tightly, he said, "I know baby, I know. But I'm here and I won't ever leave you." He curled his fingers under her chin, lifting her to look up at him. "I love you, Casie, and I will stay with you and protect you. We will work through this together. Got that?"

The long lashes swept up and down over her large green eyes so childlike but with adult hauntings shadowed in them. "Thank you, Neco."

He bent and covered her mouth with his, kissing away her fright and the loneliness he could hear in her voice. He kissed her until the server cleared his throat.

After their dinner plates were cleared they shared a strawberry cheesecake. He ordered coffee, his fingers webbed around the cup as they were too big to fit into the handle. He was staring at the coffee.

Saying, "Neco," Casie waited until he raised his eyes to her. "I know I'm constantly being a whiny crybaby. You are so patient and stalwart all the time. I want you to know I do appreciate everything you do for me, and everything that you…are. The man that you are."

A warm smile reflected his feelings for her. "Thanks for saying that, Casie. I care for you and want you to know we're in this together. Right?" He held his hand out, palm up.

She set her hand in his; he closed his fingers around it.

He said with a slight squeeze, "I think you were a lot braver than you give yourself credit for." He didn't say out loud that she managed to get away from whoever her attackers were, and likely that was at least twice, that had to take a lot of moxie.

Especially if she was scared out of her mind, and, he leaned over and gave her a light kiss, there was little doubt in his mind that she had been frightened to death.

They were both quiet on the drive home.

Neco was thinking about the time they drove back from the clothes shopping and Casie had asked permission to touch his hair. His smile made him think Casie does that a lot to him, makes him smile.

He had loved her fingers combing through his hair, then she had stroked his shoulders, and tried to squeeze his biceps and giggled when she couldn't. Then when she rubbed his chest- he shook his head. It wouldn't do him any good to get wood now, at least not more than he already had.

He shot a glance at her.

Casie was staring pensively out the window, deep in thought, she'd barely uttered a word.

Neco suppressed his sigh. He had hoped they would finally be intimate tonight. Sadly, after the shit she told him that she was remembering at dinner surely put a damper on any erotic feelings she might have had.

Exhaling in frustration, and patience, it was all right. Like he told her, she was worth waiting for.

Parking the truck, Neco went around to open her door and help her out. She turned to face him.

"You look stunning, Casie." He breathed deeply. The way the dress hugged her breasts, exposing just a hint of the mounds, the material was silky and her nipples were poking through the thin material. He knew his eyes were bee-lined on them but he couldn't make himself look away.

"You look pretty handsome yourself, Neco."

He glanced up at her face, she had a funny slight smile. Her lids were half-mast only a stream of green slipped out. He thought she looked...turned on...but no, she was probably just tired.

"Thanks, baby." He wrapped his hands around her waist and picked her up to lift her out of the truck.

The thing was, he didn't want to set her down. He wanted to hold her against his body and kiss her until she was wet and willing for more, a lot more. It was tough, for him, still, he will wait for another night when the residual doom and gloom from earlier wasn't hovering over them.

"Uh, Neco," she sounded teasing, but he figured she was worried someone would see them. He set her down and walked her to the door.

Infusing lightness and faux cheerfulness into his tone with a halfhearted smile, Neco said, "I guess we'll make it an early night, get some rest."

Inside, Neco went to flip on a light switch, Casie put her hand over his to stop him.

They were in the country so there weren't many outside lights. Scant spheres of twilight speared gently into the front window creating velvety shadows through the room.

When she stopped him from turning on the lights, with a twinge of concern, he asked, "What's wrong, Casie?"

Chapter Twenty-Six

The car doors thumped closed and Harry and Don started through the parking lot of the King's Palace.

Seeing a stream of men going in and out even though it was only late afternoon, Harry jabbed Don in the side with his elbow.

"Listen, Don, we are here for one reason only. To get the girl. We are not here to gawk at, touch, or try to get a date with any of the talent. You got that?"

Rubbing his side where Harry's hefty elbow caught him, Don, growled, "Fuck you, Harry, quit hitting me for fuck's sake. If I want to look at some naked broad, or feel up a barmaid what's it to you? I can grope broads and look for the little bitch at the same time."

At Harry's objecting grunt, Don griped, "You already fucked it with me and that waitress at the diner, I coulda had a date tonight. She blows good, I can tell. I'd have had her on her knees before-"

"Shut up, for cripes sake, Don. We get the girl and take her to Pryce, you can go back and get Ms. Tits. Let's go." He grabbed the door handle and pulled the door open then followed Don inside.

Typical blaring strip club music reverberated throughout the building.

The two men stood just inside the doorway letting their eyes get adjusted to the dim light after being outside in the sun. Both scanned the long bar checking out every patron sitting at it or standing around the area.

They carefully scrutinized each female behind and around the bar.

Harry turned to his left squinting through the smoky dusky room teeming with customers, while Don checked the right side. Then they both carefully scoured each table in the middle and scattered around the three stages.

Only one girl was dancing, she was at the center stage. She was in the process of weaving her hips back and forth and peeling off her clothes.

She did it so awkwardly and slowly, fumbling getting her top off that it was obvious she was as high as a kite. Her shrill giggles skidded through the room every time she almost stumbled.

The men cheering her on didn't care how high or drunk she was as long as her clothes came off.

Harry carefully checked around the stages to see if the girl they sought was perhaps in the back serving, or maybe even getting ready to get on the stage and dance. His attention returned to the center stage.

He brushed the front of his pants as his cock jumped. *Yeah*, he would love to see Pryce's sweet little bird naked and writhing on the stage under the strong light.

Recalling the shy innocent young thing he'd chased down twice, and beaten when he'd gotten his hands on her, she'd have to be drugged or forced to be up there, even better. *Yeah.* That's hot. Humiliation. Forcing women to submit, yeah, rape, he had no problem admitting it turned him on.

He palmed his crotch picturing the bitch naked on her hands and knees with a chain around her willowy neck. He was hoping that she would make an appearance any second. He glanced over at the other stages but they remained empty.

Seeing Harry staring at the empty stages and rubbing his cock over his pants, Don snickered. "You're picturing the bitch up there, aren't you?"

Harry ignored him.

"Hey," Don said with a quiet mean voice, "this time, I say we get our share of the bitch before we take her to Pryce. At this point, she will have been passed around anyway, so he won't care. I want first dibs. I want to push her on her face and jerk that sweet ass up and shove my cock up her ass, it has to be insanely tight."

Harry didn't bother even looking at him, his snarky snort said enough. "You are such a tool, shithead. Pryce will, actually he has, killed for that girl. He finds out you fucked her in any of her holes he'll cut off your dick with a rusty knife and watch you bleed out."

Pressing a hand to his ribs, Harry's face clouded darkly remembering the thrashing Pryce had three other of his employees give him for beating the girl that day in the car. His hand moved to his balls, and then another beating for letting her get away.

Don and Landers had gotten only one pounding for letting her escape. He slapped Don's arm with the back of his meaty hand. "Come on, let's ask around."

Don with his narrow shoulders hunched and scowling like his candy had been snatched out of his hand, strode through the crowd to the bar.

Harry showed the girl's picture to several barmaids. They all shook their heads and quickly walked away.

"Fuck," Harry muttered. "They recognize her, bitches aren't talking." He snagged a female employee and asked her who the manager was. The girl pointed to a woman by the front entrance talking to several people.

Harry and Don approached the woman.

Around thirty with almost a blonde crew cut and heavy liner around her small eyes, her cheeks and body were angular and thin.

Nervously eyeing the thuggish looking men, the other people wandered away.

"Miss?" Harry had the picture in his hand.

When the woman turned to him with raised brows, Harry held up the picture. "I'm looking for my cousin. She ran away and her mom is so worried about her, she can't eat or nothin'. We was told she mighta worked here. Do you remember her?" He could see by the angry frown he'd hit paydirt.

The woman glared at the picture and flicked it with her finger and thumb. "Yeah, I remember the twat. Rex gave her a bunch of help. Put her up at my place for a couple of days, gave her a job," she sneered and hit the picture again and shrugged her bony shoulders.

Wearing a tank top and tight pants she ruffled her fingers through the back of her short hair. "He had high hopes for the bitch, wanted her-" she clapped her mouth shut, she was blabbing too much.

Harry could hardly contain his grin. Beside him, Don was nodding like a baboon. "Yeah?" Harry said politely with a neat smile, "Miss, uh..."

"Sasha O'Connor. I'm the manager. Take that ungrateful slut back to her family, and good riddance."

Trying to think of how to ask without pissing her off further, Harry rubbed at his burly chin, said mildly, "You, uh, sound kind of...angry. Did she do something, uh, bad?"

Sasha slapped her hands on her square lean hips and rolled her eyes. "You would say so. After all Mr. King did for her, she ups and walks out right in the middle of her shift."

Harry's eyes lit and burned. "Oh yeah? She was a dancer?" His gaze narrowed and shifted to the stage, big tongue came out and swirled around his thick lips. "Up there? Nude?" It was an effort to keep his hands from brushing the front of his pants.

Shaking her head, the manager ran a hand over the top of her short hair. "No," sniffed inelegantly. "Little bitch was too good to take her clothes off. No, she was a barmaid."

One shoulder lifted as her mouth twisted with a vulgar sneer. "Huh, that would have lasted only so long. After Rex had his fill of her, he would have had her on the stage, whether she wanted to or not." Her eyes slit, mean lips turned up. "He has his ways. Ya know what I mean?"

"Oh." Suppressing his thoughts of the girl on the stage, naked, those pretty green eyes unfocused from drugs, on her hands and knees, bare tits bouncing as a whip smacked her naked ass, *maybe scared, crying, yeah, that would be*- Harry put the picture away.

A hand in his pocket, Harry pushed a toe around the wood paneled floor. "Maybe, uh, do you possibly know where she went?"

Crossing her arms over her flat chest, Sasha nodded with a scowl. Dark brown brows rode down over her lined eyes. "Yeah. Her boyfriend came storming in, snatched her away from one of our best customers. Tough guy took down two of our bouncers and dragged her out the door. Mr. King was, let's say, beyond livid."

Beside Harry, his blond hair tufted around his narrow face, Don was making notes on his cell, poking at the tiny buttons with his knobby fingers.

"Wow." Harry nodded in commiseration. "How damned ungrateful. Her papa will surely give her a whipping when we get her home." That was true in a way, Pryce will flog the hell out of her. Harry would only be so lucky to watch it. "She was taught better manners than to walk out on a job."

He tried a little flirtatious smile. His thick lips tugged up the hefty face exposing fairly white teeth. "So, uh, do you possibly know who this asshole boyfriend is? I mean," he nudged her arm lightly with his elbow, "when we get her, we can give him a beat-down he won't forget for treating you good people the way he did, ya know?"

Sasha's gaze rolled down Harry's stocky body, flitting over his big blocky shoulders and barrel chest, then paused at his crotch. A tiny smile split her thin lips. "Na, I don't know where he lives. Rex, uh, Mr. King might, but he's out of town."

A snicker gurgled from her thin lips, "Yeah, Rex was fit to be tied. Would have gone after the guy himself but he already had

245

some trouble brewing with the law so he," realizing she was giving out too much information, she broke off.

"So," her eyes scrolled down then up Harry. "You that big all over?"

Beside him, Don choked, then covered it coughing into his gangly hand. He kept his eyes on his phone.

A shit-eating grin spread over Harry's thick face covering his surprise, he'd thought she was a dyke. Maybe she was bi, he was okay with that.

He nodded with very serious inflection. "Yeah." He gave her body the once over with a leer. "You wanna find out how big later tonight?" He winked one tiny round brown eye at her.

She was more manly looking than female. Sasha's eyes drifted down his body again, her skinny lips curved up in a lascivious smirk. "Sure. I get off at ten. We can have a drink here before we..." Her hand pushed at the back of her short hair like she was being flirty.

"Well, that'd be really nice, babe." Harry drew a thick finger down her arm and watched her shiver, her small braless tits jiggled with it. He ignored Don's snort.

"So, uh, back to my cousin. I mean, I gotta find her before her dear sweet mother has a heart attack. Maybe you got an address for her?"

She started to shake her head, but then recalled the day Casie had been brought to her apartment. "Actually, we sent a car for her, it'll be on the Town Car's manifest. I'll be right back, don't you move, hot stuff." She patted Harry's face before hustling off to get the address.

"Oh yeah, nice." Don extolled. This time he jabbed his elbow in Harry's side. It didn't do much, Harry had a lot of meat and muscle on him.

Chapter Twenty-Seven

*C*asie dropped her hand off of Neco's and strolled to the sofa.

Standing with his hand still on the light switch watching her move through the dim living room, curious, he followed her to the sofa.

Casie gave him a small push making him shift backwards to sit on the arm of the couch.

"Casie what-"

"Neco," she purred. The lilt in her throaty voice pervaded with shy subtle arousal whizzed like a satin bullet straight to Neco's ears, tingling all the way up to the tips.

Her words slowed, her voice soft, huskily sweet and sexy, she said, "Are you trying to get out of our evening plans?" She pushed to stand between his legs.

He sat perched on the couch arm, his legs spread to accommodate her. The expression on his face made Casie smile. His expression was a combination of uncertainty and surprise, and then his eyes narrowed in suspicion that she was only teasing him.

She looped her fingers around his tie and drew them down the length of it in a long sexy drawl of silk on skin.

The tie sliding under her hand all the way to the end, then she let it drop with a fluff on his stomach.

247

Neco looked down watching her sensuous sifting movements. He was reminded of her fingers delving through his hair that day in his truck. It was visually erogenous watching her play with his tie, but he'd prefer those fingers were dancing on his bare body.

She pushed her small hands under the lapels of his jacket moving up to his wide shoulders to slide the jacket off.

His face still a mask of unsure suspicion, he assisted her by shrugging out of the jacket, and although he looked uncertain, his eyes were pinned on hers studying her expression. Was she kidding, or not? He was waiting for her to tell him.

Showing him instead, her hands went back to his tie. She painstakingly untied it, so slowly he wanted to rip it off and throw it, but then again, she was undressing him, *he thinks*, and he was going to enjoy it however far it went.

Without breaking their eye contact, Casie tugged one end of the tie until it slid around his collar with a hiss, and off into her hands, she dropped it on the floor. With one finger, she toyed with the top button of his shirt.

"Baby," his voice thick with building desire that was quickly pushing through the locks he'd placed on his libido. "Don't stop there…" Neco set his palms on the couch arm on either side of his thighs.

She was right where he wanted her. Her hands on him, standing between his legs. If he spread them further and she moved closer, their sex would touch.

"Hmmm, you know I don't know what I'm doing, you will have to help me…guide me…" Her lips turned up in a seductive little catch.

He had to clear his throat to get the words out, they were shaky. "You're doing…ah great honey, just great. Keep going."

Her head was tilted down. She rolled her eyes up at him with a secretive short smile, then she looked down and unbuttoned the top button. And the next and the next down to his lean belly, she stopped when she reached his belt.

Pushing aside the shirt, she stared at his chest like she'd never seen a man's chest before. Dark hair made his chest rocky with slabs of thick muscles even more powerfully masculine.

His head bowed near hers, inhaling her fresh scent. Neco whispered, "Touch me, baby." Tightening his thighs around her hips, he kept his hands on the sofa, his fingers digging into the cloth.

She couldn't take her eyes off his strapping physique. Splaying her fingers, she set one palm on his chest, then the other. Burrowing her fingers up through the hair, she molded her hands over each hard hunked rise and steel groove.

Neco's rumbled groan urged her to explore his massive chest. She obliged, moving up to frisk his broad shoulders, down to the ridged abs, and lower to his tapered hips.

He was about to encourage her to go down further but she slid her hands back up to just below his pecs and held them under them. Then she unexpectedly bent her head and licked a nipple.

"*Shit Casie-*" his gasp sucked the air right back in. His groin twisted, balls tightened.

Without lifting her head, her voice all husky giggles, she whispered, "You did this to me, Neco, and I liked it, do you?" and licked the other nipple then drew it into her mouth and sucked.

Electricity zinged from the wet pull of her mouth and tongue and shot right to his crotch. Growling, "Casie," he wanted a long night and that wasn't going to happen if she kept her mouth on his body. He circled her waist with his hands and drew her back.

Apparently she was very focused with what she was doing because she hazily looked up at him with passion filled bewilderment. Then her brows lowered. "Did I do something wrong?"

A chuckle shivered out of his mouth. "No, honey, you are perfect, but I want to be inside you, and if you keep doing what you're doing, I won't get that far."

Pink and confused, her eyes on his chest, she mumbled, "I don't know what you mean."

"First, I need to kiss you, Casie." Neco wrapped a big hand around the side and back of her head pulling her mouth to join his. Covering her lips, he slanted his head to the side and brought up his other hand to cup the other side of her head pressing their mouths together tighter.

Casie's hands went back to caress his blocky chest, her mouth opened eagerly to accept his tongue.

Their tongues tasting and tangling, licking and savoring, besides relishing how soft and sweet tasting she was, Neco could still tell she was following his movements, that she acted like she has never been kissed before.

He figured it had to be like riding a bike, your muscle memory would just automatically do it, but she was pure fresh innocence. It was so hot. It was like she was his, all his, and he was ecstatic he would be the one to teach her everything.

If she got her memory back and was a little different, maybe had experience with lovemaking, it would still be exciting, like mixing two women into one. Not like just banging two different women, but like making love to a woman that had many facets.

Right now she was purity intensified and she was all his. He skimmed his hands down the front of her over the curves of her waist, then stroked them back up to cup her breasts over the thin dress that snuggly cradled them. His groin just melted into hot gold.

Her body stiffened faintly, her shyness and inexperience making her slightly anxious.

Against her mouth, he murmured, "Relax sweetheart, stay out of your head and just feel." Fusing their mouths together, he explored her silky mouth and felt her breasts.

He filled his hands with them, kneading and cupping their fullness. A growl burned in his chest, his body fired up in an instant, flaming brilliantly, too savagely excited he squeezed too hard, too fiercely and a tiny whimper misted into his mouth.

Leaning from her, Neco whispered, "Sorry, baby, you just turn me on so goddamned much I don't know my own strength." He tilted her head up to look at her.

The sensuous heat in her green eyes clouded like a sea storm coming. Damp lips parted waiting for his mouth to return and claim them again. His dick swelled and throbbed, straining against his pants.

Mumbling, "I'm okay, Neco," she lifted her head, her lids hooded covering her eyes, she sought his mouth with hers.

"Good," he muttered, lowering his mouth to hers. He caressed her breasts more gently. Stroking his thumbs over her nipples, he lightly pinched them, rolling them between his fingers before grasping and filling his hands again with her plump globes.

With a heavy passionate sigh, Casie slightly pulled her mouth from his but kept their lips touching. "I didn't mind your rough handling, Neco." Her lips pursed shy at her words. "I, uh, liked it. It's okay to feel me, touch me, with…exuberance."

Her luring lids rose, releasing gleams of shyness and lust. The plush lips parted dazed as she looked up at him. Lashes fluttering over the green orbs, she smiled against his mouth.

Her words ignited a full body shiver up and down the span of Neco's body. The reaction went to his hands and he greedily fondled her soft curves, top and bottom, with more frenzied intensity until the moans he wrung from her lips rivaled his own gruff rumbles of desire.

He needed to feel skin. Keeping their mouths sealed, Neco reached around her neck, under her hair and slowly untied the halter strips of her dress.

Holding the sleek strips in his hands, he pulled them down. The silky bodice billowing softly on her skin, her flesh quivered with the light material stroking, tickling her bare bosom as it exposed it, her nipples tightly puckered.

Neco separated from her to gaze at her exquisite beauty. His big hands circling her waist, he squeezed her hard from the thrust of lust that made his already rigid erection pound.

"Baby, you are…indefinable, so other-worldly, like a radiant pearly goddess."

Her hands on his thighs for balance, Casie looked down at Neco's fiercely admiring eyes blazing blue brilliance on her creamy plump, naked breasts.

When he skimmed his hands up to cover her full flesh, his fingers clutching the smooth plethoric globes, her spine arched, a faint gossamer gasp chafed from her parted lips. Her neck fell back and her head dropped, the long wavy hair feathered her now bare waist.

Filling his hands with her soft feminine flesh, Neco ground her breasts between his long fingers. "Ah, Casie," he rasped, cupping them roughly, deepening breaths filled his lungs sending more blood to his already engorged sex, and firing suds of dizzy lust to his already fogged brain.

He kissed the top swells of her flesh mounded in his hands, peppering kisses and licks, stopping to suck until red marks blemished her milky skin. He pulled an entire areole into his hungry mouth. More shivers struck his lower torso at her whimpered purr, and pebbled the tight nipple under his tongue.

Her fingers raked into his hair, twisting locks around her fingers. She wasn't aware she tugged so hard he winced with striking painful pleasure. He could feel her tugging fingers like they were right on his cock, like she was roughly stroking it, scraping it with her nails.

Neco pushed the top of her dress down to the curve of her hips then leaned in to take a nipple into his mouth. He licked it, sucked it. As her moaning whimpers grew louder and breathier, he nipped it then licked across to her other breast to take that nipple into his mouth to be treated to his sandpaper soft tongue.

He cupped under her breasts, mounding them up for his voracious mouth to devour.

Her breasts wet and red with his ministrations, tonguing a nipple, Neco stroked his hands down, to her waist, to her hips. Sliding them down as he passed her hips, his thumbs faced inward he brushed them over her thin dress, and down against her sex as he brought them to her thighs.

Her hips jerked when his thumbs pressed her core as he passed it to grip her thighs. A slight uneasiness stiffened her legs, her fingers still twined in his hair.

Casie gazed down at the top of his head, dark against her pale skin. He slanted his head up, smiled tenderly, calmly at her nervousness.

"Don't be afraid of me, Casie," he murmured softly. Still perched on the edge of the couch arm, Neco widened his legs, still fencing her hips then delicately nudged her legs apart. His heated gaze latched onto her anxious green orbs.

"Stay out of your head, baby, just feel my hands loving you. Okay?" He studiously watched her, patiently waiting while she worked to get back out of her head and back into her body.

Soon the soft razing sounds cauterizing her throat while he fondled and sucked on her breasts whipped and heated his blood so intensely he knew he would bring them both to great soaring heights of passion.

"Baby," growls heavy in his chest drummed in discordant grunts, seethed harshly when he slipped his hands up under her dress.

The growls deepened when he gripped her slender thighs, then moved his hand slowly up until he cupped her female mound with his hand over her panties. The heel of his palm pressed against her delicate core. "Your sweet body was fucking made for loving."

"Neco," she admonished his language with a nervous giggle that turned to a sudden groaning cry when he brushed his thumb over her sex.

"*Uh*," the groan gurgled out. Her legs trembled, her fingers gripped his hair almost tugging it out by the roots. He moved a hand pressing to keep her thighs apart, his other hand stroked her sex, his thumb gentled up and down.

"*Neco…*" his name a divine shiver, she released his hair to lean over and set her hands on his shoulders.

Her posture moved her breasts to nudge his mouth. His lips parted to suck on one. Lifting the hand on her thigh, Neco moved it to clutch her breast while he suckled it.

Against her skin, he murmured, "Open your legs for me, honey." The hand still between her thighs pushed them further apart. She was still slightly stiff with her innocence, but she let him spread them further.

Stroking her over the silk panties, he could feel her dampness through them. "Ah, baby, you are so damned receptive, you are wet already for me." He smiled at her embarrassed cut inhale.

"It's the way it's supposed to be, Casie. Your body is telling me it wants me," his big fingers slipped inside her panties to stroke her bare skin, "inside you."

With a sharp inhale, she cried, "Neco, I...don't know, maybe you-" gasps choked out at his every caress of her womanhood.

He could tell without even looking at her she was blushing, it only made his smile broaden.

"The- the way you talk, it's- *ohh...*" her moan tumbled out when his fingers rode up her slit.

He chuckled, his hand clenching her breast. "I will talk dirty to you, baby, until your ears turn so red they'll pop off, but right now we'll ease into this."

He drew a thick finger slowly up her slit, rubbing his thumb and squeezing the folds of her tender, tight skin. Her hips shook, legs trembled, his hand was soaked with her silk. He licked and nipped her nipple then moved his hand out from under her dress.

Casie stood topless with her legs slightly spread and her hands clutching his shoulders. Neco straightened her a little.

Dragging his palms roughly down her naked breasts to her ribs then to where the dress nestled just below her slim hips, he pushed the dress down the rest of the way past her hips, down her willowy thighs until it fell to the floor.

She stood in just her swathe of white silky panties and heels.

Neco leaned back to drink her in. "God, you take my breath away, baby." A small chuckle escaped his turned up lips. "Those damned panties, so sheer and virginal white, barely wrapped around your little pussy is so fucking hot." He moved his hand to cup her mound again over the sheer panties.

"*Neco, please,*" his language mortified her, yet turned her on too. Her body quivered with the contrasting feelings forcing her sex into harder contact with his hand.

Hearing and feeling her contradicting emotions, Neco chuckled again at her pushing against his hand. He slipped the tips of his fingers of both hands over the top of the panties and pulled them down, then lifted one of her legs then the other to remove them.

Leaning over, he unbuckled the thin straps on her high heels and slid off one then the other. She stood totally nude in front of him.

His hands went between her porcelain legs. "Like a naked angel, baby, just like a naked angel." Groaning, he pushed her legs apart a tad more. He cupped a cheek of her bottom to hold her then stroked his thumb up her slit.

Her breath rushed out hard, a muted hiss in his ear. He moved his fingers around her sex, getting them wet and slippery with her silk, then slid them around and around her bud until it swelled and her moans were coming shallow and breathless.

When her breaths cropped more ragged, he slid his middle finger just inside her.

With a grated surprised gasp, she lurched forward gripping his shoulders. Her breasts pressed against his face. Her legs immediately went rigid.

"Okay, baby, relax, trust me." The strain of holding himself back from laying her down and ravishing the shit out of her right now, savage and hard and fast, clenched his jaw. A vein hammered at his temple, his lids lowered over narrowed eyes.

He hesitated a second for her to get used to the feeling of him invading her body, then he drew his finger out a hair then pushed it carefully back inside her tender sheath.

His smile returned when silk covered his hand and her legs widened slightly. Tiny moans hovered in her throat urging him to keep pushing his finger until it was all the way inside her.

Feeling her legs now rigid with desire instead of nerves, Neco moved his finger in and out and around while rubbing his thumb over her bud and around her slit.

When the rasping sounds grew louder and her hips were moving to meet the thrusts of his finger, he tightened his grip on her bottom.

"Neco...I- I- feel...uh..." a blast of harsh groans filled her chest, her fingers dug into his shoulders.

"Yeah, baby, go with it, let go, baby. I have you, come for me." The faster his hand moved in and around her core the faster, shallower, louder her breathing until her thighs squeezed his hand and her sheath gripped his finger and she arched back with a taut scream.

Her hips rippled against his hand, another hoarse scream ripped from her constricted lungs. "*Neco-*" her pussy clenched his finger, and she fell forward over his shoulder.

His heart elated hearing his name on her lips as she screamed out her climax, Neco kept maneuvering his hand, adding a second thick finger in and out until her body shook with a hard shudder.

Her hips thrust in violent spasms then she fell limp over him with a harsh expelled cry. Gasping over his shoulder, her sheath trembled all around his fingers.

Casie's legs wobbling like rubber, Neco slipped his hand out from between her thighs to roll under her knees. His other hand around her back, he moved off the couch to bend slightly and lifted her up in his arms. He moved to the center of the sofa and set her down on the cushions.

Sitting with her back against the couch, her head lolled back, lashes fluttered over dazed limp eyes.

Neco knelt in front of her, put his hands on her thighs and spread them apart.

Her eyes cracked open. Seeing him between her legs, Casie was suddenly vividly aware that she was buck naked, he was fully clothed, and his eyes scrolled all over, up and down her body like a paintbrush.

It was like he was physically stroking her breasts, weighing their heft in his avaricious hands, then over her concave belly, down the slender legs then back up to settle on her core where they flickered with fiery want.

"Neco…" Casie quickly moved her hands to cover her sex. Her move made her arms press against her breasts, pushing them together. Neco's rapacious gaze rode up to them. The hot light in his eyes made Casie's skin sizzle with their heat.

He grasped her wrists moving her hands to the side so he could devour her with his eyes. "No baby, don't hide your beauty from me. It seems like I've waited forever to see you like this, in your buffed glory." Shifting between her legs, forcing them further apart, he looked down at her pink shiny womanhood and licked his lips.

Seeing him leaning towards her apex with his mouth open, Casie tugged at her hands, tried to close her legs. "No, Neco, what are you-"

He pinned her hands to the couch and bowed his head placing his mouth full over her whole sex.

"Oh, Neco, oh my gosh, what…" she cried, her head flipped forward then back arching over the back of the couch as his mouth closed over her. The heat of his breath burning her tender flesh.

His hard-on raging in his pants, Neco chewed over Casie's tender baby-pink nether lips. Sucking in her female folds, foraging her entire mons, he licked down her slit and up.

Her bleating huffing trills let him know she was already back up to the pinnacle. Her hips bucked and wriggled at his mouth, and he let go of her hands to clamp down on her thighs to hold her still.

Her head draped back, Casie's eyes were closed as she gasped, "Oh my gosh, Neco…it's…incredible, you- *ohh*, I- I'm going to- to-"

He bit hard on her bud with his lips and pushed his fingers into her.

"*Neco!*" his name on the edge of a rising scream, Casie gripped the sofa cushions. She lowered her head briefly to see him between her legs. His dark hair brushing her light skin, his big hands holding her thighs immobile.

When he rolled his tongue around her clit, her head dropped back and the cries rifled up her throat, mincing out in jagged little weeps.

Feeling her body rising to the cliff of release, Neco reached up and grasped her breast, palpating it with vehement strength in his big hand, at the same time he ran his thumb around her clit and plunged his fingers in and out.

The cry climbed up her throat, her body stiffened, a pretty pink flushed over her body. Neco kneaded each breast, and just as she fell over the cliff, he pinched a nipple and thrust another finger up her to fill her, stretch her to make ready for his body to claim her.

Her scream came out in spurting gasps and shaking thralls all over her body. He kept working her until the harsh quaking broke down to reverberating tremors and the screams dipped to choppy breaths of soft, whimpering mewls.

At the last shudder, Neco pulled his hands from her then before she could catch her breath, he stood up, scooped her up in his arms then stalked quickly out of the room, down the hall and to his room.

The cool silver moonlight streaming into the room was enough illuminant to see her creamy body against his dark shirt.

Her arms clinging around his neck, through trembling lips, weak and spent, Casie stuttered, "Ne- Neco, what are you doing?"

He bowed his head and captured her lips, kissing her gently then with increasing heat. "It's what *we* are doing, baby, this is all about us together."

Chapter Twenty-Eight

He laid her on the bed.

She instantly went to sit up and hide her nudity from his prying eyes.

Grunting, "Uh huh," bending over, Neco spread his fingers across her chest and pushed her gently on her back then grasped her legs straightening them, parting them. Taking each of her hands he moved them to lie beside her head.

Smiling down at her, his hands on his hips, he said, "There, just like that. Don't move, my beauty." He knelt and quickly removed his boots and socks then stood back up to breathe her in.

Feeling vulnerable and displayed, Casie forced herself to not move. "Neco, I feel," the blush strolled up her face to brighten her cheeks, "um, exposed."

She blinked up at him. "I'm," her lashes lowered, "naked, and you," they swept up to meet his blistering blues that engulfed her body, the blush deepened, "are fully clothed."

His grin stretched ear to ear. "Yeah. It's kind of a dream of males, to stand completely dressed and look down at their woman lying splayed naked on his bed, so he can enjoy her pure beauty and study every inch of her without obstructions, knowing he is going to claim her as his in a moment."

His pupils glittered up and down her body striking static shocks all over her bare skin. "And, right now baby, I'm living the dream."

Casie couldn't help but smile at his frank talk while he plundered her body with his eyes. "That's, uh, nice, but, I would feel more comfortable, if you would..." her own gaze swept his brawny body. "I mean, you're staring at my body while I can't see yours, um."

He strode to his dresser, picked something up and went right back to stand over her. "I will remedy that right now, my sweet. I had to take a break for a minute or our night would be too short.

"You turn me on like insanity, baby. I find it hard to control my libido when I'm around you. And honey, the way you came apart in my hands, ah," he sighed. "I almost came with you both times right then and there. Now," he undid each cuff, then gripped his shirt where it was still tucked into his pants.

He tugged it out of his pants, pulled it up and over his head and tossed it on the floor. Smiling at the way Casie's eyes grew wide scanning his bare chest, he put his hands on his belt.

Those green eyes dropped and widened further, her cheeks bloomed with color.

"Yeah, baby, you tell me if you like what you see."

"Hmmm," her eyes glued to his hands that worked his belt buckle.

A short chuckle made the muscles on his chest flex. Her eyes flew up to them. The green effervesced with heat, crackling at his powerful masculine chest like she wanted to tickle her bare feet in his mat of thick hair.

The heat in her eyes pulled the smile from his face. His eyes tight with hers, his features rugged with male desire hardened as he unbuckled his belt, unbuttoned his pants then pulled the zipper down.

Casie lying naked and spread eagle with her eyes tracing his every move made his dick so hard it could punch a hole through a steel door.

He pushed his pants down his legs along with his underwear to the floor then stepped out of them. He stood for a moment watching her looking at his nude virile body.

Her gaze ran from his face down over the bulky chest, huge arms, over the taut abs, his flat belly, and down to his manhood that was long and thick and hard as iron. His hand went to it, he fisted it, and Casie blanched, her gaze shot up to his face.

"I won't hurt you, baby, I promise," his voice hissed like low rough velvet. The blue eyes darkened to the purest night sky, he moved the couple of feet to the bed and set one knee on the mattress.

Her eyes on his raging hard-on, Casie drew her legs up protectively and her arms crossed over her breasts.

"Shh," he whispered like gentling a frightened animal. "It'll be all right, honey, it will be good, trust me." He moved onto the bed, the mattress sinking with his weight.

She flinched when he grasped her ankle but didn't resist when he pulled it down, then the other and pushed her legs apart.

He knelt between her legs and slid his hands from her knees up her thighs to her woman's cleft. Her legs shuddered at his touch, he held her thighs to keep her from closing her legs.

"Casie," he said quietly, her eyes were scrunched tightly closed. "Look at me baby, give me all of you, your body, your trust, your...love." His voice so poignant and richly sensual it drew her lids up and her eyes pierced his.

"That's it, baby, stay with me." He drew his fingers with long sinuous strokes over her nether lips, fluttering along her soft wet slit. When her body relaxed, he prodded her legs further apart, brushed her clit and pushed a finger inside her, then another.

It was as difficult as before, she was so tight Neco could be pretty sure she had not been with another man. Absurd pride and love overwhelmed him. She was his, wholly.

When her soft body started trembling and her hips urged up to meet his hand, Neco moved to kneel up closer between her legs. When he stopped touching her, her gaze drifted down with apprehension.

He had taken a condom off his dresser and now opened it and rolled it down the long hard magnitude of him.

Her eyes wide and wildly apprehensive at the size and the steel hardness of his manhood, she shifted her body up, away from him.

Neco grasped her hips, wrapping his fingers around them to hold her immobile, then he lowered his body and positioned himself between her thighs. When he pressed the softer round tip of his shaft against her opening, in a sudden panic she struggled to move from him.

"Baby, relax, look at me." Holding his throbbing organ, he rubbed it gently against her tender vulva until her eyes met his and her female sex moved rhythmically against him.

Her puffy lips parted, lids lowered, she kept her eyes on him as he carefully nudged inside her.

"Neco," her face stiffened along with the rest of her body. "You- you're…big."

He let out a short chuckle. "I know." He pushed in an inch further. "I'll go slow baby, so your body can adapt, stretch to take me. I hurt you, you tell me. Okay?" His hand stroked tenderly through her hair.

Casie's, "Okay," came out in a breath. She labored to relax as he worked his way inside her.

He stopped halfway in and lowered to his elbows so their faces were close. Bracing himself his biceps bulged, he asked quietly, "You okay, Casie?"

Now he knew why he always chose big and bawdy women, he could be as rough and hard and fast as he wanted and get what he wanted quickly and move on. With Casie, he brushed his fingertips down her face, he had to take care. She was so tight and dainty and soft, and he wanted to be inside her forever.

The weak smile loosened the nervous planes in her face. "Yes. I feel, I mean, filled, you are filling my…body, oh!" She felt him throb against her tender inside walls, her sheath squeezed him and he groaned, almost losing it.

His laugh a deep rumble in his chest, he said, "Ah, baby, you feel amazing, incredible, I'll never get enough of you." He pushed slowly, drew back a little to gather her natural lube then forward, still not reaching the end of her.

Curving over her, he kissed her. Seizing her mouth, his lips and tongue canvassed over the tops of her lips, then under them, ransacking her inner cove of sweet sugar, taking her with him in searing spiraling flight.

Neco's heart thundered with lust and love and feeling at home. He pushed his engorged shaft until he was embedded all the way inside her glossy tight passage.

Pausing to slow his racing pulse, Neco palmed her breast, feeling it firm and swell in his hand. As her heartbeat accelerated, her nipple pebbled between his fingers before he sank his tongue deep in her mouth chasing her tongue, and sculpted her lush globe between his strong fingers.

Casie's whimpered purl strummed into his mouth, her breath hitched, he could feel her heart pounding against his hand.

He slowly drew almost all the way out before pushing slowly back in.

They moaned together as his man's root thrummed and her sheath gripped him, pulsing all around his hard flesh. The third time he moved out then back in was easier, smoother, her silk lubricating them like warm cream.

Watching the way his biceps bulged and flexed with his movements, Casie curled her hands over them to feel the play of muscles. "You are so strong, Neco, *uh*," a soft grunt gasped out when he pushed more quickly, and suddenly harder into her.

"Yeah?" His hair flopped over his eyes. He grinned at her, then he arched back from her as he plunged deeper into her channel in a serpentine thrust that raked friction over every sliver of her clitoris, rebounding hard over sweet spots all the way up her sheath.

It was tantalizing, electrifying, and it tore a scream from her lips.

"Neco!" Spurting hisses panted through her clenched teeth and intense shudders shook Casie to the core.

When he did it again and again, like rapid fire thrusting deeper, driving harder each time, his raw growls coiled with her breathy wails that tunneled through her constricted throat before breaking into spastic cries as he continued his assailing frenzy.

He wrapped his arms around her shoulders to keep her from getting shoved away from him with his violent thrusting. His primal blitz escalated, with unrestrained prowess firing through his veins, deeper animal growls and harsh grunts caged in his chest, Neco wildly, repeatedly penetrated her woman's slit.

His power unleashed, his driving so hard into her stung visceral sparks inside Casie's brain, obliterating her conscious thoughts, she was pure feeling. Pure flying sensation.

She would be afraid of the intensity of the feelings, and of his strength, if he hadn't brought her into such a mindless tempest of splendor. Her brain buzzed, she couldn't think, only feel. Her body bucked up to collide with his, meeting his thundering rhythm.

His brain a vortex of acute stimulus, Neco had never felt such extreme sensations. He struggled to get a grip on his control. He couldn't hurt her, she was too delicate, too precious. With supreme effort, he slowed, moved so languorously it was almost as exquisitely exhilarating as his savage driving into her.

Breaths shallow and rapid, Neco's chest billowed into her soft femininity. He cupped the sides of her head, smoothing damp hair off her face.

Through the sweat dripping from his bangs, a keen smile broke his fierce concentration seeing her lids were flipping over eyes drugged with profound passion, her breathing as tumultuous as his.

"Baby," he whispered, stroking her hair back, watching her lashes flutter over flushed cheeks as she heard his voice. Her eyes opened a slit to gleam misty up at him.

"Casie, you okay? I," he brushed her panting lips with his. "I don't want to hurt you, do I need to lighten up? Stop? Tell me, honey."

He stroked her hair, touched her lips with his thumb. His smile loving and soft, heat burned between their naked skin. He continued moving rhythmically, languidly in and out of her, his smile deepened feeling her little hips match his every thrust.

A beauteous tremulous smile broke over her face damp with perspiration. She caressed his face rough with faint evening stubble and sweat. "I'm fine, Neco. I didn't know it was possible to experience such...phenomenal feelings before, don't stop, don't t- *uh-*"

Before she got the last word out, he shot into her, hard and fast and furious with desire.

"Okay, baby," he panted coarsely, "hang on, I'm taking us home, stay with me-"

Her voice full and hushed, her hands clutching his shoulders as he jolted her body with every plunge. Between grunts he punched out of her, she spurted huskily, "I love you, Neco."

That broke him. Huffing, "Oh God, baby," he reared back, teeth grit and jaw locked, his hooded eyes voltaic with vicious heat. "Look at me," he commanded hoarsely, tense with his release building like rocket fuel. "Come with me, baby."

Her eyes cracked open, trusting, loving, connecting with his. She gripped his shoulders, bucking her hips up to his as he charged at her so hard she couldn't stop the moans he forced out with every surge he drove into her.

Neco felt like he was bludgeoning his beloved with his iron club, but her moans of pleasure drove him on. He thrust faster, deeper, snapping his hips at hers.

He could hear the rasping screams of pleasure building in her chest, her body turning rigid. Their eyes still locked but Casie's were going blank as the tidal wave of pleasure overrode her, taking her crashing against the shore.

Wailing, "Neco!" Clinging to him, she sobbed, her eyes wide with excruciating wonder. "Like shooting stars! I see, feel- a- a-

barrage of shooting stars…" A massive shudder took her over. Her voice eked out as she went over the crest, convulsing with inaudible cries in Neco's arms.

Feeling her carried away with her climax, her channel seizing his shaft, trussing it with creamy silk and clutching again and again in tighter and tighter contractions, Neco let go.

He surged into her with a riot of powerful thrusts, bestial sounds forced from his chest. The sensations striking his body beyond mind-blowing bliss as he headed to his release.

Rising up, his arms straight and rigid, body straining with the agony of the explosive burn roiling up his cock, he suspended himself, momentarily buried deep within her, feeling his male organ swollen and throbbing against her tender sheath.

Then, he let it wash over him, dropping down, his body slamming and grinding so hard against her, he shot like a cannon firing his seed, feeling the burst all the way from his balls and up his shaft. His roar of release muffled with his face burrowed in Casie's neck.

He was breathing so hard he thought he was going to die. Didn't matter, Neco collapsed on Casie, he was already in heaven. His chest pumped hard against her soft woman's body.

Growling and groaning against her neck, he forced himself to roll slightly to the side of her, but stayed inside her with his arm and leg thrown over her trembling body.

It took a long time for Neco to come back down to earth where he could pull together a coherent thought, and his racing heart and heaving breathing slowed.

Casie strung her arms around his neck, he had buried his face in her hair. She could feel his heart banging out of his chest into hers. His body was covered in a sheen of sweat and the hair around his face was damp.

She held onto him tightly, feeling tremors and small jerks still rolling around his body. He was warm and big and all encompassing, she felt warm and protected, satiated, and loved.

"Neco," she murmured, stroking his hair. In between hugging him, she drew her fingers through his thick waves. He didn't move. His incoherent mumble in her hair made her giggle.

Gathering his wits and waning energy, Neco rolled onto his back, pulling out of her.

With a gruff groan he shifted to the side of the bed and rolled off it barely staying on his feet and trudged to the bathroom. He was gone a few minutes.

When he came back with a wet cloth in his hand, his hair was damper and combed back, and his breathing had returned to normal.

His smile grew huge at her lying on the bed waiting for him with her own sated little grin. As he approached the bed, he watched her studying his body with peaked interest. He slid onto the bed and pulled her into his arms.

With her curled against him, he cleaned her with the cloth then dropped it on the floor, and drew the covers over them. Caressing her face, Neco lifted her chin to kiss her. He couldn't help smiling with his lips on her mouth.

Casie pulled back, her hand on the side of his face. She asked, "What are you grinning at, Neco?"

His gaze roamed all over her face like he was memorizing her features, but he didn't have to, he already had. He held both arms around her.

"Just, I..." He kissed her again, his smile broadened. "I had hoped we would get here, to this, to this point. I was so afraid we wouldn't. I'm just," he sighed, hugged her tight, her arm slid around his waist. "So happy baby, so blessed."

She nodded, her head brushing up and down on his shoulder. "Me too. I'm glad you kept pushing through my defenses, Neco. We will do as you said, take each day as it comes and deal with whatever happens, together."

Smoothing her hair off her face, his eyes glowing with his feelings, he said, "Baby, Casie, I love you."

She tilted her head up to kiss him, whispered, "I love you, Neco."

Squeezing her against him, feeling her lush breasts pressing into his chest Neco said, "Good. Because as soon as we can clear up your history, and we will, we are getting married."

Her laugh puffed the hair at his neck. "Are you telling me, or asking me?"

His arms tightened. "Doesn't matter, as long as we get there." This time he took her on a long, heady, savory kiss.

His already hardening erection pressed against her. "Uh, Neco," she asked with a sultry quiver, "how soon can we do it again?"

Chuckling into her hair, he combed her tresses with his fingers, and replied, "We need to wait a bit, baby. I could tell, ah, well, you were so small, so tight, you are going to be sore. And I'm not going to do anything that hurts you or puts you off from making love with me because we didn't wait a few hours for you to be okay."

He ran his finger down her nose and smiled. "But I'm glad you want to do it again."

Snuggling into him, she said with a yawn, "Oh, I do. Can't..." yawn, "wait."

As sleep overtook her, she murmured, "And...other stuff...I want to touch you, Neco...all of you..." Her voice trailed off, "And lick you like you did...me...all over..."

His erection already pulsing against his belly, Neco tucked the covers in around them then cuddled her tight in his embrace.

The smile on his face was still there as he fell into sleep.

Chapter Twenty-Nine

He held off until morning then he dragged her into the shower.

Amongst the soap and steam and her giggles they made love.

And after breakfast they christened the kitchen table before they managed to get out the door.

Neco had some errands to run.

They spent an hour in the center of town before heading back home. One hand on the wheel, Neco stretched the other one to reach for her hand.

When they twined fingers, he smiled over at her.

Casie's head was resting on the back of the seat, but she was facing him. Her own fetching smile intimated she clearly adored him.

His timbre deep, contented, Neco said with a slight squeeze of her hand, "I love you, baby. In only these couple of months I realize I could never live without you. You know that, right?"

Her head nodded against the seat cushion. She had wanted to sit in the seat next to him but he knew he wouldn't be able to concentrate on driving with her hot little body so close.

"So, um," still shy, her voice soft and only faintly audible. "You, uh, said I can you know, do the stuff to you that you, uh," her face glistened with a flush of pink, "did to me."

Feeling the heat rise up his neck and his shaft harden, "Oh yeah?" he teased. "Like what?" She looked so serious as she was considering what she wanted to do to him, Neco about burst with love, she was so damned adorable. And she was his. Forever.

"Well, first, I'd like to take my, time touching you, all over, everywhere." Her eyes lowered with her shyness, the pink in her cheeks darkened, and the green in her eyes smoldered with anticipation.

"Then, I'd like to…" her entire face was red, her gaze dipped down to his jeans then she peered up through her long lashes. "Taste you. You know, like below…"

One brow arched in amusement. His pants continued growing tighter, he teased, "Below?"

Her head ducked as she nodded. "Um, yes, your…" Unable to push the word out of her embarrassed lips, she leaned over instead and gripped his swelling dick through his pants.

He yelped, "Shit, Casie!" The truck veered, he had to struggle to get it back straight on the road.

"Baby," he huffed, lifting her wrist off him. "You need to save it for when we get home. I told you I can't concentrate on driving with any part of you on me, or vice versa. However," he wiggled his brows at her with a cocky grin, "remember where you left off as soon as we clear the front door, okay?"

Her head bobbing cheerfully, she agreed, "Don't worry, I will."

He glanced quickly at her, his face suffused with his deep feeling for her lighting his eyes. "I love you, Casie. I can't wait until we get home, baby, and get my angel naked so we-"

BLAM!

Neco just caught a glimpse of the huge black truck that smashed into the side of them before his truck spun.

The airbags burst, Casie screamed, and they slammed into a tree.

His head bashing on the side of the door knocked Neco out cold.

"*Ahh*," Neco groaned. His aching head whirled with jolts of red and flashes of white. He couldn't get his eyes open. Struggling to push out of the tunnel of blackness and pain, he put his hand to his throbbing head, and felt something wet on his hand.

Finally managing to pry open one swollen lid, he peered through the slit at his hand. It had blood on it. *What the fuck-*

His dizzy brain wincing in confusion, he rubbed at his eyes to clear the disorientation.

Then he remembered- the black truck slamming into them- deliberately- Casie-

He swung his head. Pain shot through it, he looked to the passenger side of the truck. The airbag had blown, the door was wide open, the seat was empty. Smoke spiraled around and up from the still running vehicle.

Casie was gone.

Neco felt a vice squeezing his heart so hard, he couldn't draw a breath through his panicking lungs. Turning the engine off, he realized the door had crushed in against him, trapping him. He couldn't get out.

Trying to keep calm, he fumbled his phone out of his pocket, swiped and pushed a button.

"Yeah, bro, wattsup?" Josh answered.

His head pounded so hard he could barely think. Blood slid down from his temple, his voice slurred, "I need you."

The tone in Josh's voice narrowed, he said quickly, "Neco, man, you're not fucking drunk are you? You break up with-"

Neco didn't know if he was going to pass out again, his breath threw the words out in a rough gush, "I'm in my truck, trapped, we were hit, they took Casie."

As serious as a heart attack, Josh said, "What street are you on? I'll call 911 while on my way there now."

Neco could hear burning rubber through the phone. "No, don't call the medics," he gasped for air, the fingers holding his cell were covering it in blood.

"Just get here, Provence Ave, call Logan and Chaz," he gasped another wheezing breath, "might need them. Lo bring his computer, bring fire…power…"

He didn't hear his brother's response, the phone slid from his fingers as he blacked out.

He didn't know how long he'd been out. The blinding pain in his head pulsed. Neco could hear his brother's voice, and a grinding noise, metal on metal. He cracked an eye.

Josh had a crowbar shoved into the side of the truck trying to pry it apart.

Logan was climbing in the passenger side, he said, "Just get it open enough Josh, to release his legs so I can pull him out."

"Hey," Neco groaned roughly, "nice of you to drop by, Lo." His face scrunched in pain, the side of his face was leaking blood.

"Geez, bro, you look like hell. Josh said you didn't want the EMTs, but I think we need to call-"

Neco cut him off, "No. Just get me out. I need to find Casie."

A screech of metal and Josh got the driver's door open just enough that Neco's trapped legs were freed. Logan grabbed Neco around his chest and pulled him towards the passenger door.

Both men grunting, Neco groaning, it was a struggle, but when Neco got to the edge and Logan hopped out, their other brother Chaz was there. The brothers shoved their shoulders under Neco's arms to hold him up.

They started dragging him away when Neco said, "Wait." He bent with a painful wince back inside the truck, reached in and grabbed the keys then opened the glove box.

Thank God, except for bruising it appeared his legs were okay. They weren't broken and he wasn't paralyzed as he had at first feared from the door crushing in on him enough he'd been trapped.

Removing a gun, he stuffed it in the back of his jeans. His brothers went to help him walk, but he shrugged them off, staggered a few steps before walking with surer steps to Josh's truck.

"Hey," Josh tossed the crowbar into the back of his truck and hurried to his brother. "Shit, Nek, you need to go to the hospital."

Neco shoved past him and climbed into Josh's truck. He sat on the passenger side with his legs out the door and asked Josh, "You got something I can clean off this blood?" He said to Logan, "You bring your computer?"

The three brothers stood staring at Neco like he'd lost his mind.

He had a big gouge down the side of his temple that was still bleeding, his hair was a wreck, blood on his clothes, burn marks on his face from the airbag.

"Neco, you need-"

Neco spoke over their youngest brother Chaz, "Josh, I need something to wipe off this blood." To Logan, he said, "Lo, power the fucker up."

The brothers still stood gawking at him.

"Now goddammit!" he shouted, hurting his head. Dragging a hand down his face, Neco took a heavy breath. "We were hit on purpose. It was done deliberately to take Casie. Probably the guy who tried to rape, maybe did rape her, beat her, and maybe the guy she saw murder a woman."

He glanced around at the shocked expressions on his brothers' faces. "Get me a fucking towel, get the fucking computer up, and get us the fuck out of here."

Josh was the first to blink and stir. "Yeah, okay, here," he ran to the back of his truck, rummaged a second then pulled out a cloth and a homemade first aid kit.

He handed the cloth to Neco, then opened the kit and took out alcohol wipes and dabbed at his brother's bloody face.

"All right," his computer under his arm, Logan trod over to them with Chaz at his heels. "What do you want the laptop for?"

Wincing at the swipes of alcohol on his open cut, Neco said, "We were hit on purpose. I need to get some video of the vehicle so I can track it."

"Uh," Logan stretched his neck and looked all around them. "You took a hit to the head, Neco, look around. This is one long rural road. There's not a car for miles and the closest house is way down the road. There aren't any cameras here."

"Ow, shit, Josh," Neco cursed ducking his head.

"Sorry," his grin showed he really wasn't, then the grin straightened. "Seriously, Nek, what is going on?"

Neco pushed him away. "What's going on, is some killer took Casie and I need to find her before he…assaults her, fucking beats her again, and likely kills her."

He motioned with his head up the street and said, "There are no cameras here, but at the main junction miles up the road there is a bank, a bar, gas stations, and a few other places at the intersection.

"The only way to get to here is through there. I know what the vehicle looks like that hit us. Can't be too many huge black trucks passing by there today, on the way to this out of the way location."

The brothers stared at him, all three thinking, listening, suddenly intent on what he was saying and what to do to help him.

"I need you to hack around and find those cameras," he said to Logan.

Logan didn't hesitate. He set his laptop on the hood of the truck and started pounding the keys.

Ordering, "Everyone get in," Neco slid all the way inside Josh's truck, "we can head to town while Logan surfs. Chaz, call a couple of friends to come get your and Logan's trucks and a tow for mine."

The brothers hustled in.

Chaz got in the back pulling out his phone. Carrying his computer, Logan didn't pause tapping at the keys as he slid in beside him.

Josh hopped in the driver's side and had the truck moving before the door was closed.

Chapter Thirty

$\mathcal{C}$asie's head was fuzzy, filled with cotton, her ears roared with the echo of a loud bang, and murmuring voices.

She rolled her head back and forth, knives of pain stabbed in it. She tried to open her eyes, but couldn't. It felt like they were made of lead, so heavy as if glued shut.

She went to rub her aching head with her hand, but she couldn't move her hand.

Fighting through the cloud that permeated her brain, feeling so sluggish and weak it felt like she had been drugged, Casie tried to move the other hand. She couldn't move it.

What- her legs, she pulled at them, they were also immobile.

She started thrashing her limbs, cries buried in her throat rose in frightening fragments as she became aware that she was restrained. Her wrists and ankles were tied to something.

"Finally, my little princess, you are finally awake."

She froze.

That voice. It was hauntingly familiar. It crawled icy fingers up her spine, goose bumps of terror popped all over her skin.

Underneath her, Casie could feel softness, a thick cushioning. A pillow cradled her head. Struggling to push against the thick molasses that her lids felt like, she nicked them open.

Without moving her head, she could see down her body, and the terror shot up tenfold from her bare toes to her head. She was lying on her back on a bed.

Soft sheets ruffled around her, and she was wearing, *oh my gosh*, make that barely wearing, some kind of brief nightgown. It was mostly sheer chiffon with pale burgundy satin bows at the bodice, which was currently spread open exposing much of her breasts. The bottom of the chemise only fell to her belly button.

Her face flushed, her areoles were faintly visible in the mostly transparent fabric. Her panicking gaze moved further down and her stomach clenched. The only other thing she was wearing was a strip of sheer panties that just barely covered her sex.

"Ah, I see that you like my choice of lingerie. But don't worry, I didn't dress you, my pet, your Aunt Dimitria did that. She knew I would like to view my present for a while before completely unwrapping it."

Even as the man spoke sending her brain into terrified overload, Casie tried to think back. They were driving- yes, she and Neco were in the truck headed home, then- she blinked and it hurt.

Right, there'd been a terrible crash. They'd been hit. She remembered the horrifying ramming as her body jolted, mercifully, the seatbelt kept her inside the vehicle.

Her skin withered against her frame as she remembered the men reaching in and hauling her out.

She screamed for Neco, but he was out cold, or dead, in the truck. She only caught a glimpse of him slumped over, his head bloody as they carried her away.

Her screams begging them to let her go to him, to help him, cut her throat raw. They must have drugged her because she can't remember anything after that.

Casie could feel her burning throat tightening, her heart hammered against her ribs sending her pulse racing. Her panicked breathing showed in her breasts rising and falling in rapid paroxysms.

She turned her head, her eyes flew up to the man standing over her, staring down at her. His mouth was wide with treacherous glee, and blinding lust glowed down her body from his carnivorous dark eyes.

Her mouth convulsed open and closed. Her throat so hoarse, her utter was a breathy rasp, "U- Uncle Vito-" A flash of pure terror rode her body as her full memory suddenly returned with a hideous blast.

The smile settled into a predatory grin that blighted his handsome maestro's face.

In a fine black suit, a perfect match to his slicked back, black hair, Vittorio Pryce indeed looked like he should be conducting an orchestra, elegantly waving a baton. His face tilted and raised in arrogant pageantry as if a spotlight shined on it.

He leaned over the bed and picked up pieces of Casie's hair. "Ah, my sweet precious Summer, have you missed me?" He slid his fingers down the length of her hair, tugging it painfully as he went.

Casie jerked her head away from his hand. Her lungs filled with dreaded fright. She remembered. Oh God, she remembered everything. Her life. She was Summer, Summer DelRay, not...Casie. Neco's Casie. *Oh my gosh, Neco-*

"The man in the truck," she rasped, taking a wheezing breath in between words, "with me. How is he, is he okay?" She hated that she sounded pleading and weak, but she feared for Neco's life.

A frown pulled Vito's black raven's brows down between his dark eyes. "There will be no talk of another man, my dear. *I* am the only man that will ever be in your life from now on."

"But- but- please, Uncle Vito, I need to know, please tell me!"

Vito said flatly, "He is dead." He didn't really know, but he didn't want her to have any hopes that the guy would come for her.

He suddenly stuck his hand in her hair and viciously gripped it, sharply jerked her to face him.

Leaning over, he moved his face near hers and snarled, "He may have fucked you, my princess, but you are back here where you belong. You will soon forget about him when we..." the corners of his lips tipped up in points, "play."

A voice on the other side of her sneered, "She made quite an impression out there, Mr. Pryce."

Casie tried to turn her head to look at Don Demelien leaning a shoulder against the wall leering at her, but Vito kept his fist in her hair, holding her stationary.

A frisson of even deeper fear sliced up her back. Where Don Demelien was, the brute Harry Fletcher must be nearby.

Don snickered and crossed the room to stand on the other side of the bed. He looked down at her.

Casie's eyes slew sideways up at him. Her palpable terror made his dick harden. The man loved when people, especially vulnerable women feared him.

He nodded. "Yeah, there are a few people out there hating on you, babe. In particular, two broads; a waitress and the manager at that strip joint you worked in."

His voice sharp, Pryce snapped, "Strip joint?"

Nodding again, Don didn't take his eyes off Casie. His brazen stare rolled continuously up and down her body, pausing at her breasts almost completely visible in the sheer lingerie, and her sex in the tiny transparent panties, then his eyes continued their roving again up and down.

"No such luck that she was a dancer, sir, your niece was just a barmaid. That's how we found her. First the bitch at the diner pointed us to the strip club."

The side of his face creased in a leer. Sick glee in his voice, Don said, "I met up with the waitress earlier while you were waiting for this one to wake up. And Harry," his chuckle was hideously sadistic, "yeah, our boy got the manager at the King's Palace, Sasha I think her name was.

"Don't worry," he said quickly with a nasty grin, "after we were done with them, it'll be awhile before their bodies turn up. They won't be telling anyone about us, or you."

Vito snapped annoyed, "Whatever." He shook his fist jerking Casie's head back and forth, smiling when she flinched.

"That's it, princess, you and I, it's only us now. Though, I think your aunt and Don want to watch. As his reward for finding you, Harry will be up in a minute too. I told him he had first rights after I'm done. Isn't that right, Dimi?"

Casie's face turned white, her eyes flashed from Vito to her Aunt Dimi standing behind him.

Dimi crossed her arms over her chest, the crisp fabric scraping together with her movements. She fittingly wore her regular spider-black. A satin dress with a full skirt, black heels, the noir hair twisted up in a tight chignon.

"Aunt- Aunt Dimi! Please, you can't let-"

Vito shook her head violently, ordering, "Shut up. You've caused enough trouble. I will teach you how to behave. Believe me, you will learn, quickly."

He moved his face close to hers again. "It's amazing how quickly people learn to obey commands when there's pain involved." Casie's rising terror ignited an avaricious flame in his dark eyes.

"Your severest punishment will have to wait a few days, enough for you to heel. The accident has bruised not only your cheek, but also elsewhere so Dimi tells me. Already injured, you won't be able to tolerate as much punishment as I plan on meting out to you."

His grin curved up so tight it was like a rigid curved line, then he widened it exposing sharp incisors. "And I want you to last as long as possible. However, right now you're getting a lashing taste of what's to come."

"Aunt Dimi, help me!" Casie cried.

Dimitria's black eyes glittered across the room at her niece, by marriage, not by blood. She stood like a crow statue, silent, only salacious interest gleamed in her dark irises. Her coarse gaze traveled as Don's had, pausing at Casie's breasts and between her legs.

Casie couldn't help but shiver at her lewd perusal. The shiver made her aware of the pain in her breasts. Her uncle still grasped her hair, she lowered her eyes.

Looking down, she could see bruises of fingerprints on her pale mounds, and a bite mark on an exposed swell of one breast. Her mouth dropped, her eyes shot up to her uncle in dismay. "You- you- bit me?"

Vito just smiled at her.

"You bit me like an animal? You filthy-"

He pressed his fingers over her mouth to shush her. "Hush now, princess, it won't be the last time, so save your fury. I had to do something to appease myself while waiting for you to awaken." Vito soothed, and released her hair, then he brushed tendrils off her face.

"I have already waited too long. A lifetime, well your lifetime, I must have you now." He glanced at Don and said, "Bring me my crop."

An excited obscene smirk lifted Don's thin lips. He pivoted, hurried to a dresser in the huge bedroom, snatched something off it and scurried over to Vito and handed it to him.

Then he returned to his place on the opposite side of the bed, and smoothed his blond hair back with his sweating palms before dropping his hands to hang at his side.

Vito slipped his suit jacket off, folded it then neatly laid it over a chair. Then he untied his tie and slid it from around his neck and set it on the jacket.

Casie's wide green eyes watched his every move.

Her fear excited Vito, even more than it did Don. Vito lived for the terror of others, especially his lovely niece. He walked to the end of the bed, and set his hands on the mattress.

He stared up at Casie from the V of her legs, then climbed onto the bed on all fours, up to between Casie's thighs. The bed dipped and shook as he crawled closer to her.

She could now see what was in his hand. Her heart skipped a beat, a riding crop. As much as she tried, she couldn't keep the terror out of her eyes. "No, Uncle Vito, please!"

She struggled against her restraints, but it only caused her breasts to jiggle and the sheer material shifted, exposing more of her bosom's flesh, and kept the observers' eyes glued there

Vito inched up and knelt between her bound, spread legs. "Ah, God, Summer, I've waited since you were a small child for this. You have no idea, how I've dreamed, how many women suffered for what I wanted to do to you. Finally now," he sighed loud and deep with satisfaction.

Casie's gaze fell to his crotch, if possible, she blanched further. His lengthened erection pressed against his black slacks. He was getting excited because he was about to whip and sexually assault her.

She couldn't control the quaking that shook her entire body. She knew it would do no good to beg, her fear and pleading only turned him on more.

Her eyes flit to Don then Dimi, who were watching, their stares hard and unblinking, tongues licking their dry lips, and it apparently turned those sick freaks on too.

As scared as she was, Casie's mind was crying for Neco. She prayed he was all right, that he wasn't too seriously injured in the crash.

A thought struck her, she hoped Harry and Don hadn't...harmed him. The savage pair were as capable of sadistic brutality, and murder, as her uncle.

The riding crop made a whipping sound before it slashed across Casie's breast, she screamed as her body jolted off the bed. The restraints held her down. Her body contorted in burning agony.

Chest pumping with harsh breaths, she cried, "You are a vile, depraved- *iee-*" screams wrenched from her throat, her spine recoiled as he brought the crop down across her bare belly.

Vito laughed down at her like a maniac. "Are you having fun yet, princess?"

Hard little sounds heaved in her chest as she gasped for air and relief from the stinging burning pain. She couldn't prevent the tears from streaming. Hiccupping sobs jerked from her throat as she cried, "You- you're a demon, a demented maniac." Casie turned her head away from him.

Vito moved closer to her, the mattress shifted under his weight, his knees pushed against her spread thighs. His licentious eyes high as if intoxicated, seething with warped eroticism, stared down at her sex covered only by a sheer strip of chiffon.

"Look at me, Summer, watch the raging lust on my face while I fuck you as I've always longed to," he growled fiercely at her. Nudging her thigh with his knee, he jabbed the end of his crop against her ribs.

Casie kept her face turned from him. Her body shook with hysterical fear and pain, and unhinging anger that pooled in her stomach. Through choking sobs, she murmured, "You're a deviant, disgusting pig."

"Now, now, princess, that's no way to talk to your loving uncle, your soon to be husband. Your dear uncle that is honoring you with marriage. That is after I reward Harry and Don with you, then you're back to me, forever, my little darling girl."

Her eyes drowning in tears sprang to him. "What?"

He nodded, harshly prodding the crop's handle against her ribs then to the underside of a breast. A smirk cut his face seeing her try to twist from the crop.

He pushed it making her soft globe joggle. "Yes, my dear. Marriage. It's always been my fantasy. You and I, we will be married so I can keep you for as long as I desire." He moved the butt of the crop to bump, then rub over her sex.

Spewing hate at him from her green eyes, Casie spat, "I would never marry you, you vile lunatic, never!" She turned her face from him.

Vito glanced at Don and told him, "Hold her head. I want her looking at me while I show my lovely niece what sexual domination means." His gaze returned to Casie squirming under him.

Don leaned over and put his hand on her neck to hold her, his fingers encasing her chin, forcing her to face Vito.

Leaning closer to her, Don whispered in her ear, "I get you when he's done, bitch. You think he's sick, you ain't seen nothin' yet. I got toys to keep you juiced too, baby. Ya ever heard of the horse bench?" His fingers gripped tightly around her slender neck.

When Casie was glaring at her depraved uncle, forced to look at him, Vito released a smug smile, and suddenly snapped the whip to slash across her sex.

He drank in the shriek of agony that tore from her lips as her body bucked on the bed.

Casie's chest blew rapidly in and out. Her stomach contracting, tears poured down her face, she could feel the wetness of them as they slid into her ears. Her sex screamed with burning pain.

Aunt Dimi stood silently behind Vito, not a muscle moved. Her cheeks flushed and her pupils dilated at every lash her brother struck at Casie.

Holding the whip in one hand, Vito's other hand went to his belt.

Delighting in the new frantic shift in Casie's horrified eyes, he crowed, "I'm tired of waiting for you, princess. I bet you've never been whipped and fucked at the same time, am I right?" The terror that flashed across her face was satisfaction enough for him.

Casie struggled in renewed hysteria, she pulled and yanked at her restraints, jerked her legs, twisted and bucked her hips, but she was securely bound.

Through sobbing, grinding teeth, she swore, "You will have to kill me, Uncle, because the second I can, I will either get away, or kill myself. Or you." Her eyes tapered tightly at him. Sniffing, and gulping, she said, "I will never be with you, never."

"Shut up, bitch." Don shook her with his fingers digging around her neck, cutting off her air and making more bruises.

"It's all right, Don, I love the threats and the fear, even her little temper turns me on, it's so cute." While talking, still on his knees between her legs, Vito tugged his belt loose and unbuttoned his pants.

While he pulled the zipper down, he stroked the whip across her heaving plump breasts that rose and fell hard and fast with her panic, pushing the sides of the chemise further apart. The only part of her that was still covered was her nipples.

They puckered from her pain and fear, poking straight through the transparent material.

Casie struggled, squirming, jerking at the ties, screamed, "Let me go you animal!" She shrieked as the whip came down across her sex again, bucked and screamed as it struck her breasts. Gasping, sobbing, she cried out in agony.

"Never, my pet, never," Vito ground through clenched teeth. His face hardened and turned serious as he reached in his pants, wrapped his hand around his cock and pulled it out. "Tonight you and I mate. Afterwards you'll tell me where you hid the phone."

Casie screeched at him, "Go to hell you monster! You're nothing but a coward!"

She'd finally said something to piss him off. No one calls Vittorio Pryce a coward, no one. Especially in front of others.

He snarled at Don, "Give me your knife, I need to cut off her panties." He had leaned over her too far, Casie dug her nails into his arm and scraped it as hard as she could.

"You bitch!" Vito howled and slapped her. Even as he grasped the top of her panties he slapped her again and again. Then in a fury, he struck her body with the handle of the riding crop.

Casie screamed and screamed…and screamed, and he struck and struck and ripped at her panties as he raged at her while stroking his bulging distended cock.

Chapter Thirty-One

Logan located several video security cameras around the intersection that the truck had to pass through to get to Neco's street.

The brothers went to the convenience store first. Chaz peeked inside the window. There was one clerk.

A young teen whose head was bowed over the phone he was tapping on. The streets were fairly empty.

Chaz said, "It's clear."

Josh, Logan and Chaz kept watch as Neco stood on the truck to get onto a side window ledge and took the camera down. They did the same thing at two other locations.

Taking the cameras, they removed the chips and put them in the laptop then quickly scanned the videos until Neco said, "There. Run it back."

Logan made it go slowly in reverse. "Stop. There," Neco pointed. "The black truck. Find a pic of his tags."

They had to view another video to get a close-up of the license plate.

As soon as they got a clear picture, Logan hacked into the DMV system to run the plate. "The truck belongs to," he ran his finger over the screen. "A Vittorio Pryce. It shows he owns a fleet of them. Do you recognize the name, Nek?"

Neco shook his head. "No. Let's go, we'll GPS the address."

The four men jogged quickly back to Josh's truck, and Josh peeled out and down the street heading for another town, Chesire.

It took so long to get there, Neco was barely keeping a lid on his racing heart.

Josh finally turned down Lambruster Avenue. It was a sparsely populated street. Each house was huge, more like estates that dotted far apart down the avenue.

Most homes had security gates, and when they reached 1100 Lambruster Avenue, they saw it too was surrounded by an iron security gate.

Chaz piled out of the back seat and ran to the gate. He pulled tools out of his pocket and in seconds the gate swung open. He raced back and hopped back into the truck.

Josh drove slowly up the driveway so they could scope it, try to figure how many people were there. Numerous cars were parked all up the drive.

That didn't bode well for a quick and easy in and out. Josh parked on the side of another truck to block his from view.

"Nek, we need to recon-" Josh broke off as his brother grabbed something out of the tool box then sprinted to the building. Josh's voice low, he called out, "Nek, man, wait!"

The three brothers ran up to flank Neco. They stopped when they reached the front entrance.

"Come on, Nek, really? You want to just freakin' barge in the front door? There may be men and guns inside," Josh tried to reason with him. "We need to check the place out first, form a plan."

"I'm going in. Now. If she's inside she may be hurt, or…" He couldn't get the word 'dead' past his lips. "You guys wait out here." He ran up the steps to the front door with an ax in his hands and struck the door handle twice and it came apart.

"Cheap door," Logan muttered as he and Josh and Chaz burst inside the house right behind Neco.

Just as they blew inside, a man walking through the vast foyer stopped and gawked in shock at them.

"Hey," he said, "what the fuck are you doing?" He pulled a gun out of a holster, but before he could get it completely out and aimed, Josh had vaulted towards him and took him down. He punched him a few times and he was out.

Logan said to Neco, "Bro, dude's armed, there's likely more around. We need to be care-" He was talking to air.

Neco sprinted over to a counter that was filled with security monitors.

"Look," he said quietly when he reached them. The others joined him.

The area was filled with monitors that viewed a dozen or more rooms. The one that faced the outside, that should have shown the men arriving, was dark. Some lazy fool hadn't turned it on.

Harry Fletcher wandered in the room. By the time he noticed the men, Josh and Logan had grabbed him, and Josh put a gun to his head.

Josh warned him, "Be quiet or you're dead."

They hustled him over to where Neco was staring at the monitors.

Neco glanced briefly at the big bulky man with tiny brown eyes before turning right back to the monitors. Without preamble, he demanded, "Where is she?"

Harry opened his mouth to deny he knew what Neco was talking about but Chaz slammed his fist into his belly. Harry doubled over with a groan.

"We don't have time for games," Chaz said, pulling out a knife. He poked the blade into the man's groin and watched a green hue cover his florid face.

"Yeah," Chaz said, "you got it. First I'll cut off your dick then the rest of you piece by piece. We ain't the cops and don't have to play by any rules. Answer the man."

The husky man's eyes flit to Neco. "Ah," he hesitated and Chaz sliced his arm with the knife then jabbed it back into his groin this time stabbing into his flesh.

"*Aggh*, what the hell!" Harry shrieked trying to twist from the brothers' hold.

"Talk," Chaz commanded. "Where is the girl, you have one chance only."

"Fuck!" Neco burst out.

"What is it?" Josh asked. Releasing Harry, he moved next to Neco. He looked at the same monitor.

There was a black and white flickering picture of Casie tied to a bed with a man bent over her. The man was whipping her while a blond man and a dark haired woman watched.

They couldn't hear her, but they could see her writhing, her face contorted in pain and her mouth opened in an agonized scream.

Neco snaked his hands out and gripped Harry's neck. "Tell me, where is she?" He slugged the man and then violently shook his neck. "Tell me now!"

"Okay, okay, shit." Harry spat blood, sweat flung from his damp hair. "She deserves what she's getting' man, I'm supposed to get to help-"

Neco crushed his fingers around his neck. "You have half a second to tell me where she is then I snap your fat neck you sick prick."

Harry's eyes flicked around at each of the brothers then back to Neco. It suddenly dawned on him that this was the man who Summer must have been staying with.

He croaked, "I'll show you where she is," he couldn't move. Neco gripped his neck and Josh and Logan were holding his arms while Chaz had his knife poking more violently into his groin.

Tightening his hands, Neco growled, "You make one sound, one move, my brother here will gut you. I'd rather he didn't have to, you and me have some business to discuss later."

Neco's obsidian glare lanced right through the man. He had a feeling the bastard was involved in kidnapping Casie in the beginning, and likely the one who had beaten her.

Like lightning, he shot his fist out punching him in the nose, bones cracked and blood spurted with Harry's howl. Neco nodded to his brothers to move him.

Chaz tied Harry's hands behind his back as Josh and Logan pushed him to start walking. They went upstairs and were heading down a hall when a door opened and half a dozen men poured out.

"Shit," Chaz swore.

The brothers shoved Harry at the group of men as all of them hurtled at the brothers in attack. In seconds the hall was filled with grunts and groans and punches.

A woman's screams flooded down the hall.

Neco bashed a man in the jaw, he dropped like a sack of dirt and Neco raced to where the screams were coming from.

They were piercing, blood-curdling, Neco's own blood froze.

"Keep it together," he told himself as he raced to find which room the screams were originating from.

There were many closed doors along the corridor and the screams had stopped, along with Neco's heart. *Was she dead?* Another gut-wrenching scream pealed out.

Neco judged the door it was coming from.

He raced to it- jumped in the air and slammed into it crashing it open with his boots.

When he landed inside, he somersaulted and sprang to his feet, and was already running.

He had seen on the monitor where the occupants were all placed. He ran across the room and vaulted over the bed shoving the man lurching over Casie with a whip into the blond fuck that had his hand over her neck.

Neco couldn't tell as he was moving if she was still alive. His peripheral mind saw in a blur that she wasn't moving and her eyes were closed. She was no longer screaming in agony.

As Neco took the two men to the floor, the woman in black slipped to the door. But Josh stood in front of her blocking the exit. Shaking his head, he smiled amicably, "Nope, everyone stays here."

He nudged her to back into the room. Logan and Chaz came in behind him. At once they saw Casie tied to the bed and Neco on the other side of the room fighting the two they had seen in the monitor.

Both men were strong and even Pryce was an experienced fighter, they went right after Neco, battling him like fiends. Neco dodged their slugs and threw his own powerful punches.

Just as all of the brothers pushed into the room, a flood of men came charging in after them shouting.

The brothers immediately sprung to fighting. Several of the men ran across the room to the other side to help Pryce take down Neco.

Neco shouted, "Chaz! Get my girl!" and ducked a swing from Don who had been a boxer in his day.

Chaz slugged the guy he was fighting, knocking him out, he sprang across the room to Casie. He went right to the restraints, not waiting to see the state of her condition. Untying her arms then legs, she didn't move as he freed her limbs.

Now, Chaz looked down at her. She was wearing practically nothing that covered little, and she had bruises and lash marks all over her body.

His stomach turned at the sight of the torture inflicted on her helpless body. Neco was going to be sick when he got a good look at her.

That's when he saw the marks on her chest and almost tossed his breakfast. "Neco, she's got fucking bite marks on her tits-"

Neco froze and almost took a bash to the head, he ducked just in time. "Get her the fuck out of here!" he barked and jumped at one attacker, slamming him in the head.

The man went down, Neco grabbed another's arm and broke it over his knee, that man's scream came after the sickening crack.

Chaz slid his hands under Casie's back and knees to lift her when she gagged.

Unable to speak through her raw throat, she whispered, "*Blond*," wheezed in, and on her exhale she wheezed, "*knife*."

Lifting Casie up in his arms, Chaz yelled, "Neco! Blade! Blond!" just as Don swung his knife at Neco.

Hearing his brother, Neco dodged the knife and blasted his fist into Don's stomach. A steel jab to the jaw sent him crashing to the floor.

Neco took out the two other men then went after Pryce, the one who had been whipping Casie and was about to run away.

Josh and Logan quickly took down the rest of the men.

They were wrapping plastic flexi-cuffs around their wrists, when Josh looked over and saw Neco on top of the older man with the black hair and was pummeling his face. Punch after punch, the man's face was a broken mess of blood and jagged bones.

Josh raced over and grabbed his brother's arms. Logan split from the room.

"Stop, you can't kill him, Nek, stop, bro!" Josh held Neco's arm behind him, shouting "Get a grip, stop!"

Neco wrestled him for a second then let go of the man's collar and his head dropped with a thunk on the floor.

Heaving, Neco dragged his sleeve across his forehead wiping the sweat out of his eyes. His hands were drenched in blood. He kicked the man on the floor, but the mess laid out there was out cold. He looked to the bed.

It was empty, the restraints lay on the sheets. There was no blood. The bastard wanted to inflict as much pain to Casie without breaking her skin and scarring her.

"Where is she?" he growled to Josh who was crouching beside the men Neco had taken down and was tying flexi-cuffs around their wrists behind their backs.

Standing up, Josh huffed, wiping his face with his shirttail. "I think Chaz took her downstairs out of range of the fighting. Logan went to clear the rest of the building, he took the older woman with him."

Dragging his sleeve across his face, still panting, Neco strode for the door. He hurried down the stairs and to the main room where they had left the first group of thugs.

When he entered the room, he saw Logan had cuffed the older woman to a chair, the other bound men were scattered in a line against the wall. Most weren't conscious.

Neco's eyes went to the couch. Casie was lying on it with Chaz leaning over her. Neco trod quickly to them and knelt down by the sofa.

Chaz was unbuttoning his shirt. Casie's skin had no color, her eyes were closed and she lay still.

Neco reached a shaking hand out to touch her face. It was cold, but he saw the pulse in her neck beating.

The chiffon thing she was wearing gaped to expose most of her breasts. His stomach heaved, he saw the bite marks, he thought he was going to puke.

Croaking, "Aw for fuck's sake, baby," tears stung the backs of his eyes. Hell, he couldn't even remember ever crying even as a child. He grasped the edges of the lingerie top and pulled them together. It was better, but the material was quite sheer.

His gaze shifted to the tiny panties then shot up to his brother who was studiously trying not to look at her while taking his shirt off.

Neco slid his arm around her back and carefully lifted her while Chaz slipped his shirt on her. Neco lowered her back down then buttoned the shirt up.

Casie's face contracted in pain, her lips parted with a wrenched breath. When the skin around her eyes puckered, her lips twitched with a soft cry, Neco gently set his hand on the side of her face careful to avoid the bruises.

His aching heart flowed out with his words, "Baby, you're safe now. You're here with me, Neco, and my brothers." He wiped the back of his hand over a tear that had escaped and rolled down his face. She was so badly hurt, but he was desperately relieved she was alive.

Her eyes flickered, the lashes feathered over her cheeks before fluttering open. The green eyes streamed straight up to Neco's worried blues. "Neco," she rasped, "you came for me."

LOUISE FURLEY

Her hoarse sigh wrapped around Neco's heart and squeezed the hell out of it.

"Ah, Casie, I will always come for you." He bent and kissed her on her forehead. "Always. I love you, baby."

Around them the bound men coming around groaned and muttered, cursed, cried and squirmed against their binds.

She struggled to sit up. Neco urged, "Wait, honey, you'll hurt yourself, just lie back," he put his hands to her shoulders.

Casie shook her head and kept moving. She said hoarsely, "No, I'm fine Neco." Her smile was weak but calm. She insisted, so he rolled his arm around her back and helped her up to lean against the cushions, and sat down beside her.

Chaz grinned at her, then stood up and joined his other brothers to search the mansion.

Neco cupped Casie's chin. "Baby, I need to get you to a hospital."

She shook her head, the wavy amber hair ruffled around her. "No, really, I'm okay."

At his look of concerned disbelief, she said, "He only slapped me, and…" She looked away, shame filled her eyes.

"Baby, don't-"

"He struck me with a whip. It was…agonizing, but," her hand went to her breast, "he didn't draw blood, even when he," her head lowered in humiliation that someone would do such a thing to her.

"Ah, sweetheart." Neco gathered her in his arms, pressing her head gently against his chest. "You have nothing to be ashamed of. You didn't ask for this or deserve to be treated this way by that deranged monster."

He kissed her head. "Who is he, Casie? Why did he take you, beat you? Are you remembering things?"

She leaned back with a deep breath. Her throat sore, she said quietly, "He is my uncle. Vittorio Pryce."

At Neco's raised brows, she continued, "He…apparently…uh, has always wanted me, even when I was a child. He said he wanted to possess me, marry me. And torture me."

293

One shoulder rose in embarrassment. "I...don't know why. I've hardly seen him over the years." Her eyes slid sideways to her aunt who was sitting like a regal queen in her chair.

Dimitria did not look at Casie.

"The woman?" Neco asked seeing her gaze light on the older woman. Tied to a chair, Dimitria's snooty nose lifted in the air as if she was above all the scum gathered around, including Neco and his brothers. However, her mouth was pinched tight and fear lurked in her dark eyes.

Blinking hard, Casie said, "She's my aunt. They both...were going to...sexually assault me...while he tortured..." Her pained gasp broke in a gulp.

Bewildered green eyes rose to Neco's adoring face. "I...don't understand it, Neco."

His arms tightened around her. "They are just sick fucks, baby, the world is full of them. They won't ever be able to get their hands on you again. The police are on their way."

She wrapped her arms around herself and snuggled closer into Neco's embrace. "I... remember, Neco, what happened." Her sigh beleaguered and weary, she shivered and burrowed further against Neco's broad chest.

"My uncle, he was trying to rape me when his wife attacked him and he- he killed her. I saw him. That was why I was running. Somehow I had managed to take photos of him doing it with my phone. I hid the phone. That's why I was...beaten, they wanted the phone."

She rubbed her eyes and sighed back into his arms. "I remember, I threw myself from the moving car to get away from them."

Her smile soft and loving, she tipped her head and brushed a kiss over his lips. "They were searching for me. They would have located me eventually. That's when you found me, and rescued me."

"And loved you." He kissed her back, carefully, her face was swollen from Pryce's slaps. Neco would have killed the fucker if Josh hadn't stopped him.

He abducted, beat, whipped, fucking *bit* her, and was going to inflict more torture and rape her, then keep her prisoner to do it again and again. Neco's hands curved into tight fists. The bastard should be dead.

"Baby, I-" he stopped at her suddenly terrified look. "What is it, baby?"

In sudden fright, she tried to crawl deeper into Neco's arms as if to hide. "Him, he," she pointed at Harry who was being brought in by Josh. "He- he's the one who beat me in the car."

Neco gently took Casie by the shoulders and carefully set her aside, then bolted from the couch, tore across the room and flew at Harry knocking him off his feet.

When the big guy landed with crash, Neco jumped on top of him and started wailing at him.

Muttering, "Aw, damn, Nek," shaking his head, Josh walked slowly over to stop his brother. He waited until Neco had inflicted critical damage to the man before he pulled him off him.

"Can't kill this one either, Nek," he said with a small chuckle. "Not that he doesn't deserve it, but if you're in jail, you won't be sharing the sack with your little hottie."

That gave Neco pause. He stood up with arms bowed, fists bloody, sweat dripping from his hair, his face grimacing in rage.

His gaze flicked to the couch where Casie watched him wide-eyed and afraid. He rushed back to her side as the police barged in.

Epilogue

Three months later

The rest of their guests ate and drank, laughed and danced around Casie and Neco, but the couple was totally unaware of them.

His hands clasped around her lower back holding her close as they swayed to the music, Neco gently claimed his bride's lips.

When they parted slightly, her hands twined around his neck, she smiled up at him. "Neco, really, I am fully healed, you don't have to treat me like I'm crystal."

Because of her injuries, since Neco brought her home from the hospital he had denied them both sex. "So, what are you saying, my beautiful wife?" He bent and sucked her lips until she giggled.

"I'm saying, how soon can we get to our honeymoon?"

He brushed bits of her curls off her cheek, smiling, his desire for her radiating from his loving eyes. "You talking about the trip or the consummation of our marriage?"

Casie ducked her head with a blush and peeked around at the crowd.

They were surrounded by friends and their families that had a few hours ago witnessed their joining. Neco's parent's back yard was perfect for the ceremony.

Flowers clustered, and ribbons rippled around the joyous throng.

Pulling his head back down for a deeper kiss, Casie whispered, "Both."

His grin as big as all outdoors, Neco swooped her up in his arms, bent and kissed her then strode through the crowd of well-wishers around to the side of the house.

"Hey!" Josh jumped in front of them with a laugh. "Where do you think you're going?"

Smiling down at his beloved bride, Neco said, "First, we're going to spend a week in bed."

"Neco!" Casie's cheeks burned bright at Josh's chuckle.

"Yeah, and then we're heading to Hawaii for a few weeks, then we're coming home and building our own house and, hopefully," he grinned down at her. "Start a family. Right, Wife?"

Nodding, Casie strung her arms around his neck as he kept walking. She agreed gleefully, "Right, Husband!"

They had plenty of time to travel, the hearings for her uncle, aunt, Harry, Don and some of the others wouldn't take place for at least a year. All were denied bond.

Not that it mattered, the beatings Neco and his brothers had dealt to Vittorio, Harry and Don ensured none of them would be walking normally again, ever.

Those three plus Dimitria were facing life in prison for kidnapping, aggravated assault, attempted rape among other charges.

Sasha from the King's Palace was found in the river strangled and brutally beaten. Tempest, the server from the diner has gone missing. The authorities assume she shared the same fate as Sasha. The two had the misfortune to hook up with Harry and Don, and paid for it with their lives.

None of them would ever bring danger to Casie's doorstep again. If they somehow managed to get out and try to get near to her, Neco's wrath would so destroy each of them that pieces of them would never be found.

Neco carried his bride away from the party to his waiting truck and set her inside then got behind the wheel.

As he pulled from the curb, he clasped Casie's hand. His smile tender, he said, "You ready, Wife? To begin our forever after?"

Belted in the middle section of the bench seat, Casie turned to face Neco as he drove.

"I'm ready for our future together, Husband. I'm ready to start making our family right now," and she plucked at his buttons, opening them as he headed towards home.

The End

Dear Reader, thank you for choosing
<u>Neco's Rescue</u>!

I know you could have picked any number of books to read, but you chose this story and for that I am extremely grateful.

I hope you enjoyed this novel, and if you did, **please leave a review where you procured it,** *and look for other exciting titles in my name!*

About the Author

Louise Furley loves writing romance with a huge helping of suspense. Sunny Florida is home where Louise is a graduate of St. Thomas University with a master's degree in Mental Health and lives with Bob, her own hero.

Louise is the author of numerous published novels. When not researching or writing, she is dreaming of unique plots, and discovering fresh ventures she hasn't yet experienced in the world.

Ride along with her as she travels new and thrilling journeys!

If you loved this adventurous romance, please check out the first few chapters of <u>Liquid Velvet</u>!

Chapter One

Anyalia Marvaux scuttled across the lawn from the main house to her grandfather's cottage. The small building was tucked way in the back yard and canopied by a shroud of maple trees.

Scant illumination in the clouded twilight shines from the windows of the two homes. Bereft of their leaves, gnarly branches reach out like black skeletons beckoning with twigged fingers to come deeper into the darkness.

Thick blades of cool dewy grass tickle her bare feet as she quickly shuffles through the soft lawn. On the cusp of spring, the air is crisp, she should have thrown on shoes and a jacket but she was in too much of a hurry to escape her parents' haranguing.

Knocking lightly before entering, Anya closed the door behind her, never seeing the dark figures skulking stealthily from tree to tree in the shadows.

Warmer inside, chemical smells mingling with the slight woody scent of the old bungalow coiled comfortably around her. The familiar aroma lessened some of the tension that pinched the back of her neck and tightened her mouth from her stepmother's continuous disapproval.

Her feet moved silently over the ancient rug, so threadbare it was like fine gossamer on her tender soles. Hurrying through the living room of mismatched, worn and lumpy furniture, she called out, "Granddad? Where are you?"

Just a few lamps were lit, leaving only dim halos of light to guide her way. Hearing a responsive grunt, she kept going, leaving the tiny living room to head to Märtin Dauphine's laboratory.

Hesitating on the wood planked threshold, Anya watched her grandfather alternate from writing notes, to toiling over copious beakers filled with a variety of liquids spread out on a metal table. Several vessels containing only vaporous gasses lined in neat rows alongside them.

The rustic cottage and the simple glass vials looked incongruous with the top-of-the-line machines anchoring the walls. Whirring sounds blending with dissonant beeps made an anomalous but familiar music to Anya's ears.

The sight of the man with short, messy grey hair, of average height, weight, and average everything else, brought an affectionate smile to Anya's tense face.

Glasses hovering on the end of his substantial but not overlarge nose, dressed in all brown with a white lab coat overlay, even with a spine of steel, Märtin Dauphine was so average he would blend into a crowd, easily becoming invisible.

"Ah, *mon chère, petite fille*, my dear granddaughter." Not looking up, he said with a slight chuckle, "I can hear your burdened sigh all the way over here."

Anya tilted her head with a soft smile. Light yellow curls woven with fine filaments of brilliant flames bounced around her shoulders and down her back. Expressing another heavy sigh, she trod over to get a better view of what he was working on.

After a few moments of silence, Märtin set down his pen and paper, rolled a stool to the table and sat down on it.

"What is it, *petite fille*?" He shoved the glasses to the top of his head causing the grey hair to spike haphazardly, and regarded Anya with the pure affection of a grandfather for his beloved granddaughter.

Pushing over a stool to the opposite side of the table, Anya plopped down with another beleaguered sigh. "Oh Granddad, stepmother and papa cornered me earlier, ganging up on me with the same, sorry old lecture." Her tiny yet full lips turned down.

Märtin crossed his arms. One grey brow arched, he asked, "They still want you to go make up with Raoul?" His aged voice held a tsk of annoyance.

She nodded, fiery blonde curls sprung over the front of her blouse. Anya crossed her legs and looked down with chagrin at the damp hems of her jeans. Great. Her stepmother, Maisa, would know she had been here.

"Yes," she sighed, then her soft features hardened. "They don't know what happened, *Grand-père*, I never told them. I just said we broke up and of course they blamed me. Said I was too young at seventeen to know what I wanted. Huh," she snorted, "at least I know what I don't want."

"It's been what, over two years now since you refused his calls, although he still perseveres. I would think your parents would give it up, especially considering your father's chronic absent-mindedness. But-" he said abruptly as Anya made a face.

"I know, it is undoubtedly Maisa's tenacious stringency that keeps that tact open. It has always been clear that she is perversely jealous of you. She thinks you steal her light, and wants you married off and stuffed fat with a baby."

His voice went from slight exasperation to gruff. "You never told me what happened with Raoul either." One eye squinted in accusation at her.

Nodding, Anya didn't meet his gaze. "No, and I'm not going to. I know if you knew what he did to me-" she broke off at the lowering of his grey brows. "Never mind. I never told you because I knew you would have gone after him-" she broke off again at the darkening of the older man's face.

"Anyway," she exhaled hard, "as usual, Maisa wants me to quit my new job at the museum on weekends, and stop my studies at university, and I've only just gotten started. She thinks the museum is too lofty and pretentious, and school is a waste of money even though I'm on scholarship. And, as you said, Maisa says I should be married, barefoot and pregnant and chained to Raoul's kitchen sink."

She didn't dare tell him she believes Raoul even paid Maisa big money to talk Anya, *push* her, into marrying him.

Märtin's lip curled up at her account of things, then his eyes lowered to her feet. He said with a fond grin, "Ah, you have the bare feet part down pat."

Scraping a few fingers over his grey evening bristles, Märtin shrugged. "As I said, I don't know what happened between you and Raoul, but, you are a young woman, don't you want a husband and children, a family of your own?"

Anya set her elbows on the table and dropped her chin on her fists. "No. I want nothing to do with the male species. Except of course you, *mon grand-père*, my granddad. My experiences so far have not been positive."

At the inverting of his brows, her mouth twisted before she explained.

"When I was 12, as you know, we left the isolation of the sheltered consulate in Mingronue, such a tiny country no one ever even heard of, to come here to Washington. Maisa and Papa thought we should join civilization in Shrivesport.

"The first moment I was alone, Mr. Fridely, our neighbor, pounced on me, and if Mrs. Johansson from down the street hadn't chased him with a broom, well, I don't know what would have happened." If not for the content, the picture would have been comical.

Grooves around Märtin's mouth and eyes deepened in anger, his lips thinned. Rolling his hands into tight fists, he said, "Then your parents moved to this rural area in Wildhaven where I've lived for years. I wasn't present at Shrivesport, or I would have seen that Mr. Fridely never inappropriately touched another woman again."

The corner of Anya's lip ticked up with a slight grin. "Yes, and that is why I won't tell you about Raoul. Anyway, being home-schooled by an elderly tutor kept me away from other kids my own age, ensuring I was even more secluded and naïve so that day at church when Giles Smart asked me to go get ice cream with him, I was so excited. Then," she paused, one shoulder rose and fell in despondence.

"He attacked me too. And, yet again with Raoul. So, you see, I want nothing to do with men. Ever. They don't look at me as a person, just a thing to- to appease their...uh, animal needs. I am but a body to them, they care not about my mind or my personality." She sniffed with her tiny nose tilted up.

His grey head nodding, he replied, "I know, my Anyalia, you have this, ah, how do I describe it, ethereal, exotic beauty you inherited from my daughter, your dear sweet mother, that men lose their minds around you. And, it's not likely to end.

"It was dreadfully unfortunate your poor mama died when you were only two, you never got to meet her. You keep up with your French in her honor." He shook his head, then smiled away the bemusement from his memories of his beloved daughter.

"You need to find a man you can tame, like your *grand-mère*, your grandmother, my precious Emmaline did to me. I was on the edge of drowning in delinquency when she molded me with her soft, sweet, gentleness." His hazel eyes blanked as his mind reverted to a world from a long time ago.

"Uh huh." Anya picked at a button on her shirt. "But you, Granddad, are one in a million. There are no other men out there with your honor, integrity, bravery. I mean, you chased that bear away that day at Montagne de Céüse, in the Alps, remember?" Her lips bowed up in an affectionate smile.

The far-away look tunneled from Märtin's eyes, leaving a fissure of emptiness, a dull aching, a longing that nothing would ever fill again.

"Papa is a good man, don't get me wrong," Anya said. "But he's so vague and absentminded. If it weren't for his pension and Maisa's iron-handed overseeing, his bills would never get paid."

"Anyway," her sigh gloomy she went on, "it's kind of you always trying to build up my confidence. But, Maisa and papa have always told me how homely I am."

She mimicked her stepmother's cool unpleasant voice, "It's unfortunate, *Ahn-yah-lee-ya*, that you are too plain and dull. Much too thin, too small and delicate to be of any use other than as a wife and mother."

Anya held a dainty hand up to hold off her grandfather's angry retort. "No, don't say anything, I have a mirror, I know what she says is true. But Granddad, it doesn't bother me, truly. All I desire is to work with you on your subcontracting projects with the military, and do my bio-chemistry studies.

"I've only had a couple of semesters and already I can see that due to your mentoring I am light-years ahead of the other students. Besides," she smiled, "you are the only family I need."

Leaning back on her stool, she said, "Can I stay with you a while right now? I can help, and you can tell me about you and grandmother."

Märtin regarded his granddaughter sadly. Maisa had always been jealous of her extraordinarily beautiful stepdaughter and thus had treated her coldly, and often, cruelly, disparaging Anya's looks and intelligence at every opportunity.

Maisa has kept her secluded in this rural countryside because she goes crazy with jealousy whenever any men young or old, pay attention to Anya.

If she could have drowned her like a kitten and gotten away with it when Maisa had maneuvered Eduard into marrying her, she absolutely would have. Now, Maisa's hope was for Anya to become swollen with Raoul Lombardo's child and then maybe the men would not eye her like she was a precious jewel they desired to own.

A sardonic snort groused from Märtin. Even heavy with a baby, Anya would still always be dazzling, like his wife. Even while pregnant, Emmaline had shone like a diaphanous gem.

And Eduard, Anya's papa, being a weak and often confused man, did as his wife told him, mostly just parroting the things she said.

So, when Maisa drilled it into Anya's head that her looks lacked, when in fact she had a luminous beauty that drew men like mindless fish to an exquisite hook, Eduard babbled the nonsense right along with her.

Märtin smiled, fond and proud of his intelligent, sweet granddaughter. "Of course you can stay with me. Come, I will show you where I was at when you came in." He tipped his glasses back down on his nose.

While they worked, Märtin told her stories of his deceased wife. "Ah, one day we were invited to a grand party at the Fondateur Hotel and Ballroom. We ate, danced, drank, then slipped away for some, you know," he winked, "private time. So we snuck out the back of the dining room through a servant's door and scurried down a hall to the end." His lips curved in mischief at the widening of Anya's already large eyes.

"The Fondateur is listed on a historic registry and the family resides there as well. The familial portion of the estate is forbidden to outsiders, but," he grinned with a conspiratorial wink, "we did sneak in." He chuckled at her surprised look.

"Darling granddaughter, I wasn't always just a grey-haired staid old scientist, I did once have a wild side. A few times I managed to corral your sweet grandmother into a not quite lawful adventure."

"Grandad!" Anya's outburst was half appalled, half enthused.

"Anyway," Märtin went on, "there were these ornate glass, double doors with flamboyant peacocks engraved in them, we opened them and found ourselves in the most opulent, magnificent room I've ever been in.

"Cathedral ceilings with stained-glass windows from floor to ceiling. All white luxurious furniture and rugs, drapes of satiny gold, immense stone fireplace. Everything, paintings, mirrors, were all gilded in gold. But, there was one thing that I'll never forget."

Getting up to go around the table to stand beside him, brilliant green eyes huge with wonder, she asked, "What? What was that, Granddad?"

"Ah, honey, it was a huge painting of Romeo and Juliet on Roman velvet. All deep reds, burgundies and forest greens. The look of love on the couple's faces was extraordinary, they veritably beamed at each other. Your grandmother and I kissed under the painting, and then, uh," he cleared his throat.

"Well, never you mind missy what happened next. Anyway, I was just there last week for that conference and it brought all those memories of that night with Emmaline flooding back. I miss her so..." he stuck a finger under a lens and dabbed at an eye.

"It was a remarkable night for us, and I want you to remember the story, keep Emmaline and me alive in your heart even after I'm gone."

He took a breath, mouth firmed, lids levered over his serious hazel eyes, he said oddly, "And in your brain. Okay?"

Anya moved closer to her grandfather and gave him a huge hug. "Of course, Granddad." She rebuked him, "Now, no more of this morbid talk of you...leaving. Can we keep working?"

Märtin rolled a thin arm around her slim shoulders and hugged her close. "Yes, yes, we can continue. Just never forget the stories I tell you. Especially that one."

They worked quietly for an hour then Anya could hear her stepmother calling for her.

Reluctantly setting down a glass cylinder on the table, she peeled off her plastic gloves, removed the protective goggles and sighed. "I have to go, Granddad."

"Of course. I will see you at lunch tomorrow, eh? We'll review the notes for the next steps."

Anya smiled wanly, kissing his proffered cheek. "Yeah, okay. Night, Granddad." Leaving the cottage, she locked and closed the door behind her.

Anya came looking for her grandad the next day when he didn't show for lunch. When she reached the cottage, Anya froze and then screamed, and screamed, and screamed.

His front door was broken in, and there was blood on the stoop.

Chapter Five

Between them, the two strapping males dragged the bloody, moaning man to a chair and pushed him down on it. They tied his wrists to the chair arms and his ankles to the chair legs.

Barely able to draw a breath from the beating the two had given him, the man begged with gasping wheezes, "Please, please, no more, please."

Déisi Zukov wiped the blood on his hands on his black jeans and shoved his raven's hair out of his eyes, pushing it back off his forehead. Hooded lids concealed most of the eyes as black and dead as burnt coals.

He said to the man in heavily accented English, "Rankin, you know the only thing we want to hear out of you is where the funds are that you stole from Anton de Vos." Like a snake's sudden strike, Déisi lashed his hand out and gripped Rankin's neck, squeezing his windpipe with fingers as thick and strong as iron pegs.

Rankin's eyes bulged, veins in his sallow skin enflamed and enlarged. Déisi clinched his throat so tightly he couldn't even gag.

"Bro, dude," Kaloyan said calmly without moving. "He can't tell us anything with that death grip you have on his throat. Actually," crossing his arms over a harshly muscular chest, he perused their prisoner, "I'm surprised he can speak at all after you knocked out most of his teeth."

Ignoring his brother, Déisi's fingers dug deeper into Rankin's throat. The man's skin lost all color and his eyes started rolling as he was losing consciousness.

Déisi abruptly released him. Rankin's head flung forward as he choked and hacked, chest heaving. Blood from his wounds streamed down and off his face, spilling and mixing with buckets of sweat that splattered into pink puddles on the floor.

Sucking in a beleaguered painful breath, Rankin whined hoarsely, "All right, all right, I'll tell you, then you'll let me live?"

Kalo shrugged one shoulder. "*Da*, sure, I'll let you live. Tell us."

Rankin stared up at the brothers with their strange accents, identical brawny chests and shoulders bulky with muscles, biceps bulging, and the sheer lack of compassion in either of their eyes. Kalo's dark blues, or Déisi's fathomless black tunnels.

"Okay," he exhaled, then spat out blood and a tooth, the tooth clicked across the floor. "It's stashed in my cabin. I got a cabin near Loon Lake."

He let out a heavy aggrieved breath. "In the rafters. 1212 Terrace Lane." Rankin peered up at the brothers with hope through stringy sweaty hair. He knew better than to lie, he would only suffer worse beatings.

"*Bună*, good," his voice deep and dark, Déisi suddenly lunged and sliced across Rankin's upper arm with a knife. Not even blinking at the man's shriek, Déisi dragged the blade across Rankin's jeans cleaning the blood off it.

Rankin cried, "Wha- wha- you said you'd let me live!"

"Huh," Kalo snorted. "*I* said *I* wouldn't kill you, I didn't say anything about my brother here. When you took what was Mr. de Vos' you knew what the repercussions would be. We might have let you live with maybe a broken back and mutilated limbs, a punctured kidney, but, alas," Kalo glanced at his stone-faced brother.

"There was that little matter of when you stole the funds, you set fire to the manager's house to eliminate him as a witness. He didn't live there alone; you knew he had a wife and three kids under the age of five. According to the neighbors, their screams could be heard for quite some time. They say it was a pitch black night except for the blazing flames that lit up the sky around the house.

"Unfortunately, the fire was so intense the responders couldn't get to the family and were forced to just stand there until there was nothing but burning embers, and eventual silence."

Kalo sighed with a wan smile. "You see, your actions brought undue attention to Mr. de Vos."

"Uh, but- but, I- I-" Rankin whimpered, watching the blood ooze out of his arm making a wide scarlet trail from his bicep to his forearm. "Someone's pissed about a little collateral damage? Shit-" Choking on the blood that slid down his throat, he coughed, expelling even more of the viscous red fluid.

Déisi slammed his fist into the side of Rankin's head. More blood sprayed the wall as his head snapped to the right.

Rolling his eyes at his brother, Kalo said to Rankin as his head bobbed and his eyes wobbled, "*Yah.*" Kalo nodded. "So we decided to make sure you suffer like those people did, as well as a few others you tortured before slaughtering."

He smiled brightly at the injured thug. "And you are! See, all's well that ends well, right, Déisi?" He nudged his brother who didn't move, or lower his blank gaze lanced straight at Rankin.

"Who- who the hell are you fucking foreign bastards anyway?" Rankin cried, his eyes glued to his lifeblood seeping away.

Smiling amicably, Kalo told him, "We are Kalo and Déisi Zukov. We're from a tiny obscure country you've never heard of near Romania. *Mi bréthaïdne*, ah, I mean my brother here is actually the one Anton de Vos hires, I'm just additional muscle for this mission.

"Déisi is Mr. de Vos' *jαúdraç*. In America he would be like, oh, I guess he'd be like an enforcer. Mr. de Vos has business internationally, from China to Russia, Algeria to Ireland, Brazil to the States. And boy, I'll tell ya, that means a lot of enforcing is needed. You'd be surprised how many people welch on deals, rob Mr. de Vos, attempt take-overs, deliberately deflate his stock.

Déisi remained a silent rock.

"*Yah,*" Kalo nodded, dark blond hair flopping with his movements, "you'd be surprised at how many shysters there are out there."

Grinning amiably at Rankin, he said, "*Na* offense, dude." He snapped his fingers. "Oh, did I mention what they call my brother?"

When Rankin made no response, Kalo cheerfully told him, "They call him, *a čelu vlad.* I'm sure you've heard of him. In English it means Death Comes."

Already ashen, Rankin's face paled until not a drop of color touched his skin. He looked from one man to the other, at Déisi's black pits of emptiness then back to Kalo with his plea. "Listen, please-"

"Ah, sorry, my friend. So," Kalo smiled jauntily. "I'm off to get the money. If tis not there I will call *mi bréthaïdne* and I'm sure you can imagine what he will do to you. Because, for now, he's only going to sit and watch you bleed out."

Before Rankin could speak, Kalo turned to Déisi. "All right, bro, I'm outta here. After I return the money I'll be joining our other brothers in Katmandu."

Aware his brother repelled most physical contact, Kalo nonetheless gave him a fist bump to the arm. "I'll call you when I get the bucks."

"*Bună,*" Déisi grunted with a brief nod. He grabbed a chair and dropped it in front of Rankin, and sat down.

"Mister, wait-" Rankin's rasped shout was barely audible at Kalo as he saluted them and left the room.

Rankin's terrified, bloodshot eyes shifted slowly to Déisi. "Uh," he swallowed hard, "you gonna just sit there and stare at me?"

Another short nod, face like sculpted iron, hooded lids so low only a glitter of dark light shone under black lashes, Déisi scratched at the dark scruff on his hard jaw and crossed his arms over the big chest.

Settling back in the chair, the dim light from the window a pale stripe across his sharp, angular cheekbones, he muttered, "*Da*. Until you bleed out. Then I dispose of your body."

Chapter Three

*T*he blast of frigid air smacking red into her cheeks reminded Anya that she had forgotten her jacket.

The bitter wind cut right through her thin, ivory blouse ruffling the collar along with her long hair, and the pale blue jeans weren't much more protection from the cold.

"Darn it all, it's been so long since I've been at work, and I need the money so badly." Turning back to her car to grab her jacket, she mumbled weakly, "I hope there are donuts or something, I had to flee so quickly I couldn't get anything into my stomach."

With her head down as she rifled around inside her purse looking for her keys, she didn't see the black bus pulling up on the side street.

A cold hard hand suddenly clamped over her mouth, and an iron band of muscle roped around her arms, pinning them to her body and lifted her off her feet.

She was too surprised to scream even if the huge hand wasn't covering half her face. A door to the bus stood open and Anya was only able to give a few futile kicks of her legs before she was rustled into the car.

As soon as she, and the monster that held her cleared the door, a man reached over, closed the door and the bus took off.

The man crushing her to his body carried her to the right side of the vehicle. He removed his hand from her mouth and set her on her butt on the bench seat then dropped down beside her.

Gulping rapid shallow breaths, Anya shoved her long curls out of her face and opened her mouth to scream or protest or question, but her eyes widened into shocked green plates, her lips stayed parted but no words came out.

The extra-wide bus was set up like a huge party bus. Long, beige leather bench seats stretched along the sides, the windows were dark tinted, and a small refrigerator door was open revealing a variety of alcoholic beverages and sodas.

Blinking back her astounded panic, Anya observed the group of people seated in the bus.

The men looked unsavory, unshaven with mean eyes, and the women looked, well, bawdy. They were all staring avidly at her with avaricious interest.

Her head whipped to the man beside her who had abducted her off the street. Again she opened her mouth to demand an explanation then froze when her shocked eyes collided with his black discs of chilling emptiness.

His mere presence raced alarming fingers of fright up her spine. He was tall, maybe over 6'5. Dark hair tousled from the wind outside flopped over an ebony eye, he shoved it back with annoyed impatience.

Her trembling gaze shuffled around his face looking for a trace of kindness or compassion, but his harsh, hard-carved features were only grim and forbidding.

Oddly, Anya thought, for a thug, he wore an expensive looking grey suit, and a thin black silk tie, he ran his large hand down neatening it. The slacks were sharply creased; his dress boots masculine and polished.

But the swank suit did nothing to hide the massive shoulders and bulging arms. The dark eyes regarding her were hooded, hiding his thoughts. To Anya he had a callous look, such a tough exterior. A scar jagged from the end of his temple to the beginning of his cheek, made her think of gangster musclemen she'd seen on TV that hurt people.

314

One of the men sitting opposite of them, stood up. The man started over towards Anya, the greedy leer on his face clearly indicating his intent.

"Yeah, nice, fucking nice, Zukov, let's get this party started." As the man moved closer to her, he rubbed his palms together. This man was tall and muscular as well, with thin, straight, light brown hair parted on the side. His face was pocked and his brown eyes bared his unmistakable malice.

Zukov, the man next to her spoke in low, brusque, heavily accented words, "*Na*. No party, sit down."

"Huh?" The approaching man's head snapped from Anya to the man beside to her. "The hell you say. Bitch is steaming hot, man, young and fucking tender. De Vos don't give a shit what shape she's in when you get her there, as long as she's alive."

His nasty gaze swung back to Anya. Smarmy eyes dropped to her breasts, his tongue swirled around his thin lips. "Yeah, and damned stacked too. Time to fuck, baby, come to daddy-" he took another step.

Her arms rigid, hands gripping the seat, Anya pressed her jean-clad legs together, and rounded her shoulders in front of her as if she could stop him from touching her.

The man next to Anya leaned forward. "I said *na*." Zukov's voice deep and dark as the night, he spoke in a low tone but the menace carried. "Go back to your seat, Dassey."

Darryl Dassey's forehead furrowed. "What the fuck? Come on, man. Okay fine, you go first then I got seconds. The others can draw straws for their turn-"

"Sit. Down." The words hard clipped came with black brows drawn like rapiers over dark ominous eyes.

Dassey hesitated, then scowled. "Fine, you foreign asshole. At least let me strip her so I can have those bitchin' tits and her pussy to look at during the drive. You can hold her legs apart so I can get a bird's eye view." His leer shifted to Anya. "I bet she's all pink and pretty down there, eh?"

Wrapping her arms around her body, Anya's head was roiling so crazed with fear, she could hardly think. Her petrified eyes darted from Dassey to Zukov sitting like a big bull beside her.

Zukov sat back in a relaxed pose. Strong hands, the backs sprinkled with black hair and tattoos splayed on his thighs, but Anya could feel the strength radiating from him coiled and ready to spring.

Behind Dassey the other people watched with wicked interest.

Dassey moved within a couple of feet and reached out for the buttons on Anya's blouse- Zukov stood up and backhanded Dassey so hard the man stumbled backwards slamming down awkwardly back on his seat.

Anya jumped up behind Zukov and made for the door.

She had her hand on the handle when Zukov snapped his arm around her, jerking her away from the door and moved with her back to their seats.

He sat down, spread his long legs and pulled her to sit on the bench seat in front of him. His angry breath rough in her ear, his body strung around her felt like a thick, grey-suited iron fence. "Stupid bitch," he snarled.

His hand on his red cheek, Dassey cawed from across the bus, "Yeah, dumb as dirt. We gotta be goin' 70, you woulda been splattered all over the fucking highway!"

"Let go of me!" Anya pealed, struggling to get loose of Zukov's hard fingers wound around her upper arms.

Tightening his knees around her legs to hold her immobile, he grasped one of her hands, pulling it behind her back and snapped a handcuff on her thin wrist. Then he jerked her other hand back and clamped them together.

Gasping, appalled and terrified, turning her head without looking at him, Anya whispered desperately, "Why? Why are you doing this?"

Not answering her, he put his hands on her waist and lifted her to sit beside him, then he pulled her to lean back against the wall in a corner. Smoothing his tie back down over his abdomen, he maneuvered his big body so he was blocking her in.

Anya pulled her legs up with her knees protectively pressed against her chest and huddled as tightly to the side wall, and as far away from Zukov as she could get. Hearing snickering, she peeped over at the other people sitting around the bus.

The group of men and women were staring at her and making lewd comments.

One man snickered, "Can't wait to see the little girl buck naked and legs spread wide for me."

The others laughed crassly.

To see what happens with Anyalia and Déisi,
Liquid Velvet can be purchased from any of your
favorite book suppliers!

Louise Furley

www.ingramcontent.com/pod-product-compliance
Lightning Source LLC
Chambersburg PA
CBHW020907200626
46814CB00001BA/216